P9-DHT-575

A Little Country Christmas

A Little Country Christmas

CAROLYN BROWN

A.J. PINE

ROCHELLE ALERS

HOPE RAMSAY

FOREVER

New York   Boston

This book is a work of fiction. Names, characters, places, and incidents are the product of the author's imagination or are used fictitiously. Any resemblance to actual events, locales, or persons, living or dead, is coincidental.

The Perfect Christmas copyright © 2020 by Carolyn Brown
A Christmas Cowboy at Heart copyright © 2020 by A.J. Pine
Home for the Holidays copyright © 2014 by Rochelle Alers
Joy to the World copyright © 2020 by Robin Lanier
Compilation copyright © 2020 by Hachette Book Group, Inc.

Cover design and illustration by Daniela Medina
Cover photographs by Shutterstock.com
Cover copyright © 2020 by Hachette Book Group, Inc.

Hachette Book Group supports the right to free expression and the value of copyright. The purpose of copyright is to encourage writers and artists to produce the creative works that enrich our culture.

The scanning, uploading, and distribution of this book without permission is a theft of the author's intellectual property. If you would like permission to use material from the book (other than for review purposes), please contact permissions@hbgusa.com. Thank you for your support of the authors' rights.

Forever
Hachette Book Group
1290 Avenue of the Americas, New York, NY 10104
read-forever.com
twitter.com/readforeverpub

First Compilation Edition: September 2020

Forever is an imprint of Grand Central Publishing. The Forever name and logo are trademarks of Hachette Book Group, Inc.

The publisher is not responsible for websites (or their content) that are not owned by the publisher.

The Hachette Speakers Bureau provides a wide range of authors for speaking events. To find out more, go to www.hachettespeakersbureau.com or call (866) 376-6591.

ISBNs: 978-1-5387-3577-0 (mass market); 978-1-5387-3575-6 (ebook)

Printed in the United States of America

OPM

10 9 8 7 6 5 4 3 2 1

ATTENTION CORPORATIONS AND ORGANIZATIONS:

Most Hachette Book Group books are available at quantity discounts with bulk purchase for educational, business, or sales promotional use. For information, please call or write:

Special Markets Department, Hachette Book Group
1290 Avenue of the Americas, New York, NY 10104
Telephone: 1-800-222-6747 Fax: 1-800-477-5925

Contents

A Little Country Christmas

The Perfect Christmas

Carolyn Brown

To Zane, Isabella, and Carter Seay
With much love

Dear Readers:

I'm so excited to be joining Hope Ramsay, A.J. Pine, and Rochelle Alers in this anthology, and I hope that all our readers love these Christmas stories. *The Perfect Christmas* brings the Longhorn Canyon Ranch series to an end. An author just knows when it's time to finish a series, but it's never easy to leave the characters and move on to the next book. These wonderful characters have been in my head for more than two years, and I must admit that I dragged my feet (or maybe I should say my fingers) more than a little bit when I got close to the last bit of *The Perfect Christmas*.

I'd like to send out a thank-you to everyone who helped make this story possible—to my fabulous editor, Leah Hultenschmidt, who draws every last emotion right out of my stories, and to the whole team at Forever; to my agency, Folio Literary Management, and my agent, Erin Niumata; to my husband, Mr. B, for everything he does so that I can continue to write; and to all my readers who buy my books, tell their neighbors and friends about them, leave reviews, and write notes to me. I appreciate and love every one of you.

Until next time, happy reading!

Carolyn Brown

Chapter One

Cowboys do not cry.

That's what Landon Griffin kept telling himself as he listened to Vince Gill sing "Blue Christmas" on the radio that cold evening in Sunset, Texas. His mother had passed her love for everything Christmas on to him, and she would want him to enjoy their favorite time of the year. Teresa Griffin hadn't been a model mother, but from Thanksgiving to New Year's, every single year, she had made wonderful memories with Landon. As he thought of those good times, tears welled up behind his eyes and spilled down his cheeks.

He parked his truck in front of the Quiltin' House in Sunset, Texas, and pulled a red bandanna from his hip pocket to dry his wet cheeks. Snowflakes that seemed to be as big as half-dollars drifted aimlessly out of the sky, as if there were no such thing as gravity pulling them to the ground. He and his mother had always wished for a white Christmas, but that would definitely have been a miracle in Southern California, where he'd been born and grown up.

He'd never even known he had two half brothers in Texas until his mother had passed away. Not having any other family, he was eager to seek them out. So he'd come to the Panhandle last summer, and Pax and Maverick Callahan were everything he'd thought a big, warm family should be. And just like family should do, he was quick to help out. To his surprise, he found he loved working on the ranch. There was something about taming the land and caring for the great big shaggy beasts, the exhausting work, and the sense of accomplishment every day that he couldn't get enough of. So when an opportunity arose to learn more from his brothers' friends in Longhorn Canyon, he jumped at the chance.

He opened the truck door, grabbed the sack of groceries from the passenger seat, and shivered against the first burst of icy wind that sent the snowflakes into a frenzy. He made his way across the yard to the old house that had been someone's home for years before Claire Dawson turned it into a quilt shop.

He heard little Sally weeping as if her heart was broken when he stepped up on the porch. At less than a year old, she was way too young to be crying over memories of Christmases past, but Landon's eyes glazed with more tears just listening to her. He knocked once on the door frame and then went right on inside to find the little girl hanging on to her mother's leg. Landon set the bag containing sugar and cinnamon on the floor, dropped to his knees, and held out his arms. Sally had just started walking the week before and didn't always trust her legs, so she dropped down on her hands and knees and crawled over to him. When he picked her up, she laid her little head on his shoulder.

"What's the matter with the princess?" He patted her on the back as he stood up with her still in his arms.

"She's cutting two-year molars, and nothing seems to help." Dixie Boudreaux carried the bag to the kitchen. "Thanks for getting these things for me."

"No problem. I was in town to buy feed anyway," Landon said.

Sally leaned back, tucked her delicate little chin down to her chest, and looked up at Landon with big blue eyes, still floating in tears.

"I'm right here, princess," he told her. "Want me to rock you and see if that will fix those old nasty teeth trying to come in?" He set her down long enough to remove his coat and hat.

She held up her arms and said, "Lan-Lan rock."

He tossed his coat and cowboy hat on the cutting table. Then he picked up the toddler and sat down in the rocking chair with her. He had sure gotten attached to the child in the past three months that he'd been working at the Longhorn. Leaving her in a couple of weeks to go back to his brothers wouldn't be easy.

He glanced over at Dixie, who was standing on her tip-toes to put the cinnamon away on the cabinet shelf. The first time he met her at Longhorn Canyon Ranch at the Labor Day picnic, he had reached out his hand to shake hands with her and stepped in a gopher hole. He dropped to his knees about the same time that she took hold of his hand, and it looked like he was proposing on the spot.

"Pleased to meet you," he'd said.

"Even if I'm bad luck?" Her blue eyes twinkled.

He had stood up, dropped her hand, and tried to ignore the vibes but, how could he? She was a pretty woman with all those curves and dark brown hair. And of course, the ranch families and hired hands kept teasing him about proposing to the first single woman he met in Sunset, Texas.

The attraction had only deepened through the day when he saw how not only her own daughter but the other little babies at the ranch flocked to her. Her sweet nature with everyone had warmed his heart and soul, and he had wanted to know more about her. He'd started making excuses to stop by the quilt shop a couple of times a week, and they'd become friends. He wouldn't let it go beyond that—not when he didn't plan on sticking around too long. Why start something that he couldn't finish without breaking either her heart or his in the process?

"Hey, what's your favorite memory of Christmas?" he called out.

Dixie thought for a moment. "I don't really have any good memories of this time of year," she finally answered. "Tell me about yours instead."

He was sitting in one of the two rocking chairs in what used to be the living room. Nowadays, the walls were lined with shelves filled with bolts of fabric. A long table with a sewing machine on one end and an area for cutting on the other sat in the center of the room.

"Well, the first thing that comes to mind is decorating a Christmas tree. We always did that the day after Thanksgiving. When I was little, we made ornaments in school, and Mom kept every single one—even the hideous ones. And it was always my job to put the star on top." He smiled at the memory.

"We never had a tree at our house," Dixie shared. "Just couldn't afford it. Or presents. But sometimes the fire department delivered something for us, like those give-to-the-needy-children things that towns often do."

"That must have been hard." Landon's heart broke at the

idea of Dixie never having a real Christmas experience like he'd had. Teresa may have left him with the nanny most of the year, but she always made sure they celebrated the holidays. They'd decorated a tree together. She took him around to see the holiday lights. They used to make and decorate cookies—the frosting being his favorite part of course. Well, maybe the eating, come to think of it. And then, after all the gifts were opened, they would go see whatever new movie was playing at a nearby theater. The presents on Christmas Day were just the last thing on his list of memories and didn't mean nearly as much as getting to share a month with his mother.

"I usually just tried to pretend the Christmas season was like any other time of year." Dixie shrugged. "I got by with telling myself I didn't need any of it. But I'll be honest, it *was* hard as a kid."

Landon felt a distinct pang in his heart. "Princess Sally needs a Christmas tree, and so do you, Dixie," he said. "As soon as you close the shop, we'll bundle this little girl up and go cut down a small cedar at the ranch." Sally waved her little fists in the air as if she were in total agreement.

"How would we even decorate it? We don't have any ornaments." She tucked a stray strand of hair behind her ear and cocked her head to one side. Landon could tell by her expression that she was warming to the idea.

"See all those quilting scraps?" He pointed to the cutting table. "I can cut circles out of those, and you can sew them together. They'll be like little round ornaments, and we can string some popcorn for a garland or maybe we could just bunch up some strips of burlap and use it for garland, and we'll make a star out of that cardboard box. We could glue some of that gold-lookin' fabric to it…"

"And maybe put some glitter glue around the edges. Yes...that could work. What about lights?" she asked.

"There's already lights around the window frame," he answered. "We'll set it right over there in that bare spot in front of the window. The sun will light it up in the day, and the moon and stars will be the lights for it at night."

"You've got quite an imagination there, cowboy. And an answer for everything it seems," she said with a smile. "How could I possibly say no?"

He grinned back at her. "I've got to take that load of feed out there to the ranch, but I'll be done unloading it by five. Can you and Sally be ready a few minutes after that?"

"Sure!" she said with enthusiasm.

"Down," Sally demanded.

"She may not know many words, but she knows what she wants." Landon set her on the clean floor.

The baby crawled over to a cardboard box that held her toys, picked up her favorite teddy bear, and then went right back to Landon and reached up with one arm.

"Go," she said.

"We can't go right now," Dixie started to explain.

Sally's chin quivered, and tears flooded her cheeks.

"It's only thirty minutes until you close up." Landon picked up the child and settled back down with the baby and the teddy bear in his lap. "I can wait that long, and then I won't have to drive back into town. She can play with Little Bit and the kittens while I unload the feed."

"She loves that little miniature donkey, but it's all right if she gets disappointed once in a while. You're spoiling her, you know," Dixie told him.

"And I intend to keep doing just that. After all, I'm only here another couple of weeks before heading back out to my brothers' ranches." He picked up one of the little girl's books. "Let's read about Frosty the Snowman. If we get a white Christmas, and the folks out at the ranch tell me we just might, you and your mama and I might make a snowman like Frosty right out there in the front yard. We'll take a picture of you in front of your first Christmas tree and one with your snowman and one of you sitting on Santa's lap."

"Looks to me like she's quite enjoying your lap right now," Dixie said and smiled.

"I saw a flyer that said Santa was going to be at the Sunset Volunteer Fire Department, and Hud is dressing up like Santa this year. The local ladies in the community are going to have cookies, and the fire department is giving away bags of fruit and nuts. We need a picture of Sally to go with all the others we'll take while we're—" He stopped before he said something about the whole Christmas experience. "So we can make a Christmas album for her. If you make one every year, then she can look at them all when she's grown and remember all the good times."

"Do you have a set of albums like that?" Dixie swept up scraps of fabric from the floor.

"I did," Landon sighed. "They were stored at my friend's house in Paradise, California, but when his house burned up in that big wildfire last year, we weren't able to save them."

"I remember hearing about that fire, and I felt so sorry for those people. I know what it's like to be in a fire," she said. "I'm sorry that you lost all those pictures." Dixie patted him on the shoulder as she headed down the hall. "If I'd had something like that and lost it, that would devastate me."

"I've got to admit to a few tears, and big boys aren't supposed to cry," he said.

"Neither are big girls, but believe me, I've sure shed my

share of tears over a lot less than that," Dixie said. "Maybe tears are just a way to let the grief out of our souls."

"I like that thought." He smiled. "To tell the truth, I hadn't grieved much for my mother until then."

"That gave you an outlet for your pain," she said. "I should get our coats and hats."

"And maybe a blanket or quilt to wrap this baby up in while we chop down a tree," Landon suggested. That wasn't what he wanted to say to Dixie—not by a long shot. He wanted to tell her that he'd had feelings for her from the first time he saw her and that they'd deepened through the past three months as he'd gotten to know her better. He had known what it was like to be raised by a single mother, so he could understand Dixie's struggles. He admired her too much—liked her too much—to ever give her a moment's heartache or pain, and he wasn't sticking around that part of Texas.

* * *

Dixie took time to brush her hair, pull it up into a ponytail, and apply a little lipstick before she gathered up her heaviest coat and a little snowsuit that Retta had given her when her own child, Annie, had outgrown it. Just to be on the safe side, though, she picked up a quilt like Landon suggested, along with the diaper bag.

She hadn't been a bit surprised at the little spark of electricity that popped when she touched Landon on the shoulder. From the first time she shook hands with him at the ranch and he'd stepped in that gopher hole, there had been chemistry between them. If she'd tried to get him out of her mind, it would have been impossible, what with all the teasing from the ladies at the two ranches about

Landon's "proposal." Since that day, their friendship had kept growing, and she'd learned to admire him more and more. His heart was as big as Texas, and he was constantly doing sweet little things, like making sure she and Sally had a Christmas tree.

Dixie stood back in the shadows for a few moments and listened to him read. He hadn't quite picked up the Texas drawl that all the other cowboys out on Longhorn Ranch had, and with his shaggy blond hair and scruffy beard, he didn't look much like them either.

Oh, but he sure looks fine to me, she thought.

Landon looked up, caught her eye, and smiled. "You got those coats ready? This little princess says she's ready to go. My mama would have loved her. She told me that she always wanted a daughter, but all she got was three old ornery boys. I still have trouble forgiving her for not telling me about my two brothers until I was grown."

"I have trouble forgiving my mother for turning her back on me when I got pregnant, and Sally's father for leaving us. But it doesn't stop the sun from coming up every single morning." Dixie took the baby from him and slipped the snowsuit on her and zipped it up, then pulled a stocking cap onto her head and tucked her wispy blond hair up under it.

"In other words," Landon said as he laid the book back on the table and stood up, "life goes on, and our forgiveness don't matter much one way or the other?"

"Oh, it matters. Not for those who did us wrong, but for ourselves. Unforgiveness and hate can take up a person's whole heart and then there ain't room for love," she answered. "So, when we get ready to forgive those who've been ugly to us, we free ourselves from the burden of carrying all that crap around."

"Then why is it so hard?" Landon kept Sally in his arms and opened the door for Dixie. "And who made you so smart?"

"I'm not smart, Landon," she told him. "I've figured out that it's just human nature to want to get even, not forgive. I hated Sally's father for leaving, but then it finally came to me that he didn't even know how I felt, and if he did, he wouldn't care. So why was I hanging on to those feelings when I have a better life right now than I ever had before—and a lot better than if he had even stuck around?"

"Oh, no!" he said.

"You don't agree with me?" she asked.

"No, not that," he answered as he opened the back door to his truck. "We need a car seat for the princess."

"It's in the house. I'll go get it." She turned around and jogged back to the shop through the inch of snow that was on the ground. She still wasn't sure about this whole idea of putting up a tree in the shop. Maybe she should ask Claire before she did such a thing. After all, Dixie only worked at the Quiltin' House, she didn't own the place. Claire was married to Levi, the foreman out on the Longhorn Ranch. Working for her the past year had been wonderful, and she had become a close friend. Dixie valued their working relationship and their friendship too much to jeopardize either one.

When she returned, Landon was sitting in the driver's seat, letting Sally play with the steering wheel. They were both having so much fun that she couldn't tell him she was having doubts about bringing a tree into the shop without asking. If Claire said that she didn't want a tree in the shop, then Dixie would just move it into her bedroom.

"Give me a minute or two to get this thing roped down, and then you can hand her over." Dixie talked as she worked. "First time I did this when I came to live here, we were in Claire's car and it took me forever to figure it out, but Sally was only three months old at the time. I've had a lot of practice since then." One of her insecurity tells was to chatter when she was nervous. Most of the time she wasn't all jittery when Landon was around. He'd been in and out of the shop lots of times when Claire asked him to pick up something in town. She'd spent Thanksgiving at the ranch with all the extended family, and he'd been there too. But this was the first time she'd been alone with him in a vehicle, and it seemed an awfully lot like a date—and that made her tense.

She got the baby seat fastened down, and Landon handed Sally over the front seat to her. "I've never even tried to get a baby seat fastened into position," he said. "Never been around babies until I came here to work a few months on the Longhorn Ranch. It's like a big extended family out there. I feel like Emily is my sister as well as Tag and Hud's, and I can't even begin to tell you how much I've learned from Cade and Levi and Justin. I didn't even know I liked babies until I moved over here from out in the western part of the state. Retta and Cade's little girl, Annie, stole my heart, and Claire's son, Wyatt, and Emily's little Hayden, why, they're the next generation of cowboys."

"There's even more on the way. Rose is pregnant with twin boys," Dixie said. "And you, Landon Griffin, are a natural baby whisperer the way they all take to you." She got into the passenger seat of the truck. "Nice vehicle here."

"Thank you. I saved up my money from working for my brothers and bought it just before I came over here." He started the engine and backed out onto the street. "I've never driven or even ridden as far as that trip was. Mama hated road trips, so we flew everywhere. What's been the longest drive for you?"

She didn't want to talk about road trips. She would rather ask him why he had to leave, but then that might open up a can of worms she didn't want to deal with. She'd followed in her mother's footsteps when it came to men. If forty good men were standing in front of them with roses in their hands and singing a love song just to them, they would pick the forty-first one who wasn't worth crap—the one who wouldn't work, wouldn't stay with them in tough times, and was more interested in a six-pack of beer than buying them a rose. She didn't trust men, but she also didn't trust herself to pick out a decent one.

"Did you hear me?" he asked.

"I'm sorry. I was woolgathering. My longest trip was from southern Louisiana to over around Abilene." She noticed a spiral of smoke coming from a nearby chimney and then caught a whiff of it. The fire that had almost taken her life and Sally's had happened more than a year before, but the smell of smoke still made her shiver.

"Cold?" Landon asked.

"No." Dixie shook her head. "It's the smoke. Gets to me every time."

"I heard that you and Sally were in a fire. What happened?" He drove straight to the barn on the ranch and pulled the truck through the double doors.

"Sally and I were hitchin' rides, goin' toward Sweetwater, and we got stuck in Bowie," she answered. "We were going to sleep in the park, but we saw an abandoned house where we'd at least be out of the cold weather, so we went inside. It caught on fire, and Hud Baker rescued us. I spent a night in the hospital, and Hud took Sally to Rose's place. The next day Claire offered me a job, and this is where

I've been ever since. The whole extended family out at the Longhorn Ranch has become my friends since then."

Landon laid a hand on her shoulder. "I'm so sorry you had to go through that."

"I keep telling myself that the worst thing in our lives turned out to be for the best, but I suppose the smell of smoke will always remind me of the fear of dying and leaving Sally without either parent." She glanced over at him and their gazes locked for a few seconds. Then he turned back to watch the road. She wanted to read something into that moment but was afraid to let herself. To Landon, she was a good friend, and it was best to keep it that way.

She sighed and said, "Maybe it's just to let me know that I shouldn't take anything, not even the air I breathe, for granted." She caught another whiff of smoke when he opened the truck door, and a vision of Hud coming through the gray fog to lead her and carry Sally to safety popped into her head. Had she and Sally slept in a park that night and hitched another ride the next day, she would never have met Landon. Sarah, one of the elderly people who lived down the road from her, often said that everything happens for a reason. Dixie believed it—almost. If everything really did happen for a reason, then why would fate bring Landon into her life, only to have him leave again?

Maybe it's to teach you that you need someone other than a baby and a few friends in your world. Claire's voice was loud and clear in her mind.

I don't need anything more than what I've got, Dixie argued.

Chapter Two

Landon hopped out of the truck with intentions of helping Dixie, but she was already sliding out of the passenger seat when he got there. "I'll get Sally out of the seat so she can go see Little Bit. He'll be glad to have some company." He pulled an apple from the console and handed it to Dixie. "Y'all can give him his treat tonight. I usually find a reason to come out here and bring him an apple or a carrot so he doesn't get lonely."

He freed Sally from her car seat and carried her over to the stall where the miniature donkey was already flipping his tail from one side to the other in excitement.

Sally wriggled and said, "Down, Lan-Lan."

He lowered her to the ground, and she plopped down right beside the bottom rail of the stall and reached up for the apple. When Landon put it in her hand, she held it out toward Little Bit, and as if he understood how small her hand was, he peeled back his lips and very gently took it from her.

Beau, the ranch dog, slipped under the railing from another stall and came over to lay beside Sally, and then Gussie, the cat that lived among all the houses on the ranch, curled up on the baby's other side.

"That's a modern-day nativity scene," he whispered.

"Where are the shepherds and the three wise men?" Dixie asked.

"They'll be in the church play. This one tonight is just for us." Landon draped an arm around her shoulders, and a sense of peace surrounded him like a warm blanket on a cold winter night. He didn't want to remove his arm and end the moment, or leave the scene, but if they didn't go soon, they'd be cutting down a tree with nothing but the light of the moon to guide them. With a sigh, he took a step back and said, "I'll get the feed unloaded in a few minutes, and then we'll go find a tree. I know just the place to start."

While he hefted the feed from the truck onto his shoulders, he stole looks over his shoulder at Dixie. She'd sat down beside Sally in the hay that had been strewn on the barn floor. He had never had a feeling like what he'd experienced moments before, and now that it was gone, he wanted it back. He loaded the last two bags of feed onto his shoulders and stacked them with all the others on the far side of the barn, then made a quick call to Cade, the ranch owner, and returned to Little Bit's stall.

"We really should be going," Dixie said. "Daylight is fading."

Sally stopped petting the donkey and stood up. "Lan-Lan, go," she said as she held out her arms for him to take her.

"Little corn has big ears," Dixie said.

"Evidently," Landon agreed as he stood and picked up Sally. "I'll have to remember that when I want to sneak something past her."

"Now where do we go?" Dixie asked.

"Cade said we could grab a tree stand from the barn and that we might have luck finding just the right-sized tree up by the cabin."

He settled Sally back into her car seat, held the passenger door for Dixie, then jogged around the back of his truck and slid in behind the wheel. He drove from the barn to the old cabin at the back side of the ranch, whistling "Jingle Bells" the whole way. "You ever been back here?" he asked as he parked.

"Nope, but I've heard the stories about it. Just about every couple on this ranch and on the one next door have used this cabin to live in at one time or another," she answered. "Claire says it's magical. That when one of the cowboys moves in here, his true love finds him."

I wouldn't mind getting stuck back here with you, Landon thought.

"Oh, really?" Landon raised an eyebrow. "So that's why the boys in the bunkhouse won't even drive back here. They're afraid they'll meet someone, fall in love, and have to give up their weekends at the Rusty Spur."

"I wouldn't know about that, but I think this is a beautiful spot. Not that it matters. We're here to get a tree and take it home, so we don't have anything to worry about," Dixie said.

He unfastened his seat belt and turned around to say something to Dixie, but he couldn't utter a word. With a beautiful sunset behind her, all he could think about was taking her in his arms and kissing her until they were both breathless. "What?" she asked. "Is something wrong?"

"Do you think that us being even this close to the cabin might have an effect on us?" he whispered.

"Not when you're going back out to the Panhandle in a couple of weeks," she said.

He tried to hide the disappointment on his face and remind himself that he was excited to see his brothers again. "So, what's your type?" he asked, gesturing to a stand of trees nearby. "Tall and skinny, or short and fat?"

"I always imagined I'd have a tall, handsome one," she answered, her eyes sparking.

Lord love a duck! That cabin might be working its magic yet.

* * *

That man is going to make a wonderful father someday, Dixie thought as Landon unbuckled Sally from her seat. He'd been so kind to them. Shortly after they'd met, he had stopped by the shop to bring in some flour and sugar he'd picked up for Claire. He'd sat down on the floor and played with Sally while Dixie put the groceries away, and then he'd stuck around for a while longer talking to Dixie. She'd never had a man—not one of her stepfathers or Sally's father either, for that matter—treat her like what she had to say mattered, but Landon did. That started the friendship, but these days it seemed like when she was around him, her heart beat a little faster and her pulse raced—that was attraction, not friendship.

She'd vowed not to put her life, her heart, and her trust in another man after what she'd gone through in the past. Sally's father had been sweet and kind at times in the beginning but he'd changed when the going got tough. Landon might do the exact same thing.

She shook her head to clear the thoughts and made herself think about making him a quilt for Christmas. She should applique a snowflake on one square so he would remember this night. Claire had bought a whole bolt of bright red fabric that was printed with white snowflakes for her Christmas Quilt Club, and there was at least half a yard of it left. That, along with a Christmas tree, should commemorate this evening.

Oh, and I'll trace Sally's little hand on a piece of fabric for a square, also. She made plans for more pieces of the quilt as they walked from the truck to the stand of cedar trees.

"What do you think of this one?" Landon pointed at a tall, thin tree. It was only a few inches shorter than he was, and he had on his cowboy hat.

"It's a little too tall, and it's got all those gangly branches." She waved her hands as she talked.

A squirrel climbed down the tree next to the one Landon had picked out, and Sally pointed at the ground. "Down," she said.

Landon put her on the ground, and though bundled up in the snowsuit, she chased after the squirrel as fast as she could. When the animal ran up a nearby tree, Sally went right to it and pointed.

"I guess she's chosen her tree," Landon said.

"It's the ugliest one in the whole area." Dixie pointed toward another tree. "What about this one over here, baby girl?"

Sally stared at the cedar tree and said, "No! No! No!"

"She can sure say that word plain enough," Landon chuckled. "If she likes the ugly one with the squirrel, then that's the one she should have." He went back to where the truck was parked and brought out a saw.

"I've got some fabric that has animals on it," Dixie told him. "I could make ornaments that look like squirrels, and maybe elephants and giraffes. You sure you don't want me to try to talk her out of that poor ugly tree? It looks like the Charlie Brown Christmas tree."

"It might not be beautiful now, but it will be when we get it decorated," Landon told her.

"It'll take a lot of ornaments to make that pitiful-lookin' tree pretty," she laughed.

He dropped to his knees and she giggled.

"What's so funny?" he asked and then realized that he was on his knees right beside her. "Have folks been teasing you ever since we met too?"

"Oh, yeah," she answered. "We've got to admit, it was kind of funny."

"Yep, it was," he agreed as he started sawing through the base of the tree. The brave little squirrel hung on until the minute the tree began to fall, and then he jumped to the ground and ran away.

"We'd better get this loaded before the princess follows that pesky animal to a ten-footer." Landon threw the tree over his shoulder as if it were as light as a bag of marshmallows.

Dixie could imagine his muscles bulging under his denim coat and wondered what it would be like to have those strong arms wrapped around her body.

Stop it! she scolded herself. *Don't let yourself go there. He won't even be around after the New Year. He'll find someone out there in west Texas to hang out with.*

He tossed the tree in the back of the truck and then turned around to Dixie. "Since we're here, would you like to see inside the cabin?"

"Don't you need to ask someone or get a key?" she asked.

"Folks leave it open all the time unless someone is living here," he said as he led the way over to the cabin. He held the door for Dixie, holding Sally in her arms, and then reached around to switch on the lights. "Especially after Claire got stuck in the snow and had to take shelter here. Did she tell you about that?"

"Yep," Dixie answered. "She said that she and her little niece would have frozen if it hadn't been for the cabin."

She stepped farther into the cabin and looked around. A stone fireplace was to her right, a small kitchen area to her left. A coffee table that looked like dozens of pairs of boots had been propped on it sat between the well-worn sofa and the fireplace. Beyond all that, in what was like a little cubbyhole, sat a king-sized bed covered with a brightly colored quilt—no doubt one of Claire's creations.

"The bathroom is through that door and the other one is a closet," Landon explained. "They offered this to me if I'd stay on here at the Longhorn Canyon."

Dixie set Sally on the floor, and she crawled over to the coffee table and pulled herself up on it. "Why did you come here, anyway? I would've thought you'd want to stay close to your two brothers after you found them."

"I love my brothers and their families," he answered. "But I got this itch to go somewhere else, like something was pulling at me to go."

"Seems to me that you'd do the same jobs no matter which ranch you decided to live on," she said.

"Yes, but..." He paused. "I guess I'm just not ready to settle down, and I need to do more, work on more ranches, meet more people, and travel more before I settle down. Have you ever felt like that?"

"Just every week," she admitted for the first time. "But it's not to leave Sunset or this area. It's to have a place of my own for me and this baby, a place that doesn't have a shop in the living room. Sometimes I feel like she's never going to have a normal life with so many people coming and going all the time."

Something like this is what I'd love, she thought, looking around the cabin, but she didn't say it out loud.

Landon chuckled. "You want to dig in and put down roots. I want wings to fly to the next ranch."

"If you want to travel and see things, then why are you going right back to your brothers' ranches?" she asked.

"It's only for a week, and then I've got a job offer just over the border into Colorado. I'm supposed to drive up there and talk to them the second week in January," he explained.

"When you finally settle down, where do you think it might be?" she asked as she turned toward the door.

"Who knows?" He shrugged. "In another ten years, I might be right back at either Pax's or Mav's ranch. When I get ready to put down roots, it would be nice to have family around me. But until then, ranchers always need help."

Dixie bit back a sigh. That sealed it right there. Even if they became more than friends, she would never be willing to drag Sally from one place to another every few months.

"If we're going to make decorations, we probably should be going," she said as she took one last look at the sweet little cabin.

"To tell the truth, I hope the decorations help the looks of that pitiful tree. I'd hoped to find something really pretty for you." He picked Sally up and followed Dixie outside.

"I've got lots of scraps," she said. "We'll just fill in all the bare spaces with decorations. The tree doesn't have to be perfect. Just think about if it could talk. It would be bragging to all the pretty trees that the cute little girl picked it over them."

"You should write children's books," Landon told her.

"I could never do that, but I do tell Sally stories like that all the time," she admitted.

"I bet you could if you tried. You should at least write

down the stories you tell Sally and keep them in a journal for her." He buckled Sally into the car seat and then checked the tree in the back to be sure it would ride well.

"Maybe I will, but right now we've got to turn this tree into a pretty one, not tell stories about it," she said.

Chapter Three

"How about pizza for supper?" Landon asked as he drove down the pathway toward the road leading west to Sunset. "The convenience store is open so we could get some slices, or some chicken nuggets if that sounds better, and then get busy decorating the tree."

"I've got a slow cooker of chicken and dumplings ready to eat at home," Dixie answered. "Be a shame to waste it. Why don't we just have that before we start making decorations?"

"You don't have to twist my arm. I'm always ready to eat a home-cooked meal." Landon made a left-hand turn onto the road.

"So, you've got the itch to move again?" she asked.

"I feel like a fish out of water," he answered. "I love it here, and I've kind of made a shirttail-kin family right here. Emily is my sister-in-law Alana's friend, and my brothers both worked out here on Tag and Hud's ranch next to the Longhorn, but I'm just not satisfied yet..." He paused.

"You feel like there has to be something more to life than this? I love my job, too, and the folks at the ranch are good to me, and I feel guilty when I want more. Is that kind of the way you feel?" she asked.

"Exactly," Landon agreed. "I can't put my finger on it, but I'm restless even when I'm happy."

"Well, you've got some time to figure all that out," she told him.

"Yes, I do, and until the first of the year, we've got something to do every single day so that you can have a perfect Christmas." He slowed down and turned right into the driveway of the Quiltin' House. "I can almost smell that chicken and dumplings. I'll get the princess out of her saddle and bring her inside if you'll go on and dish them up."

"Saddle?" Dixie laughed.

"She's not a princess who rides in a low-slung sports car. She's a cowgirl princess who shows up all the boys on the ranch. She can outride and outshoot them and is prettier than the whole lot of them too." Landon got out of the vehicle, rounded the front end, and opened the door for Dixie.

Just that small gesture made Dixie feel like a queen. Sally's father had been Dixie's only boyfriend, and he had not had an ounce of chivalry. Truth be told, he was a selfish bastard who had left her high and dry when his mother offered to let him come back home if he would leave her and *that brat* behind.

"Thank you." Dixie grabbed the diaper bag and hurried up on the porch to get away from the howling north wind. "Good thing we got the tree when we did," she said as she unlocked the door. "If we'd waited until now, we would have had to put rocks in the princess's pockets to keep the wind from blowing her all the way to Dallas."

Landon carried Sally into the house, set her on the floor,

and removed her little snowsuit. "That's funny, but so true. Maybe we should carry a bucket full of stones in the bed of the truck for both of you. I'd hate to try to find y'all if you got carried off to Dallas. That's a pretty big place."

"So, you'd come lookin' for us?" Dixie removed her coat.

"Of course I would. Your roots are here, not in the middle of a big city."

The baby's little lower lip quivered when Landon walked back out the door without even sitting down for a few minutes. After all the excitement of the evening, Dixie might have felt the same if she hadn't known he was coming right back. When he brought the tree into the shop, Sally's blue eyes got as big as saucers, and she clapped her hands. She watched as Landon removed his coat and hat and then got busy putting the tree in the chipped and rusted metal stand. When it was upright, Sally pointed at the top, walked all around it, and jabbered words that even Dixie couldn't understand.

"I think she's looking for the squirrel," Landon said as he lopped the ends off a few branches in an attempt to give it a better shape. "Maybe we should make a stuffed squirrel first."

Dixie headed toward the kitchen. "Before we do anything, we're goin' to have some supper."

She had been out to the ranch for Sunday dinner after church many times, but she'd never had anyone sit down to a meal with her here in the shop. Her hands shook as she took three bowls from the cabinet and set the table.

Settle down and enjoy his company, Sarah's voice scolded in her head.

A picture of the elderly woman, tall and thin with chin-length gray hair, popped into Dixie's head. She was part of the Fab Five, as the group of senior citizens called themselves who lived not far from the shop. No one would ever guess that she or any of the other members of the Fab Five were past seventy. They were active in everything in town and had been on a couple of long cruises since Dixie met them. They all spoiled Sally terribly, bringing her prizes and toys every time they went anywhere, even if it was only into Bowie for groceries. Sarah was Dixie's pick of them all, and if she had a problem, she often went to Sarah for advice.

"What are you thinkin' about?" Landon asked.

His deep voice startled Dixie so badly that she jumped. "Sarah was fussin' at me."

"On the phone?" Landon picked up Sally and carried her into the kitchen.

Dixie tapped her forehead with a finger. "Right here. She gets into my head sometimes and scolds me."

"The whole bunch of them meddle in all of the folks' lives out at the ranch, but it's just because they love all y'all. That reminds me. We'll have to go to the church program Sunday night. They're going to put on a skit." He settled Sally into her high chair. "What can I do to help with supper?"

"Pour the sweet tea. It's already made up in the refrigerator," Dixie said. "I'll slice the bread and set the pecan pie in the oven to warm up."

"Holy smokes!" Landon grabbed Dixie around the waist and spun her around a couple of times before setting her feet back on the floor. "This ain't just supper. It's a feast."

Her heart pounded, and her pulse kicked up a dozen notches. "No, a feast"—she stopped to catch her breath—"is what we have at the ranch for Thanksgiving."

"We'll have to agree to disagree," he told her. "If you ate whatever the cowboys cook up at the bunkhouse all week, you'd understand. I can't wait to tell them about this meal.

They're going to be so jealous. Merry Christmas to me," he singsonged as he put ice and tea into the glasses.

Dixie couldn't remember the last time she'd enjoyed an evening so much. Usually, after closing the shop, she and Sally had supper, and then she spent the rest of the evening with the baby before her seven-thirty bedtime. After that, she either cut out the pieces for a quilt or maybe watched some television before she turned in. Tonight, Landon had given her and Sally a taste of the joy of the season. They had a tree. Ugly as the poor thing was, standing over there in the corner with too many branches in some places and gaping holes in others, it was theirs, and Landon would be sharing in the fun of making decorations.

She hummed as she spooned the dumplings into a large crock bowl and put it in the center of the table. Then she added a platter of sliced bread and a small divided plate with two kinds of cheese. Landon seated her before he took his place and then waited for her to say a simple prayer.

"We didn't say grace when I was growing up, and we didn't go to church," she said after she finished. "But after the fire, I decided that I needed to go to church, and that I'd raise my daughter to respect God."

"We didn't pray over our food either," Landon said. "But I got used to saying grace when I moved to Daisy to be near my two brothers. Everyone out there, and everybody here on the Longhorn Canyon Ranch, respects God, like you said."

She dipped up small bowls full of chicken and dumplings for each of them, and then put a few spoonfuls on a saucer to cool for Sally. "She can eat a lot of things by herself, but not this."

"I'll help." Landon cut a dumpling into pieces and blew

on a spoonful until it was cool enough to feed her. "Here you go, princess."

Sally closed her eyes and made an "mmmm" noise when she tasted the food in her mouth.

Landon put the first bite into his mouth and said, "I agree. These are great."

Dixie could feel the heat rising up the back of her neck. Not once had her ex-boyfriend ever complimented her on anything that she cooked. More than once, he had come in from work, taken one look at the supper table, and said, "I'm not eating this crap. I'm going down to the convenience store and get myself a burrito."

"Thank you." Dixie kept her eyes on her plate and hoped he couldn't see her scarlet-red cheeks.

I will not think about the past, she vowed. *I will enjoy the memories I have already made today and look forward to what is ahead during this holiday season.*

When they finished eating, she cleaned Sally's face and hands, set her on an area rug with some of her toys, and turned around to find Landon clearing the table. "I can take care of that," she told him.

"Oh, no!" Landon rolled up his sleeves above the elbows. "You cooked and fed me a great supper. It's only fair that I help with the cleanup. I don't know where everything goes, so if it's all right, I'll wash, and you can dry."

Dixie couldn't keep her eyes off his muscular forearms. A vision of him wrapping her up in his arms popped into her head. The temperature of her body jacked up at least ten degrees, and her voice sounded strange in her own ears when she said, "That's fine and thank you."

He washed the tea glasses first, rinsed them, and set them in the drainer. Her hands shook when she picked the first one up, and she dropped it on the floor. It shattered, sending glass all around her legs and feet. Landon scooped her up in his arms and carried her to the living room. He set her down on a rocking chair and grabbed the broom.

Landon makes me feel like a queen and this rocking chair is my throne.

"I'll clean it up. Just don't let the baby come into the kitchen until I'm sure there are no more slivers on the floor," he said. "Are you hurt? Did you get cut? I didn't realize you'd kicked your shoes off until I looked down."

They both noticed a blood spot on the top of her sock at the same time. "Where's your medicine cabinet? In the bathroom?"

"What you need is in the cabinet to the left of the bathroom sink," she answered.

He picked up the baby, set her in Dixie's lap, and handed Dixie the first book he could lay his hands on. "Here, you hold Sally so she doesn't get into the glass, and I'll take care of your foot." Then he patted Sally on the back. "Mama is going to look at a book with you, baby girl."

"Lan-Lan, go?" Sally's little lower lip stuck out.

"Only down the hall," Landon assured her and glanced down at Dixie. "Bathroom, right?"

Afraid to blink for fear she'd wake up and find that this was all a dream, she just nodded. Her foot was bleeding, and it should hurt, but she didn't feel a thing. Did all queens feel like this when their knight in shining armor picked them up?

Not armor, she thought. *Landon is a knight in shining cowboy hat and boots.*

In minutes he returned and dropped to his knees in front of her. "If it needs stitches, we'll have to go to the emergency room," he said as he eased the sock off her foot. "Nope, it's more of a puncture and it's not deep. Thank goodness you were wearing socks, or it might have been worse." His big, rough hands felt like silk as he cleaned the wound, applied ointment, and then covered it with a Band-Aid.

Dixie's heart pounded and her pulse raced. "Thank you," she said and was surprised when her voice sounded like she'd been sucking air from a helium balloon.

"No problem." Landon patted her on the knee and then started back down the hall to put away the supplies. "Keep Sally entertained, and I'll clean up the glass, then do those dishes."

"I can stand up and dry dishes," she protested.

"Of course you can, but let me do it," he threw over his shoulder.

While Sally pointed at the pictures in the book about a puppy dog, Dixie listened to Landon singing bits of "Have Yourself a Merry Little Christmas" and humming through the words he didn't know.

Landon would never leave his wife and child behind without so much as a backward glance, she thought as she looked down at her bandaged foot.

He finished the cleanup and came back into the living room. "Are you sure you feel like running a sewing machine tonight? Will it hurt your foot too much to sew?"

"It's barely a scratch." She handed Sally up to him. "Your turn to entertain her while I work on some ornaments to dress up our tree."

Landon sat down on the floor and played "name that stuffed animal" with Sally. While she tried to say the animal's names, he peeked over at Dixie. She cut circles from red and green velvet and then ran a stitch around the outside edge. Then she gathered it up and stuffed the result with leftover quilt batting to make a perfect little round ball. In less than half an hour, she had two dozen ornaments ready.

"Let's put these on the tree so Sally can see them before I put her to bed. It's already past her bedtime," Dixie said.

Landon had just finished hanging the last one up close to the top, when Sally crawled between his legs, grabbed one from a low limb, and the tree came crashing down to the floor. The limbs brushed against her face and startled her so badly that she began to cry. Landon gathered her up in his arms, checked her to be sure she wasn't hurt, and kissed her a dozen times on her cheeks and forehead.

"It's all right, baby girl. We should have fastened it down better. Don't you worry. Mommy and I will get it all fixed so it won't fall on you again," he chuckled.

Dixie righted the tree and stood back staring at it for a full minute. "What are we going to do?"

Landon handed Sally off to her, went out to the porch, and brought in two heavy flowerpots. He situated them at the base of the tree to hold it steady and then tried to knock it over, but it stayed upright. "It's not beautiful, but it works."

"Beauty is in the eye of the beholder." Dixie set the baby down and retrieved a bolt of fabric printed with Christmas trees. She stretched it out on the table, cut two lengths the same size, and sewed up the ends and sides on the sewing machine.

Sally toddled right over to the flowerpots and was about to stick her hands in the dirt when Landon picked her up again. "Guess my idea wasn't so good after all."

"It was a wonderful idea." Dixie stood up and carried her two new sacks to the tree. "We'll just cover the pots with these," she said as she worked, "and tuck the ends under the bottom like this. Now Miss Nosy Pants can't get into them."

"You are a genius, and now it doesn't matter if she takes the ornaments off and plays with them."

"What do you mean, 'if'?" Dixie pointed at the baby,

who had already taken several of the little balls from the lower limbs.

"We can always put them back on each evening," Landon told her.

"And now it's time for Sally to have her bath and go to bed," Dixie said.

"And I get to rock her to sleep after her bath?" he asked.

"She always loves for you to put her to sleep," Dixie said. "Sure you've got time to stick around that long? It's getting late."

"I can always make time for you and Sally, and besides, your foot has to hurt, so I'll take on the bedtime duty tonight." He grinned. Dixie picked up the baby and carried her into the bathroom.

Help with supper. Help with the baby. Help with decorating the tree and then rehanging the ornaments that Sally kept taking off without even scolding her. That was more than she'd ever seen her father, her boyfriend, and her stepdad all do combined.

"Lan-Lan," Sally said when Dixie set her in the tub. "My Lan-Lan."

"No, mine." Dixie played along with her. Sometimes she would say "my mama," or sometimes it was "my baby" when she wanted her favorite doll in the bath with her.

Sally drew her chin down to her chest, and she looked up at her mother from under blond lashes. "Mine." She pointed to her chest.

"I can be both," Landon said from the doorway. "I kind of like being y'all's Lan-Lan."

Heat flooded Dixie's face so fast that she didn't have time to even attempt to control the blush. "Trouble is that tomorrow it might be that we're arguing over whose baby doll or whose mama is hers."

"That's all right," Landon said. "Tonight, right now at this moment, I get to be her Lan-Lan and I like it."

Sally reached up and flashed a bright smile. "Lan-Lan hold?"

"Yes, I will soon as your mama dries you off and gets you ready for bed. I get to read to you tonight too. Isn't that great?" Landon said.

He didn't say that he *had to read* to her, but that he *got to read* to her. His tone and his sparkling eyes left no doubt that it was a privilege, not a chore to rush through. Dixie's heart swelled with happiness and sucking on a lemon couldn't have wiped the smile off her face. She could really get used to this kind of arrangement.

Every night while Dixie brushed the tangles from Sally's blond hair and put sweet-smelling baby lotion on her body, she gave thanks for all her blessings. That night when she put pink pajamas on her daughter, Landon Griffin was on the top of that list. When she finished getting the baby dressed and carried her out of the bedroom into the shop, Sally reached out to Landon and said, "My Lan-Lan."

"That's right, princess." He took her from Dixie and went straight to the rocking chair. "I've picked out four books. Which one do you want me to read first?"

Sally pointed at the one with a squirrel on the front of it and settled down with her head on his chest. Before he had finished reading half the book, her eyes fluttered shut, and she was asleep.

"That didn't take nearly long enough," he whispered. "Does she always fall right to sleep like that?"

"She's had a really big evening." Dixie left the table where she had just finished making the star for the top of the tree. "Slip her over into my arms and I will..."

"No need for that," Landon said. "Just lead the way, and I'll put her in her crib."

Ever so gently, he stood up with the toddler still in his arms and followed Dixie down the hallway. He noticed a door to the left that led into a room with a huge machine. That had to be where they made their quilts. Then she turned right into a bedroom with a crib only a few feet from a big four-poster bed. He laid the baby down on her back, and Dixie covered her with a blanket that looked like it had seen better days.

"It's her favorite, and she'll fret if she doesn't have it next to her face," Dixie explained in a soft voice.

Landon bent forward and kissed Sally on the forehead. "Sleep tight, princess. Dream of squirrels and Santa Claus and puppies."

"Why puppies?" Dixie headed out of the room.

"Because that's what I dreamed about my whole life. I asked Santa every year for a yellow puppy, and I also asked my mama for the same thing. I would have traded all the toys I ever got, and even the fancy bike with the special wheels, for a dog, but Mama said that she wasn't having an animal in or around the house," he explained as he followed her back to the shop part of the house. "If I ever have the privilege of being a father, the first thing I'm getting my child is a puppy."

"So, you think fatherhood is a privilege?" Dixie asked.

"Just one of the greatest in the whole world," Landon answered. "One of my favorite memories of my dad is the time he took me to the rodeo. I wasn't much more than five, and I wanted to be a real cowboy when I grew up. The only sporting event my dad liked was golf, and he hated anything to do with animals. Looking back now, I can see that was a really big sacrifice for him to take me."

If only. Dixie stopped her thoughts right there. She wouldn't live in the past.

Landon bent and kissed Dixie on the forehead. "Thank you for a wonderful evening. I'll be by tomorrow right after work to build a snowman out in the backyard if that's all right with you."

"You ever lived in a place where you could build a snowman?" she asked.

He shook his head. "How about you?"

"Nope, but I think it would be fun." She grinned. "Oh, and don't eat supper before you come over."

"You don't have to tell me twice. Can I bring anything?" he asked.

"Just a healthy appetite." She walked him to the door.

"Will you wait to put the star on the tree until I get here?" he asked. "I want a picture of Sally's face when we first put it on the top."

"Sounds good." She didn't want him to go. What she wanted was another kiss or two, maybe even a little south of her forehead.

When he'd closed the door behind him, she slumped down in the rocking chair and touched her forehead to see if it was as hot as it felt. Surprisingly enough, it was cool.

"I can't go there," she muttered. "I can't afford to get my heart broken twice. That was just a friendly kiss, not a romantic one, and I won't make it into something more, no matter how much I want to do just that."

She pushed up out of the chair and went to the cutting table where she deftly cut a green tree from a remnant of fabric and appliqued it to a twelve-inch quilt square. When she finished, she cut out a tiny little gold star and carefully stitched it to the top of the tree. After that, she created a red square with a snowflake in the middle and carried both appliqued squares to her bedroom.

"Day one," she said as she tucked them away in a dresser drawer.

She took a quick shower and was in bed by eleven o'clock but tossed and turned until midnight. When she finally fell asleep she dreamed of a yellow puppy, with a red bow around its neck, chasing a squirrel across the yard toward a tree all decorated with cloth ornaments.

Chapter Four

"Good mornin'." Sarah threw her coat and gloves on a rocking chair when she entered the shop. "How's my girl? Oh. My. Goodness. When did you get a tree?"

"Lan-Lan!" Sally said proudly.

"Landon says we need the whole Christmas experience," Dixie said. "So, we cut down the tree and made ornaments last night, and tonight we're going to build a snowman. Then we're going to go see the Christmas lights and make cookies."

"That's wonderful," Sarah said. "You should talk him into staying in this part of the world. Cade says he's the best hired help he's ever had, and that he could be a foreman of the Longhorn Canyon within a couple of years if he stuck around."

"Not me." Dixie shook her head. "What if he stayed and then resented me after a while?"

"Miracles happen during Christmas." Sarah cocked her

head to one side and then the other. "That is one ugly-ass tree. We've got an extra one at our house you could use."

"Sally picked it out," Dixie explained.

"Then it's the right tree even if it isn't the prettiest," Sarah said with a smile. "Patsy threw a fit about me driving down here in the snow, but I told her that I used to ride a four-wheeler to gather up the cattle in worse weather than this. Besides, I want to play with Sally and eat some cookies right out of the oven. I smell cinnamon. Are you making snickerdoodles this morning?"

Dixie nodded. "Yes, ma'am. I don't expect many customers in this weather, but Claire and I always have cookies and coffee ready just in case. I bet Patsy had a smart-ass remark about you on a four-wheeler, didn't she?"

"Oh, yeah." Sarah opened one of the baby's books. "She said that she used to ride a mechanical bull, but that didn't mean she was stupid enough to do it now."

Dixie could visualize Patsy popping her hands on her chubby waist and telling Sarah that she was too old to drive a quarter of a mile in the snow. "You sure you only need one yard of this fabric? Better get as much as you need while you're here. You might have to whip Patsy to get to drive down here again."

"By damn, I'll walk if she hides my keys," Sarah declared. "Right now, I'm going to enjoy some one-on-one time with this baby girl before I eat some of those cookies. You got coffee made?"

"Pot is almost full. I'll bring you a cup," Dixie offered.

"Thank you," Sarah answered and then started reading a book to Sally about a puppy who was all alone at Christmas.

"I dreamed about a puppy last night," Dixie said.

"Every kid needs a pet. When you get your own place,

I'm going to go to the shelter and adopt a puppy for y'all," Sarah told her.

"I'm sure Sally would like that, but it'll be a long time before we save up enough to get our own place," Dixie said as she handed Sarah her coffee.

"If you'd let us help, we could rent you that little place next to ours, and then we could babysit this sweet little girl every day while you work," Sarah said.

"Thanks for the offer. I really appreciate it, Miz Sarah. I love all of you, but I need to do this on my own." Dixie cut Sarah's fabric, made up a ticket, and laid it to the side. With icy roads and bad weather, this might be her only sale that day. She was returning the bolt of cloth to the shelf when the phone rang.

"The Quiltin' House. Merry Christmas," she answered.

"Is Sarah there?" Patsy asked.

"Yes, ma'am," Dixie answered. "You want to talk to her?"

"Nope, but please call me when she leaves," Patsy said.

"Be glad to," Dixie told her. She had barely put the phone back on the stand when it rang again. This time it was Claire.

"Hey girl, I'm not even going to try to come to the store for the next few days unless you need me," Claire said.

"I can hold it down. I doubt that we will have many customers, and we're all caught up on orders until after the New Year." Dixie thought about the throw she was making for Landon and kind of hoped for a couple of slow days so she could finish it. "Oh, and we put up a tree in front of the window in the shop. Is that all right? Landon cut it down for us, and I made ornaments from scraps."

"Sounds cute. Take a picture of it with your phone and send it to me. I don't know why I haven't thought of doing something like that before now. Can't wait to see it," Claire said.

"It's not quite finished yet, but sure. I can take a picture of it now," Dixie told her.

"Great! Then I'll see you in church Sunday if not before. Right now, I'm just staying in with the baby. He's cutting teeth and so cranky it's not even funny," Claire said.

"I'm in the same boat with this girl of mine. See you in a few days," Dixie said.

The call ended and Dixie made a mental note to send a picture as soon as she got the first batch of cookies from the oven. She put a dozen on a tray and took them to the little table in the living room where Claire always had cookies ready for the customers.

Sarah reached for a cookie and dipped it into her coffee. She pinched off a small corner for Sally before she put it in her mouth. "Good, ain't it, baby girl? Just a little coffee with a snickerdoodle makes it a thousand times better. Those are the cutest ornaments on your tree. So original and fitting for a quilt shop. Love the little squirrel. Are you going to make more animals?"

"Plannin' on it." Dixie told her the story of the squirrel. "I'm too cheap to buy a tree or ornaments." She snapped two pictures of it from different angles and sent them to Claire. "That's money that can be saved up for a car so we can be more independent, and before you say anything, I need to do that on my own too."

"You're as stubborn-headed as Patsy," Sarah said.

Dixie giggled. "Thank you. I want to grow up to be just like the Fab Five."

"Oh, honey, if you mixed us all up together and put us in one little ole thing like you, it would be more dangerous than a box of dynamite." Sarah laughed with her. "Now why don't you get busy and make some more ornaments? If you cover it up with stuff, it might look like something other than a Charlie Brown tree. What are those two pillowcases covering up, anyway?"

Dixie nodded in agreement. "The flowerpots from the porch are under the sacks. Sally can't get into the dirt inside them that way, and they're propping up the tree so it won't fall over again. I've got to admit, even though the tree isn't beautiful, the experience of getting it and sharing time with Landon was amazing."

"That boy really likes you," Sarah said.

"I really like him, but...," Dixie began.

Sarah held up a hand. "There are no buts in relationships."

Dixie wanted to believe that, but she'd had too many disappointments in her life to let herself think such a thing.

"Would you look at the time? It's my day to make lunch so I'd better get on home. If you change your mind about the tree," Sarah said as she picked up her coat and hat, "just let me know, but it is looking better with each thing you hang on it."

Sally stuck out her lower lip in one of her famous pouts when Sarah walked out the door.

"Turn that frown upside down," Dixie told her little girl as she scattered toys out on a quilt on the floor that Dixie used for a play mat. "We've got lots of fun things going on, like working on Landon's throw. What do you think, sweetheart? Let's put a snowman on a quilt square today since we'll be making one out in the yard tonight."

"Lan-Lan, snow." Sally nodded and picked up a stuffed donkey that Sarah had bought for her back on her first birthday. "Lil Bit, snow?"

"No, Little Bit won't be here to play in the snow with us, but we'll go see him again, soon." Dixie made a snowman

out of white satin, sewed small buttons on his face for a
nose and eyes, and even appliqued a red-and-green scarf
around his neck. Then she designed a square with a string
of Christmas lights tangled up in the middle.

* * *

The day dragged by for Landon like a snail trying to go
from the barn to the bunkhouse in the snow. He spent the
morning hefting fifty-pound bags of feed onto his shoulders
and carrying them from the truck to the troughs for the cattle
and trying not to think about the feelings he'd had when
he was with Dixie and Sally the night before. No matter
what he did, he kept going back to the aura that surrounded
him in the barn when the three of them were all reaching
between the old wooden rails of the stall and petting Little
Bit. Not even when his mother was alive and the two of
them were enjoying all the events of the holiday season had
he ever known such peace. Could it be an omen that he was
supposed to stay in that area and find what Dixie called his
passion right there? He checked the time on his phone and
sighed loudly when he saw that it wasn't even noon yet.

*You are so excited about seeing Dixie again tonight that
you are wishing away the hours.* His mother's voice was
loud and clear in his head. *Why are you leaving this place
when you care so much for her?*

She's a friend, he argued.

Just a friend doesn't make you feel like this, my son,
she said.

"She's had a tough life," he muttered out loud. "And I
want to give her the kind of Christmas you always gave me.
This is for her, but it's also therapeutic for me."

He crawled up into the cab of a tractor. In the next

two hours he hauled six round bales of hay from where they were stored in one pasture over to another one where a hundred head of cattle had been brought up closer to the barn.

The day lasted a week, or so it seemed, but finally it was quitting time. He rushed through the bunkhouse, took a quick shower and changed clothes, and drove to the Quiltin' House. He parked his truck and jogged across the yard. He cleaned his boots on the welcome mat and then knocked on the door.

Dixie threw it open a minute later. "Come on in. You don't have to knock. This is a business, you know."

"But it's after business hours, so now it's your home." He couldn't take his eyes off her.

"That's sweet," Dixie said. "I'm glad you're here. The first thing Sally said this morning was your name, and every time the door opens, she thinks you're here."

"Lan-Lan!" Sally started toward him.

"I made spaghetti for supper," Dixie said. "I hope you haven't eaten."

"That sounds great, but let's go build our snowman first before we lose the light," he said. "We don't have enough to build a big one, but we can build a snowball man, and take pictures of our girl with him."

"You've given this some thought, haven't you?" Dixie went to get their coats from the bedroom. He'd said *our* girl, but did he really mean it? she wondered. Or had it just been a slip of the tongue, so to speak?

"I've been working alone today, so yes, ma'am, I've thought about this all day," he admitted. "This will be my first snowman, too, so it doesn't matter if it's not as big as King Kong. I can't wait to send pictures back to Mav and Pax. They don't have a bit of snow out there, and they're going to be so jealous. If we take a picture from the right angle, we can make it look like it's six feet tall."

Landon reached for the snowsuit Dixie was holding. "I'll put it on her. Are we going to put our snowman in the front yard or out back?"

"In the front for sure," Dixie said. "It'll be cute, and it can be our outside decoration. Claire and I planned to wrap some lights around the porch posts and put a wreath on the door, but we got busy with last-minute quilt orders."

Landon zipped up Sally's snowsuit and carried her toward the door. "Ask Mommy if she's got something for the eyes and the nose. We could use a carrot, and maybe some buttons."

"I'll bring them right out." Dixie headed to the kitchen.

Landon set Sally down in the snow and laughed when it came almost to her knees. "Princess, you could use a pony to ride right now so you wouldn't be butt-deep in this white stuff," he said.

Dixie returned with a carrot, several buttons, and a long, thin piece of plaid fabric in her hands. "I figured he could use a scarf, and this was destined for the trash can."

Her blue eyes sparkled like a reflection of the summer sky on the ocean water, and she looked so darn cute in that knit cap that he wanted to kiss her. He glanced down to see that she was wearing shoes, not boots. If only he knew her size, he would buy her a pair of boots for Christmas.

I can't do that, he thought. *Clothing or boots is not something a guy buys his girlfriend for Christmas.*

Girlfriend! He was struck speechless at the thought. Was he really ready for that?

Good grief! He shook the notion from his head. They hadn't even gone out on a date, much less talked about taking their friendship to the next level.

Dixie snapped her fingers. "Earth to Landon."

"What? I'm sorry, I was daydreaming," he admitted.

She held up the strip of fabric. "Scarf?"

"It's perfect," Landon said.

Sally sat down on her butt, picked up a fistful of snow in her mitten and licked it, then giggled and shivered. Then she crawled through the snow right behind Landon as he began to roll a snowball across the yard. In only a few minutes the yard was bare, and his snowball was about the size of a softball.

"Looks like our snowman really is going to be small," Dixie laughed.

"Nothing is going like I pictured," Landon said. "I wanted a perfect tree, and now there's not enough snow to make a decent snowman."

"Hey, perfect, like beauty, is in the eye of the beholder." Dixie gathered up a handful of snow and threw it at him.

He stepped to the side to avoid getting hit and slipped and fell on his back.

"Are you all right?" Dixie dropped down on her knees beside him.

"Can't...," he sputtered, then managed to get out one more word, "breathe."

Without any forewarning, she pinched his nose shut, opened his mouth, and began trying to resuscitate him. When she blew into his mouth, he coughed and sat up.

"It worked!" Her eyes widened out as big as silver dollars. "I saw that done on television, and thought it was crazy, but it really works."

He sat up, grabbed her around the waist, and pulled her onto his lap. "Need mouth-to-mouth resuscitation." He pulled her lips to his in a steamy, hot kiss that came close to melting what snow was left in the yard.

Sally crawled up in his lap right along with her mother and touched his face with her snow-covered mitten.

"I guess we shouldn't make out in front of the baby," he whispered.

"I thought that I was reviving you, not making out," she teased.

"I might need more to keep from dying. That was a nasty fall and you caused it when you threw snow at me." He raised an eyebrow.

She gave him a peck on the cheek and stood up. "I wouldn't let you die," she joked.

"What about when we get done with supper. If I feel faint, will you make sure I don't die?" He reached up and took her hand in his.

"Oh, hush." She moved Sally to a bare place on the ground. "You weren't ever going to die. You're just a big flirt. Do you tease all the girls like this?"

"I saw a bright light beckoning me to leave this world." He let go of her hand and stood up with Sally in his arms.

"That was the moon, silly cowboy," she told him. "This baby girl's little nose is red. Let's get our snowman done so we can take the pictures and go inside. Hey, speaking of pictures, I sent Claire one of our tree and she loved it."

"Well, I'm not surprised." Landon packed together a nice-sized snowball. "It is the prettiest tree in the whole state," he said as he finished making their tiny little snowman. "And we're about to have the cutest midget Frosty in Texas too."

"Our tree really doesn't look bad when we consider what it looked like at first," she told him as she tied the scarf around the snowman's neck.

Sally clapped her little mitten-covered hands together and hugged the snowman. Then she kissed him on the button nose, took a step back, and said, "My Fossy."

"That's right, baby girl," Landon agreed with her. "That is your Frosty, and now we need some pictures of you with him."

"Lan-Lan." Sally stretched her arms up toward Landon.

"Guess you'd better let me take the picture since she wants you to be in it," Dixie said. "This way when I tell her that you were the one that helped make this Christmas special, she'll have a face to go with your name."

Landon dropped down, set Sally on a knee, and pasted on a smile, but he didn't feel the happiness he had before. He didn't want to be nothing more than a picture in a book that Sally could look at through the years ahead. He wanted to be part of her life like he was right at that moment—for the rest of her life.

Chapter Five

Landon had wrestled with his feelings all night, sleeping sporadically and waking to question his decision to move back to the other side of Texas. Sure, he had family there, but he'd made a family right there in Sunset in the past few months, and Levi had offered him both the cabin to live in and a job if he wanted to stay on at the Longhorn Canyon. His old nanny, who had passed away years before his mother, would tell him to follow his heart.

Finally, at daybreak, he got up from his bunk. He was still trying to figure out which road to take when the door opened and a blast of cold air seemed to blow Levi Dawson, the ranch foreman, into the bunkhouse. Levi removed his coat and hung it on a nail inside the door, then made his way into the kitchen.

The ranch foreman was just over six feet tall, had light brown hair that he kept cut close, and green eyes. He was a big guy, outweighing Landon by at least twenty pounds, and his chest was as broad as a Dallas Cowboy football player's. "You the only cowboy up and around?"

"Yep." Landon nodded. "Thought I'd go ahead and get breakfast started. What are you doing out so early? I don't usually see you around for another hour."

"Claire has breakfast with all the ladies this morning," he answered. "She told me to eat a bowl of cereal or else come to the bunkhouse. So here I am. Want me to make the biscuits?"

"I'd appreciate that a lot. I can do them thwock biscuits, but when it comes to scratch, mine make hardtack look like feather pillows."

"Thwock?" Levi removed his hat and set it on top of the refrigerator.

Landon grinned. "That's when you take a can from the refrigerator and thwock it on the side of the cabinet to open it."

Levi chuckled. "I can do a damn sight better than that. Got something on your mind that's keepin' you from a good night's sleep?"

"How'd you know I didn't sleep?"

"Just a guess since you look like hell and you're up before dawn." Levi got the flour and other ingredients from the pantry and set about making a huge pan of biscuits.

"That old cabin still up for grabs?" Landon asked.

"Anytime you want it," Levi answered. "Has Dixie gotten under your skin?"

"Maybe." Landon took the crisp bacon out of the skillet and put it on a paper towel to drain and started frying a second pound.

Levi chuckled. "We'll be glad to have you long as you want to stick around, but I've got a feeling that your brothers will want you to come home at some point if you stay in

Texas. You might want to talk that over with Dixie before you make any final decision."

"I can't ask her to leave the only stable home she's ever known," he said.

"That would be her decision," Levi told him. "Yours is to decide where you want to live. You've got a job here, and I'm sure you've got one with either of your brothers," Levi told him as he slid the pan of biscuits into the oven and then clamped a hand onto Landon's shoulder. "Every one of us on this ranch has been where you are right now. We questioned ourselves, our motives, and even our hearts when we knew they were steering us right. You ain't alone, and if you need someone to talk to, just holler at me."

"Are you happy being the foreman of this ranch? Don't you want a place of your own?" Landon asked.

"I couldn't be happier than I am right now. I've got a wonderful wife, a son, and we're plannin' on havin' a couple more kids. I'm treated like a son here on the ranch, and I never wanted the responsibility of havin' a big place of my own. This right here is enough job for me."

"You think I could be happy being the foreman on one of my brothers' ranches?" Landon expertly cracked two dozen eggs into a bowl and whipped them with a fork.

"That's a question only you can answer. I can't do it for you. Ask yourself if you want to work for one of your brothers or if you want to go it on your own right here," Levi said. "I'm going to kick those sleepin' cowboys out of their bunks. Is the coffee ready?"

Landon pointed to the other end of the cabinet. "Two full pots."

"Then maybe they won't cuss me too bad," Levi said.

* * *

Dixie had customers in and out of the shop all day. She wasn't so busy that she needed to call Claire, but she certainly didn't have time to get bored. Several of the quilts that customers wanted to give as Christmas presents had been picked up throughout the morning. That afternoon a few ladies came in with gift cards they'd gotten at the various holiday parties around the area and wanted to buy fabric so they could start their projects right after the New Year.

The second that she flipped the sign on the door from OPEN to CLOSED her cell phone rang, and her heart dropped. Between customers she had told Sally all about Santa Claus and how they were going to go see him that evening, and she had a horrible feeling that Landon was calling to tell her that he couldn't make it. She stared at the phone without even seeing the caller ID for two rings, then she realized that the call was from Claire.

"Hello," she answered.

"How did things go today?" Claire asked. "I had planned to come in for a few hours, but I got busy wrapping gifts and time got away from me. Now it's almost time to go to the fire station to get Wyatt's picture made with Santa Claus. If I didn't have you to work for me, I'd sell the shop. I still love having my own business, but..." She paused.

Dixie looked at her phone to be sure that they hadn't been cut off, but then she heard Claire's voice.

"...don't tell anyone," Claire went on. "I'm going to surprise Levi on Christmas Day. I'm pregnant again, and I just love being a stay-at-home mama. Never thought I'd say that, but there it is."

"Congratulations," Dixie said, "and my lips are sealed, but please don't sell the shop."

"I won't, not until you get tired of working there. Then it's going on the market. We'll talk about giving you a raise after the first of the year, because you're basically going to be running it by yourself," Claire told her.

Dixie's thoughts spun around so fast that she had trouble latching on to one long enough to form a decent reply. Finally, she said, "Thank you for having that much faith in me."

"You've earned it many times over," Claire assured her. "I understand from Levi that you and Landon are taking Sally to see Santa last night. We should put Sally on one of Santa's knees and Wyatt on the other for a picture. Wouldn't that be cute?"

"I love that idea. I could put one in the memory book that Landon is making," Dixie said.

"I sure wish that guy would stay with us. Levi says he's the best help we've ever had on the Longhorn Canyon," Claire told her. "But we can't tie him down if he doesn't want to stay. See you later."

The call ended, but Claire's words about tying Landon down kept going through Dixie's mind as she got Sally dressed in a cute little red velvet dress for her Santa Claus picture.

A lonely tear escaped from one of her blue eyes and slowly made its way down her cheek. She swiped it away with the back of her hand. She wouldn't need an album to remind her of Landon. A picture of him in his weathered black-felt hat, tight jeans, and chambray work shirt would be burned into her mind forever. Add that to the sight of his clear blue eyes lighting up every time he looked at Sally, and the feel of his lips when he brushed a good-night kiss across her forehead. Then she had her own personal album of Landon Griffin that she could bring to mind anytime she wanted.

A hard rap on the door sent her down the hall with Sally

in her arms. She opened the door to find him standing there, all decked out in his best cowboy hat, a leather jacket, and shined cowboy boots.

He smiled. "There's my girls."

His girls? That put an extra beat into Dixie's heart. "Come on in. We just have to get our coats, and then we're all ready to go."

"Oh. My. God!" He stepped inside the house and closed the door behind him. "Y'all are both so gorgeous that it takes this rough old cowboy's breath away."

"We thank you." Dixie almost blushed. She had curled her dark brown hair, applied a little makeup, and chosen a pretty dark blue sweater to go with her best pair of jeans.

"I might need to carry a big stick to beat off all the men who'll be trying to sweet-talk you tonight," Landon said.

"Oh, hush!" She grinned as she got Sally into her coat and hat. "It'll be me needin' to use that stick to whip all the women who'll stop whatever they're doing to flirt with a sexy cowboy like you." Even in her nicest sweater and jeans, Dixie felt like she paled in comparison to him.

"We'll probably take a backseat to the princess," he told her. "She looks like she belongs in a television commercial for one of those movies they play this time of year."

"Lan-Lan." Sally reached for him.

He picked her up, set her on one arm, and helped Dixie into her coat with the other hand. Then he carried the baby out to the truck and strapped her into the car seat. "Now we're off to see Santa Claus and the elves. Have you thought about what you want to tell him to bring you?"

"If she understood what all that means, she'd probably ask for a squirrel. She's taken that ornament off the tree a dozen times today, and then fussed at me to put it back on so she could do it all over again," Dixie said as she fastened her own seat belt. "If you could still fit on Santa's lap, what would you ask for?"

"A puppy," Landon said without hesitation. "Like I told you before, that's what I asked for every single year until I told Mama that I didn't believe in Santa anymore."

Dixie made a mental note to make a quilt square with a yellow puppy on it that evening when they got back home. *And put a red bow around its neck*, she reminded herself.

When they arrived at the Sunset Volunteer Fire Station, the first thing they saw on the bed of a pickup truck out front was a pen full of puppies. A cardboard sign proclaimed that there were plenty more at the Bowie shelter available for adoption at a special Christmas rate. Landon stopped and let Sally reach through the wire fence and pet a couple of the cute little pups. They licked her hands and whined, and it saddened Dixie to not be able to adopt the yellow one with the big feet and brown eyes for both Landon and Sally.

"You're not fooling me," Dixie whispered. "You're the one who really wants to get your hands on those critters."

"Busted!" He laughed and shrugged. "Looks like there's a full house in there so we'd better get on inside."

A pregnant lady with three little boys came out of the station when Landon opened the door and stood to one side. The lady stopped and said, "What a beautiful baby. She looks exactly like her father. Y'all make such a cute little family. I'm finally getting a girl. Took a fourth time, but we're all excited."

"Congratulations," Dixie said.

"Merry Christmas," the lady told them and shook her head at the oldest little boy, who was pointing at the truck with the dogs. "No, Thomas, you can't have a puppy. Y'all have a nice evening. I've got to get out of here before my husband lets these boys take all those dogs home."

"How about that? We make a cute family." Landon's eyes met Dixie's.

"Of course we do," Dixie teased, but in that moment, she wished it were a truth.

Landon blinked a couple of times. "I can't believe you just said that."

"I didn't hear you telling her that we were just friends." Dixie waved at Claire and Levi, who were already in line.

"I didn't want to burst her bubble." Landon took his place behind half a dozen people.

"Me either," Dixie said.

"Did you ever sit on Santa's lap?" Landon asked.

"Nope," Dixie answered. "Mama took my half brothers to the mall once to sit on his lap, but I refused. I could tell he was"—she lowered her voice to a whisper—"that he was just a man dressed up in a suit and that his beard was fake. Besides, after too many stepfathers to count, I'd lost all faith in miracles at Christmas."

"So, you never believed?" Landon's brows drew down.

"It's hard to believe in much of anything when everything about life is just one tough hill to climb after another," Dixie said. "Until I got stranded in Bowie, I was the poster kid for bad luck, but not anymore. Sally is going to believe and she's going to have miracles, not hills."

"Yes, she is," Landon agreed.

When it was their turn to get Sally's picture made, she sat on Santa's knee like a little princess and even smiled for the cameras. When Santa asked her what she wanted for Christmas, she said, "Lan-Lan."

"Just a minute," Claire called out from halfway across the room. "I want a picture of our two babies with Hud—I mean Santa Claus."

"Thank goodness I hadn't planned to leave before

Christmas Day," Landon chuckled as Claire hurried across the room and put Wyatt on Santa's other knee.

Wyatt started to whimper. Sally reached out a hand toward him, and the whining turned into wails. "No, no, no!" Sally told him, and he cried even harder. Then she puckered up and tears began to roll down her cheeks.

"Lan-Lan, go," she said between sobs.

Landon picked her up at the same time Claire rescued Wyatt. "Guess that didn't work too well," she said. "He hates the words 'no, no.'"

"I'm so sorry," Dixie apologized.

"Don't be. It'll be the picture we love the most." Claire smiled and headed back across the room to where Levi waited.

"Who or what is Lan-Lan?" Santa looked up at Landon.

"That would be me. She doesn't know a lot of words yet," he explained.

"I don't know if I can get you in the sleigh, but if that's what she wants, I'll do my best." Santa winked.

"Thank you." Dixie smiled at Hud.

"What about you?" Santa asked her. "What do you want for Christmas? I don't see a ring on your finger. Maybe you want Lan-Lan too?" he teased.

"I learned a long time ago that wishing for special things don't make them appear," Dixie shot back at him.

"So, I'm special?" Landon asked as he stepped to the side and let the folks behind him have a chance.

"Of course you are, and you are welcome." Dixie batted her eyes at him flirtatiously.

"I'm welcome for what?" he asked.

"Didn't you see those women behind us gawking at you? I let them think we were a family so you could get out of this place with your pants on," she teased.

"Then I thank you. A cowboy needs a good woman to take care of him," Landon said. "Let's bypass the sack with an apple and an orange in it, and drive into Bowie for some ice cream."

"Ice keam!" Sally said and clapped her hands.

"She knows exactly what that is, and she loves it, especially chocolate," Dixie said.

"Then let's get out of here. I vote McDonald's for burgers and milk shakes." Landon held Sally in one arm and guided Dixie out of the crowd with his other hand on her lower back.

Sally narrowed her blue eyes and said, "Icc keam!"

"Yes, ma'am, baby girl. Let's have some ice keam—and some real food too," Landon said.

The trip to McDonald's was only a five-minute drive, but the line was long at the order counter. That suited Landon just fine because the evening was already going faster than he wanted.

"Ice keam." Sally stuck her bottom lip out and pointed toward a poster that featured a triple-dip banana split.

"You bring that precious baby on up here and get in line in front of us," a sweet little gray-haired lady said. "We've got our Sunday school class here for treats after our Christmas program, so we'll be awhile."

Dixie smiled. "Thank you."

"That's a beautiful little girl. She has her father's eyes for sure," the woman said.

"We get told that a lot." Landon couldn't keep the grin off his face.

"You'd better be ready to fight off the boys here in a few years," the elderly gentleman with her said. "That little girl is going to turn a lot of heads, but then I guess her mama sure turned yours awhile back, didn't she?"

"Yes, sir, she did," Landon replied. It wasn't a lie. Dixie had caused him to take a second and a third look when he met her the first time. With her dark brown hair and those clear blue eyes, plus that cute little figure she sported under those skinny jeans and her T-shirt, any man would have had trouble keeping it down to just one glance. But it was more than her looks that drew Landon to her. She was an amazing mother to Sally and had the sweet attitude that he imagined angels in heaven would have. When she looked at him, he felt like he was ten feet tall and bulletproof.

They ordered their food and Landon paid the young man behind the counter. "Thanks again," he told the Sunday school couple as he and Dixie took Sally to a booth in the corner.

"No problem. Y'all have a Merry Christmas," the guy said.

"Does that embarrass you?" Dixie asked in a low voice when she slid into the booth.

"Nope," Landon answered. "Kind of makes me feel good. Like a practice run for when…" He stopped before he finished the sentence.

"When you have a real family?" she asked.

"Does that make you uncomfortable?" he countered, avoiding her question.

She shook her head slowly. "You're going to make a wonderful father, Landon, so tonight I'm enjoying a night out on the town and pretending like you are really Sally's daddy."

Landon was not expecting that answer, and for a moment he thought he'd imagined her saying the words. "What about the rest of it, Dixie?" he finally asked.

"Yep, I'm pretending we are a family too," she answered, "and it's a good feeling. I should thank you for renewing my trust in men. Until I came to Sunset and met the cowboys out on the ranch, I thought all men were bastards. I still wasn't sure until you came into my life. Now I can see there are a few good ones left."

He could feel his cheeks flush, but before he could figure out some kind of response, the number for their order was called. Landon gratefully slid out of the booth to go get it. When he returned with the tray, Sally shook her head and said, "Ice keam."

"After you eat your fries and chicken." Dixie set about making bite-sized pieces of the French fries and nuggets. "Then you can have ice cream."

Thirty minutes later Sally looked like she had taken a bath in the ice cream machine. She had it in her hair, between her fingers, and even behind her ears. The cone was a soggy mess, and the tray was covered with melted ice cream that Sally had tried to clean up with her bare hands.

Dixie pushed the napkin dispenser over to Landon and said, "Have fun."

He took out a fistful and leaned over to wipe the baby's hands, but before he could make the first swipe, she patted him on his cheeks, leaving sticky handprints down in his five o'clock shadow.

"My Lan-Lan!" She grinned and kept patting until he got ahold of one of her hands and wiped it. She immediately ran the clean hand around on the messy tray and patted his arm.

"Tray first, and then kid." Dixie leaned back, crossed her arms over her chest, and smiled.

"You might have told me that in the beginning," he said.

Sally leaned over and laid her face on the tray the minute he finished wiping it down. She looked up at Landon and smiled. "Lan-Lan go."

"Not yet, baby," he answered. "I've got to show Mommy what a great daddy I am."

"Lan-Lan, Da-Dee!" She raised up, clapped her hands, and left a smear of ice cream on the tray.

"In our pretend world, I am." He attacked the tray with another bunch of napkins, and then tried to get her face clean again, but she got a handful of hair that time.

"Need a little help there, cowboy?" Dixie asked as she brought out the wet wipes from the diaper bag.

"Never turn down help." He repeated one of her earlier lines. "Getting her cleaned up is like trying to nail Jell-O to the smokehouse door."

"Pretty good sayin'." Dixie had Sally cleaned up in only a couple of minutes, and then she focused on Landon. "Turn around here." She got him by the chin and twisted his face around so she could see him, wiped all the ice cream from his cheeks, and then expertly got it out of his hair. "Now I think we can go home and finish up by giving her a bath."

"You sure you don't want to give me one too?" he flirted.

"Not tonight, cowboy." She leaned over and kissed him on the cheek. "We've had enough excitement."

Chapter Six

Dixie could not believe that she'd felt comfortable enough to be honest and admit that she had been playing like they were a real family that whole evening. She replayed every moment of the time they'd had together later as she put together a quilt square with a Santa hat on it and one with a yellow puppy that had a red bow around its neck.

By the time they had gotten home from their visit with Santa Claus, freezing rain had started falling, coating the trees and the roads with ice. That put an end to his idea about going over to Bowie to see the Christmas of Lights Festival on Wednesday evening. When she suggested that if the roads weren't too bad he could help her make cookies to deliver to all her friends on Christmas Eve, he'd been as excited as Sally always was when he arrived at the Quilt Shop.

Now it was midnight, and she had tossed and turned for the past hour. She sat up in bed, beat on her pillow, straightened her covers, and flopped back down to stare at the ceiling.

She finally fell asleep and dreamed she was standing on the porch with Sally in her arms. They were both waving good-bye to Landon as he drove away, and tears were rolling down both their cheeks. She woke up saying "my girls" and "home" over and over again.

Then Sally was standing up in her crib and saying, "My Lan-Lan," over and over again. Dixie threw back the covers, picked Sally up, and hugged her tightly.

"Were you dreaming too?" She kissed the baby's little cheeks. "We've never been like this with good-byes, not even when your father left us. We'll just have to be brave and love the memories we're making with Landon these days."

She changed Sally's diaper and carried her to the kitchen. "Let's have pancakes this morning, and then we'll make a batch of chocolate chip cookies—just in case someone comes in today. I doubt that anyone will be out on the roads, but we'll be ready if they do."

"Nanny?" Sally asked.

Dixie settled the baby into her high chair and kissed her on the top of her blond hair. "Never know what one of your nannies might do, but I don't expect them to get out in this kind of a mess."

* * *

Levi arrived in the bunkhouse that morning right after the hired hands had finished breakfast. "All right, guys, it's a mess out there. We've got the cattle pretty much contained in two pastures, but we've got to break ice in their watering troughs at least twice today. I'll take Landon with me, and we'll take hay and feed out to the west pasture. The rest of you take care of the east pasture. I don't have to tell you to check every head of cattle."

Landon pulled on a pair of mustard-colored insulated coveralls and a ski mask, stomped his feet down into his boots, and followed Levi out the door.

"Do you ever wish that you were doing another job when weather like this sets in?" Levi asked as he climbed into one of the old ranch work trucks and started the engine. He put the truck in gear, backed out a ways, and then headed toward the pasture.

"Nope." Landon shook his head. "Weather is part of ranchin', whether it's hot enough to boil your brains or cold enough to turn your blood into ice pops. You got to love it to be able to do it."

"That's the gospel truth. You are a natural-born foreman. I sure do wish you'd stick around. I'm willing to give you a foreman's assistant title, and you know you're welcome to move out to the cabin," Levi said.

The two of them got out and, working together, they hitched up a trailer already loaded with two big round bales of hay. Without being told, Landon went straight to the stacks of feed and hoisted two bags onto his shoulders.

"I've been givin' that some thought, but I'm not sure I'm ready for a title. If I was to stay, I would sure like to live in the cabin though." He carried the feed to the truck and tossed it in the back. "Do you think we need four or six this morning?"

"Four should do it now, and then we'll take more out this evening," Levi said as he leaned against the truck fender. "You talked to your brothers?"

"Nope." Landon loaded two more bags and got back into the truck. "I got to figure out things for myself before I talk to them."

Levi slid in behind the wheel, started the engine, and headed out across the ice-covered ground. "The cabin is yours anytime you want it. We haven't had weather this bad since back in the late nineties. That one knocked out our power and we were without electricity for five days."

"What did you do?" Landon asked, but his mind wasn't on the ice storm or the electricity.

"In between taking care of chores, we all snuggled up to the fireplaces," Levi answered.

"Ranchers through thick and thin," Landon chuckled, but the picture in his mind was one of Dixie and Sally and himself in the old cabin at the back side of the ranch. They were cuddled up together on a quilt in front of the stone fireplace, and the logs were blazing on the andirons. Just thinking about that made him happy.

Now think about leaving here and going back to the other side of Texas and figure out which one makes you happier, the pesky voice inside his head suggested.

I know that I have to make a definite decision before the first of the year, he argued, *so get out of my head and leave me alone so I can figure things out on my own.*

"Speaking of huddling around the fire, telling tall tales, and soaking up enough warmth, that's what the hired hands do in between jobs on these cold days. I'm not interested in tall tales. I think I'll go out to the tack room and do some cleaning," Landon said.

Levi nodded. "Best way to sort things out is with hard work."

"That's what my old ranchin' friend used to tell me," Landon said.

"We're both lucky to have had good advice." Levi stopped the truck in front of a gate leading into a pasture, and Landon hopped out to open it. Mesquite tree branches sounded like shotgun blasts as they broke with the weight of the ice. Cows bawled and made their way toward the feed bins. A cottontail rabbit darted so close to his foot that he could have touched it with the toe of his boot. Cold permeated his coveralls, and yet he was so happy that he couldn't imagine being anywhere but on a ranch—and he was happier right here in Sunset than he'd ever been anywhere else.

When Levi dropped him off at the bunkhouse after chores, Landon discovered that he was the first one to get back, but he didn't linger long. Since he wasn't on the list for kitchen duty that day, he got into his truck and headed back to the barn. The tack room was a mess, so he skipped lunch and spent the rest of the day putting it to rights. Then right before suppertime, Levi picked him up for the evening feeding.

"Looks good in here," Levi said. "Matter of fact, I don't think this place has ever been this clean. You want to call it a day and go on into Sunset to see your girlfriend?"

"A future ranch foreman wouldn't do that now, would he?" Landon said. "And Dixie isn't my girlfriend."

"Is she going to be?" Levi asked.

"Don't know yet. She'd have to agree to that," Landon answered.

"Won't know unless you ask her. She's as valuable to Claire as you are to me. Claire would sell the shop tomorrow if she didn't have Dixie to run it for her." Levi headed out of the tack room toward his truck.

"Oh, really?" Landon followed him and helped load a couple more bags of feed.

"Dixie will have a job as long as she wants it, and Claire will still make quilts to ship out to her customers, but she'll be doing her part at home," Levi explained.

They repeated what they'd done that morning, and when

they were finished, Levi dropped Landon back at the barn. He got into his truck and didn't even stop at the bunkhouse. He was already running an hour behind, and he didn't want to miss another minute of the time he could spend with Dixie.

* * *

Dixie had just pulled the second sheet of sugar cookies from the oven when she heard the familiar *rat-a-tat-tat* on the front door. She knew by the knock that it was him, but he was earlier than she'd expected. She hadn't even had time to take her hair down from the usual ponytail, and she was barefoot, but she couldn't leave him standing out there in the cold, so she opened the door.

She smiled. "Come right on in."

"Hello, gorgeous," he said as he stepped inside the house and brushed something from the tip of her nose before he removed his coat and hat. "Little flour on your nose. You must've already started the cookies."

If this was the way a ranching wife felt, then Dixie liked it. "I figured y'all would have extra work today and you might not get to come into town." She hurried back to the kitchen, set the cookies on a cooling rack, and peeked around the corner.

Landon picked up Sally, and she laid her little head on his shoulder. Oh, yes sir, she did like this contented feeling more than a little.

"Feeding took longer than it does in better weather," he said, "but I wouldn't miss decorating cookies for anything. Is that pot roast I smell? Have y'all already eaten? Should I put the baby in her chair, and help feed her?"

"We had supper," Dixie answered, "but I'm sure Sally

would love to eat a little something with you. She's been sayin' your name all day."

"Well, I've been thinking your name and hers, too, so we're even." Landon settled the baby into her high chair. "Is it all right if I give her bites of one of those warm sugar cookies to nibble on while I eat?"

"Sure you don't want me to fix her an i-c-e c-r-e-a-m instead?" she teased.

"Shhh!" Landon put a finger over Dixie's lips. "She's so smart she can probably already spell that word. And the answer is no, thank you very much."

"Then a sugar cookie will have to do." Dixie grinned.

She'd just slid the second two batches of cookies into the oven when, suddenly, Landon caught her by the hand, twirled her around, and kissed her. The whole world stopped moving when his lips touched hers, and then it started spinning at warp speed. Heat flowed through her body like hot lava and she wanted more than just a steamy, hot kiss. Then the kiss ended, and she didn't know what to say to fill the awkward silence.

"What...," she started, but the words wouldn't come out of her mouth.

Landon's eyes twinkled, and he pointed up to the mistletoe that hung right above them. "Don't know why I haven't taken advantage of that before now."

"Me either, cowboy." She smiled up at him.

"Whew!" He wiped his brow in a dramatic gesture. "I didn't know if I'd get slapped or booted out the door."

"Neither one," she said. "You better have some supper, though, so you'll have the energy to decorate cookies with me."

"I'd rather use my energy to make out some more." He got a plate from the cabinet and helped himself to some roast, potatoes, and carrots.

"Is that what you want for Christmas more than a puppy?" she teased.

"It'd be a close decision." He winked at her.

"Well, when it's the thing you want the most, we'll talk about it," she told him.

While he ate, she whipped up several colors of icing to decorate cookies shaped like Christmas trees, Santa faces, and even Rudolph and Christmas stockings. Hopefully, they could get six dozen done, then the next night, they could make snickerdoodles, gingerbread squares, and lemon cookies so each person would get a variety. She'd made a list, and she needed about thirty plates to give out on Christmas Eve morning.

"That's more friends than I had in my whole life before I moved here," she said.

"What? Are you talking to me?" Landon asked.

"No, to myself," she answered. "I was thinking about all the people I want to deliver cookies to. And that's more friends than I had all combined in my whole lifetime."

"Do I get a plate of cookies?" Landon asked.

"Of course. You are my friend." She patted him on the head and smeared a bit of icing on his upper lip. "And for helping me decorate them, you get to taste the icing. Have you ever decorated cookies before?"

"Yes, ma'am." His tongue flicked out and licked the icing from his lip. "Mama and I used to make them every year. I'm an artist when it comes to Christmas cookies."

"Really?" Dixie asked.

"Oh, yeah." He smiled up at her. "I call my work *Christmas abstracts*. The only way you can tell it's a Christmas tree is by the shape."

He finished his food and rinsed the plate before putting it in the dishwasher, and then he took Sally out of her high chair and turned her loose on the floor. She crawled over to the quilt on the floor and opened one of her books to read.

"Here's the first three dozen." Dixie set the cooling racks on the table and then brought out the small bowls of colored icing.

"How long until the next batch is ready?" Landon asked.

She checked the clock on the stove and said, "Five minutes."

He pulled her down onto his lap, tilted her chin back with his fist, and kissed her. The first time their lips met, there was steam. The second time, he deepened the kiss and a blaze built up in her insides that all the fire trucks in Bowie and Sunset combined couldn't put out. Her breath came in short gasps, and she couldn't force herself to get up to check the cookies, not even when the timer dinged. One more minute wouldn't hurt. They might be a little browner around the edges, but they could cover that up with extra icing. She quit paying attention to the clock and then she smelled smoke.

"Sweet Jesus!" She finally twisted free of his arms and hurried to the stove.

"No, just plain old Landon Griffin," he said.

"We burned three dozen cookies." She threw the oven door open and smoke billowed out into the room. The smoke alarm went off, and Landon grabbed a chair, hopped onto it, and did something to stop the loud noise. Dixie set the pan of cookies in the sink and turned on the cold water, then ran to the kitchen window and opened it. Landon hopped down off the chair, picked up two tea towels, and threw one her way. Both of them began fanning the smoke out the window while Sally pointed at the now silent smoke alarm and jabbered in baby language that Dixie was sure had cusswords in it.

"You didn't freeze up," he said. "There was smoke, and you acted like a fireman."

"I did, didn't I?" she gasped.

"It won't take long for the smoke to clear," he said.

"Lan-Lan! No! No!" Sally frowned at him.

"Guess we heated the kitchen up too much," he chuckled.

"Those were some hot kisses," she agreed.

"It was worth it, wasn't it?" he asked.

"Yes, of course it was, but you do realize that every one of those kisses is just going to make it harder on me when you go back to the other side of Texas?"

"What if I didn't leave, but I just stayed here and worked for Levi?" he asked.

"Don't tease me, Landon, and don't even talk to me about that until you know for sure." She couldn't bear to get her hopes up and then have them crushed, so she changed the subject. "I haven't burned a cookie in all the time I've been working here."

"How many times have you made out with a cowboy while you were baking them?" He shut the window.

"I don't kiss and tell." She sat down across the table from him and applied green icing to a Christmas tree and handed it to him. "Now you can put the rest of the decorations on this."

He took the cookie from her and added sprinkles and some crisscross lines to represent garland.

She covered a Santa hat with red icing and pushed it across the table toward him, then turned to check on Sally. She had crawled over to the Christmas tree, reached for the squirrel ornament from a bottom limb, and set up a howl. Landon was the first one to her, but Dixie wasn't far behind him.

"What's the matter, princess? Show me what hurt you."

Landon checked her fingers one by one and finally found a tiny piece of dried cedar sticking out of her palm.

"Damned old tree has got some dead stuff on it. It's gone dry." He gently pulled the thing from her hand. "We need to get some water in the pan so it'll last until Christmas. I'm so sorry, baby girl." He kissed her hand a dozen times.

He might not be so good at cleaning up an ice cream mess, but he sure knew how to take care of a boo-boo. Boyfriend who didn't yell at her for burning food. Father who comforted Sally over a tiny little wound. Yes, sir, this was the good life.

She tried to take Sally from Landon to check her finger, but the baby shook her head. "No! No! No!"

"It's not bleeding, Mommy. I think she'll be fine," Landon whispered.

"Lan-Lan down," Sally said.

He put her on the floor, and she pointed her finger at the squirrel. "No! No! No!"

Dixie giggled.

"What's so funny?" Landon asked.

"She thinks the squirrel bit her. She probably won't mess with that ornament again," Dixie said.

"Things sure aren't turnin' out like I'd planned them," Landon said.

"Folks plan, and then God laughs," she said.

"Ain't that the truth," he agreed.

Chapter Seven

Landon had sat beside Dixie in church a couple of times before, but the Sunday morning of the Christmas program was a whole new experience. Maybe this new feeling was a result of the kisses they'd shared the night before. His heart swelled with happiness, and, suddenly, the excitement of California beaches paled in comparison to the joy of sitting in church with Dixie so close to his side that air couldn't have found a way between them.

"Packed church today, ain't it?" Dixie whispered.

He leaned over close to her ear. "Folks come out for entertainment and food more than they do for preaching."

The preacher left the front row of pews and took his place behind the pulpit. "We're glad to see such a good turnout today. The Lord does love to see every pew filled. Welcome to all y'all this morning, and please, remember that the ladies have planned a potluck in the fellowship hall right after our morning Christmas program. I'll turn this over to the preschool Sunday school teacher at this time."

"Just think, in only three years, Sally will be up there singing with that age group," Dixie said.

"She'll be the prettiest one up there too!" Landon's heart clenched again at the thought of not being around to see the baby grow up.

"Look at that little girl on the end with her blond curls. I hope I can get Sally's hair to do that when she's big enough to have a part in the program," Dixie said.

I believe I'm falling in love with Dixie, Landon finally admitted to himself.

Falling? Levi's voice popped into his head. *I believe that ship done sailed and you've fallen already.*

Okay, now what do I do about it? he asked.

Figure it out, just like the rest of us had to do, the voice told him.

Landon enjoyed watching the little kids doing their parts with simple Christmas songs, and the next group did a fantastic job playing the Christmas bells. As smart as Sally was, he could imagine her with a serious expression on her face and ringing her little red or yellow bell at just the right time. The older kids came on the stage next and did a skit and sang a couple of songs, then the teenagers presented the story of Christmas with verses from the Bible and a nativity scene. Would Sally ever play the part of Mary, and would her boyfriend be Joseph?

The idea of her having a boyfriend with no father around to protect her bothered Landon so much that he squirmed in his seat. Worse than not having a father would be having a stepfather like the one Dixie talked about having when she was growing up. What if Dixie made another bad choice and ended up with a loser like Sally's biological father? He shuddered at the thought.

Dixie nudged him with her shoulder. "You okay?"

"Just letting too many thoughts run through my mind," he admitted, "but I'm fine."

"The Fab Five are up next," she said. "I can't wait to see what they do."

The curtains opened, and all five of the elderly folks were sitting in rocking chairs around a decorated Christmas tree. Patsy, Bess, and Sarah wore long red-flannel nightgowns, with green dust caps covering their hair and big fluffy house slippers on their feet. Larry and Otis wore red long-handle pajamas and cowboy hats and boots. The music started and they chimed in at the right time with "Rocking Around the Christmas Tree." When that song ended, they hopped up out of their chairs, joined hands, and sang, "All I Want for Christmas Is My Two Front Teeth." They ended the program by putting on long coats and singing "Let It Snow" before finally taking a bow.

"That was so cute." Dixie clapped and stood up to give her friends a standing ovation. Everyone in the church followed her example, and then the crowd all started toward the fellowship hall for the potluck dinner.

Landon took Dixie's hand in his and led her in the opposite direction toward the nursery. "I bet our baby girl is ready for us to come rescue her."

"Probably so," Dixie agreed. "She's around adults most of the time, so she's kind of shy around other children, even the kids out at the ranch."

He didn't even realize his mind was made up until they reached the nursery and Sally reached up her arms and said, "Lan-Lan!" He picked her up, and then retrieved

Dixie's hand. This felt right, and he would never look back with regrets.

* * *

If only…

That's where Dixie's thoughts were as they went from the nursery to the fellowship hall. On one hand, she couldn't wait to see all her friends again. On the other, she wished that she and Landon could sit down on a back pew of the now-empty church and just enjoy some time together.

If only she would never have to face a day without Landon in her life. If only he would stay in Texas, and they could get into a serious relationship that involved more than a perfect Christmas and a few kisses.

Dixie was so deep in thought that she was surprised when she looked up and realized they'd already crossed the sanctuary, and Landon had opened the door into the fellowship hall for her. The buzz of the conversation was such a contrast to the few minutes of quietness she'd just experienced that it took a moment for her to adjust to the noise.

"Well, don't y'all just look like the perfect little family." Sarah touched her on the shoulder.

"The Fab Five was my favorite part of the show." Dixie avoided responding to the comment. "I loved that rocking chair scene. It was so cute."

Sarah took a bow and raised up with a wicked little grin on her face. "When you and Landon are old and gray like us…"

"Speak for yourself." Patsy fluffed up her kinky dyed hair with both hands.

Sarah gave her the evil eye. "Okay, smarty-pants," she quipped before turning her attention back to Dixie. "When you and Landon are old like us, you can do that scene, and we'll put it in our will that you inherit our rocking chairs."

"Thank you, but—"

Landon butted in before she could finish. "We'd love to inherit the rocking chairs."

The preacher tapped on a glass with a spoon and cleared his throat.

"If everyone will bow their heads, I'll say grace and then we can start digging into all this good food," he said.

The noise level dropped from practically raising the roof to total silence. Landon let go of her hand to remove his cowboy hat and held it over his heart. In the next few brief minutes while the preacher gave thanks, Dixie felt the loss of his touch and wanted it back again.

"Amen," the preacher said.

"Amen!" several of the elderly folks echoed with a nod. Cowboy hats were settled back onto several of the guys' heads, and a line started at the long tables that were filled with food of every description.

"What did you bring?" Landon asked Dixie.

"You brought it in before services began," she reminded him.

"All I saw was a dish all covered up with aluminum foil," he told her.

"It's what Sarah calls Watergate salad. I thought it would go well with the ham and turkey that the Fab Five cooked for today," she answered.

"Point it out when we're going through the line," he said. "Anything you make has to be good."

That comment alone was a huge Christmas present for Dixie. She could scarcely even imagine a life where she'd hear things like that every day.

"We'll save y'all a place beside us," Levi said, turning

around. He had Wyatt in one arm and the other was thrown around Claire's shoulders.

Claire was short, but standing beside Levi, she looked even smaller. She and Dixie were pretty close to the same height—five foot three inches in their bare feet. Being outside in the summer had put natural blond highlights in Claire's brown hair. Her brown eyes were filled with love when she looked up at her husband.

Dixie wondered if she looked at Landon like that and couldn't help but steal a glance up at him. They locked eyes and then he whispered, "Sometimes I feel like you can see right into my very soul."

"I feel the same way about you," she said, "and to tell the truth, it's kind of scary."

"Not for me." He draped his free arm around her shoulders. "I like the feeling that we can talk to each other without words."

When it was their turn to go through the line, he removed his arm and reached to pick up a plate. She shook her head. "You're holding Sally, and she'll be grabbing for your food. I can fill both our plates and take them to the table. You just tell me what you want."

"Yes, ma'am…" He nodded.

Retta and Cade, one of the three couples living on the Longhorn Ranch, came up behind her and Retta whispered softly just for Dixie's ears. "Are y'all a couple now?"

"I don't know," Dixie answered, but she could hope.

Chapter Eight

Like a lot of men, Landon always waited until the last minute to do his Christmas shopping, not that he was lazy, but most often simply because he couldn't figure out what to buy. That was especially true this year. Dixie was making cookies for all her friends, and that was a bit of a new idea for him. He and his mother had made cookies, but they had never given any of them as gifts.

He'd racked his brain trying to come up with something when the guys at the bunkhouse asked if he wanted to be a part of what they gave the ranch families every year. Each year, they all put in a few hours of their own time and chopped a rick of firewood for each of the five married couples. They delivered it on Christmas Eve—just before they all left to celebrate the holiday with their own relatives.

That took care of the ranch bunch, and he could chop an extra rick all by himself for the Fab Five, but he needed something very special to give Dixie and Sally. He had four days to come up with an idea, and he had begun to feel the pressure.

He was busy loading feed into the back of his truck when Hud showed up in the barn that morning. "Got your Christmas shopping done yet?" he asked.

"Nope," Landon said. "Do you?"

"Not yet," Hud said. "Have you made up your mind to stay on at Longhorn?"

"Yep," Landon repeated. "But I'm not telling anyone just yet."

He'd spent time with Hud and his wife, Rose, as well as with Tag and his wife, Nikki, but he didn't know them as well as he did the folks from Longhorn Canyon. He was aware that Tag and Hud were Emily's younger twin brothers, but something told him that morning that Hud wasn't there to talk about Christmas.

"I may be stickin' my nose in where it don't belong, but how are things between you and Dixie?" Hud asked. "Rose and Claire were talkin' last night about how they've never seen her so happy."

Landon removed his hat and raked his fingers through his hair, and then he chuckled. "Y'all have bets going, don't you? And you're out here getting some inside information, right?"

"Busted!" Hud laughed out loud. "So you're not staying."

"Every one of you will have to wait to find out. I will tell you this much. I'm moving into the cabin until summer, and then I'll make a decision," Landon told him.

"If that girl loves you as much as you love her, staying a few more months will be the best Christmas present you could ever give her."

"I didn't say I loved her," Landon protested.

"Some things you don't have to say," Hud chuckled. "It's written all over your face every time you say her name."

* * *

On Monday Dixie worked on making a quilt square with a string of lights while Sally played with the ornaments that she had taken off the lower limbs of the Christmas tree, but the squirrel had only gotten dirty looks.

Dixie needed one more quilt square to complete the quilt, and she wasn't quite sure what to make. Then she remembered she hadn't made one to commemorate the church program they'd attended the day before. She found a scrap of fabric that was printed with Christmas trees and cut one of those out and laid it on a red square. When she had finished stitching around the edges of the tree, she carefully drew a rocking chair on a piece of paper. The first two attempts didn't work, but the third was the charm. She didn't realize how much intricate work would be involved until she pinned the rocking chair to the square.

"He's worth it," she muttered.

She had finished sewing the squares together with alternating red and green squares by quitting time that afternoon. She fluffed it out in front of Sally and asked, "What do you think, baby girl?"

"Doggie." She pointed at the puppy square.

"That's right, and you've learned a new word. You are such a smart girl." Dixie dropped the quilt top on one of the rocking chairs and bent to hug Sally. "You're going to grow up to be something amazing."

Sally stuffed the puppy ornament in her mouth and grinned around it.

"Or maybe you'll be a comedian." Dixie giggled and hugged her again. "Whatever you are, I want you to be self-confident and happy."

When Dixie heard a truck door slam outside, she grabbed

the quilt, raced to the back room, and hid it in an empty box. She grabbed her coat and Sally's from the bedroom on the way back up the hall and then answered the door.

"Sorry about making you wait. I was in the bedroom getting our coats," she said when she opened the door.

"No problem," Landon said. "I'll help get Sally ready." He talked as he put the baby's coat on her. "We're going to see all the pretty lights. They aren't nearly as pretty as you or your mama, but they'll make you smile, and then we'll go out for pizza and ice cream."

"Ice keam." Sally clapped her hands.

"And we'll clean her up together, right?" Dixie smiled up at him.

"Yes, ma'am. You ever hear that song by Blake Shelton called 'I'll Name the Dogs'?"

"Of course I've heard it. Blake is one of my favorites," she said.

Landon grinned. "Well, you know how he says that you can name the babies, and he'll name the dogs? I figure I'll take out splinters if you'll clean up ice cream messes."

"Think we could write a country song like that?" Dixie asked.

"I bet we could," he chuckled.

"We make a pretty good team, don't we?" She picked up her purse and the diaper bag.

"We sure do," he answered. "Have you ever been to a festival of lights?"

She shook her head. "That costs money, and Mama needed her cigarettes and beer."

"Well, get ready for a surprise." He sat up, and Sally crawled over into his lap. "I don't expect this to be as big as the one in Hollywood, but I'm looking forward to sharing it with you and this sweet little girl. All you have to decide is whether we have pizza and ice cream before or after the show."

"Maybe before, so Sally doesn't turn into a whiny monster," she suggested.

"This baby?" Landon carried her out to the truck. "Never happen."

"Oh, yes, it can. If she's hungry, she's unbearable. They do have pasta at the pizza place, don't they?" she asked. "She doesn't do well with pizza, but she loves pasta."

"Yep, and they have an ice cream machine so we can either put some in a cup or make cones," he answered. "I didn't think about her not being able to eat pizza. We can go somewhere else if you think we need to. There's a buffet on the same road that will have vegetables and ice cream too."

"Pasta is great, and I love pizza." Dixie opened the rear door and helped him get Sally into the car seat. "I think we're ready."

"Doggie?" Sally cocked her head to one side.

"No doggies tonight, sweetheart," Landon told her. "They might have a Snoopy dog in the lights, but it won't be a real one."

Dixie sucked in a lungful of air and let it out slowly. She knew exactly what Sally was talking about, and it wasn't a real doggy, but an image on a quilt. In another year, the baby would be talking enough to tattle about Christmas presents. Dixie would have to be careful about what she showed her.

"Are we ready?" Landon got behind the wheel and started the engine.

Dixie picked up her purse and nodded. "Let another wonderful adventure begin."

"Have you really enjoyed all the events, even though most of them were catastrophes?" Landon asked.

"More than words can say," she answered. "Simply going out for pizza, pasta, and ice cream is like getting a Christmas present to me. Add in getting to experience a light show for the first time"—she stopped before she said, *with you*—"makes that two big presents."

"For real?" Landon put the truck in gear and backed out of the driveway. "If you could have anything in the whole world for Christmas, what would it be? Money wouldn't even be an issue, so would it be diamonds, a fancy new car, or what?"

"You want the truth?" she asked.

"Yes, I do." He made a right turn toward Bowie.

"I'd want one more week like this last one," she answered. "This has been the stuff that dreams are made of. When I was a little girl, I always dreamed of having a perfect Christmas like all the other kids at school talked about, and now you've given me just that. I've never had so much attention poured on me in all of my years combined, Landon. And I just love our little Christmas tree."

"An ugly tree that is already getting dry and shedding. Next year, we're having an artificial tree with soft needles, so it doesn't bite the baby," he declared.

Dixie held her breath for a minute, letting hope get a toe in the door. "And you helped me make my first snowman."

"It wasn't even a foot tall," Landon laughed, "but we did have fun playing in the snow."

"And we've got lots of cookies made," she went on.

"After we burned a few in the process," he reminded her.

"You've come to see us every night this week," she finally said.

"That was the stuff dreams are made of for *me*, Dixie." He reached across the console and laid a hand on her shoulder. "Why would you only want one more week? Why not a lifetime?"

"That would be asking for too much, and I'd feel selfish," she answered. "I'll just be happy with what I've had and count every minute of this Christmas as a blessing and a miracle. Especially when I know you'll be moving on soon. Have you decided what day you are leaving?"

"Pretty much," he replied.

"You wouldn't leave without sayin' good-bye to us, would you?"

"I promise I won't." He took her hand and gently squeezed.

Driving to Bowie took only ten minutes, and Dixie let her thoughts wander, reliving the moments she'd had with Landon. The most beautiful things in life weren't perfect. They were feelings and memories and smiles and laughter. Landon had made her believe there were good men in the world...and she had flat out fallen in love with him. The ugly tree, the tiny snowman, the burned cookies—a perfect Christmas was a feeling, not everything turning out flawless. Every time she thought about this year, she would wrap the warmth of that emotion around her like a warm blanket on a snowy night and think of Landon.

There were only a half dozen vehicles in the pizza place parking lot. Monday night was buffet night, so they didn't have to wait to be served. Landon loaded up two kinds of pasta on a plate for Sally, along with some tiny bits of ham and cheese from the salad bar so that there would be a few things she could eat all by herself. Then he fed her bites as he ate his meal. Every one of his gestures, every moment she spent with him, every smile he flashed her way was a memory, and there could never be another Christmas as perfect as this one had been—not even if she lived to be a hundred.

They were back in the truck headed for the entrance to the light show in less than an hour. Dixie hadn't known what to expect, but it certainly wasn't what she saw. From the time they crossed under the brightly lit arch and started the drive through the park where the lights were on display, she felt like a little kid.

"Go slow so I can take pictures for our album," she said as she snapped photo after photo until her battery went dead.

"Here, now you can use mine, and I want a couple of selfies of you with the displays behind you in the window," Landon told her. "And don't forget to turn around and take some of Sally. I've been watching her in the rearview, and her little mouth has been a perfect *O* ever since we started the drive."

"Neither one of us has ever seen anything like this. I thought maybe we were just going to drive around and look at people's houses all fancied up," she said.

"Did you do that when you were a kid?" Landon asked.

"Once," she replied, but kept snapping pictures. "The stepdad who was with us then took us to look at the lights, but he and Mama got into a big argument on the way home, and she kicked him out. But hey, I got to see something pretty before the bad stuff happened that time around."

"Do you always find something positive, even in terrible situations?" he asked.

"I do my best," she answered, and wondered exactly what she would find positive when she and Sally were telling Landon good-bye.

Don't weep when he goes. Give thanks for the time you got to spend with him.

Chapter Nine

By Christmas Eve night, there were boxes of cookies in every room at the Quiltin' House. Landon worked for half an hour loading the boxes with plates covered in plastic before transferring them to the truck. Then he and Dixie got Sally strapped into her car seat so they could begin their delivery rounds. First stop was the Fab Five house, where they took in five separate plates full of cookies—one for each of the elderly folks. Then they drove out to the ranch and were able to catch the bunkhouse guys before they all left for a couple of days with their kinfolks. That taken care of, they swung by Claire and Levi's house and were invited in to visit for a little while.

Levi and Landon left the ladies in the kitchen and disappeared into the living room with a couple of beers. "When are you moving into the cabin?" Levi whispered.

"Already did," Landon said. "Got all my stuff in there

today. I love the place, but good lord, that bathroom is tiny."

"Yep," Levi chuckled. "It sure wasn't designed for a couple to shower in, but Claire and I managed to defy the odds a few times. Does Dixie know yet?"

"I'm going to tell her tonight. I even put up a tiny little tree, and I have a present wrapped for her and one for Sally waiting underneath it," he said.

"Did you call Pax and Maverick?" Levi asked.

"Yes, and I'll be going back out to west Texas the first day of June, so teach me everything you can between now and then. I'll be working for Maverick at first, and maybe later, I'll help with both ranches," he answered.

"Nervous about telling Dixie and the move?" Levi asked.

"You can't imagine how jittery I am," Landon answered.

* * *

Dixie and Claire sat at the table and sipped from cups of hot chocolate while their babies crawled around the table legs and giggled as if that was a funny game.

"I made Landon a throw for Christmas, but now I wonder if it's too cheesy. It's got a square to remind him of each thing we did this past week," Dixie said.

"He'll love it," Claire assured her. "Did you manage to make one with kissy lips on it?"

Dixie's face immediately flushed with a bright red blush. "I did not!" she protested.

"Too bad, because that's what he'll remember more than anything. When he kissed you, did your toes curl?" Claire asked.

"Yes, they did, and my insides went all hot and mushy," Dixie said.

"That's great," Claire said. "That's the way I still feel when Levi kisses me, and I hope it affects me the same way when I'm ninety."

Dixie wanted to say, "Me too," but she couldn't. "Did you tell Levi about—" She paused, then looked over her shoulder and whispered, "…the baby yet?"

"Not until morning. One of his presents is the first ultrasound picture," Claire answered.

"That's a great idea," Dixie told her.

"Hey, are y'all ready to go?" Landon came around the door and into the kitchen.

"What's a great idea?" Levi crossed the room and bent down to pick up his son.

"Santa doesn't reveal his secrets until Christmas morning," Claire told him.

"We really should be on the way," Dixie said. "It's been great visitin' with y'all, but—" She stopped and stared at Landon. "That's the first time I've ever heard you say 'y'all.' You usually say 'you guys.'"

"Guess this Texas lingo is rubbing off on me." He reached down and gathered Sally into his arms. "Let's get your coat on, sweetheart. We still have places to go, and then you can open your present from me."

They drove to the big ranch house and then to each of the other places where Dixie wanted to give cookies. The clock on the dashboard flipped over to 8:30 when they were finished, back in the truck, and ready to go home. The only box left in the back of the vehicle held a plate of cookies, and the quilt, all wrapped up in gold paper for Landon. She wasn't sure where or when he wanted to exchange gifts, but she was ready no matter what.

Instead of driving down the lane and toward the road leading back to Sunset, he made a left-hand turn and headed to the barn. If he wanted to have Christmas out there, that was fine with her. The little throw she had made for him wouldn't seem like such a small present in a barn setting.

"Bit!" Sally squealed when she recognized the barn.

"We'll see Little Bit tomorrow if you want to," Landon told her. "Right now, we've got somewhere else to be."

"And where's that?" Dixie cocked her head to one side and raised her dark eyebrows.

"It's a surprise," Landon answered.

As far as Dixie knew, the cabin was the only place located that far back on the ranch, but she couldn't imagine why they'd be going there. Had he realized how much she'd loved the little place and wanted to have Christmas there?

She could see a trail of smoke from a distance, and hoped the cabin wasn't on fire. Then she remembered the fireplace. He'd started a fire for warmth, and they were going to have their Christmas there for sure. Just thinking about the peace and coziness she'd felt when she was there put a huge smile on her face.

A few snowflakes drifted down out of the sky as he parked as close to the porch as he could. He opened the passenger door for Dixie and then took Sally out of her seat. "I thought we'd have our private Christmas right here. I've got a pan of lasagna ready to put in the oven, and a bottle of wine chilled. Let's go on in and spend the rest of this evening together."

Tears welled up in Dixie's eyes. Once she'd heard someone say that home wasn't a place but a feeling just like the memories of Christmases, and that evening, she knew that she'd come home. Rose and Hud had taken care of her after the fire. Claire had given her a job. The Fab Five had befriended her and spoiled Sally with love as well as presents. Retta had given Sally her daughter Annie's outgrown clothing. Then there was the rest of the folks on the two intertwined ranches who had become her friends. And now Landon had brought her to the cabin for Christmas—that was enough to bring tears of joy to her eyes. She swiped at her cheeks with her coat sleeve and picked up the last box of cookies.

"What's that?" Landon asked.

"Your present from me and Sally," she told him.

"You didn't have to do that," he said. "I've eaten at least a dozen cookies every night all week, and I got mine right out of the oven."

"It's just a little something to remember us by." She carried the box to the porch. "It's nothing fancy."

He swung the door open and the aroma of fresh bread wafted out to greet her. "You made bread?"

"No, I baked bread this evening. It came in a roll and all I had to do was put it in the oven. The lasagna came from the frozen food department. I can make a mean breakfast and a fairly good pot of chili for the bunk-house, but I'm not a good cook," he admitted as he sat down on the sofa with Sally. He removed her coat and carefully set her on the floor. Then he got up and slid the pan of lasagna into the oven. "I put up a little fence so she can't get close to the fire. Let's have presents while supper heats up. Sally can have hers first."

The baby didn't know what to do with the gift that he brought out from under the tiny tree that sat in the middle of the kitchen table. Finally, Landon helped her remove the paper and opened the box for her. She grabbed the stuffed yellow dog and held it close to her chest.

"Doggie!" she said and kissed it a dozen times on the nose.

"Now yours." Dixie handed him the box.

"But you already gave me cookies," he said. "What's this?"

"Open it." She was so excited to see his reaction that she didn't even think about the other gifts that were still sitting under his tiny tree.

Landon tore into the box and brought out the throw. His eyes widened and he shook his head from side to side. "I can't believe you did this for me, Dixie. It's too pretty to use. Maybe I'll use it for a wall hanging right above the fireplace." He wrapped his arms around her and tipped up her chin for a long, passionate kiss.

When he ended the kiss, she thought of what Claire had said, and yes, sir, her toes had curled.

"What did you just say?" she asked.

"I said, I would hang it above the fireplace." He got up from the sofa and brought two gift bags back to Dixie. "Neither one can match the quilt."

She slid a piece of wood with a big red bow tied around it from the first bag. She looked up at him, and he sat down beside her. "I didn't know what to give you, darlin'. That's just a single piece of the firewood that's stacked against the back of this cabin. It's ready for the fireplace and will keep us warm this winter when you come to visit or if I'm lucky enough to have you live here with me. I've found that home is where the heart is, and mine is right here with you and Sally."

"For real?" she asked.

"Yes, darlin', for sure. I'd be miserable without you in my life. I'm hoping that when we've been together fifty years our kisses are still hot enough to burn cookies. Now open the other one," he said.

She tossed a couple of pieces of tissue paper from the bag and brought out a small box. Inside she found a bracelet with a tiny red heart charm attached to it. "It's beautiful," she whispered.

"I can't take my heart out of my chest and give it to you, so that will have to do. I don't want to rush you, but I want you to always be in my life. I'm giving my heart to you for Christmas, and each year we're together I'll add another heart to it," he said as he fastened the bracelet around her wrist.

"Oh, Landon." She didn't even try to stop the tears from flowing down her cheeks. "This really is a perfect Christmas, and I love my presents, but most of all I love the fact that we don't ever have to say good-bye."

He picked her up and set her in his lap. "Now we're the perfect little family for real, and I want it to last forever."

She cupped his face in her hands and kissed him again. "I've liked being your friend all these months, but that's grown into something more. I love you, Landon Griffin, and this has been the most perfect Christmas of my whole life."

"Yes, it has, and I've fallen in love with you, too, Dixie, and even with all the craziness, it has been perfect."

She smiled. "That's the way our life will probably be— mishaps, giggles, and memories as we raise Sally together."

"And lots of Merry Christmases," he added, then kissed her again.

Also by Carolyn Brown

The Longhorn Canyon Series

Cowboy Bold
Cowboy Honor
Cowboy Brave
Cowboy Rebel
Christmas with a Cowboy
Cowboy Courage
Cowboy Strong

The Happy, Texas Series

Luckiest Cowboy of All
Long, Tall Cowboy Christmas
Toughest Cowboy in Texas

The Lucky Penny Ranch Series

Wild Cowboy Ways
Hot Cowboy Nights
Merry Cowboy Christmas
Wicked Cowboy Charm

Digital Novellas

Wildflower Ranch
Sunrise Ranch

About the Author

Carolyn Brown is a *New York Times* and *USA Today* bestselling romance author and RITA finalist who has published more than one hundred books. She presently writes both women's fiction and cowboy romance. She has also written historical and contemporary romance, both standalone titles and series. She lives in southern Oklahoma with her husband, a former English teacher who is also an author of several mystery books. They have three children and enough grandchildren to keep them young.

For a complete listing of her books (in series order) and to sign up for her newsletter, check out her website at CarolynBrownBooks.com or catch her on Facebook/CarolynBrownBooks.

A Christmas Cowboy at Heart

A.J. PINE

For S and C, who make all of my holidays magical.

Chapter One

Deputy Daniela Garcia always set two alarms. One for 4:15 a.m. and the other for 4:25. That allowed for one snooze and then one kick in the butt when she tried going back to sleep after said snooze. Some people liked time in the morning for coffee and contemplation. Not Dani. A good three-mile run through Meadow Valley while it was still asleep—with streetlamps and porch lights to guide her along the way—gave her plenty of time to contemplate. The coffee came later.

It was 4:29 now, and thanks to a time-honored practice of sleeping in her running gear, all she had to do was brush her teeth, splash some water on her face, throw her hair into a ponytail, and slip on her running shoes. She checked the weather on her smartwatch and sighed. Thirty-nine degrees. Looked like she'd be grabbing her track jacket too.

She stretched, put her earbuds in, and situated a water

bottle in her waist belt. Then she loaded her holiday playlist before storing her phone in the belt as well.

"All I Want for Christmas Is You," by Mariah Carey, blared in her ears, and she couldn't help but grin.

She glanced at the closed door to her roommate Casey's bedroom and shrugged before heading out of the apartment and down the stairs. Between Dani's daytime shifts on duty and Casey's late nights managing Midtown Tavern—the one-stop shop for any sort of nightlife in Meadow Valley, above which their apartment sat—the two barely saw each other.

Dani burst through the door and onto the dark and still-quiet First Street. She drew in a deep breath through her nose, the crisp smell of winter in the air, and headed up the street toward the town square.

As she ran, she made a mental note of each storefront's holiday display and tried to imagine what sort of lights would be hung to give each window, roof, or awning—or all of the above—its finishing touch.

Because today was the seventeenth of December, the day the countdown to the First Street Holiday Lights Parade started, and this year the Sheriff's Department was going to kick the butt of every other shop, tavern, inn, and building. *Not* that it was a competition.

But it sort of was. An unwritten and unspoken competition of sorts where the only reward was bragging rights. Sure, it evoked some good-natured ribbing and maybe some mild trash talk, but winning meant being the talk of the town for the whole next year, and that was enough for her.

Dani ran into the square and made a loop, eyeing the three government buildings that occupied the space—the red-bricked and white-pillared courthouse, standing with elegance beneath the gray sky; the Meadow Valley town hall, equally regal, like a miniature White House; and then the sheriff's office. Its one story was dwarfed by the other two buildings, and its brown-brick facade—some of it starting to crumble—was a far cry from the curb appeal of the other two. But that was nothing compared to what was happening on the inside. The roof leaked when it rained. Maybe that wasn't often, but still. And the power seemed to go out whenever the wind picked up. Plus, one of their two cells was so badly rusted that if you actually locked some-one in it, it might never open up again. Not that Meadow Valley was overrun with crime. In fact, since most of the county was farm- and ranchland, and everyone in town *knew* everyone in town, she doubted Sheriff Thompson or any sheriff before him ever actually had occupants in both cells at the same time.

Still. The place could use an upgrade, and Mayor Grady kept promising that the sheriff's office would be on the top of his list for allocation of town funds in the New Year. He just hadn't had a chance to follow through before dying. *Peacefully*, of course. In his sleep. He was eighty-three.

"And now we have to deal with Mayor Grinch and *boost-ing* the economy and bringing in more tourists and blah, blah, blah," she muttered as she slowed her pace, giving the stink eye to the town hall.

If his platform had been cutting the lights parade from his budget, Peyton Cooper never would have won the emergency election. He threw *that* little nugget into his acceptance speech. "The parade can still happen," he'd said, "but preparation cannot take place during working hours. Tourism is growing in this town, thanks to the Meadow Valley Ranch joining our ranks. But we need to concentrate on serving our public the best we can, which means actually *working* during daylight hours."

"Actually working during daylight hours," she mimicked. "Because I'm too good for small-town shenanigans." The hypocrite of a mayor seemed to have forgotten he'd grown up in Meadow Valley. And once upon a time Dani could have sworn he'd even participated in a small-town shenanigan or two.

She felt a tap on her shoulder and gasped, then pivoted toward her possible assailant and grabbed him by the wrist, quickly wrenching his arm behind his back and using her chin to pause her playlist from her watch as her other hand cupped the man behind the neck.

"Deputy?" His deep voice was calm and assured. "While I do admire your reflexes and have no doubt the street—empty as it might be—is safer with you patrolling it, is this really how you want to greet your elected official, especially after just calling him a grinch and—dare I say—parroting his mayoral acceptance speech in that awful voice? I don't really sound like that, do I?"

Dani winced.

Shit.

She'd just apprehended Mayor Grinch—er *Cooper*. At least, that was what she called him to his face.

She released her grip and took a step back while the mayor shook out his arm and straightened to his full height, which she estimated to be about six foot three—quite a bit taller than her five-seven frame. But let the record show that she'd still subdued him. The corner of her mouth twitched, but she fought the urge to grin.

She cleared her throat. "Mayor *Cooper*," she said, thinking before speaking so as not to risk the whole grinch thing again. "My, um, apologies. Guess I'm still not over Mr. Big-City Politician practically canceling the Meadow Valley Holiday Lights Parade."

She smirked.

He gritted his teeth, and a muscle in his jaw pulsed. Once upon a time she might have noticed that said jaw was chiseled and maybe even a little sexy. But Deputy Daniela Garcia was no longer a high school sophomore crushing on the senior boy who never even noticed her. Besides, *sexy* wasn't a man who turned his nose up at small-town traditions. *Sexy* wasn't a man who cared more about the bottom line than the community who helped him become the big-city hotshot he was today. And sexy *certainly* was not a man who basically wanted to cancel Christmas.

"I didn't cancel *anything*," he said coolly. "I just thought it might be more fiscally responsible for the whole town to scale back on *all* festival activities. Do you know most businesses have to hire extra help so the decorating can get done during daylight hours and shops can stay open? If folks want to do the whole light thing on off-hours and weekends, that's fine by me."

"It's *winter*," she said. "Off-hours don't include any daylight hours."

"Folks do get days off around here, don't they? No one's working a seven-day week." He scratched the back of his neck, and in the glow of the streetlight, she could see the ends of his light brown hair, just above his ears, damp with sweat. Now she eyed his track pants, lightweight jacket, and trail-running shoes.

"I didn't know you were a runner. I've never seen you on my route," she said, not acknowledging what sounded like a dig to all the hardworking folks in her town. Sure, maybe things moved at a different pace here than they did in Chicago or wherever else Peyton Cooper had been for the past decade and a half, but that didn't mean anyone worked any less hard than he ever did.

"I'm sure there's a lot you don't actually know about me, Deputy. Though I see you've got your mind made up." He crossed his arms. "And just so we're clear, your apology a few minutes ago? Was that for using physical force or for the name-calling?" He raised a brow.

Her cheeks burned, and she was grateful the sun still wasn't up. That self-assured attitude was one of the reasons she'd had a crush on Peyton Cooper in high school—and had made a total fool of herself because of him many Christmases ago. But he wasn't the same guy anymore. Now all his bold confidence did was remind her of how she'd humiliated herself and how he'd left Meadow Valley the second he graduated, turning his nose up at small-town living and heading to college in Chicago for all the big city could offer a young politician on the rise. Why he came back was beyond her. And how he *won* the election when Mabel—owner and proprietor of Meadow Valley's one and only bakery, the Mad Batter—would have been perfectly suitable in the role was an even bigger mystery. Okay, so maybe Mabel was pushing eighty herself…Jeez, why did no one under sixty-five want to run this town?

"The first one," Dani finally said. "The physical force. You weren't supposed to hear the—uh—name-calling, so an apology for that would be empty because all it would mean was that I was sorry you caught it—"

"But not that you actually said it," he interrupted. "Because it's what you think. It's what everyone thinks, isn't it?" He shrugged. "How about we look on the bright side. At least no one has to worry about me shirking any of my mayoral duties, since the town hall is bowing out of the lights parade altogether."

Her eyes widened. "You're not—you're not participating? I don't get it. You used to love the holidays. You were the winter formal king your senior year. They—they crowned you with a Santa hat, for crying out loud."

His eyebrows arched, and she regretted letting that last part slip out.

"You remember—" he started, but she cut him off. She was *not* about to delve into high school nostalgia with the guy who certainly didn't remember her like she remembered him.

"So that's it?" she said, bringing the conversation back to the matter at hand. "Not even one tiny string of lights?"

Frowning, he shook his head. "Gave most of my staff a full two weeks off for the holidays. Not enough hands on deck. Plus, Christmas isn't really my thing anymore, so it's a win-win." He pulled a pair of wireless earbuds from his pocket and put them in. "Anyway, I was just going to say good morning before when you—you know…"

"Almost broke you like a wishbone?" she said, hands fisted and resting on her hips. She could do boldly confident too.

He laughed. "I'm harder to break than that, Deputy. Have a good run. I'll just head back the way I came so we don't have any more unfortunate encounters." From his other pocket he pulled a small flashlight, then took off toward a side street that led nowhere other than the outskirts of town.

"Ugh," she groaned. He didn't get to just push her buttons like that and then run off into the sunrise.

Except that was exactly what he did.

Chapter Two

Peyton Cooper *knew* about the Grinch nickname, but he'd enjoyed the blissful ignorance of never having *heard* anyone refer to him as such. Out of sight, out of mind—that was his motto. Well, more like out of *ear*, out of mind. But thanks to Deputy Garcia, who probably didn't realize she was talking over whatever was blaring in her earbuds, Peyton heard it loud and clear.

Didn't she get it? He was going to make this town better than it had ever been. He was going to do for Meadow Valley what he wasn't able to do as the youngest elected village trustee in the Chicago suburb he'd hoped to use as a stepping-stone to his own mayoral seat someday. So someday had come sooner than expected, and maybe it wasn't exactly the big city he'd planned on, but he was here. Trying to make a difference. And Deputy Garcia was—she was so—so—

He growled under his breath. She acted like she knew

everything about him and his agenda when she'd barely said two words to him back in their teen years. Now she was all sharp-tongued and angry at him for wanting to do his job. *Christmas* had nothing to do with it. And those damned caramel-colored eyes of hers that had looked away all those years ago when he—a pretty well-liked guy at their high school, if he did say so himself—had tried to say hi to her in the halls now held his gaze until *he* was the one who turned and walked away. Okay, so maybe he *ran* away, but he was out for a morning run. He couldn't fault himself for that part.

Leave it alone, Coop, he told himself. *Nothing good will come from finding her attractive.* Even if he had then. Even if he did now.

She still wants nothing to do with you.

He laughed, shook his head, and continued running up the road, back toward what was once his family's home but was now a house and stable in disrepair. He hoped the pilot light had stayed lit on the hot water heater so he didn't have to take another cold shower.

Baby steps, right? Little by little he'd get the place up and running again. He owed his parents that much—and the town too. Grinch or not, he had Meadow Valley's best interests at heart. Maybe that wasn't what sent him hightailing it out of Chicago, but it's what pushed him to run for the open seat when Mayor Grady passed away.

Peyton made it to the steps of his childhood home clocking in at four miles. Sweat dripped down the back of his neck, and his T-shirt clung to his chest—both signs of a good ol' stress-purging run.

He kicked off his shoes inside the door and stripped off his clothes on the way down the hall to the bathroom, a perk of living alone. He might be mayor, but that didn't mean he was a neat freak. He'd get to the laundry when he was good and ready.

Naked, mentally exhausted but also cleansed, he squared his shoulders and turned the shower on, pushing the lever as far toward the *H* as it would go.

He waited a good fifteen seconds and then let out a relieved breath when the room began to fill with steam.

"Well done, Mayor Cooper," he said to no one in particular. If *Mr. Big-City Politician* could fix a hot water heater, there was no telling what else he was capable of, right?

He stepped into the hot spray and let the water wash away his encounter with Deputy Garcia. Daniela Garcia. Dani, if he remembered correctly.

He closed his eyes and braced a palm against the cool tile of the shower wall.

Dani Garcia, with caramel eyes and unbridled disdain for the man who avoided what most thought to be the happiest time of year.

Sure. One long, hot shower would definitely erase it all from his mind. At least that was what he kept telling himself.

So imagine his surprise when he showed up to the Meadow Valley town hall—his running gear replaced by his navy suit and silver tie—to find the unforgettable Deputy Garcia sitting in full uniform on the bench outside his door, her jaw set and eyes narrowed as she muttered something to the man on the bench beside her. Deputy Teddy Crawford was the only other officer who worked in the sheriff's office aside from Sheriff Thompson himself.

Peyton approached his office assistant, Keith—a twenty-two-year-old local with political aspirations of his own—and rested an elbow on his desk.

"Do I have a meeting with the deputies?" he asked softly. Dani still hadn't noticed his arrival.

Keith shook his head. "They just barged in here... Well, *she* was more the one to barge. Deputy Crawford at least wished me a good morning and tipped his hat. But you apparently did a number on her."

"What?" Peyton whisper-shouted. "Did a number? Did she say—I mean, *what*, exactly, did she say?"

Keith sighed. "All she said was that the sheriff sent them over and that you'd know why they were here."

Peyton had *no* idea why they were here.

"Do I have any other meetings this morning that might preclude my being able to invite them into my office?"

Keith sighed, then blew a shock of sandy brown hair off his forehead only for it to fall in exactly the same place again. "Nope. This office is pretty much a ghost town. Nothing on the agenda until after..." He paused and then leaned forward and whispered, "the *holidays*."

Peyton rolled his eyes. "Just because..." He took a deep breath before continuing, "*Christmas* isn't my thing doesn't mean any mention of it is off-limits."

"You can barcly chokc out the word." Kcith winccd. "And you *did* suggest canceling one of Meadow Valley's most-loved traditions, but when the town balked, you countered with that whole *only during off-hours* mandate, and if we're being honest, Mr. Mayor—which you know by now I always am—when anyone does mention, um *Christmas*, you get a little sulky."

Peyton's jaw tightened.

"Exactly like that!" Keith said, his eyes brightening. "So forgive me if I'm out of line, but it might work in your favor to fake it 'til you make it with all the holiday stuff."

"Fake it 'til I make it?" Peyton cleared his throat and straightened his tie. "And sulky? I'm a grown man. I don't get—sulky," he insisted, then realized he was maybe, possibly, sulking. So he painted on his best mayoral grin and pivoted toward his uninvited guests.

"Deputies," he said, and both Dani and Teddy stood. "To what do I owe the pleasure of this visit?" He gave Deputy Crawford a firm shake and then held his hand out for Dani. She hesitated for a brief moment and then wrapped her hand around his with the same strong grip she used when wrenching his arm behind his back.

Peyton laughed softly. "So nice to greet you face-to-face this time, Deputy Garcia, rather than waiting to hear you read me my Miranda rights." They kept shaking as he made the joke, and it felt oddly like a game of chicken as to who would let go first. What felt odder was his urge to *not* let go, even as her eyes narrowed and her jaw tightened.

Deputy Crawford laughed. "Am I missing something?" he asked. "Because this sounds like a story I'd love to hear."

Dani looked down at their still-joined hands and snatched hers back. Then she smoothed out nonexistent wrinkles from her perfectly starched shirt. "It's nothing," she said evenly. "Just a misunderstanding."

Peyton clapped Teddy on the shoulder of his tan uniform shirt and nodded. "I'm sure Deputy Garcia would love to tell you all about our *misunderstanding* later. But right now, how about you both come inside and let me know why we're meeting first thing in the morning."

He unlocked his office door and motioned for Dani and Teddy to enter before he followed them inside.

He flipped on the light and then strode behind his desk to where a coffeemaker sat on the windowsill prepped and ready to go. He pressed the power button, then turned to face his visitors.

Teddy had already made himself comfortable in one of the two leather armchairs facing his desk. Dani, however, was strolling the perimeter of the room, brushing her hand along the oak-paneled walls and running her fingers down the thick blue drapes that covered the window on the side wall.

Peyton cleared his throat. "That's Grady's doing," he said. "The drapes, I mean. Well, the whole room. Leather chairs and floor-to-ceiling window coverings. It's all so—"

"Stuffy? Uptight?" Dani said, finishing his thought yet somehow accusing him of something. "Don't suppose you've stepped foot in the sheriff's office since you took up as mayor. We could use some fancy walls and drapes. Or maybe just a roof that doesn't leak."

"Your roof leaks?" he said, and the deputy scoffed, which somehow felt like another accusation.

He decided to ignore her needling for the time being. After all, they weren't here to discuss the state of the Sheriff's Department. Or were they? He still didn't know, so he dove into full-fledged customer service mode. If you can't beat 'em, charm the hell out of 'em. "Exactly, Deputy Garcia. You're very observant." The aroma of fresh-brewed coffee filled the space between them, and he inhaled deep. "Coffee, Deputies?" he asked.

Deputy Crawford held up a travel mug Peyton hadn't noticed before now. "Already on my second cup, but thank you."

"I'm just getting started," Dani said—as did Peyton. At the same time.

Teddy glanced between them and laughed again. "That was amazing," he teased. "Did you two plan it?"

Dani collapsed into the chair beside her partner and Peyton turned back to the now-full coffeepot.

Another standoff.

Neither of them responded.

"Okay, then," Teddy said. "Awkward," he added with a

mumble that was probably only meant for his fellow deputy but Peyton caught it nonetheless.

Awkward. Yeah. That pretty much summed up the morning so far, and it was only nine o'clock.

"How do you take yours?" he asked over his shoulder.

He waited for her to say *cream and two sugars*, just like his, and then braced himself for yet more ribbing from Deputy Crawford after.

"Black," she said. "And I hope you brew it strong."

That he did. Maybe he couldn't stomach the bitterness of drinking it straight, but that didn't mean he liked it watered down. Not even close.

He pivoted back toward his guests, a mug of coffee extended over his desk toward Deputy Garcia.

She raised a brow as she peered into the mug, the rich, dark liquid letting off steam.

She breathed in and sighed. "Not bad," she said, then leaned over his desk to peek into his mug. She chuckled. "Didn't take you for the cream-and-sugar type. Actually, didn't take you for the drip type at all. I'm surprised you don't have your own little barista. Only the fancy stuff for city folk, right?"

Peyton shrugged. "Guess you're just chock-full of misconceptions today."

"*Any*way," Teddy said, and Peyton realized he needed to shift his focus from all things Deputy Garcia to *why* she and her partner were here.

"Right," Peyton said. "Let's get down to business." He relaxed into the high-backed leather chair that—while it, too, had belonged to Mayor Grady—he wasn't against keeping even after he tailored his office more to his liking. But that would come later. After the house. For now the space was functional, and that was all that mattered.

"As you know, Mayor Cooper," Deputy Crawford began, "the—uh—Holiday Lights Parade is next week. On Christmas Eve."

He paused, and Peyton guessed the other man was waiting for him to get *sulky*, but he wouldn't give Keith the satisfaction, even if his assistant wasn't in the room. So instead he forced a grin, possibly too big of a grin judging by the two deputies' puzzled expressions. Maybe he was overcompensating for the sulking—that he hadn't even done—but he didn't want anyone mistaking his reaction for anything other than pleasant.

"Excellent tradition," he said, letting the muscles in his face relax a little. "As are all Meadow Valley traditions—as long as they don't cost the town more money and time than they're worth."

Deputy Crawford took a long swig from his travel mug before continuing. "The thing is, Mr. Mayor, with all due respect, Meadow Valley is what it is *because* of traditions. Occasions like this that bring the whole town together. It seems maybe you've forgotten how special that is. Even though you've been back almost six months and acting mayor for half of that time now, it's been awhile since you've been around for the lights parade. The sheriff was worried about you...How did he put it? About the mayor's office bowing out of the parade. He assumed it was because you were short-staffed, seeing as it's only you and Keith until after the first of the year."

Peyton gave Dani a knowing look. "Wow. News sure does travel fast, doesn't it, Deputy Garcia?"

She raised a brow. "I was concerned that you might need help but not know how to ask for it." Then she paused to take a sip of her coffee. "And of course my suggestion of finding you a few extra hands—*after* office hours, of course—blew up right in my face."

"How's that?" Peyton asked.

"He sent *us* as reinforcements," she said. "Which means I'm pulling double duty because there's no way I'm letting the sheriff's office lose."

Interesting. If Peyton had to describe her tone in nothing more than one word, he might call it *sulky*.

He bit back a smile. "I didn't think the parade was a competition," he said. But then the other part of her sentence sank in.

He sent us as reinforcements.

His smile fell. "While I appreciate your *concern* for my lack of extra hands around here, the square technically isn't part of First Street," he said. "If the town hall takes a break this year or next year or indefinitely—"

"Indefinitely?" Deputy Garcia asked, incredulous. "Maybe we have too many festivals for your liking, but this one? It's the oldest and dearest to so many residents. And also, you're wrong. Because First Street ends at the square."

"But the address of all three buildings on the square is *On the Square*. Not First Street. So the town hall taking a breather for *this* year to start, while the first-year mayor gets his bearings, really shouldn't affect Meadow Valley's coming together and all that," he argued.

She set her coffee cup down on her side of his desk and pressed her palms against the polished wood. "Some would say that the square is the *heart* of First Street and that having the largest and most prominent building in the square *not* participate in a time-honored tradition would absolutely affect the town's coming together. *And all that.*"

Peyton opened his mouth to counter yet again but caught Deputy Crawford's gaze volley from Dani to him. He'd been watching them like they were locked in the final point of a tennis match, and if Peyton had to make a prediction, he'd say he was neither *beating* nor *charming the hell out of anyone.*

The last thing he wanted was to add any more fuel to the fire *or* to live up even more to his nickname of Grinch. So he relented. To an extent. He was a politician after all.

He leaned back in his seat and crossed his arms.

"Okay, Deputies. I see and value your point. But I'm working on reallocating the fiscal budget so that it better suits the town, which means whatever sort of light treatment the town hall gets, it will have to come from what Mayor Grady left in the storage room, and it will have to be done after hours so as not to interfere with our daytime responsibilities—just like everybody else. Seeing as how the Sheriff's Department consists of no more than the sheriff and the two of you, that's going to make for a busy week. For both of you. But I'm willing to shake on it if you are."

He stood, walked around his desk, and held out his right hand.

"Do we have a deal?"

Peyton was relieved when Deputy Crawford stood first.

"Just one question before we shake," he asked. "Since this is happening after hours, and we have lives outside of work"—he glanced toward his partner—"well, at least I know *I* do." He chuckled, and Dani rolled her eyes. "Would it be permissible for Deputy Garcia and me to split our time working on the mayor's office?"

"Absolutely," Peyton said, giving Deputy Crawford's hand a firm shake. "Send over whoever draws the short straw at five o'clock this evening. We'll iron out the details then." Except he realized that might mean time alone with Deputy Garcia.

He should have backtracked. He should have insisted the

two deputies work together and knock a half-assed lighting job out in one evening, especially since he still wanted no part of it. But instead he found himself pulling his hand from Teddy's and grabbing Dani's with renewed purpose.

"Looking forward to getting reacquainted with both of you," he added, and even though he thought lasers or death rays or something equally catastrophic might shoot from Deputy Garcia's golden-brown eyes and obliterate him on the spot, he couldn't help but grin.

Chapter Three

At the end of the day, Dani and Teddy flipped a coin to see who would be on call for the sheriff's office and who would be *ironing out the details* with Mayor Cooper.

Dani readied herself, the quarter perched on top of her thumb.

"Call it, Crawford," she said, and sent the coin sailing into the air.

"Tails," Teddy said matter-of-factly, like he knew whatever he called would be correct.

The coin clattered on top of the desk the two deputies shared, Dani sitting on one side and Teddy on the other.

Tails.

"Two out of three?" Dani asked, and her partner shrugged.

"If it makes you feel better."

She tossed the coin again and nodded toward Teddy to call it once more.

"I'm liking my odds with tails," he said.

Again the quarter hit the desk, spun, and landed on tails.

"Are you some sort of sorcerer?" Dani asked, then added, "Three out of five?"

Teddy laughed. "Garcia, I'll give you four out of seven, five out of nine, six out of ten—whatever floats your boat, but the odds are in my favor."

Dani narrowed her gaze at him. "And why is that?"

Her partner grinned. "Because I can read people, Deputy. It's part of the job. And what I read between you and the mayor this morning?" He shook his hand out like he'd accidentally touched a burning pan on a lit stove. "Sizz-*ling*. The universe wants this to happen."

She rolled her eyes. "False," she said. "He just makes me so crazy with his '*Christmas isn't my thing*,' and '*The mayor's office doesn't really count*,' and '*Are you apologizing for calling me a grinch?*' and—" She growled softly. "Besides, if you really thought that, you'd have been ribbing me all day about it. You're just pulling stuff out of your rear end to cover for your otherworldly powers when it comes to coin tosses."

"I'm a professional, Deputy Garcia. I save my ribbing for when we're off the clock." He laughed. "Also, I've known you since we were kids. Don't think I forgot the two-year crush you had on that Grinch. Figured it was a sensitive subject I should let marinate before bringing it up. Consider marination complete." His dark brows rose. "*Wait.*" He leaned forward, resting his elbows on the desk and his chin in his hands. "When did you call him a grinch to his face? There's no way I missed that in the good mayor's office this morning. You were supposed to fill me in on a *misunderstanding* that happened earlier, right? No time like the present."

Dani crumpled up a piece of paper on her desk and

tossed it straight at her partner's nose, but he straightened and caught it. *Damn his good reflexes.*

"O-*kay*," the other deputy said. "Still a sensitive subject." He shrugged and pushed himself back from the desk and stood. "Enjoy your night, Deputy. Pop by Midtown Tavern when you're done. I'll let you buy me a beer if I haven't already found a lovely tourist to do it herself."

She stood as well. "*You're* on call, Deputy Crawford. It's just soda for you tonight. But feel free to buy *me* a cold one when I get there." She doubted her meeting with the mayor would take long. The sun had already set, so the most they could do was discuss how and when to fit in decorating the Town Hall by Christmas Eve.

Dani grabbed her quarter and shoved it back in her pocket, offering Teddy her best self-satisfied grin, but there was no rattling him. There never was.

"No worries, partner. I don't need a pint to enjoy myself. There are still tourists," he said.

She sighed and pushed in her chair. "Ever thought about any of the locals? A relationship that lasts longer than a one- or two-week vacation?"

Teddy laughed. "Variety is the spice of life, my friend. I'll tell you what though. I'll consider your suggestion when you admit you still have a crush on City Boy over there." He nodded toward the window that looked out on the town hall.

Dani forced a laugh. "Enjoy your variety," she said. "The only things I have a crush on are this job and this town and doing right by both."

Teddy gave her a puzzled look.

"You know what I mean." She groaned. "It sounded better in my head. I'm married to the job. I don't complicate it with relationships or crushes or any of my old high school fantasies. I'm an adult *and* I act like one." She squared her shoulders and raised her chin.

Her partner gave her a pat on the back.

"I *will* enjoy my variety," he said. "And *you*, Deputy Daniela Garcia who's married to all this"—he spread his arms to indicate their dilapidated office—"enjoy that adulting."

He winked at her, tossed his hat onto his head, and strolled out the door.

She knocked on Sheriff Thompson's door, the only private office in their small building.

"Come in," he called from inside.

Dani opened the door slowly and poked her head in to find the sheriff with his head down, finishing some paperwork on his desk.

"Sir, just wanted to let you know that Crawford is on call tonight and I'm...I'm heading over to the mayor's office to help him get started on the whole lighting thing that he'd prefer to avoid."

The sheriff waved, eyes still glued to whatever he was working on.

"Thanks for the update—and for helping Mayor Cooper get back into the spirit of things around here. He means well but still needs a nudge in the right direction."

Dani grimaced. "I'm not so sure about the spirit part of it, but we'll get the lights and whatever else up—*unless* you'd rather I put my whole focus into *our* building. I mean, it *is* the sheriff's office, and I *am* deputy sheriff. And since I'm not on call, this is technically off hours for me."

Sheriff Thompson finally looked up. His dark hair was in need of a cut, and she swore she could see a little more gray in it than yesterday. Dark circles rimmed the underside of his eyes.

"You okay, Sheriff? You look—exhausted," she added.

He laughed, which set her more at ease. "You don't pull any punches, do you, Dani?"

She smiled back at him. "Never have."

"I'm fine," he said. "Just working out the details for something personal. Nothing to worry about. But do I need to worry about *you* playing nice with Mayor Cooper? I know you're not thrilled about splitting time between our place and his, but I do want to remind you that *you're* the one who came to *me* concerned that Mayor Cooper wasn't going to participate in the lights parade."

She'd knocked on his door ready to argue, but she could see now that whatever Sheriff Thompson was dealing with, he didn't need added drama. Plus, technically, he was right. She'd gotten this whole ball rolling by opening her mouth in the first place. She might as well put her good intentions into action.

"I'll play nice," she relented. "As long as you promise not to do our office all by yourself when I'm not looking. I want to help. I want the Sheriff's Department to stand out. I want us to—"

"It's not a contest, Deputy," the sheriff said, the corner of his mouth turning up.

Dani blew out a breath. "Except, sir, that it kind of is. Which is why I need you to *promise* you'll let me do my part. I know you have enough on your plate as it is."

"Deal," he said with a small laugh, and she closed his door, leaving him be.

She grabbed her jacket off the back of her chair and threw it on, opting to leave her hat on the desk since she technically wasn't on duty.

"Ready or not, Mayor Cooper," she said softly to herself, "here I come."

She ignored the little flip in her belly at the utterance of his name. Crushes were a thing of the past, as were fantasies of being noticed by someone who never even knew she was there. Tonight was strictly business.

* * *

Dani wasn't sure what she expected to find when she arrived at the mayor's office, but it wasn't Peyton Cooper in a Midtown Sluggers—the town's coed softball team—T-shirt and jeans, his five-o'clock-shadowed jaw set as he tried to untangle a massive nest of holiday lights.

She watched him, probably for several seconds longer than she should have. But he looked so—different than all the other times she'd seen him out and about town. Where Mayor Grady had always topped off his look with a cowboy hat and bolo tie, Peyton Cooper walked the streets of Meadow Valley in three-piece suits and wingtips. Maybe Grady had been ostentatious in his office design, but he'd still looked the part of a small-town mayor. Until today, Peyton had seemed like a fish out of water, even after having lived in Meadow Valley most of his life.

Dani had been too caught off guard earlier in the morning to pay attention to what the mayor looked like in his running gear, and she was sort of regretting that at the moment. Maybe it wouldn't have been so jarring to see him like this—like just a normal guy. A really good-looking normal guy whose jaw was maybe a bit scruffier and his eyes a hell of a lot more intense than the teenage boy she'd admired from afar. Except right here, right now, while she was all but stalking the man, he was as unguarded as she'd ever seen him since his return. The image evoked a nostalgia she wasn't expecting, and her stomach flipped again.

Hey… genius… don't be fooled. He might be the same guy who made your silly heart go pitter-pat, but he's also the same guy who crushed that silly heart without a second thought.

She cleared her throat, and the mayor looked up. "Keith was gone, so I figured it was safe to just come on in."

He shook the tangled web from his hands—his triceps flexing as he did—and dusted off his jeans. Dani was sure they were clean as could be, yet as he stepped out from behind his desk, she could see the denim was faded and well-worn. It even looked like there might be a paint stain on his right knee.

"Evening, Deputy Garcia," he said, extending a hand. "I let Keith take the afternoon off. When I'd initially thought the mayor's office would, uh, bow out of the festivities this year, he asked if it would be all right if he helped out at Mrs. Davis's bookstore." He shook his head and laughed. "I'm a grown man—the mayor even—and I still can't seem to call her Trudy like everyone else."

Dani shook his hand. "I think Keith is dating Trevor, one of Mrs. Davis's—I mean *Trudy's* employees. Guess old habits die hard, right?" she said with her own nervous laugh. She was much more aware now of the calluses on his palm, of the sudden warmth that radiated from his skin to hers. Both observations startled her so much that she snatched her hand back, and the mayor raised his brows in question.

"Static electricity," she lied. "Felt a little shock."

The corner of his mouth quirked into an almost-grin.

"Yeah," he said. "Felt it too. Sorry about that. Must have been the lights."

He glanced over his shoulder at the pile of lights on the table.

"Is that what Grady left you to work with?" she asked.

He turned back to her and nodded. "Look, I meant what I said about stepping back from all this. But I'm not a big enough jerk to leave you this mess and expect you to deal with it on your own. I'll help you get the lights untangled, but I need to draw the line there. I hope you understand."

She shook her head. "I don't. But I'm not going to keep fighting you on it. That won't get us anywhere." She nodded toward the wad of lights. "Speaking of getting anywhere, how long have you been working on that?"

He laughed. "Probably a good hour already." Then he shrugged. "I guess you *really* drew the short straw, being the one to have to start on this unwanted assignment—and start it with the Grinch."

Dani groaned. "First of all, it was a coin toss. No straws involved. And second—look, can we start this day over? Forget about—well, every rude thing I said or did or *thought* up until now? This will go a lot quicker if we can put all that behind us."

He laughed, straight from his belly—which rippled under the thin cotton of his T-shirt. *Not* that Dani was looking, but keen observation was a part of her job. And his voice—deep and full of joy—elicited a smile from her as well.

"Your saying and doing were few and far between," he said. "But I imagine you've been thinking all sorts of things all day."

She rolled her eyes. "Don't flatter yourself, Mr. Mayor. I do think about things other than you and your hatred of the holidays."

He raised a brow. "But what you're saying is that you *did* think about me today."

She threw her hands in the air. This man was impossible.

He leaned back on the edge of his desk. "And I don't hate the holidays," he said, his voice softer, almost solemn. "These days it's just easier to focus on getting through this time of year than to make such a big deal about it."

"Getting through it?" she asked, incredulous. "You talk like you don't have anything to celebrate. I mean, you're the mayor of your hometown. At thirty-two. I know it doesn't compare to Chicago, but it's something, right?"

His jaw tightened.

"I got fired, Dani. That's why I left Illinois. I came back to regroup, and then Mayor Grady died. I needed a job. Everything else happened so fast. I want to do something good here before I figure out my next move."

"Oh," she said. "And your parents aren't coming back to spend the holidays with you?"

When Peyton hadn't moved home after college, they'd followed their only son to where he'd set up his new life, selling their home and property to an investor who—for whatever reason—never did anything with the house or the land. Every small town seemed to have that house on the outskirts that sat empty for years, the windows boarded shut and the grass overgrown. For Meadow Valley, it was the Cooper residence. If Peyton hadn't come back, she guessed that soon enough, kids would start making up stories of the place being haunted—if they hadn't already.

He shook his head, and for a second it looked like someone had socked him in the gut, but she blinked and the expression was gone.

"They can't come back this year," was all he said.

"Oh," she said again. "So you lost your last job and are alone for the holidays. I can see how that would suck. I'm sorry, Coop."

Coop. What was she doing calling him by the high

school nickname she'd never used because she'd never said two words to him while they were there?

His brows furrowed. "I didn't know we were on a nickname basis. Also, I didn't realize you *knew* my nickname."

Dammit. She did it again, just like she had this morning when she'd mentioned the winter formal. Her cheeks flushed. "Of course I knew. You were president of the school the two years we were there together. *Everyone* called you Coop. It was on every campaign poster. Kind of hard to miss. I guess...I don't know...you seemed like the old you. Not that I *knew* the old you."

Oh my god. What was she doing? It was like an instant replay of the humiliation she'd felt years ago, except this time he was watching her go through it.

"*Any*way," she said, "we should really get to the whole light-detangling situation so you can rid yourself of this silly holiday business. In fact, you know what?" She strode toward his desk and wrapped the mass of lights into her arms. "I can just take these back to my apartment and work on them there."

Maybe he was letting his personal feelings about the holidays spill over into his thoughts about how the town celebrated it. And while she didn't agree with it, she could understand it. Plus, the thought of keeping the guy here untangling Christmas lights when it was the last thing he wanted to do didn't make the rest of her night sound too fun. At home she could at least take off her bra. God, that sounded amazing after the day she'd had.

"Wait," he said, blowing out a breath. "I said I'd help with this part, and I'm a man of my word. And I think I can make the night a little more bearable for both of us." He strode toward a small mini-fridge that sat on the wide window ledge next to his coffeemaker and retrieved two bottles of beer. "How about a refreshment?" he asked, turning to face her again.

She sighed. An adult beverage would *really* hit the spot right now. If Deputy Crawford couldn't relax with a cold one tonight, she might as well pick up the slack. The mayor did seem genuinely committed to helping her sort out the lighting mess. And truth be told, she was kind of dreading doing it by herself.

Dani offered him a conciliatory smile and popped the top off her bottle using the edge of the mayor's desk.

"Refreshments, Mr. Mayor. You just said the magic word."

Chapter Four

 Two hours, three beers, and a whole mess of wire and glass later, Peyton and Dani had somehow accomplished the impossible. The perimeter of the mayor's office was now lined—twice over—with the untangled lights.

"This is it," he said, holding the plug at the ready. "The moment of truth."

Dani winced.

"What?" he asked.

"Well, do you think maybe we should have—?"

"Tested the lights as soon as we uncovered the plug? Oh yeah. One hundred percent." But he'd gotten sidetracked by their rhythm. By listening to her talk about life in Meadow Valley since he'd been gone and her family and living with Casey above the bar and—all of it. Every word that came out of her mouth—now that the whole grinch thing was behind them—put him at ease. He could have listened to her for two hours more, but he'd stolen enough of her time for one night.

Dani laughed. Her hair—no longer in the tight ponytail she wore under her hat—bounced in dark waves against her shoulders, and Peyton had to fight the urge to forget the lights altogether and tangle his fingers in that hair and...And what? She was here because of a coin toss and because she didn't want to see him ruin her favorite holiday. He needed to get his head on straight and stop thinking things he shouldn't be thinking.

"Okay, then," he said. "Did we, or did we *not* waste the last two hours of our lives?"

"Wait!" Dani said as she collapsed into the chair behind his desk and started pounding the top with her palms. "We need a drumroll!"

He listened to the beat of her hands against the wood and then finally plugged in the lights.

The perimeter of his office lit up like a bright white picture frame.

Dani sprang up and pumped her fist in the air with a loud "Woo-hoo!" Then she strode to where he stood and high-fived him like it was something they'd been doing for years. "Nice work, Mr. Mayor! I never thought I'd say this, but we make a damn good team, don't we?"

He nodded then breathed in deep. Now that she was closer, he could smell the scent of cherries and something else...Almonds maybe? Her shampoo.

"You smell great," he said without thinking. Then he thought. "*And* that was a completely inappropriate thing to say. I apologize."

She shook her head and bit her bottom lip before her mouth curved into a small smile.

"It's okay," she said softly. "I mean, I like knowing that

I smell good. It's better than smelling bad, right? And after this day, which started before the crack of dawn—for both of us, even—it's good to know I haven't turned too ripe. You know what I'm saying?" She rolled her eyes. "Jeez, what the hell am I saying? A cute guy says I smell nice, and I launch into a manifesto on ripeness?" She took a step back, holding her hands up as if stopping him from pursuing her. "And *that's* my cue to exit. Good night, Mayor Cooper."

"You think I'm cute?" he asked, holding back a grin. He wasn't letting her off the hook that easily. He'd spent the past few hours untangling Christmas lights, which should have put him in what Keith would have deemed his sulkiest of sulky moods. Yet he'd smiled more tonight than he had in months. He'd laughed as much too. And it was all thanks to Dani. If, on top of all that, she thought he was easy on the eyes, far be it from him to let such an admission go unnoticed.

"What?" she asked. "No. I didn't say—"

He took a careful step closer to her and nodded. "But you did say, Dani. And if there's one thing I've gotten to know about you since coming back to Meadow Valley, it's that you're honest and direct and always say what you mean. You're not afraid to speak your mind, even if it means telling a grumpy old mayor when he's being a selfish ass. I admire that. I might even find it attractive."

She lowered her hands, her shoulders relaxing. "Peyton..." His name came out like a sigh, and god, he liked the sound of it. "Look, I didn't know about your last job or that you're alone for the holidays this year. And I never called you selfish."

"Just a grinch," he said with a grin.

This time she blew out an exasperated breath. "I apologized for that too." Then recognition bloomed in her expression. "Wait. Did you just say you found *me* attractive?"

He shook his head, still smiling, and took another small step closer. "I said I found your blunt honesty attractive."

She rolled her eyes and groaned, and he laughed.

"I think you're beautiful, Deputy. *All* of you," he added. "I know this is going to sound crazy, but I kind of had a crush on you in high school."

Her eyes widened and her cheeks flamed. "You—you did not. You liked Cady McKay. You were the winter formal king and queen together. You..." She slapped her hand over her mouth.

He raised his brows. "Cady McKay asked me to the winter formal with one of those silly Christmas Grahams she made the student council sell. I'd have been a jerk if I said *no*."

Dani stared at him blankly.

"You remember the Christmas Grahams, right? *Graham*? With an *h* because she loved that movie with that British actor... What was his name?"

She swallowed, then cleared her throat. "*The Holiday*. With Jude Law. His character's name was Graham," she said flatly.

"Yes!" he said, pumping his fist in the air. "The freshman and sophomore student council members had to sell these mugs with Jude Law's face plastered all over them, and you could fill it with a small gift or whatever and send the cup to anyone in school. She sent one to me with an invitation to the dance, so I said yes. That doesn't change that I had my sights set on someone else. But every time I saw you in the hall or the cafeteria and attempted eye contact, you'd look away or talk to someone else and pretend like you didn't see me." He paused for a moment, then added, "I'm not sure if you remember, but it was a small school. And I like to think I had a bit of a presence when I entered a room."

She scoffed, but he continued.

"It was pretty obvious you wanted nothing to do with me, so after a while I stopped trying."

She took the final step to close the distance between them, then exhaled a long breath.

"I looked away whenever you were nearby," she said, "because I was afraid if I actually made eye contact that you'd know."

"Know what?" he asked.

"That like almost every other girl in school, *I* had a crush on the golden boy, Peyton Cooper." She shook her head and buried her face in her hands before setting her gaze on his again. "I swore that after…" She shook her head again. "Forget it. I'm not the same girl I was then."

Peyton reached his hand toward her face, afraid he might spook her into leaving. But she didn't move, so he tucked a lock of her hair behind her ear.

"And I'm not the same guy."

She wrapped her palm around his wrist, lowering his hand. Dammit. He'd spooked her.

"I still don't agree with your views on the lights parade. Or what you think of Meadow Valley's time and investment in its festivals in general," she said.

He nodded. "Agree to disagree, then," he replied. "I can live with that."

"And whatever either of us felt in high school, that was then. Promise me you won't bring it up again."

He'd thought they'd made some sort of a breakthrough, realizing that their attraction had a history. For both of them. But the finality in her tone said otherwise.

He nodded once more. She hadn't left yet. So he waited. He'd liked her then, even more so now, and hoped that he hadn't blown it completely.

She let go of his wrist and blew out a breath before extending her right hand.

"So let's start fresh. Hi. I'm Deputy Daniela Garcia. It's nice to meet you."

Peyton smiled and shook her hand. "Mayor Peyton Cooper," he said. "But you can call me Coop. When it's just you and me."

She bit her bottom lip, and good lord, it made him want to do the exact same thing.

"Do you anticipate it being just you and me *often*?" she asked.

He shrugged, though his heart was beating a mile a minute. "I think that depends on how compatible we are when it comes to greetings other than shaking hands."

She swallowed. "Are you going to kiss me, Mr. Mayor?"

"If you'll let me, Deputy," he said.

And she did.

Her arms wrapped around his torso, and he dipped his head. In the space of a breath, her lips were on his, and his hands were in her delicious-scented hair, cradling her head in his palms, and it was everything that had been missing from his hollow life for the past year.

Her lips parted in a smile against his as he savored the taste of her on his tongue, the cherry-almond air that enveloped them.

"Just for the record," he whispered, barely taking his lips off hers. "You said I was cute before I said you were beautiful."

She laughed softly. "Less talking and more kissing, please."

He rested his forehead against hers, unable to erase his own smile from his lips. "Call me Coop again," he said softly.

He liked his nickname when she said it. It made him feel like part of the old him was still there. It made him feel like he wasn't alone, simply trying to get through what was once his favorite time of the year.

"Coop," she said, then kissed him again.

"Dani," he answered back, their kisses moving from sweet and patient to somewhere more urgent and full of a shared need.

"Coop, I..."

He waited for what came next, for her to kiss him again and again. Hell, he could kiss this woman until the sun came up if she'd let him.

But she let go of him and took a step away, her lips swollen and cheeks flushed.

"I can't," she said, and then grabbed her jacket from the back of one of his chairs, threw it on, and bolted through the door.

He stood there stunned, not moving for several long seconds.

She'd called him cute.

She'd initiated, so he knew she wanted to kiss him when they started.

She'd called him *Coop*. Twice.

He grabbed his phone from his desk, readying himself to call her—then realized he didn't have her number. She'd said she lived with Casey over the tavern. He could show up at her apartment like some stalker. And then what?

You've been out of the game too long, Coop. You have no idea how to do this.

So he collapsed into one of the guest chairs facing

his desk, in a room framed with bright white lights, and scrubbed a hand over his jaw.

What had he done wrong?

He had absolutely no clue. All he knew was that he had kissed Deputy Daniela Garcia, and he really wanted to do it again.

Chapter Five

Dani slapped the crisp twenty-dollar bill into Deputy Crawford's palm.

"So, are we completely done with coin tosses?" he asked.

She nodded. "You keep winning. I'm just trying to keep things fair. Plus, I have better things to do when I'm off duty than work."

Teddy laughed. "Like what? Your idea of enjoyment *is* working. Especially when it involves prepping for the lights parade. You *love* this stuff. In fact, I'd go so far as to say that you live for it. So what's the deal, Garcia? The sheriff and I got *our* lights up the first night, so all that leaves for you is—"

"A quiet night at home," she interrupted. "Casey's working, so I have the whole place to myself. And don't you go thinking that a few lights mean the Sheriff's Department is *done*. I have ideas. Things in the works. But tonight is all about *me* time, even if I have to pay for it."

And since being on call rarely ever amounted to any sort of law enforcement activity, it also meant a hot bath, a cup of tea, and whatever was on Netflix that she hadn't yet watched. "I *can* relax, you know," she added. "Also, I may head out to the Everything Store in the morning and see if I can't find something to make our little building stand out more this year."

"It's *not* a competition," Teddy said.

"I know," she replied. "But it still is. A little. And while I appreciate you and Sheriff Thompson hanging the same twinkling icicle lights we hang every year, it's not enough. You and Sheriff Thompson fight me on this every year, but I'm tired of using the excuse that our building is *literally* crumbling to keep us from doing it up big like everyone else does. This year we're upping the ante. If the Everything Store can transform its facade into a new Disney character every year, shouldn't *we* be able to do more than generic twinkle lights?"

Teddy raised a brow. "Mayor Cooper got under your skin with the whole 'The square's not part of the parade' bit, didn't he?"

Dani huffed out a breath. Of course it had gotten to her. Sheriff Thompson had used the same reasoning last year. Sure, he'd thrown something in about the structural soundness—or the lack thereof—as far as keeping anything weight-bearing off the roof, but twinkle lights? Twinkle lights when the Everything Store would likely ignite with the likeness of Elsa or Anna? Not *this* year, folks.

"Mayor Cooper did no such thing," she lied. And he certainly hadn't gotten under her skin with that kiss either.

Teddy shrugged. "Suit yourself. But I'm guessing the store is cleaned out of holiday lights by now." He folded the twenty and stuck it in the pocket of his jacket. "This is the second night in a row you've paid me off, and Mayor Cooper has stopped by the office twice in the past two days, which is two more times than he's been here since he blew back into town. Are you sure there's nothing else to this?"

Dani zipped up her jacket and put her hat on her head.

"Mayor Cooper was here? I didn't realize," she lied. Of course she knew he'd stopped by. She'd seen him through the window by her desk each time he strode down the town hall steps. And each time she'd found a reason to slip out the back door before he made it to their office.

I just saw Sam Everett outside with Scout. I'm going to go bring her a dog treat.

Casey just texted. Locked her keys in her truck. I'm going to go jimmy her out.

There'd been no dog, though Dani did love that pit bull. And—you guessed it—Casey had never texted. But Dani couldn't face Coop—er, Mayor *Cooper*—after running out on him the other night. After *kissing* him. After he kissed her back.

That kiss was—*wow*.

She'd been kissed by men before. Some of them had even made her weak in the knees. But Peyton Cooper? In her wildest dreams—and she'd had a few—she couldn't have imagined the electricity or the way her heart would pound. She couldn't have known it would be everything she never knew she was missing.

Him saying he had a crush on her in high school was nothing more than a line. And it had worked—until his lips touched hers and everything came flooding back. The stupid Christmas Graham. The invitation to the dance. Dani putting her fragile teenage heart on the line and him being so sure it was anyone other than her.

It was silly. She was a grown woman now—a confident

grown woman who knew what she had to offer. But when Peyton Cooper was nearby, it brought her straight back to that ego-shattering day.

"Hellooo? Garcia?"

She heard her partner's voice like he was trying to speak underwater.

She blinked, and his words and her surroundings came back into focus.

"Huh?" she asked. "What was I saying?"

Teddy crossed his arms and leaned back in his desk chair with an accusatory grin.

"I don't know, Deputy," he said, then kicked his feet onto the top of his desk, crossing one steel-toed boot over the other. "You said Mayor Cooper's name and then got all far off and dreamy-eyed."

Dani glared at him. "I was not—I don't get *dreamy*-eyed."

Deputy Crawford glanced out the window. "Speak of the devil. Here comes Mr. Mayor right now."

Dani gasped. "He's what?" She slapped her palms down on her side of the desk so she could lean forward and get a better look. Her heart raced, and her stomach rose high into her throat.

But the square was vacant.

"You're the worst," she said through gritted teeth, straightening to her full height.

Teddy chuckled. "And you, my friend, are *very* concerned about Mayor Cooper's whereabouts and making sure *your* whereabouts are, well, as far from his as possible."

Before she could give him a piece of her mind, a loud thump sounded behind her. She spun, palm on the gun in her holster, then let out a breath when she saw the culprit—drywall from the water-damaged ceiling that had crashed to the floor.

Teddy was standing beside her, hand on his own weapon and ready to back up his partner if backup was needed.

"Everything all right out here?" Sheriff Thompson said as he poked his head out of his office.

Dani groaned. "Just another piece of the ceiling deciding it's had enough."

The sheriff pinched the bridge of his nose. "I'm trying," he said. "But the budget is tight."

"What about the Everett brothers, Sam and Ben?" Teddy asked. "They built that whole ranch with their bare hands. I bet they wouldn't charge you any more than the cost of materials and maybe their time."

Sheriff Thompson sighed. "They're good men," he said. "And I'm sure you're right. If I asked, they'd step up. But they're running a twenty-four-hour business. They have their hands full with that. And after their father's recent passing, the holidays are going to be hard enough. I don't want to add to their burden."

Dani's heart squeezed. She couldn't imagine losing a parent, not like that. Her father leaving her mother when she was a teen was devastating, and even though she still blamed him, was still so angry at him, he was alive. Maybe one day, when she was ready, things would be different. But the matter at hand right now was the Sheriff's Department.

"Can I ask you something, Sheriff?" Dani asked.

The man let out a chuckle. "Would it matter if I said no?"

"No," Dani said matter-of-factly. "Why is it that we get the short end of the stick? The fire department is state-of-the-art. They even have a gym out in back. And the town hall…Don't even get me started on the over-the-top decor going on over there. But we sit here, day in and day out, with rusting cells and a falling ceiling."

"Mayor Grady," Teddy said from behind her. "May he rest in peace and all that, but we all know he was terrible with finances."

"Which was pretty much his whole job," Dani added. "Allocating tax dollars."

The sheriff held up his hand. "Look, we're not going to speak ill of the dead." Dani opened her mouth to protest, but he continued, "Even *if* you're both right. We just need to move forward. I've been meeting with Mayor Cooper this week—"

"What about?" Dani jumped in. "Unless... You were just about to tell us that, which you were. Of course you were. I'll just zip it from here on out." She mimed zipping her lips, then noticed her pulse quicken and her palms dampen at another mention of Mayor Cooper, and she decided her *me* time should really start now before her physiological reaction to the man in question gave her partner any more fuel with which to rib her about her two-year crush. "But actually," she added, quick to ignore the zipping of said lips, "I'm officially off the clock and on call, so I am going to skedaddle and keep on keeping on, and I'll see you two gentlemen tomorrow."

She spun on her heel and headed toward the door before she could gauge either one's reaction.

Skedaddle? Keep on keeping on?

What was the matter with her?

Mayor Peyton Cooper and his stupid kiss and his stupid *I'm just doing this mayor thing until I figure out my next move* attitude. Ugh. Dani wasn't some consolation prize for a man who fell into a job he clearly didn't intend to keep long-term. And she had no intention of letting him humiliate her again.

No thank you.

It was just a kiss. She'd get over it just like she'd gotten over her two-year crush on the guy. She wasn't some head-in-the-clouds teen anymore. She was a grown woman. A practical, doesn't-waste-time-on-unavailable-men-who-don't-truly-value-her woman. And just like Peyton Cooper's time in Meadow Valley would eventually pass, so, too, would whatever this was. Not that it was anything.

Just a kiss.

A ground-shaking, bone-melting, hot-as-hell kiss that she barely even remembered after two days.

She laughed as she strode out of the square and down First Street toward Midtown Tavern and her apartment. And she glanced back toward the town hall only once.

Okay, twice.

Fine. It was three times. Not that she'd admit that to anyone if they asked.

When Dani got there, she thought about stopping into Midtown to catch up with her roommate, but a hot bath and a cup of tea sounded much more appealing, so she headed straight upstairs and through her apartment door.

She dropped her hat and keys on the small table inside the entrance—their catchall for mail, flyers, and whatever else didn't have a specific storage space—and hung her jacket in the front hall closet. Then she stepped into the small galley kitchen, grabbed the teakettle from the blue and white tile countertop, filled it with water, and plugged it in to heat up.

Next, she made her way to her bathroom. One of the perks of the apartment was its setup. To the right of the kitchen was Dani's bedroom and bathroom. To the left, Casey's. The only rooms they shared were the kitchen and the living room.

She turned on the water, closed the drain, and dropped

a eucalyptus-spearmint bath bomb into the tub. She kicked off her work boots and stripped out of her clothes, leaving it all in a heap on the bathroom rug as the tub filled. Then she strode barefoot and, well, bare *everything* back into the kitchen just in time for the kettle to whistle that it was ready.

She rifled through her tea box, not for one second worried about anyone walking in on her naked in the kitchen. Another perk of the roommate setup and their alternating schedules.

Chai won the silent debate in her head. Only decaf for the evenings, or else she'd never sleep, which would make getting up for tomorrow's run so much more painful than it should be. She knew it would be a quiet night. It always was. And she wanted to get in a good six hours of sleep before her 4:30 a.m. wake-up call.

Mug in hand, she padded back to the bathroom and set her tea on the side of the tub before climbing into the steaming, fragrant water.

She lowered herself into what could only be described as pure and utter bliss. When the water reached its optimum level—just covering her breasts—she used her toe to turn the faucet off, closed her eyes, and sighed.

This—*this* was better than decorating a town hall that didn't want to be decorated with a mayor who likely saw her as a fun fling until he decided what to do next.

So why was she thinking about the Meadow Valley town hall and Mayor Peyton Cooper when she had eucalyptus, spearmint, and chai?

She took a sip of her tea, blew out a long breath, and closed her eyes.

Clear your head, Dani. This is your night. No work. No stress. The apartment to yourself.

But her head was full of noisy thoughts that wouldn't leave her alone, so she submerged herself in the water, hoping the complete and utter quiet would silence it all.

And for a couple of seconds, it did. But then she swore she heard a pulsing or a beeping, almost like—an alarm.

An alarm?

No way. An alarm*!*

Dani bolted upright, clearing the water from her eyes and ears to make sure her mind wasn't playing tricks on her. But there were her work pants, vibrating on the floor, her phone lighting up the holster where it hung from her belt, and the emergency alarm blaring.

"You've got to be kidding me," she said aloud as she scrambled out of the tub. Of course she knocked her tea off the ledge, spilling it onto her pants but luckily missing her phone.

She glanced at the screen and saw that the call came from a security system she didn't even know had been installed at the old Cooper property.

Great. First she runs out on Mayor Cooper in the middle of kissing him, and now she was going to have to tell him that someone was robbing his family's abandoned home?

"Shit!" she hissed as she hightailed it into her room and threw on the first thing she could find, which was her running gear for tomorrow morning. She dressed as fast as she could, not caring that her hair was a wet, tangled mess. Then she unthreaded her belt from her work pants, strapped it around her waist, making sure her gun and phone were secure, and sprinted out the door.

She radioed the sheriff and Deputy Crawford to let them know she was on the call.

"Let us know if you need backup," Sheriff Thompson radioed back. "Over."

"Copy that," she said. "Over." Then she hopped onto the police-issue motorcycle parked behind Midtown Tavern and took off toward the ranch.

She made it from her apartment to the property in nine minutes. She was prepared to park a few yards away so any intruders wouldn't see her coming, but she could see the light illuminating the front porch and a man on a ladder fiddling with something over the front door. A man who—even from a distance—was unmistakably Mayor Peyton Cooper.

"Fan-freaking-tastic," Dani said to herself, then groaned.

"Looks like a false alarm," she radioed Sheriff Thompson and Teddy. "No backup needed. Over and out." Then she rode the rest of the way and up the property's gravelly, weed-covered main drive.

She parked the bike, took off her helmet, and quickly finger-combed her still-sopping-wet hair.

"Evening, Mr. Mayor," she called out to him as she ambled up the steps to the porch.

He was off the ladder now, and he glanced at her, then at what looked like a door alarm he'd been installing, and back at her.

"I—uh—tripped the alarm, didn't I?" he asked, looking mildly chagrined. And maybe mildly adorable standing barefoot in a pair of flannel pants and a long-sleeved navy thermal shirt.

Focus on the alarm, Dani, not how handsome he is.

"Yeah," she said, arms crossed. "You tripped it. Do you know how to turn it off?"

He winced. "There's an app on my phone, but I hadn't quite gotten to that part yet."

Dani held out her palm, and he handed her the phone with the app open.

Luckily, she knew the system and was able to reset it in a matter of seconds.

"Oh no," he said, though he sounded amused. "Were you in the shower or something?"

She gave him his phone back and wrung out her hair onto the desperately-in-need-of-a-paint-job porch.

"A bath, actually. Barely had time to get wet before you did whatever it was that you did." She shivered, finally realizing she wasn't properly dressed for the below-forty-degree temperature.

He actually had the audacity to laugh. "I'm sorry," he said, but he was still laughing. Dani didn't see the humor in the situation.

"Oh, come on, Deputy. It's kind of funny, don't you think? I've been trying to get in touch with you for two days, and you've managed to avoid me at every turn. Now I inadvertently ruin your night but finally get to see you? I'm guessing that this on top of spooking you the other night means I've pretty much sealed my fate now...unless you're willing to give me another chance."

She shivered again. The temperature must have dropped in the two minutes she'd been standing there, and she was too cold to fully absorb what he was saying.

"I should..." she began, teeth chattering, "I should go."

"You're freezing," he said, then wrapped an arm around her, and god, the warmth of him against her felt good. "Come in and warm up. At least let your hair dry. Then I promise I'll let you go without protest."

Despite her better judgment, she nodded and let him lead her inside.

Chapter Six

Okay. So plumbing Peyton could do. Messing around with a wireless security system? Not so much. Yet the fortunate consequence was face time with Dani Garcia, the woman who'd been avoiding him for two days.

He padded down the steps with a towel under one arm and the quilt off his bed in the other.

Dani sat on one of the two barstools he'd picked up at a resale shop, her elbows propped on the kitchen island in front of her—the counter now stripped of its tile and sanded down. Her hands rubbed her upper arms for warmth.

"Here," he said, offering her the towel first. Then he chuckled when he noticed that her belt, which included her holstered gun, had been removed and laid on the island to her left.

"Glad to know you don't feel the need to remain armed in my presence."

She didn't laugh. Instead, she wrapped her hair in the

towel like she'd just gotten out of the shower—or bath, like she actually had. Then he draped the quilt over her shoulders, and she sighed.

"I did good?" he asked.

He liked this woman. A lot. Hell, he wasn't lying about the high school crush thing either. He thought telling her was a good thing. He thought she'd like to know that his attraction to her now wasn't some spur-of-the-moment thing, that he'd always sort of seen her as the one who got away even though they'd barely known each other back then— even though *he'd* been the one who actually left.

The hint of a smile appeared on her face as she tugged the quilt tight around her. "You did good," she told him. "Now, if you had some decaf chai, you'd almost have made up for the mug I spilled all over my uniform getting out of the tub. But I'm guessing by the looks of this place, you probably don't have much of anything yet."

Peyton winced. "I really messed up your night, huh?"

She blew out a breath. "No. I mean, you did, but I'm on call, so getting my night interrupted *is* part of the job. It just doesn't really ever happen—unless you count when we *thought* Delaney Harper had been kidnapped by her ex-husband."

"I remember that," he said. "And it's a good thing you were there to help. You're good at your job, Deputy."

"I know I am," she said, sounding a little defensive. "I mean, thank you."

Peyton rounded the island and started rummaging through a cabinet below the kitchen sink.

"No chai," he said. "But I do have some English breakfast tea. I, um, did an internship in London my junior year of college. Kind of got hooked on the stuff. It's really good with milk and sugar."

Dani shook her head and smiled ruefully.

"What?" he asked. "And while we're asking questions, do I finally get to ask what sent you bolting from my office the other night?"

She groaned and nodded toward the box of tea in his hand. "*That*," she said.

His brows drew together, and he laughed. "Because of a box of tea?"

She shook her head. "It's not the tea. It's what the tea represents. You're—*worldly*. You're bigger than anything Meadow Valley has to offer you, and you flat out told me that you're only doing the mayor thing here while you figure out your next move. I may be a small-town girl, but I'm not an idiot, Peyton."

His eyes grew wide. "I never said you were." How had he already spooked her again? With *tea*? Coming back to Meadow Valley was the hardest thing he'd ever done, so yeah, maybe he wasn't sure if he was here for the long haul. But it wasn't as if he saw her as a placeholder. Not by a long shot. There was something undeniable brewing between the two of them. If she felt the same—even if only a little bit so early on—then who knows what the future might hold? But she didn't seem to want to give him a chance.

He noticed she wasn't looking at the tea anymore, that her gaze now fell past his shoulder. He followed it toward the mugs on the counter next to the sink and couldn't help but chuckle when he saw Jude Law grinning at them through fifteen-year-old porcelain. "Yes. I keep old mugs. Especially ones that hold a bit of nostalgia. It also makes up for the fact that I don't exactly have a fancy set of dishes with matching plates and mugs and all that."

"Typical bachelor," she mumbled.

His brows drew together. "Is your grudge against Jude Law, the movie, or the high school winter formal?"

"Which of the three is the cause of your nostalgia?" she shot back.

He shrugged. "D. None of the above."

"Fine. That's my answer too. D. None of the above," she said coolly, but the heat rising to her cheeks said otherwise.

"Dani..." He took a step toward her. "I like you. And for a millisecond I was pretty sure you liked me too. Can we start over? Again?"

She stood and dropped the quilt and towel over the top of the stool.

"Look," she said, backing out of the kitchen, "I know the holidays can be lonely. I'm reminded of it every year when my mom flies to Miami to spend Christmas with my sister, brother-in-law, and my nieces and nephew. 'Come with, Daniela,' they insist. 'It's the only time we get to see her,' they say." Their yearly mantra since Julia left for a job on the other side of the country. She waved the thought away, getting herself back on track. "I'm reminded of how much it stinks to spend the holidays alone when the only *home* I have to decorate is the Meadow Valley Sheriff's Department for the lights parade. And as much as I'd *love* to have something more to look forward to than that, I'd rather be on my own than be someone's method of killing time until they up and move on again."

"And there it is," he said.

"What?"

"The whole leaving thing," he added.

She groaned through gritted teeth. "So just like that, you think you have me all figured out, right?"

He shrugged. "You've already made your mind up about me, haven't you? Don't I get to weigh in?" He was pushing her buttons. He knew he was. But she was pushing right back. Eventually, something had to give.

"I should go," she said. "Thanks for the towel and the blanket."

Okay. But wait. We were getting somewhere, weren't we? Peyton thought as he watched her turn and walk away.

But she stopped short when she faced the kitchen desk, piled with mail and one other item that he guessed would be hard to ignore.

"Peyton," she said softly. "Why is there an urn on the desk?"

So they *were* getting somewhere. They were getting here. Peyton guessed it was time to tell her everything.

He braced his hands on the edge of the island and waited for the tightness in his throat to ease.

"It's my parents," he finally said. "A car accident back in Chicago," he added, his voice low and controlled. Because he wasn't going to lose control in front of Dani. In front of anyone. He had a job to do. A home to restore. And a town that was counting on him, regardless of whatever came next for his career, if he even still had one.

She pivoted to face him again. "And you're living here instead of the town-owned mayor's residence—"

"Because it's what they would have wanted. If I hadn't left, they would have stayed here forever. I guess I feel like I'm somehow honoring their memory by restoring their home. *Our* home." He cleared his throat. "Lost my job out east right about the time I heard their place had fallen into the hands of the bank. Bought it back with what I had in savings."

She swiped at a tear under her eye.

"When did it happen?" she asked, then added, "If you're okay sharing."

"Almost a year ago."

She nodded. "Right before the holidays. It's all starting

to make sense. I didn't know," she said. "No one did. Why haven't you told anyone?"

He shrugged, but his shoulders felt heavy. His muscles tight.

"Because I didn't want everyone to look at me like that. I'm the mayor. I have an image to uphold. And now you're looking at me like I'm one of Mrs. Davis's strays."

She moved toward him, and now he knew how she must have felt the other night. His instinct was to bolt before things got too real. The only problem was that they were in *his* house. He had nowhere to go.

So he stood there, hands still gripping the counter's edge, wondering if Dani Garcia would be his salvation or if she was right, that he would cut and run as soon as something better came along. Losing both his parents was hard enough, but losing his job and possibly jeopardizing everything he'd worked for? He felt like he had nothing left but this house and the memory of a life he thought he hadn't wanted.

She urged him to release his left hand, and he did, allowing her to step between him and the island. She pressed her palms to his chest, and he knew she must have felt his heart hammering against his ribs.

"You're not one of Mrs. Davis's—ugh, *Trudy's*—strays," she said.

That got him to laugh.

"But you're also not *just* the mayor," she added. "You're someone who's obviously hurting, and I'm someone who cares about that."

He nodded slowly. "I didn't say I was leaving," he said. "The other night in my office."

"But you also never said you were staying."

"I guess I just don't know what comes next," he said. "I'm a little lost."

She worried her bottom lip between her teeth, which also made him smile. He loved that he was already picking up on her idiosyncrasies. Her tells.

"What?" she asked, her brows furrowing. Also adorable.

"This," he said, brushing a finger over her bottom lip. "You bite your lip when you're thinking."

"Coop?" she said, and this made him smile bigger, made him almost stand at attention.

"Dani?"

"You being back in town…Is that temporary?" She shook her head. "I mean, are *we* temporary?" Her golden-brown eyes looked at him expectantly.

He didn't want them to be. Coming back to Meadow Valley to spread his parents' ashes, to save the home they gave up to be near him—it was the hardest thing he'd ever done next to losing them. But Deputy Dani Garcia was a bright light in the darkest time of his life. And when she called him *Coop*—when she made him feel like the man he was before it all went to hell—it seemed like getting through this might actually be possible.

"No," he said, hoping it was the truth.

And then she kissed him.

Her lips on his tasted sweeter than any confection. Her teeth nipping at his bottom lip was sexier than anything he could have imagined. And her body—no longer shivering but radiating heat against his—was the closest thing he'd felt to home in a long time.

He brushed some sawdust off the counter and lifted her onto it.

"Sorry," he said, suddenly realizing what the place must look like with countertops removed and the wood floors sanded but not refinished. "It's a work in progress. Has been for a few months now."

"Why are you here when you could be living in Grady's mayoral estate over on the residential side of town? I get wanting to fix the place up, but you could live in a house that probably already has a working alarm system." She laughed softly. "I imagine the inside of Grady's place looks a lot like your office."

She skimmed her fingers through his hair, and he closed his eyes, letting himself get lost in one tiny moment of normal before letting out a sigh.

"If I don't live here and work on the place every free moment I get, I'll never get it done. Plus, I don't know, I kind of like being here. Feels like they're with me."

She hooked her legs around his waist and nodded. "Do you want to talk about it?"

He shook his head. He wasn't ready for that yet.

"Do you know what you're going to do with it when you're done? Fill the stable and be the mayor who moonlights as a cowboy?"

He shrugged. "Future's wide open. Just taking it one day—or night, I guess—at a time."

"One more question, then," she said, placing a hand on each of his shoulders. "And I should warn you that after you answer, I *am* going to kiss you some more."

He laughed. And god, it felt good to laugh with her. "Ask away, Deputy. And by all means, keep the kisses coming."

She glanced around the room and then back at him, her eyes bright and determined.

"Let me help," she said. It was more of a demand than a question, which didn't surprise him. "My father's best friend when I was growing up was Jorge Lopez, the best electrician in the county. He did a lot of work on our house over the years. Still helps my mom out from time to time. Bottom line is, I know a thing or two about fixing up a house."

Peyton forced a smile. He was so bent on figuring everything out himself, on doing for his parents what they couldn't do anymore. But he was in over his head.

"I know," he admitted. "I finally broke down and called your uncle a couple of weeks ago to deal with a wiring issue after I shocked myself one too many times."

Her eyes widened and her mouth fell open. "Uncle Jorge has told me *nothing* of this," she said. "And he's usually my go-to for town gossip."

"So *I'm* town gossip?" he asked.

She nodded. "Sure. The prodigal son returning and taking over as the town mayor? You're big news around here. People—and by *people* I mean other people and not necessarily me—like to know the inside scoop," she said, sliding her hands down his arms and linking her fingers with his. "Like the sexy new mayor forgoing the mayoral residence in favor of rugged living while he restores his parents' ranch with his own two sexy hands."

He squeezed her hands in his. All he'd meant to do tonight was install a security system. He hadn't planned on Dani, on telling her what he'd been keeping secret from everyone in town save Sheriff Thompson. Kissing her, though, he could do. Kissing meant he didn't have to say any more about his parents. Kissing her meant both of them ending this night on a better note than the last time his lips had touched hers.

"You realize you just called me sexy *twice* in the span of one sentence, right? And not one mention of this Mayor Grinch you almost tried to arrest the other day." Maybe he could steer this conversation into a more comfortable subject area.

She squeezed her legs tighter around his waist, pulling him closer and making him want to do things that had very little relation to restoring his childhood home. He guessed his strategy was working.

"Careful, Deputy," he teased. "Or you may forget I tried to ruin your holiday altogether."

Her gaze softened. "Hey," she said. "I get it, okay? You'd rather forget this time of year exists, and I'd rather throw myself headfirst into all things holiday-related for—reasons. So how about we meet halfway and throw both of ourselves headfirst into getting this place back up on its feet? You can start by letting *me* install your alarm so Deputy Crawford doesn't get dragged out of bed tomorrow night." Her brows furrowed, then a particularly mischievous grin spread across her face. "Or *maybe* I'll let you fiddle with it for another night or two."

He shook his head and laughed. If he brushed it all off as no big deal—turning her down—she would too, right? This was something he needed to do alone. He wasn't ready to share everything with her, not when they'd barely made it past their first kiss. She was holding something back too. He could tell and wouldn't push her. Hopefully she'd do the same for him.

"Trust me," he said. "You don't want to dive into this mess." He looked around the unfinished room. "Because you're only seeing one tiny part of it. And it's...a *lot*. A lot of work *I* signed up for that I need to do on my own—except for maybe one emergency call to your uncle."

"And to the deputy on call tonight."

He winced. "And that," he said. "But the rest has to be me. Just me. Can you understand that?"

She shook her head, then let go of his hands and draped her arms around his neck. "No. I *don't* understand not wanting help when it's offered. You took Deputy Crawford and me up on our offer to put the lights up on the town hall."

Peyton raised one shoulder. "Ah, but that was something I didn't *want* to do and wasn't going to do."

She rolled her eyes. "Okay, that was pretty grinch-y."

He laughed, glad he was able to lighten the mood rather than drag her down to where he dwelled much of the time. "Bah, humbug," he said. "So we're okay? I mean, you're good with me doing my thing here while you do your thing in town with the lights and the parade and all the holiday stuff?"

She nodded. "I don't get you, Mr. Mayor. But I can respect whatever it is that you need."

"Thank you," he said, relieved.

Since the day he learned how to ride a bike and wouldn't let his mom *or* dad grab on if he was about to fall— regardless of skinned knees and elbows—he'd wanted to figure it all out on his own. Something even then, in his six-year-old brain, told him that his parents wouldn't always be there to hold the back of the bike. He'd just thought they'd have more time than this. Now it was like some sort of atonement. Being here. Bringing everything back to what it used to be.

"Hey, Coop," she said, bringing him back to where he was—in the kitchen with a beautiful woman in his arms. "You still there?"

He cleared his throat, painted on a grin. "I am. And I'm pretty sure you said something about *more* kissing a few minutes ago, didn't you?" He lifted her off the counter, and she yelped with laughter, her knees holding tight against his hips, her torso in his arms. He let her slide down just enough so her mouth could find his, and as promised, she delivered.

Minutes flew by like seconds as he nipped and tasted her lips, the skin on her neck, the place where her running shirt dipped into a V between her breasts. When he kissed her *there*, she hummed, a sound so sweet yet at the same time so full of need he knew if they didn't stop soon, they might not be able to stop at all.

When Peyton finally lowered her to the ground, both he and Dani were out of breath, but they were also both grinning from ear to ear.

She let out a nervous laugh and ran her fingers through her drying hair. "So, um, I'm still on call. Which means I should probably focus on—you know—being on call."

He smoothed out his shirt and crossed his arms. "And I should get back to pretty much anything other than alarm installation. Unless...you want that cup of English breakfast tea."

She smiled nervously. "If I stay for tea, I'm afraid I might not go home at all, and if Casey comes back at three a.m. to find the tub filled and my uniform in a pile on the bathroom floor with chai spilled all over it, she might actually get worried. Good night, Mr. Mayor."

She grabbed her belt from the counter and put it back on. Then she kissed him one more time, her lips lingering on his before she slipped out of his arms and seconds later out his front door.

He watched as she threw on her helmet and started her bike. She was pretty in high school, and she had that *something* that had always made him wish he'd gotten to know her before he left. Now, though? She was so much more than he ever could have imagined. Strong. Sexy. Funny. Smart as a whip. If he wasn't careful, he might get in over his head as much with her as he was with this house, with running a town that used to be home but now seemed to fit like someone else's clothes.

Dani Garcia though. She made it feel like it was possible

to come back. To be who he used to be despite what he'd lost.

His phone buzzed in the pocket of his flannel pants, and he pulled it out to see a 773 area code. *Chicago.*

He normally ignored unknown numbers, assuming they were spam, but something told him to answer this one.

"Hello?" he said, hoping he didn't sound confused.

"Peyton Cooper?" the woman on the other end said.

"This is *Mayor* Peyton Cooper," he replied, adding the *Mayor* for a reason he couldn't explain.

"*Mayor* Cooper," she said. "Of course. My apologies for calling after office hours, but I'm making my way through a list of candidates. Let me be frank. I'm calling from the Chicago mayor's office. She's looking for a research analyst to help her plan a long-term budget for her new education task force, and she had *you* on her short list of people to interview based on the budget work you did in your previous position. I realize as far as title this may be a step backward for you, but in terms of salary *and* a future in the Chicago office of the mayor…"

She trailed off.

If this wasn't a joke—and it sure as hell didn't sound like one—they were aware of his previous work *and* that he'd been let go. And they still wanted him to interview?

"Mayor Cooper?" she asked. "Are you still there? I'm guessing you're wondering if the mayor knows about the financial blunder that lost you your previous job, and she does. She is also aware of the personal circumstances surrounding said blunder and is sympathetic, where it looks as if your former board was not. We'd be looking to set up a phone interview after the holidays. Should I add you to the mayor's official list of candidates?"

It's just an interview, he rationalized. For a position in basically one of the top offices in local government. He'd be an idiot to pass it up without at least considering the possibilities.

"Yes," he finally said. "Add me to the list."

"Thank you, Mr. Mayor. Someone will be in touch in the next few days with the date and time of your phone interview. If all goes well, she'll expect you for a face-to-face interview soon after. Good night, Mayor Cooper."

He could still see the taillight of Dani's motorcycle in the distance as the call ended.

It was just a phone call. It didn't mean anything. Not yet, at least.

Chapter Seven

Deputy Crawford had been right. Meadow Valley had been cleaned out of any and all holiday lights as well as lawn and roof displays. That just wouldn't do. Maybe a simple string of lights framing the entrance to the town hall was good enough for Mayor Cooper, but the same old icicle lights as last year for the Sheriff's Department? Dani wasn't having it.

On her way back through town last night, First Street had been abuzz with shop owners outside working tirelessly on what she knew would be fantastic decorations. Trudy Davis was turning the entire front window of her bookshop into a giant lighted book. The Meadow Valley fire station had lights strung from top to bottom, and there was talk of Santa in a lighted engine going up on the roof.

Everyone was making do with Mayor Cooper's time restrictions as far as working on their decorations, but Dani was still at a loss for how to make the Sheriff's Department stand out.

And then she found it.

She looked up from her laptop where she'd been frantically googling things like "Griswold Christmas decorations" and "holiday roof displays."

"Look at this," she said to Deputy Crawford.

She spun her computer to face him, a photo of a life-sized Christmas ornament made from white lights filling the screen.

"You can *stand* inside it," she said. "This guy builds these amazing displays and then auctions them off. The last bid on this one is *two hundred dollars*, and the auction doesn't close until the twenty-third."

Teddy's brows rose. "How would you even get it here if you won the auction? And where would you put it? That thing is *huge*."

She bounced in her chair and grinned. "It *collapses*. And there are plenty of pickups in town for me to borrow. If it doesn't weigh too much, the roof might be able to take it, and if it's too heavy, then I'll set it in the lawn next to the sign you forgot to string with lights. Don't worry. I did that last night on my way back…"

She trailed off as something moved in her peripheral vision.

Through her window she saw Mayor Cooper striding down the town hall steps and toward the sheriff's office.

Her first instinct was to bolt, like it had been earlier in the week. But then she remembered last night, kissing the man she'd wanted to kiss for fifteen years. Okay, so she still wanted to bolt, but now it was for a whole new reason. How were they supposed to act around each other after— after she had to convince herself to leave so Casey wouldn't come home to what had looked like the scene of a bathtub kidnapping. And maybe she'd wanted some time to think, too, about what the hell she was getting herself into.

"A*hem*," Deputy Crawford said from across their shared space, the most exaggerated throat clearing she'd ever heard.

"What?" she said, snapping her head away from the window and fixing her narrowed gaze on her partner.

"Saw the emergency call came from the Cooper ranch," Teddy replied with a knowing grin.

Dani shrugged it off. "It was a false alarm. Literally. He was installing a new system, tripped it, and I fixed it."

Teddy glanced out the window, then over his shoulder toward the back exit to their small building.

"How come you're not hightailing it out of here to see a man about a dog or something?" he asked.

Peyton was getting closer, and she noticed he was not in his usual suit and tie but in a thermal shirt and jeans, a down vest zipped over his torso and cowboy boots poking out the frayed ends of the denim.

Yep. She was staring again. And not answering Teddy's logical questions since she *had* made herself scarce the other two times the mayor had approached their building.

Dani stood, trying to smooth out the wrinkles in her shirt and pants—her *clean* shirt and pants, since yesterday's uniform was toast until she did laundry this weekend. She winced, realizing her closet consisted of mostly her work clothes and running clothes. That was her life—running and working.

"Deputy Garcia?" Teddy said, pulling her from her thoughts.

"Huh?" she said. "What?" But before he could toss any further questions her way, the front door opened, and Mayor Peyton Cooper walked in.

Coop.

Whom she had kissed Tuesday night. And last night. A *lot* last night. And oh, look, there were the lips she kissed, right there on his smiling face.

"Deputies," he said with a nod. "Good—" He looked at his watch and then back at Dani and Teddy. "Good morning, for one more minute, at least. I'm just going to…" He pointed toward Sheriff Thompson's office door, and then, without further hesitation, left the two of them standing there as he gave the sheriff's door a quick knock before heading in and pulling it shut again behind him.

Teddy chuckled from behind her, and she turned to face him, rolling her eyes, waiting for whatever came next.

"So you think he lost the suit because you called him stuffy and uptight?" he asked, leaning back in his chair. "Also, nice touch with the whole standing for his entrance like he's royalty or something."

Dani gritted her teeth and growled softly. "I thought you saved your ribbing for the end of the day," she said. "And I didn't call *him* stuffy and uptight. Just his office."

"You insinuated," he said. "Looks like the guy took it to heart." Then Deputy Crawford nodded toward the clock above the sheriff's door. "And it's high noon, Garcia. Friday before Christmas. Which means a half day, and you and me officially off the clock. Sheriff's on call, so you're free to do—whatever it is you had planned for the rest of the day."

Her eyes widened. She'd been so caught up in holiday decor shopping—in deciding whether or not to bid on the life-sized ornament while the dollar amount was still manageable or to wait a few days and hope she could swoop in and win with the final bid—that she'd completely forgotten she was off for the next forty-four hours, thanks to the half day and weekend rotation.

Sheriff Thompson popped his head out of his office door. "It's quitting time for you two," he said, then smiled. "Crawford, you're on desk tomorrow. Garcia, you've got Sunday. And then we're closing up shop until the twenty-sixth. Keep your phones charged and ringers on though."

They both nodded.

"If I could borrow Deputy Garcia for a few minutes—" the sheriff started to say, but Deputy Crawford cut him off.

"I'm outta here, folks," he said. Then he was out of his chair and halfway through the door before Dani even stood up.

She laughed and waved as the door banged shut behind him. She wondered what he had planned. Knowing Teddy, it was something far more exciting than Dani's deciding whether or not to take a new trail for her afternoon run.

"This won't take too long, Garcia," Sheriff Thompson said. "Come on in, please. The mayor has some questions for you."

Dani's eyes widened.

Had she done something wrong?

Was she in some sort of trouble?

She tried to flip through a mental handbook containing the rules of her job. She knew very well that being on call did *not* mean she had to cease living her life however she might choose to live it, so long as it didn't interfere with responding to an emergency.

Nothing that had happened last night impeded her ability to respond to the situation. In fact, she hadn't even kissed Peyton until *after* she'd assessed the situation and determined there was no emergency.

Unless a deputy sheriff kissing the town's elected official was somehow unacceptable office behavior.

She laughed out loud. "Sir, this feels a lot like getting

called into the principal's office. Am I getting called into the principal's office?"

Sheriff Thompson also laughed, a loud and rueful sound she hadn't heard in a while, and it put her at ease. Mostly.

"Just come on in, Garcia," he said. "This should only take a few minutes." He held the door open for her.

When she walked in, Peyton stood and held out his hand.

"Deputy Garcia," he said with a warm smile. Not entirely formal but not at all as—um—*friendly* as they were last night. As if he'd greet her the same way he'd said good-bye to her when she left his place.

She bit back the urge to laugh again and shook his hand, her brows furrowed.

"Mayor Cooper," she said.

The sheriff followed her in, and they all sat down.

The mayor pulled out his phone and set it on the sheriff's desk.

"Do you mind if I record this?" he asked. "I want to make sure I don't forget any repair details. Once we have a list and can get an estimate on cost—"

"Okay," Dani said, holding up her hands, her gaze volleying between the two men. "Record my suggestions? I can make you a spreadsheet and email it over whenever you want. Hell, I can even do the cost estimates. I've just been waiting for Sheriff Thompson to give me the thumbs-up, but he seems to think you have other priorities to attend to first. So what is actually going on here? I'm getting called into a surprise meeting that may or may not have me slapping my gun and badge down on the sheriff's desk for something I may or may not have done to incur some sort of violation of the rules and regulations of my job. And now you want to record said conversation? I feel like I should call a lawyer or something."

"Dani," Peyton said, resting a hand on her shoulder—the use of her first name and gesture immediately reassuring. But when the sheriff's eyes shifted to the two of them, he pulled his hand away and crossed his arms over his chest. "From what it sounds like after talking to Sheriff Thompson, you spend the most time in the building out of all three of you."

Her cheeks grew hot. Was that the nice way of telling her she had no life?

"So I want your input," he continued, "on what needs work or repairing first. A priority list so that I can take it back to the office, figure out funding, and get some estimates. I know crime in Meadow Valley and the surrounding county is minimal if anything at all, and we're damn lucky to live in a place where it's safe to walk the streets at night and folks can leave their doors unlocked."

She relaxed into her chair and exhaled.

"Is that why you're installing a security system on the ranch? Because of how safe our town is?"

He laughed. "Maybe I'm a little jaded from my time away, but I'm learning. It's also good to know that when something happens—when you or the sheriff or Deputy Crawford is needed—you have what's necessary to do your job and to stay safe while you do it. That starts with the roof over your head, the floor beneath your feet, and everything in between."

Sheriff Thompson stood, grabbed his hat off the corner of his desk, and dropped it on his head. "I already gave Mayor Cooper my take on the situation, but I'd really love your input, too, Deputy Garcia. So if it's okay with both of you, I'll leave you to it. I have a few personal things to take care of before nightfall."

Peyton stood and shook the sheriff's hand. "Jeremiah," he said.

"Peyton," the sheriff replied, then he turned to Dani, who was too stunned to speak.

Jeremiah?

Peyton?

Had Dani missed a budding bromance when she wasn't looking?

No one called Sheriff Thompson anything but *Sheriff Thompson*, in public or otherwise. It was like *Sheriff* was his first name. Of course she *knew* it was Jeremiah, but hearing it was like—it was like seeing a dog walk down the street on its hind legs.

She stood, too, not that she had a habit of formal partings with her boss but because it just felt weird to be the only one still sitting. This whole exchange, from the second she walked through the door, had felt weird.

"Enjoy your time off, Deputy," the sheriff said with a smile, and then he was out the door.

She spun back to face the mayor...Peyton...Coop. How the hell was she supposed to think of him after last night? After *two* nights of kissing this man who was a stranger but not.

"Deputy Garcia," he said with a soft smile, then shoved his hands into the front pockets of his jeans.

"Yeah?" she responded.

He shrugged. "You look like you want to say something. Probably lots of things. So I'm just waiting for it."

She narrowed her eyes at him and crossed her arms. "I feel like I'm being set up somehow. So I'm just pausing to assess the situation. If Sheriff Thompson...I'm sorry. Apparently you call your buddy Jeremiah now? If *Jeremiah*..." She shook her head. "Nope. Can't do it. No one's called him that out loud for years. I can't start doing it now. If Sheriff *Thompson* already told you what needs fixing around here, which is *everything*, then what do you need me for?"

He wrapped a gentle hand around each of her wrists. "May I?" he asked, urging her to uncross her arms and let them fall to her sides, and she nodded, granting his request to speak, trying to ignore how her heartbeat sped up the second his skin touched hers.

"For this," he said, cradling her cheeks in his palms and dipping his head to brush his lips across hers.

She wrapped her arms around his waist and let her whole body—tense with anticipation until this very minute—melt like warm chocolate against his.

She felt his lips part in a smile against hers, and she couldn't help but smile too.

"All I've been able to think about since you left last night was this," he said between kisses.

She nodded, hoping he understood the same was true for her, because talking meant giving up his lips, and she wasn't ready to do that just yet.

He must have, because he didn't say anything else, not for a few wonderful minutes, at least. Finally, though, when it seemed they both needed air, he lifted his head, and she was happy to see his lips looked as kiss-swollen as hers felt.

"What are you doing for the rest of the day?" he asked. "Other than making me a spreadsheet, though I was hoping that could wait at least until you were back on desk duty."

Her mouth fell open, but no words came out of it. At least not as quickly as she would have liked.

She was going to go for a run and then maybe contact the artist who was auctioning off the ornament, see if she might be able to get an in-person look at the piece. He was only about an hour outside of town...

"So you're *that* busy," Peyton teased. "Because I was hoping to steal you for a few hours."

Her eyes widened, and her ability to form words returned with a vengeance.

"So you assume I have nothing to do, huh?" she teased back, but there might have been a tiny bite to her tone. "Because I have things to do, Mr. Mayor. I have an afternoon run planned. And Meadow Valley has been cleared out of any and all holiday decorations for purchase, but there's this life-sized ornament and this artist and—"

"Dani?" he said, her name soft and gentle on his lips. Ugh. She *really* liked those lips.

"Yeah?"

"You don't need to give up your day for me. But seeing as the whole town pretty much shuts down from now until the day after Christmas—whether I like it or not—I had some free time and thought I might take you out. Like, on a date."

"A date?" she asked.

"A date," he said again, nodding.

"So...a *date*," Dani repeated.

Peyton laughed. "You've been on one before, right? It's when two people who like each other—and seem to *really* like kissing each other—do a thing like go out to dinner. Maybe take in a movie after. Stuff like that."

Dani blinked. "But it's not dinnertime. And the closest movie theater is forty-five minutes away."

He raised a brow. "That's why I have something else planned," he said. "It involves a horse named Ace who right now is assessing whether or not I did an adequate job cleaning up and restoring the stable on *my* property or if he should hightail it back to the Meadow Valley Ranch. Borrowed him from Sam, Ben, and Colt."

Dani threw back her head and laughed. "A horse? You think I'm getting on a horse? You, my friend, need to research your dates better. I'm not getting on a horse. The only saddle I sit in has two wheels beneath it."

"Jeremiah said he's thinking about employing a horse or two at the Sheriff's Department. Says you all don't need to travel *that* far on a daily basis and that it's better for the environment."

Her eyes widened. "Like hell he is! I can assure you there is *nothing* in my employment contract stipulating how I get from point A to point B, and I plan on keeping it that way, thank you very much."

Peyton didn't flinch. He simply held out a hand.

"Come on," he said. "It'll be fun."

She didn't take the bait.

Kiss the mayor in her boss's office? Sure. Hop on the back of a horse with him? Not happening.

"I'm good," she said.

"If you're scared," he said hesitantly, "I can promise you'll be safe. I'll be on the horse with you the whole time. Ace is the best there is. Between him and me, you're in good hands. Or hooves. Both, I guess," he added with a chuckle.

"I'm not *scared*," she said defensively. She was terrified. You didn't control an animal. Animals controlled *you*. "So, you know, thanks for the offer. But if you want to plant another one on me before I get on with the rest of my day, that would be acceptable." She tugged the sides of his unzipped vest, urging him closer.

He smiled and tilted his head toward hers but stopped short.

Her breath caught in her throat.

"There is nothing I want more than to kiss you again, Deputy. But I'm going to hold my pretty little pucker ransom long enough for me to show you that a ride in my saddle is just as satisfying as a ride in yours." He grinned. "That came out a little—um—" He let out a nervous laugh. "You know what I mean."

"But I—"

"You can go for your run," he said. "I'm happy to wait. And your ornament thing, too, whatever that is. I'm patient. I'd just really like to show you something before sundown, and Ace is the best form of transportation to get there. And I probably should have mentioned earlier that our destination *is* holiday-related."

She sighed. "Are you going to kiss me if I say yes?"

He grinned. "I am."

"And if your four-legged friend decides *he* doesn't like me as much as you do and tosses me to the curb, do I get to say 'I told you so' and send you all my medical bills?"

He laughed. "Isn't a motorcycle just as dangerous?"

She shook her head. "An injury on horseback is something like three and a half times more likely than an injury on a bike. Eli Murphy's wife..." She trailed off.

"I know," he said. "I feel terrible about him losing Tess. But Dani, I promise that I'm not going to let anything happen to you. Ace and I will keep you safe." He kissed her. "*I'll* keep you safe."

He took a step back and waited for her to respond.

"That's usually my job, you know. Keeping people safe," she said, a smile on her lips to mask the fear she very poorly disguised.

"Can I ask?" he said. "Have you fallen before?"

She blew out a breath and nodded. "My dad loved to ride. He still does as far as I know." She shrugged. "It was our thing for a while. I was fifteen the last time we went. Tried bareback for the first—and *last*—time. Lost my grip and broke my fall with my right hand. Heard my wrist snap and everything."

Peyton winced. "I'm sorry that happened. Does it make me sound like a creep if I admit to remembering your arm being in a cast? It was green, right? Figured that was why I didn't see you at the winter formal—you being injured and all."

Her eyes widened. He didn't see her at the dance because he'd assumed her invitation was from someone else. Still, she couldn't hide her surprise. His so-called crush on her in high school could have been nothing more than him feeding her a line. But her cast? Her absence from the dance? While these were the hallmarks of the worst time in her life, they should have been minor details to someone like him. Yet he recalled both as if it were yesterday. Her chest tightened at the thought. "You really *do* remember me from high school?"

He laughed. "I thought we already established my unrequited crush." His smile faded. "What happened with your dad?"

She let out a bitter laugh. "That day he was great. Got me right to the hospital. Took me to the bookstore for Mrs. Davis's homemade ice cream after and promised me that every good rider takes a tumble or two but that he'd always be on the horse next to me keeping me safe. A week later he and my mom told us they were separating, and he moved out. A year after that, he moved to Miami and remarried."

She'd always told herself the reason she'd never gotten back on a horse was because she couldn't count on the animal not to hurt her again. Her wrist healed though. It was her family's splitting up she couldn't fix.

He tucked a lock of hair behind her ear. "We don't have

to do this. The last thing I want to do is drag up painful memories for you. I'm an expert at avoiding my own, so I get it. But if you can trust me to keep you safe, on and off the horse, maybe we can make a new memory. For both of us." He held out his hand once more. "What do you think?"

Dani released a shuddering breath. Maybe it was time to let go of some of the pain she'd been holding on to for fifteen years—about her parents, about a stupid crush on an oblivious boy who maybe wasn't so oblivious anymore.

She laced her fingers through his, and he squeezed her tight. For the first time in years, she let herself trust someone other than her mom and Deputy Crawford, not only with her physical well-being but with a tiny piece of her heart.

Baby steps, right?

"Okay, Coop," she finally said. "I trust you."

Chapter Eight

Dani had decided to forgo the run, unable to tamp down the anticipation of an afternoon with Mayor Cooper. Peyton. *Coop.*

Who wanted to keep her safe.

"Nobody can harm you if I'm around, *mija*. I will always keep you safe," Dani's father would say. Even when she technically did get harmed falling off the horse, she still felt protected having her dad there. Dani knew she wasn't unique in being the child of a fractured family. But how could he tell her that he'd always be there—and then leave? Her sister, Julia, had forgiven him, had even called it an *opportunity* to be near him again when a recruiter snagged her right off her culinary school campus to train as a sous-chef at an up-and-coming restaurant in Miami.

"It's a chance to reconnect, Dani," she insisted. "It's time to get to know him as an adult, you know?"

Dani didn't know, at least not anything other than that

some of the people she loved most in the world thought Meadow Valley wasn't enough for them when it was for her. That home wasn't enough. That *she* wasn't enough.

Now she was the one so much of her town counted on. She kept *them* safe. And suddenly Peyton Cooper wanted to lift some of that burden and do the same for her.

She'd run home to change. All he'd seen her wear since they'd started spending time together this week was either her uniform or running gear. She'd had to dig into the recesses of her small closet to find her jeans. As far as warm tops went, she had the choice of either her red-and-green argyle Christmas sweater—which was usually earmarked for Christmas Eve and the lights parade—or a black-and-white flannel she could layer beneath a heather-gray fleece pullover. She went for the flannel and fleece.

She topped off the look with a black knit cap and fleece-lined gloves and then laughed when she caught a glimpse of herself in the full-length mirror on the back of her bedroom door.

If not for her steel-toed work boots—the only shoes she owned other than her running shoes and one pair of dress shoes—she looked like she'd stepped right out of an Eddie Bauer catalog.

"Eddie Bauer is suitable date attire, right? Because this is as fancy as I get," she said out loud.

This is me, Coop. Hope you know what you're getting yourself into.

Soon she was on her bike and heading down the road to the old Cooper home. He was sitting on the porch, his feet resting on the bottom step, when she came to a stop in front of the house. He was on his feet and jogging toward her before she was out of her seat.

"Have I told you how incredibly sexy you look on that

bike?" he said as she took off her helmet and locked it to the back of the cycle.

"Yeah, well, wait until you see how awkward I am on the back of a horse," she said. "You'll forget all about your little motorcycle fantasy. *Not* that I'm suggesting you fantasize about me or *have* fantasized about me or—" She stopped and straightened the cap on her head. "Congratulations, Mr. Mayor. I've nudged the needle over to awkward already."

He laughed, his eyes crinkling at the corners, and then dipped his head toward hers.

"Deputy Garcia," he said softly, his breath warm against her ear. "You couldn't look awkward if you tried. Sexy as hell on the back of a motorcycle? Sure. But awkward? Not even close." He patted the seat of her bike.

Dani swallowed. If he didn't stop saying things like that, they were never going to make it to the stable.

Wait. Wasn't that what she wanted? She thought for a second about Coop's warm house, how much warmer it might be under the quilt he'd given her last night, and how much warmer, even, that quilt might be over, say, *two* people lying next to one another in a bed.

"Let's go," he said, then straightened to his full height. "Ace is waiting for us."

Okay, then. Maybe they weren't quite on the same page.

They strode around the house to the stable, and Dani finally understood why after six months, the house part of the Cooper property was still under construction.

The stable looked brand-new, the siding painted a pristine white and the roof boasting a weather vane that made it abundantly clear it would be a windy ride. On the concrete at the entryway sat fresh hay, bundled and stacked in a short, neat pile.

"You did this?" she asked, knowing the place hadn't been touched in years before Peyton's arrival back in Meadow Valley.

He nodded. "The sooner I can get horses back on the property, the better. I've got running water and heat in the house. The rest will come in time."

She wrapped her arms around him and tilted her gaze up to his.

"It's beautiful," she said. And even though she knew nothing of horses or stables, she was sure he'd done an amazing job restoring it inside and out. "I bet your mom and dad would be so proud of you."

A muscle ticked in his jaw, but then he smiled.

"Thanks," he said, his voice tighter than she'd expected. "How about we go meet Ace?"

He grabbed a gray wool cap from the back pocket of his jeans and pulled it over his head. Then he strode to the stable door and held it open for her.

"We're really doing this, huh?" she asked with a nervous laugh, and this time his smile looked genuine. His shoulders seemed to relax.

"We are, Deputy. You remember my promise, don't you?"

He was going to keep her safe.

She nodded. "Okay, Mr. Mayor," she teased, hoping to cover the slight tremor in her voice. "Let's ride."

* * *

Dani looked down at the black-and-white spotted animal beneath her and then over her shoulder at Peyton.

"I'm still here, Deputy," he said with a chuckle. "You okay? I can sit in front if you're more comfortable with that. I just wanted you to have an unobstructed view when we get to where we're going. I'm usually a sucker for an over-cast day. Lets me get in my broodiest, grinchiest mood," he teased. She could hear the smile in his voice. "But I have to admit that today I'm thankful for the sunny skies."

"Why?" she asked.

"You'll find out. But before we get going, I need you to answer my very important question. Are you, Deputy Daniela Garcia, okay with your front-row view?"

They hadn't moved any farther than just outside the stable. Ace stood unquestioningly calm while Dani sat in his saddle and Peyton sat just behind, his arms around her waist holding the horse's reins.

"I think so?"

He laughed again. "Is that a question or an answer?"

Dani really wasn't sure. When she was on her bike, *she* was the one in control. When she was on a run, guess who was in control? Her again. And whether she was sitting behind the desk at the sheriff's office, responding to a call, or writing up an out-of-towner for a speeding ticket, Deputy Daniela Garcia held the reins. Now she was at the mercy of a four-legged creature and a man who made her pulse race every time he touched her.

"Um. An answer, I guess," she amended, looking straight ahead.

Peyton leaned forward, his chest against her back, and pressed his warm lips to her cold cheek.

"Here we go," he whispered, his breath sending a shiver through her whole body.

Whether he noticed or not, she had no clue, because seconds later, Peyton made a clicking noise with his mouth, and Ace began to trot.

They weren't going fast, but her stomach leaped into her throat anyway.

She held the reins with Peyton because she needed *something* to hold on to, even if *he* was the one guiding the horse.

At first she couldn't speak. But after a couple of minutes, she didn't want to.

She'd seen Meadow Valley's rolling hills from the side of the road on her bike, and they were beautiful. She'd always thought so. But now they were riding *through* the hills, with land on either side of them as far as she could see, the main streets of their small town disappearing behind them. How had she lived here all her life and never done this?

Peyton must have noticed her shoulders relax because from behind her, he yelled, "Ya!" And Ace's safe little trot turned into a gallop.

She sucked in a sharp breath as one of Peyton's arms snaked around her torso, as if he knew she'd need more reassurance that she was, in fact, safe.

"Still okay?" he called out as they whipped through the wind.

She nodded and let go of the reins with her left hand so she could wrap her arm over his, the one like a safety belt across her stomach.

She tilted her head back and saw a flock of geese flying in a V-formation overhead. When she straightened, she spotted a copse of trees in the distance, seemingly at the top of a hill.

Maybe the wind added an extra bite to the chilled air, but the sun shone like it was the middle of July, and the view was nothing like she'd ever seen.

They were climbing the final hill now, the one that was fenced in by the trees, and Dani wondered if this was it, if this—Meadow Valley uncultivated and untouched and her right in the heart of it—was what he'd wanted to show her.

But then they made it to the top of the hill.

"Whoa, Ace," Peyton said in a low voice, and their four-legged companion slowed to a stop so they were looking down on a small forest of evergreens. But the sun was hitting something on one of the trees that reflected back at her, almost blinding her.

"What the...?" she asked, shielding her eyes with her forearm.

"We need to get closer," Peyton said. Then he hopped off Ace's back like they were no higher off the ground than a kitchen chair.

He held his arms out for her, and she took them willingly, letting him lower her to the ground.

"Stay," he told Ace in the same deep voice he'd used to slow the horse down.

"He won't take off?" Dani asked, and Peyton shook his head.

"Sam and Ben Callahan have him trained real good. Took him out on my own earlier today to test the waters and make sure he'd respond to me as well as he did for them."

Not only had this man promised her safety, but he'd made sure the words he'd spoken were true.

She wanted to kiss him, but he'd already threaded his gloved fingers through hers and was tugging her toward the perimeter of wild Christmas trees.

Christmas trees!

She saw it now, what had blinded her when she was on Ace's back. She saw *them*. Sparkling, light-reflecting ornaments on several of the trees. There a mirrored glass snowflake sent the sun bouncing back to the hill. Here was an angel, twisting and turning in the breeze.

"It's beautiful," she said, her breath catching on the last syllable of the word. "But I don't understand."

She turned to face Peyton but found him staring straight ahead at the trees.

"When I was learning to ride as a kid, my mom and I ended up out here one day not too long after Thanksgiving. We could never fit too big of a tree in the house because of low ceilings, so when I saw these, I kind of lost my mind." He laughed.

"How old were you?" she asked.

"Seven," he said. "Maybe eight? I asked my mom if we could decorate one of *these* since they were so much bigger and better than anything we'd ever had. She got a permit from the Sheriff's Department that said we could decorate the trees anytime after Thanksgiving as long as we cleaned them up by the third of January. The permit said something about keeping the trees and animals safe, not compromising the integrity of the branches. Stuff like that. Some other folks out this way and those who could get here by horseback started joining in, and it's sort of been a thing ever since."

"*You* started this," she said, her throat tight. She wrapped her arms around his waist and stared up at him. "You started this beautiful tradition filled with Christmas spirit, and I called you a *grinch*. I am so sorry, Coop. For all that you lost."

She stood on her tiptoes and pressed her lips to his, thankful that he kissed her back, that he didn't retreat when things got hard like she had earlier in the week, the second she doubted his intentions with her were any less than true.

"I came here this morning with Ace to see if the tradition had continued after I left. After *they* left. I came to see if I could even stand to look at it without them."

His eyes shone, and all she wanted to do was take his pain and make it hers instead. But she couldn't. So she squeezed him tighter, closer.

"And it sucked," he admitted with a bitter laugh. "But somehow I knew it would be better—that I might see it differently—with you." He scratched the back of his neck. "I love this town, Dani. And I *have* missed it. I didn't leave because I hated small-town life. I left because I wanted to do something big. I wanted to make a difference, and I didn't know how to do that here without it getting swallowed up by the rest of the world. And while I still don't have all the answers, I know one thing for certain—that I would not have made it where we are standing right now without someone by my side. Without *you*."

Dani's cheeks burned, and her eyes stung from either the cold or the threat of tears. She tried to convince herself it was the former.

Her love of all things Christmas had been her refuge when her parents split and when she'd anonymously asked her crush to the winter dance. Well, it wasn't *completely* anonymous. As a dreamy-eyed freshman, she'd remembered selling her mom's famous peppermint meringue drops to a ridiculously gorgeous junior everyone called Coop. "These are *amazing*," he'd said. "Did you make them?"

She'd lied and told him yes, vowing to learn how to make them herself should the occasion arise for her to impress him again. And then, in an attempt to fill the void left by her parents' divorce, she'd gone out on a limb and sent a Christmas Graham filled with peppermint meringue drops to her longtime crush, only to watch him assume it was from someone else.

Dani's deep dive into all things Christmas had been a crutch back then. Today it felt as if it was morphing into something new. Different. Better.

Maybe we can make a new memory. For both of us.

Peyton's words echoed in her head, and she believed them.

"If I'd known, I would have brought an ornament," she finally said.

He smiled and stuck a hand into the pocket of his vest, retrieving a small ceramic Grinch figurine.

Dani threw her hand over her mouth and burst into laughter. "Where did you get *that*?" she asked. "The town's cleared out of all decorations."

He held the small creature between his thumb and forefinger and squinted into the sun as he stared at it.

"Found an old box of holiday stuff in the attic. Even though I deny it to this day, my parents swore up and down that Dr. Seuss's *How the Grinch Stole Christmas*—the old version from the sixties—was my favorite holiday movie when I was a kid."

"Mayor Grinch," she said, incredulous.

He shrugged. "Guess you knew the real me after all."

He kissed her, and it felt like something shifted between them. It felt like—she wasn't scared anymore. Not of getting back into Ace's saddle. Not of whether or not the Sheriff's Department would "win" the lights parade. Not of opening her heart to someone who might leave.

"Want to hang it?" he asked, dangling the figurine by a silver ribbon.

She nodded, and together they made their way to a tree that looked like it could handle hanging with the Grinch for the next week. They put him next to an ornament of a stack of presents, fitting for the fictional character who liked to steal others' gifts until he learned the true meaning of Christmas.

In the shade of the trees, the temperature dropped, and Dani shivered.

"I think we need to get you somewhere warm, Deputy," Peyton said, wrapping his arms around her.

Even through the layers of jackets and clothes, she still felt the heat of him against her and wanted more of it. So much more of it.

"What did you have in mind, Mr. Mayor?"

He pursed his lips like he was deep in thought, then smiled softly.

"The fireplace works back at the house. And I do believe I still owe you a cup of tea after making you spill yours last night."

"You had me at fireplace," she said. "But I won't kick a hot cup of tea out of bed." Her eyes widened and her cheeks burned. "Not that I'd have tea in bed *or* that I'd kick it out because it would spill. I just—I wasn't insinuating..." *That I want to go to bed with you.*

Except she sort of was. No, she absolutely was.

"Dani?" he said, laughing softly. Not *at* her. She could tell that much.

"Coop?"

He kissed her, his lips lighting her up from the inside. She knew without a doubt that if *she* were put on display for the parade, right here and now, she'd win. Hands down. The most spectacular demonstration of light.

Not that it was a competition.

Except it was.

Without another word, she led him back to Ace, who was waiting patiently, and let him help her into the saddle before he climbed up behind her—her big-city mayor, who, even after fifteen years, was still a small-town cowboy at heart.

Chapter Nine

Peyton filled the electric teakettle with water and plugged it in. Dani sat on the kitchen barstool while he got the fire going in the living room—the only part of the first floor he'd consider remotely finished even if the only furniture was his favorite recliner he'd brought back from Chicago and the floor rug he'd picked up at a discount home store in an outlet mall a couple of hours south.

He smiled to himself as the logs in the fireplace crackled and the golden flames licked their way up toward the chimney.

He'd come home to figure his life out. To restore the home his parents left to be closer to him. He'd come home to honor them. He'd come home to escape his own failure. He hadn't come here looking for a reason to stay.

But now there was a deputy sheriff in his kitchen, one he hadn't stopped thinking about since she wrenched his arm behind his back on a morning run went wrong. Dani Garcia found such joy in this time of year that it had started to rub off on him. If she hadn't seen the urn—if he hadn't told her about his parents, he never would have taken her to the evergreens. Hell, he wouldn't have gone himself. But somehow he knew if she was there, he could get through it.

Baby steps, right? He wasn't ready to let her all the way in. The restoration project had to be his alone. It was *his* home. *His* parents. *His* responsibility to put everything back the way it used to be as best he could. But he'd made it to the trees, and he hadn't sulked once.

Peyton inhaled a steadying breath and let it go. He'd lost his parents and his job. He'd lost his *way*. And then he found Dani.

Maybe, just maybe, this was the start of his life *actually* going right.

The kettle whistled. He rose from where he was squatting in front of the fireplace and followed the sound back to the kitchen, to the woman who was unwrapping and dropping a bag of English breakfast tea into each of the mugs he'd set out on the island.

"I'll get the milk and sugar," he said, kissing her on the cheek.

She wrinkled her nose. "Can't we drink it as it was intended? Like we should *all* be drinking our coffee?"

He laughed. "Suit yourself. You can have yours however you want. I'm going to have it the *right* way."

He moved past her to the refrigerator, and he heard her groan behind him.

"Fine. I'll do it *your* way, cowboy. But that doesn't mean I have to like it."

He grinned, even though his back was to her.

"Cowboy, huh?" he asked. It had been a long time since he'd thought of himself as anything other than a politician who was hopefully on the rise.

He grabbed the box of sugar packets and turned back to face her, a jug of milk in one hand and the sugar in the other.

"You don't have to like it, Deputy," he said with a wink. "But you will."

He set the items down on the island, then pressed his lips against her neck.

She shivered, which only made him smile more.

"Yeehaw," he whispered in her ear, and she shivered again. "Still cold?" he asked, straightening so his gaze met hers.

She shook her head. "At least not the kind of cold that requires tea to warm me up."

Her coat was off, as was the fleece pullover she'd had on underneath. She stood there in her button-down flannel, jeans, and a pair of gray-and-white polka-dotted socks, and Peyton swore he'd never seen anyone sexier.

"Maybe you need a blanket?" he teased, and she shook her head again.

"No. That's not it. I think I need to be closer to the fire," she said, then spun on her heel, ignoring the two mugs of tea as she moved into the living room.

Peyton stood there, speechless, wondering if he'd misread the entire situation until he heard her yell, "You coming, cowboy? The fire can't do the job all by itself."

He found her kneeling on the rug in front of the fire-place, rubbing her hands together in the heat radiating from the flames.

When she turned to him her golden eyes were ablaze, and he knew three things. One: The tea would go cold. Two: He couldn't care less if it did. And three: Deputy Daniela Garcia could ruin him if she wanted to, but he couldn't imagine a better way to go.

He knelt beside her and leaned back so he was balancing on his heels.

"Well, hello there, Mr. Mayor," she said with a grin. Then she worried her bottom lip between her teeth. Had he mentioned how much he loved it when she did that?

"I'm not sure if there's anything sexier than when you do that," he said. "Except for maybe the whole motorcycle thing. And the running thing. And being a deputy sheriff thing." He laughed. "I guess it's really just a *you* thing, Deputy."

She pressed her lips together, as if to keep herself from doing the thing again, but she was smiling too.

"Coop?" she said, resting her hands on his knees.

That—her calling him *Coop*—he loved even more.

"Dani," he answered, covering her hands with his.

She raised one brow. "I've never been good at this— relationships. Letting people get close. I'm not sure if you can tell, but I have some trust issues."

His brows drew together. "I'm not your dad, Dani."

"I know. I'm just—scared. If I admit how much I like you or how long..."

She stopped herself short, but Peyton wasn't letting her off the hook.

"How long *what*?" he asked.

She squeezed her eyes shut and groaned. "I wasn't just some moony-eyed freshman who got one look at you and your megawatt politician grin and swooned. Teenaged Dani thought she'd fallen for you—for two whole years."

Her cheeks were bright pink, and Peyton found it hard to take a full breath.

But then his eyes narrowed. "Are you teasing me, Deputy? Two years?" How could he have missed that?

She shook her head. "I admit I give you grief about a lot of things, but I don't mess around when it comes to matters of the heart, especially my own. Ask Deputy Crawford. He still teases *me* about it. And if he finds out about this?" She groaned again. "I'm never going to hear the end of it."

Peyton couldn't help but wonder, What if something had happened between them in high school? They might have been one of those couples everyone loved to hate—high school sweethearts who made it all the way. Or not. Peyton always had his sights set on something bigger than Meadow Valley. At least that was what he'd thought back then. He would have left, and she would have stayed. Meadow Valley was in Dani's blood.

"Dani, if I'd have known *then,* if I wouldn't have been such a clueless, self-absorbed kid—"

"Nope," she said, interrupting him. "We're not going there. Nopety, nope, nope. I've embarrassed myself enough. So can we *please* forget I said anything and focus on now? On us, right here, in front of this *very* romantic fire?"

She batted her lashes at him, and he laughed.

"Okay, Deputy. In the spirit of honesty, then," he said, "I should probably come clean. I don't think I have a crush on you anymore."

Her eyes narrowed and she pulled her hands from beneath his, crossing her arms over her chest.

She wasn't going to put up with his teasing, and he added that to the growing list of what he loved about her.

"I'm giving you five more seconds to follow that up with something spectacular, Mayor *Grinch*, or else I'm walking out that door." She looked at him expectantly.

He wrapped a hand around her wrist and tugged her gently, just enough to knock her off balance and send her falling forward and straight into his chest—exactly where Peyton wanted her to be.

He caught her and wrapped her in his arms as she tried not to smile.

"I don't have a crush on you, Daniela Garcia, because I think after this week—well, fifteen years and this week—I might have already gone and fallen for you."

Her eyes widened, and she backhanded him on his upper arm.

"Might have?" she said. "*Might* have? I pour my heart out to you, and you *might* have...? Wait..." Her brows furrowed, and he watched her mouthing words to herself like she was replaying the conversation until her whole expression lit up and her cheeks bloomed an unmistakable pink.

"You already fell for me?" she asked, the mostly feigned indignation leaving her voice.

He nodded.

"So this is *real*," she added, motioning between them.

Another nod. "I'm afraid so."

She covered her mouth with her hand, but she couldn't hide her beautiful, beaming grin.

"What are you so happy about?" he asked, knowing that whatever the answer was, it would be what he wanted to hear. Because he'd all but said those three little words, which should have spooked her, but she hadn't run out the door. Not this time.

She pressed both palms to his chest, and electricity sparked from her skin straight through his shirt.

"Because," she said. "I'm about to see my teenage crush—*naked*."

He threw back his head and laughed.

"Just to clarify," he said, hooking a finger through the belt loop of her jeans, "you'll be naked, too, when this viewing takes place?"

She nodded, and he scooped her into his arms, both of

them laughing and maybe a little nervous. But they were smiling. And she wanted him as much as he wanted her. The past and the pain stepped back, not threatening to invade the moment as she pulled his shirt over his head and peppered his chest with pulse-quickening kisses. He unbuttoned her shirt and brushed his lips over her breasts, her belly button, and across the line of each of her hips.

"It's a *you* thing, Dani Garcia," he said, echoing his words from before. And then he kissed her, the fire's glow softly illuminating bare skin.

Later—two cold cups of tea forgotten on the kitchen island, their clothes forgotten on the living room rug—they made their way up the stairs and to his room. It wasn't a question of whether or not she was staying. Dani Garcia would be in his bed, in his arms, in his life, turning everything upside down in the most *right* kind of way.

He waited for her to nod off, to let the rhythm of her breathing lull him into the deepest, most restful sleep he'd had in months.

When he woke, the morning sun shone through the slats of the wooden blinds scattering light across the sheets—and the empty space with the imprint left by Dani's body confirmed that last night really did happen. But *Dani* was gone.

* * *

Breakfast, Dani thought upon first waking in Peyton's arms. Okay, maybe breakfast wasn't exactly her first thought. It was more like *Ohmigod ohmigod. I slept with Peyton Cooper and I am a thirty-year-old giddy schoolgirl who can't stop smiling*.

And this giddy schoolgirl was still naked.

And hangry, because not only had they forgone tea for

other activities to while away the evening hours, but they'd also forgone a meal or maybe two. Dani couldn't remember. Because of the giddiness. And the lack of caloric intake to balance caloric output and *Ohmigod I slept with Peyton Cooper.*

Who was falling for her. Who thought he already had.

She could finally let go of what he didn't even know had happened in high school—her silly invitation to the winter formal. It wasn't his fault. She'd always known that. But the timing of it all with her dad leaving...She shook her head, laughing softly to herself.

He wasn't her dad, and it was time she stopped waiting for him to prove her wrong, for the other shoe to drop.

She stared at his sleeping form, his breathing slow and heavy, the big, bad, beautiful Grinch still deep in sleep.

Okay, back to thinking of *breakfast.* She would make them breakfast. Hell, she'd even make them the English breakfast tea with milk and sugar.

Her stomach growled, and she covered it with her hands, like she could shush it and keep it from waking the man still wrapped around her.

Dani slid out from under his arm and tiptoed out the door. Every step on the wooden staircase squeaked and creaked as she made her way down. She paused at the bottom and waited, sure she'd woken not only Peyton but everyone in a five-mile radius, but no sound came from the bedroom.

Wow. That man could sleep.

Good. It gave her more time. She wondered when the last time was that someone cooked for him. Well, today she would be that someone. Hopefully she'd be able to surprise him with something good made from whatever she could scrounge up in a single man's kitchen.

She padded through the living room and picked up her

flannel and undergarments along the way, her socks, too, haphazardly dressing herself—albeit only partially—on the way into the kitchen.

She laughed when she saw the two mugs still sitting on the island.

Yesterday had not exactly gone according to Dani's half-day Friday plan. It had gone so much better than she could have imagined.

And now she was here, emptying and washing out the mugs to start fresh. And it was almost Christmas, and everything felt like it was falling into place.

She found eggs and bacon in the fridge and a loaf of rustic bread on the counter. Her stomach growled again, either in protest that she wasn't moving fast enough or in appreciation for the feast it was about to receive. Whatever the reason, Dani got to work opening and closing cabinets and drawers until she found everything she needed, which wasn't that difficult. Peyton had the bare minimum as far as kitchen supplies, basically just enough for one person to get by from day to day. That would do for now.

Butter melted in a skillet on the stove while the bacon baked in the oven below. The bread was sliced and in the toaster, the teakettle plugged in, and a bowl of beaten eggs waited to be scrambled.

She heard her phone ring from the living room floor and ran to grab it before it woke her sleeping cowboy. She picked up the phone but the screen was black. The ringing sounded again, and she realized she must have been holding Peyton's phone and not hers. She dropped it on the rug and finally answered the correct phone, silencing the ring.

"*Mami*," she whispered, running back to the kitchen before the kettle whistled or the butter burned. "This isn't the best time."

She poured the eggs into the skillet and moved them around with a spatula, making sure they cooked evenly and just enough so they were light and fluffy, not dry and stuck to the sides of the pan.

"Are you cooking?" her mother asked. "I can hear kitchen sounds. I thought you only drank those chalky protein shakes after a morning run."

Dani rolled her eyes. The woman was the best cook Dani knew. Of course Mami heard kitchen sounds through a phone.

She set the phone on the counter, putting her mom on speaker.

"I didn't run this morning," Dani admitted, now plating the eggs.

She opened the oven to take a look at the bacon, decided it needed to get just a little crisper, and closed it with her hip.

"Didn't run?" her mom asked. "Are you sick? Do you need my caldo de pollo? I have some in the freezer I can defrost. Or I can make a fresh batch. I'll come over—"

"I'm fine, Mami. I just decided to sleep in for once."

Silence rang out for a beat before her mother spoke again.

"Did you spend the night with the mayor?" she asked point-blank.

"Mami," she said, louder than she would have liked.

Dani'd had the good sense to text Casey the night before and let her know she wouldn't be coming home until sometime today. But Casey didn't gossip, least of all to Dani's mom.

"What?" her mother asked. "Uncle Jorge said he saw you on the motorcycle heading toward the Cooper house. Yesterday. You skipped your run. You're cooking. I'm just putting all the puzzle pieces together."

Uncle Jorge. Of course.

"Does Mayor Cooper like caldo de pollo with a little kick? So good for the cold weather. I'm taking it out of the freezer right now. You could bring him for dinner tonight. Jorge is fixing my doorbell. Well, he's installing one of those fancy ones that has a camera on it. I was going to make him dinner anyway, so two more would be no trouble."

"I like chicken soup," a man said.

The groggy, deep voice came from behind her, and Dani spun to see Peyton standing in the entryway to the kitchen wearing nothing but the flannel pants he had on the night she'd responded to his accidental emergency call. His lean, muscular torso was bare, his chestnut hair rumpled and sleep-mussed.

"That's it, mija," Dani's mother said, still on speaker. "He knows Spanish. He's a keeper. I'll see you two at six."

Her mother ended the call.

The teakettle whistled.

Dani let out a nervous laugh and held up the two plates of eggs.

"Surprise!" she called out over the still-screaming kettle.

Peyton unplugged the kettle and turned to face her, a beautiful grin plastered across his face.

He took the plates from her hands and set them down on the island, then skimmed his fingers through her hair, pulling her to him with a bone-melting kiss.

Dani Garcia was bringing the mayor, Peyton Cooper—the man for whom she'd unwittingly pined for fifteen years—home. Tonight. For a family dinner.

What could possibly go wrong?

Chapter Ten

Since nothing was open at half past five on a Saturday afternoon other than the Meadow Valley Inn and the Midtown Tavern, Peyton crossed his fingers in hopes that the tavern could help him out.

Before he stepped inside, though, he paused, taking in the sight before him. Dani was right. Even though no lights were yet lit, there was an inflatable Santa on top of the Meadow Valley fire station roof, sitting on what he could tell would be a lighted engine once the parade was underway. Across the street, Trudy Davis stood on the window seat inside Storyland, her bookshop. Peyton could see what looked like a staple gun in one hand as she grabbed a rope of lights from an employee with the other.

All around him, shop owners worked tirelessly in the dwindling daylight. He expected to be hit with a wave of grief, for his fight-or-flight instinct to kick in, or at the very least to fall into a heavy-as-hell sulk. Instead, he felt a weight lift from his shoulders. And when he walked toward Midtown Tavern's front door, his steps felt a little lighter.

He shook his head and laughed. It looked like Dani Garcia had knocked the grinchiness right out of him.

The place wasn't too crowded, which made it hard not to notice heads turning when he walked in. He greeted the townsfolk he knew and smiled at those who were likely tourists as he made his way to a stool at the bar.

Casey spotted him as quickly as the rest of the patrons. She tucked her long blue bangs behind one ear and gave Peyton a knowing grin as she approached him.

"Fancy seeing you here, Mr. Mayor, when I'm pretty sure you have a prior engagement this evening," she said.

He sighed. "And here I thought you weren't much for gossip."

She shrugged. "It's not gossip if I'm talking directly to the source. Plus, I live with Dani. We may operate on conflicting schedules, but that doesn't mean I'm not in the know when she's taking a gentleman caller such as yourself home for dinner." Casey leaned forward over the bar and narrowed her eyes at him. "You *are* being a gentleman, aren't you, Mayor Cooper? Doing right by my girl and all that?"

She straightened and arched her brows.

He raised his right back. "Have you ever known me to be anything less?" he asked.

"Ah, but do I *really* know you, Cooper? Fifteen years is a long time. It can change a man," she said, her smile faltering.

"Hey," he said, all playfulness gone from his voice. "I was really disappointed to hear that you and Boone didn't go the distance. Always thought you two were the couple most likely to—"

"Yeah, well..." She cut him off. "He's marrying a real

estate broker from Chico. Met her when he had to drive out there for some auto part he couldn't find locally, and the rest is history. She's moving here and everything, says we're an untapped market for great real estate development." She said the last part in an overly bubbly voice that was very *un*-Casey. "At least, that's what I hear," she added. "Now, back to why you're *here* instead of knocking on Miranda Diaz's door with a bottle of wine and your winningest politician grin."

He realized she was putting the Casey-Boone discussion to rest and followed her lead.

"I'm all good with the grin. But the wine..." He winced.

Casey crossed her arms. "And I look like a liquor store to you?" She glanced around the bar, at the beer taps, the bottles of liquor on the shelf behind her, the small wine refrigerator below. "Okay, fine, I can see how that question might be a little misleading."

"Look," he said. "Everything is closed, and this whole me coming to dinner thing just sort of happened today. I'll pay you double whatever you'd charge if someone were to order it to drink here."

Casey smiled. "And here I was going to give it to you on the house. You really shouldn't show your hand so early, Mr. Mayor. So, what will you folks be eating? Wait. Forget I asked. Miranda always has her spicy chicken soup on hand. It's a staple, and it's one of the best things you'll ever taste." She walked to the bar and opened the wine refrigerator, pulling out a bottle of white. "Sauvignon blanc," she said. "Pairs great with the soup and is always a good one to kick off the evening."

She handed the bottle to him, and he let out a breath, his shoulders relaxing.

"Thank you. You're a lifesaver. What do I owe you?" he asked.

She shook her head. "Go on. Take it. If you want to re-pay me, you can get me some extra help around here. Can't seem to find someone who wants to tend bar full-time other than myself, and *I* don't even want to tend bar full-time."

He smiled. "I'll keep an eye out," he said, then held up the gifted bottle. "Thanks again for this. Also, did I hear you call Dani's mom by the name Diaz? Not Garcia?"

Casey nodded. "After Dani and Julia's dad split, Miranda went back to her maiden name. There was some bad blood there for a while, but now both parents spend Christmas at Julia's in Miami like it's what they've always done. Dani, on the other hand..." She shook her head. "She took it the hardest, which is why this time of year really hits her, you know? Anyway, like I said, you better do right by her. She deserves nothing less."

"You're right," he said, then walked out of the tavern grateful for the wine yet feeling like an ass for how he'd behaved when the whole light festival business had begun. The holidays were just as difficult for Dani as they were for him. She simply went about dealing with it in a different way. A better way. She took all of her energy and put it toward making each Christmas more special than the one before, while he'd wanted to pretend it didn't exist.

He needed time to think, to process how much Dani had changed his life in the short time since he'd let her see past the polished veneer that was Mayor Peyton Cooper.

He'd driven to town but decided to walk the rest of the way to Meadow Valley's residential area. It was cool outside but not cold, and for the first time since he could remember, he didn't want to speed by the decorated windows, the strung lights just waiting to be lit in three more days.

He'd been aimless since he'd gotten back to town, but

tonight he felt like he might have direction, something to look forward to. Some*one* who might even give him hope.

By the time he made it to the small blue cottage at 165 Locust Way, he was smiling. It didn't even faze him that the roof was trimmed in a rainbow of holiday lights. Seemed like the closer he got to wherever Dani Garcia was, the easier everything simply became.

He stepped onto the porch, his free hand raised and ready to knock on the white door that was framed on either side by white-trimmed windows, when the door flew open before he had a chance to make contact.

An older woman, a few inches shorter than Dani and with dark brown hair cropped short, opened her arms in welcome.

"Mayor Cooper!" she said, wrapping him in a warm hug. "It's so nice to see you."

He hugged her back, of course, even though it had been some time since he'd greeted a virtual stranger with such a gesture. Come to think of it, Peyton had never actually hugged someone on first meeting. He was an expert at shaking hands, but this was—unexpected. Especially when the woman knew her daughter had been cooking breakfast at his house earlier that morning.

"Mrs. Diaz," he said when she straightened. "It's so nice to officially meet you."

She clapped her hands together. "You did your homework, young man. Didn't you? I'm impressed. But please, call me Miranda."

He held out the bottle of wine. "Well then, Miranda, this is for you."

She gave him a wry grin. "You know, you're not even through the door yet, and I'm just about ready to offer you my daughter's hand."

He suddenly coughed, choking on nothing in particular, and Dani's mother laughed.

"I'm *joking*," she said. "But it was worth it just for that terrified look on your face. Which is now forever caught on camera—or as long as it stays in the clouds. How is the video in the clouds? I still don't get technology sometimes."

"The *cloud*," a man called from inside. Peyton guessed it was Dani's uncle Jorge. Miranda waved him off as if he could see her. Then she motioned for Peyton to follow her inside. "Jorge just installed one of those video doorbells. That's how we knew you were here. I get a notification on my phone, and then I can look and see who's setting off the motion detector."

He stepped into the small foyer after her and brushed his shoes off on a rug that read "Mi Familia."

My family.

His chest grew tight, but as soon as they stepped past the entryway and into the open living room/dining room/kitchen, he saw Dani stirring a pot at the stove, smiling at him over her shoulder. Next to her, sprinkling a green herb into the pot, was the tall, thin, gray-haired and gray-bearded man who'd kept Peyton from electrocuting himself last week. Uncle Jorge.

"We saw you on the doorbell cam," she said.

Peyton nodded. "So I hear."

Miranda strolled into the kitchen brandishing the bottle of wine.

"And he brought us a sauvignon blanc, *mija*. Your favorite," she said.

Peyton shook his head and chuckled. Casey was either rooting for him or figured he'd probably take a nosedive at some point during the evening, so why not at least start off on the right foot?

"How'd you know?" she asked, taking the bottle from her mom and pulling a corkscrew from a drawer.

He shrugged. "Lucky guess?" Then he reached over the island and shook the older man's hand. "Jorge. Good to see you again."

"Mayor Cooper," Jorge said with a smile. "You haven't found any more exposed wires I should know about, have you?"

He laughed and shook his head. "No, sir. But I promise not to touch them if I do. And I'd love it if you all called me Peyton," he said. "Unless we're in my office, I'm just— me, I guess."

"Okay, Peyton," Jorge said, then he followed Miranda to the refrigerator where they worked in tandem pulling out plated vegetables and cheeses and lining them up on the counter.

"What about Coop?" Dani asked with a coy smile, her cheeks turning pink. She looked down after that, focusing on filling the four stemless wine glasses in front of her until the bottle was empty.

He rounded the island and came up behind her, wrapping his arms around her waist. He kissed her softly on the cheek.

"I think we should save that one just for you," he said so only she could hear.

She sucked in a breath and he straightened, clearing his throat.

"Peyton!" Miranda said. "I got so caught up in the doorbell excitement that I didn't even take your coat."

Peyton realized he still had his down vest on over his navy wool sweater and plaid button-down. He handed Miranda a glass of wine and smiled.

"No worries. I can hang it myself. Just point me in the right direction."

The woman beamed. "The closet is right next to the front door."

He headed back to the front of the house and quickly deposited his vest. He paused, though, when he noticed the wall of photos opposite the closet. Dani and her sister, Julia, through the years, from childhood to adulthood, including what he guessed was Dani's first day as a deputy sheriff, standing so proud in her uniform and seemingly trying not to smile too big. There were family photos, too, some of just Miranda and the girls. Some with Jorge. There was even one of Dani and her parents at the hospital when Julia was born. She couldn't have been more than two.

Peyton thought about the blank walls at his family's home, wondered if when the place was finished he'd be able to go through the boxes of what he'd packed away from his parents' condo in Chicago and fill the walls with memories that now might be too painful to bear.

"Hey." Dani popped her head around the corner, then made her way to where he stood with two glasses of wine.

"Is one of those for me?" he asked, deflecting with humor like he'd grown accustomed to doing.

"Nah," she said. "I'm really thirsty." Then she laughed and handed a glass to him. "Everything okay?" she asked, nodding toward the picture-covered wall. "Mami always did go overboard with the photos."

"I'm good," he said, then took a sip of wine. "But there's something I forgot to tell you when I first got here. It's pretty important. Could change everything between us."

She narrowed her eyes at him. "And what's that?"

He dipped his head and kissed her, and he felt her lips part into a smile against his.

"*That*," he said, their lips still touching.

She laughed, and he kissed her once more before straightening and taking another sip of his wine.

"You're right," she said. "You should have been up-front about that from the beginning."

He clinked his glass against hers. "I'm glad we cleared that up."

She smiled. "Come on. My mom and Uncle Jorge made entirely too much food, so prepare to leave here tonight with enough leftovers to last you through Christmas."

"Is that a promise?" he asked. "You've seen my fridge. I need all the help I can get."

They laughed together on their way back to the kitchen, and any nerves he felt about the evening fell away.

"Okay," Miranda said, walking toward them with a small basket in her hands. "Food is ready, which means phones go in the basket."

Dani slid her phone from her back pocket and deposited it in the basket.

"House rules," she said to Peyton. "Only face-to-face conversation at the table." Then she gave her mother a pointed look. "That means you too. No peeking at the doorbell cam every time Trudy Davis walks by with one of her dogs or an Amazon delivery person stops by."

She stood on her toes and whispered in Peyton's ear. "My mom has an online shopping problem. I try to explain the importance of buying local, but the woman just loves her Prime." Dani was loud enough for Miranda to hear. Likely on purpose.

Peyton stifled a laugh while the older woman gave her daughter a light smack against the shoulder. "Hey. At least I'm not bidding half a week's worth of pay on some life-sized Christmas ornament that will never fit on the back of that motorcycle."

"She can use my truck," Jorge called from the kitchen.

"Life-sized ornament?" Peyton asked.

"Shhh, Mami. It's supposed to be a secret. You think I want the whole town knowing?" She nodded toward Jorge. "And that goes for you, too, Mr. Town Tattler. This is between me, the artist, and the Sheriff's Department. Everyone else will find out on Christmas Eve."

Peyton took his phone from his pocket as well and dropped it into the waiting basket.

"Hey," he said. "Same model."

"I know," Dani started. "Got them mixed up this morning when they were still on the fl—" She stopped short before finishing the sentence, and Peyton bit back another laugh.

When our phones were on the floor where we took off all our clothes in front of the fireplace last night?

Yeah, that probably wasn't how they should start the predinner conversation.

Miranda narrowed her dark brown eyes at them before turning to Jorge and asking for his phone.

"Smooth," Peyton whispered.

Dani snorted. "It's not like she doesn't know. I just don't need it to be family dinner fodder."

Peyton kissed her on the nose and set his glass on the table so he could help carry crocks of soup and trays of food to the table.

Dani was right. Her mom had prepared a veritable feast. But his full belly was nothing compared to the fullness of his heart—or at least the feeling that the pieces of it that had been torn or cracked were finally starting to mend.

After dinner, Miranda put the coffee on while Jorge got a fire going in the living room.

"You didn't bring in the new logs," he called to whoever would listen.

"I got 'em," Peyton said on his way into the living room. "Just tell me where they are."

"Piled on the right side of the house—right side if you're facing the front door, I mean. Left when you're walking out the door."

He nodded at Jorge. "I'm on it. Back in a minute."

Peyton didn't bother grabbing his vest from the closet but instead bounded out the door, making sure not to pull it all the way shut, then off the porch and to the left. But there was no pile of wood. He laughed and followed the perimeter of the house, through the small backyard, and around to the other side of the house—where he found the stack of firewood. He grabbed enough for at least the next three nights so Miranda wouldn't have to carry any more in before Christmas. When he got back to the front door, he nudged it open and then closed again with his hip and strode straight into the living room to set it all down.

"That should hold you until the holiday," he said, brushing off his hands and sweater. It was only when he was rid of the firewood that he noticed Jorge wasn't waiting for him by the fireplace.

Peyton spun toward the kitchen where Miranda and Jorge stood behind the island, their expressions unreadable. That was—odd. But Dani walking toward him with her phone in her hand and a stricken expression on her face? That was—unsettling. And maybe a little scary. Because he'd seen Deputy Dani Garcia fired up with anger before, but that wasn't what this was. She'd been hurt, and as soon as he found out who'd done it, he was going to make sure whoever it was *never* hurt her again.

"Dani, what—"

"Here," she said, holding out the phone in her hand. "I accidentally answered it. Guess we also have the same ringtone. The *Stranger Things* theme music." She let out a bitter laugh. "I didn't even know you liked the show. And I also didn't know you were interviewing for a position in the mayor's office in Chicago. The woman who called wants to know if eight in the morning California time works for you on the twenty-sixth. She said if the answer is yes to just text the word *yes* to the number she called from. If the answer is no, then she said there'd be no interview."

Her voice was cool and steady, but her clenched jaw and glassy eyes said everything she couldn't. That *he* was the one who hurt her.

"Dani," he started, not reaching for the phone but for her hand. Her cheek. Some part of her that he could touch to let her know it wasn't what she thought, even though it was pretty much exactly what she thought.

She brandished the phone at him.

"Take it," she said. So he did, slipping it into his pocket. "I asked you if our relationship was a temporary thing for you, and you said *no*," she added.

"It's *not*," he said. "I hadn't even gotten the interview yet when I told you that, and I meant it. But when you get a call from one of the biggest offices in local government because even after you messed up, they still think you're the man for the job, you schedule the interview. Just to see."

She swiped at a tear under her eye, but her expression wasn't one of pain or sadness anymore. It was fury.

"Is that why you showed up at the sheriff's office yesterday talking about all you were going to do to fix up our department? Was that going to be your parting gift?" She blew out a breath but didn't give him any room to protest or explain. "I asked you about our relationship *two* nights ago. When did you get the call?"

Shit. Shit, shit, shit, shit, shit.

"Dani," he said carefully. "You have to understand that I didn't come here looking for a reason to stay. But when you walked into my office earlier in the week and then showed up on my property Thursday night, I thought that maybe the universe or whoever's in charge was starting to see things differently for me. Because it sent me you."

"*When*, Peyton?" she asked again, arms crossed over her chest. "When did you agree to the interview?"

He blew out a breath. "Right after you left Thursday night."

She pressed her lips together and nodded. Then she spun on her heel and marched toward the front door, stopping to yank his down vest out of the closet.

"You need to go," she said, holding out the vest.

He turned toward Miranda and Jorge, his eyes pleading with theirs. Jorge shrugged, and Miranda just shook her head.

"So that's it?" he said, striding toward her. "I don't get to explain how hard it was to come back here without them? Or how *you* are the only one who made it bearable? I don't get a second to be confused about what I want or whether or not this thing between us is forever when it started less than a week ago? I lost my job when I missed a meeting with a fund-raiser because I ran late making preparations for my own parents' cremation—a meeting that cost the board tens of thousands of dollars. I thought I tanked my career, Dani. So when I got the call...I felt like I'd have to be an idiot to say no."

She was still holding the vest, a tear leaking out the corner of each eye.

She closed the distance between them, pressing the garment to his chest.

"I'm sorry, Peyton. I'm *so* sorry for what happened to

your parents and how hard the last year has been for you.
But you're obviously not ready to make promises to me
or to this town, and I don't fault you for that. I just—I
can't get left again. It'll hurt too much if we let ourselves
get any more attached, so let's just forget this week ever
happened, okay?"

She let go of the vest so that he had to grab it before it
dropped to the floor, so that he wouldn't be able to reach
for her before she reached for the door and held it open
for him.

"Just like that?" he asked. "After fifteen years?"

She sniffled and squared her shoulders. "For fifteen years
a part of me pined and wondered, and now I have my
answer. At least we both have closure now, right?"

He leaned down and kissed her warm, tear-streaked cheek.

"I've meant every word I've said to you the past few
days," he whispered. "Don't put more weight on what I
didn't say."

He stepped over the threshold and out the door, waiting
for a beat when it didn't slam shut behind him. But then he
heard it, the click of the dead bolt into the doorframe.

He turned to face the door.

Closure.

He pulled out his phone, copied the number from his
recently received call, and pasted it into the contact box in
his texting app, responding as requested, with one. Single.
Word.

Chapter Eleven

Peyton called her on Sunday morning, but Dani sent it right to voice mail. He didn't leave a message. She watched out the window of the Sheriff's Department for him to come bounding down the town hall steps—so she could avoid him, of course—but he never came.

He waited until that night, showing up at her apartment on Casey's one night off. When she saw him through the peephole, she had her roommate answer the door and tell him that Dani was spending the night at her mom's house.

Dani wasn't spending the night at her mom's house.

Now she was glued to her laptop at 9:57 a.m. on Monday morning, December 23, ready to win the auction for the life-sized ornament so she could dive back into what should have been her sole purpose all along—*winning* the lights parade for the Sheriff's Department.

Not that it was a competition. Except it sort of was.

"He looked like shit, you know," Casey said, pouring them both another cup of coffee. "Your Mr. Mayor."

Dani took a sip of her coffee, which was suddenly harder to swallow than the last mug had been.

"Just say it," Dani said. "You think I'm being too hard on him."

Casey lifted her own mug, held it in front of her lips, but paused. "I think you're being too hard on him."

Dani groaned. "He's interviewing for a job in Chicago. Chi-*ca*-go."

"Mmm-hmm," Casey said. "Is he though? Maybe he thought about it. Considered it. But are you sure he's going through with it?"

Dani sighed. "I'm sure he agreed to that interview *after* he told me I wasn't a temporary thing. And that just…"

"It sucks," Casey said. "I know it sucks. But maybe if you hear him out—"

Dani held up a hand. "Hang on. There's less than a minute left." She upped her bid by fifty bucks, so that she was now in the hole for $575, but in less than thirty seconds, the ornament would be hers.

She set a timer on her phone and watched it count down.

Ten.

Nine.

Eight.

Seven.

Six.

Five.

Four.

Three.

Another bid popped up for $576.

Two.

One.

Auction now closed to bids.

"What?" she cried out, her voice rising at least an octave. Maybe two. "A dollar? With *two* seconds to go? Who does that? Who *did* that, because...*What?*"

Casey leaned over the table to peek at Dani's laptop.

"Yep. You got your ass handed to ya. But look on the bright side. You just saved almost $600." She sat back down on her chair, eyes wide. "Wait, you were going to spend six hundred bucks on an ornament?"

Dani clenched her jaw and narrowed her eyes at her roommate.

Casey laughed and held up her hands.

"Okay. Okay. I won't poke the bear. Even if it's a little fun. But now that the bidding war is over, maybe we can get back to...you know...the mayor stuff?"

Dani stared at the screen, at the one shred of something she'd had to look forward to for the holidays, and threw her hands in the air.

"I give up," she said.

"On Peyton?" Casey asked.

"On all of it. On being naive enough to think it was safe to fall for him. On believing *this* would be the year the Sheriff's Department won the lights parade."

"Not a contest," Casey interrupted, but Dani waved it off.

"I give up on thinking this Christmas would knock all the others out of the park," Dani added. "I've been trying for fifteen years to make every Christmas for my family better than the last so we're not reminded of how much it sucked when my dad left. But you know what? I'm done. I'm officially boycotting any and all Christmas activities from here on out." She slammed her laptop shut, grabbed her coffee, and stood. "I'm going to take a nap," she said. "Wake me on the twenty-sixth."

Casey grabbed Dani's free hand. "Are you going to be okay?" she asked. "I have to head down to the bar soon, and I don't know if I can leave you in this grinchy state. Why don't you come to work with me tonight?"

Dani shook her head. "Thanks, but I'll survive." Then she let out a bitter laugh. "I guess *I* am the Grinch now, huh?"

Casey released her hand, and Dani trudged the rest of the way to her room where she collapsed on the bed, not bothering to take off her robe or her moccasin slippers, and willed herself to sleep.

She woke to shouting. Or was it singing? Whatever the sound was, it came from below.

For several moments she convinced herself it was pre-Christmas revelers at Midtown, but the voices sounded closer, like they were coming from the street. She remembered cracking her window the night before, wanting her room extra cold so she could burrow under the covers, head and all, and not come up.

Easy fix. She'd just shut the window and go back to sleep.

She climbed out of bed, blinking as her eyes adjusted to the waning light. Had she really slept until dusk?

She shuffled to her window, ready to slam it shut, but paused when she saw several clusters of people—some pouring out of the tavern—murmuring as they all headed in the direction of the town square.

She pulled her phone from her robe pocket and texted Casey.

What's going on outside?

Casey's reply was almost immediate.

Omg. I was just about to text you. You need to head to the square. Something about Mayor Cooper on the roof of the sheriff's department.

"The roof?" she said out loud.

What the hell is he doing? Dani texted back.

I don't know. But maybe you should go and make sure he doesn't do anything stupid? Don't you have a Chicken Little situation over there?

Oh god. The ceiling crumbling. Water damage from a roof that should have been replaced years ago. How had she even considered putting that ornament on the roof herself?

He was going to kill himself.

On my way, she texted back to Casey.

Dani didn't bother changing. Or checking how wild of a mess her hair was. There wasn't time for that. She simply tied her robe tight, grabbed her keys, and was out the door.

She started out speed-walking, pushing her way through small crowds who thought it appropriate to stroll toward the square when she needed to get there five minutes ago.

Her walk turned to a jog, which then turned to an all-out sprint.

Note to self: Sprinting in slippers will cause shin splints.

She was winded by the time she made it to the square and had to bend over to catch her breath. When she straightened, she saw him on the roof of the Meadow Valley Sheriff's Department, just like everyone was saying. But it wasn't just Mayor Peyton Cooper up there. With him was a life-sized ornament, one she was willing to bet cost $576.

"Peyton! What are you *doing*?" she called to him, exasperated.

He walked toward the roof's edge, and Dani's heart leaped into her throat.

He held his arms out wide, and she was half prepared for him to yell that he was a golden god before leaping off the roof.

"I'm doing what I should have done three months ago.

I'm committing to this town, which means all of its quirks and traditions. No matter what other stuff I need to work through," he said instead.

Okay. Good. No leaping. That was a start.

"That's great, Peyton. But can you come down so we can talk about this?" she asked, trying to control the tremor in her voice.

"In a minute," he called back. "I just need to hammer in the last nail so this thing doesn't blow away, and then run the cord off the back." He grinned at her. "Nice outfit, by the way, Deputy."

She groaned. How was he teasing her at a time like this? He bought that stupid ornament for her. If anything happened to him, it would be Dani's fault because she was too damned stubborn to give him the benefit of the doubt.

"Peyton, please!" she called after him. "The roof is a mess. You shouldn't be up there."

"Don't worry," he said. "I can see the weak patches. I know what I'm doing."

Then he took a step back. One second he and the ornament were there, and the next they were gone. A loud crash sounded inside the building.

A collective gasp rose up from the crowd as Dani raced toward the department's entrance.

Dani heard a siren in the distance, figured someone had called the fire station, and hoped it was an ambulance on the way.

She fumbled with her keys as she tried to find the right one for the door, adrenaline coursing through her veins until she somehow made it inside.

At first all she could see was dust and debris. Then she spotted the still-upright ornament on the floor between her desk and the two seldom-used cells.

"Coop?" she called out. Where the hell was he? "Coop?"

"Up here!" she heard him say, and she did everything in her power not to burst into a sob as she looked up through the gaping hole in the ceiling to see him squatting at the edge.

"What are you *doing* up there? You need to get off the roof before the rest of this place caves in!

"I thought...How are *you* still up *there*? I saw you disappear so I came inside to save you!"

He smiled. The man had the freaking audacity to smile when she'd thought she was going to run into the building and find his broken body splayed on the floor.

"Not sure if you saw, but there was a bit of an earthquake up here. Knocked me off balance," he said.

She threw her hands in the air. "Think you can get down before another quake happens?"

"Think you can get out?"

She narrowed her eyes at him. "Remove yourself from the roof, Mr. Mayor, before I arrest you for trespassing."

She made her way back to the door and outside to safety, her heart squeezing in her chest for every second he wasn't back on the ground.

Thirty seconds later he emerged from behind the building, and the crowd gathering in the square cheered.

It was all she could do to keep herself from running to him, but she had to be sure this was it, that he was for real.

He must have sensed her hesitation because he stopped walking when he was six feet in front her.

She opened her mouth to speak, prepared to launch into an inquisition about whether or not his commitment to Meadow Valley also meant a commitment to her, but Peyton spoke before she could get the words out.

"When you wouldn't take my calls or answer my texts, I stopped by your mom's house. I figured if I could get through to her that maybe *she'd* get through to you."

Dani frowned. "She didn't tell me."

He shook his head. "It was only about an hour ago, when I was on my way here. I asked her not to tell you, at least until after I finished with my surprise." He glanced back toward the caved-in building, then faced her with a nervous laugh. "Surprise?"

"You could have killed yourself," she said.

He raised a brow. "But I didn't. And also, I'm not done." He pulled a small plastic container from his coat pocket and moved a couple of steps closer so she could see the red-and-white confections inside. Her mother's peppermint meringues. "I guess I caught your mom in the middle of her holiday baking, and when I saw these, everything just sort of clicked."

Dani sucked in a breath. Now she couldn't speak even if she wanted to.

Peyton took another step toward her, close enough so that she could touch him, but she was frozen where she stood.

"*You* asked me to the winter formal," he said. It wasn't a question.

Dani nodded.

"And I was the idiot who asked Cady McKay if she knew who sent it and believed her when she said it was her."

Dani nodded again, then cleared her throat. Okay. Good. She hadn't completely lost the ability to utter sound. "It's stupid," she finally said, "that I've held on to that rejection for all these years. Everything seems so big when you're a kid, though. You know? So when my dad left and you acted like you didn't know I existed? It was—*big*." She let out a nervous laugh.

He shook the little container in his hand. "I might have forgotten it was you who sold me these amazing cookies or whatever you call them—"

"Peppermint meringues," she said.

Peyton cleared his throat. "I wasn't *done*," he said with a grin.

She winced. "Sorry."

"I *knew* you existed, Dani. I wasn't lying when I said I had a crush on *you*. But I was also out of my depth. I didn't know how to pursue a girl who seemed to want nothing to do with me. But if I'd known?" He shoved the meringues back into his pocket and held his left hand out to her.

Dani suddenly remembered that they had quite an audience—an audience who seemed to be waiting with bated breath for whatever came next, as was she.

"What?" she asked, a small tremor in her voice.

"Go to the dance with me," he said.

A collective *Awww* sounded from the aforementioned audience, and Dani's heart felt like it was about to explode. Tears stung her eyes.

She placed her palm in his, and he wrapped his free arm around her waist.

"Is this the hand you broke?" he asked, nodding to the one he held.

"Wrist," she corrected. "But yeah."

He pressed his lips to the inside of that once-broken wrist, and she shivered.

Peyton pulled her close.

"Sing something!" someone called out. "They need a song for their first dance!"

And, as if it had been planned all along, the whole crowd burst into "We Wish You a Merry Christmas," and Dani and Peyton both laughed.

The sirens drew closer until she knew the ambulance or fire truck or whatever emergency vehicle was sent had arrived.

Lieutenant Carter Bowen and his unit of firefighters approached, and after they had determined that no one was hurt, they made their way toward the building to assess the damage and any further danger of collapse.

Dani tilted her head up toward his. "You're so stupid," she said, half laughing, half crying.

"For climbing onto a roof that wasn't structurally sound?" he asked.

She nodded. "And for spending almost six *hundred* dollars on a holiday decoration."

He tilted his head to one side. "And if *you'd* won that auction, you would have been the one up there making questionable decisions."

She let go of his hand and cupped his cheeks in her palms. "You could have been hurt. Or *worse*. All because I was too scared of you leaving to believe you might actually stay. I'm sorry, Peyton. I can't imagine how hard it is for you to be back here after losing your parents. I should have cut you some slack. I should have given you the benefit of the doubt, I should have—"

"You *could* have told me the whole story. About us."

She groaned. "It's embarrassing."

"It's *our* story, Deputy. There's nothing embarrassing about that."

She rolled her eyes. "I guess it doesn't matter that I've never left Meadow Valley, because it looks like I've got as much baggage as you do."

He pressed his lips to her forehead. "I'll help you carry yours if you help me carry mine," he said softly against her ear.

She shivered again.

"You're staying?" she asked, daring to let the hope seep into her voice.

"I once thought I had to leave Meadow Valley to do something important. To make a difference. But Meadow Valley *is* important. *You're* important. I texted *no* in response about the interview, right after you kicked me out of your mom's house."

Her eyes widened. "I tried so hard to read your phone screen through that stupid doorbell camera."

He laughed. "And I've been trying to *tell* you for three days. But I should have told you about the interview as soon as I saw you on Friday. I messed up too. Which really sucks because I'm falling in love with you, Deputy. So if you don't forgive me, I might have to go back to being a grinch."

She wrapped her arms around his neck and kissed him.

"You were going to win the lights parade contest for me, *and* you're falling in love with me? I'm guessing this story of ours has a happy ending," she said.

"Not a contest, Dani."

She laughed. "Shut up and kiss me again, Coop."

And he did.

* * *

One year and one day later…Christmas Eve, to be exact…

Dani, Teddy, Sheriff Thompson, and Keith stood on the street in front of what was now officially named the Meadow Valley Town Hall and Sheriff's Department while Peyton waited in front of the door ready to plug the extension cord into the one outside outlet.

They listened for the chime of the firehouse bell, the indication that it was time to begin the parade.

The bell sounded, and they all stared down First Street as far as they could see, watching as one building lit up. Then another. And another.

"Almost!" Dani called to Coop. "Wait for it…Here we go…*Three. Two. One. Now!*"

He plugged in the cord, and the town hall lit up from base to roof, everything from twinkling icicles all the way to the life-sized ornament on the reinforced, *definitely* structurally sound roof.

Cheers erupted up and down the street as Mayor Peyton Cooper strode down the town hall steps, gathering his beautiful, pregnant wife in his arms.

"Merry Christmas, *Mrs. Coop*," he said, kissing her first on the nose, then the mouth, and then her rounded belly. "Merry Christmas, *Little Coop*," he said to the baby inside, the one who'd hopefully be riding horses with his mama before even learning to walk.

"Merry Christmas, Coop," Dani said when he straightened to kiss her again. "And look at that beautiful street. Everyone did such an amazing job."

He winked and pulled her close so only she could hear.

"Yeah, but we totally won, right?" he asked.

"Yeah," she said, her eyes locked on his. "Totally."

Also by A.J. Pine

Meadow Valley Series

Cowboy to the Rescue (novella)
My One and Only Cowboy
Make Mine a Cowboy

Crossroads Ranch Series

Second Chance Cowboy
Saved by the Cowboy (novella)
Tough Luck Cowboy
Hard Loving Cowboy

About the Author

A librarian for teens by day and *USA Today* bestselling romance writer by night, A.J. Pine can't seem to escape the world of fiction, and she wouldn't have it any other way. When she finds that twenty-fifth hour in the day, she might indulge in a tiny bit of TV to nourish her undying love of vampires, superheroes, and a certain high-functioning sociopath detective. She hails from the far-off galaxy of the Chicago suburbs.

* * *

Learn more at:
  AJPine.com
  Twitter @AJ_Pine
  Facebook.com/AJPineAuthor

Home for the Holidays

ROCHELLE ALERS

Chapter One

Peering closely at her image in the mirror over the bathroom vanity, Iris Nelson applied a coat of mascara to her upper and lower lashes and then took a step back to examine her handiwork. The smoky shadow on her lids, faint raspberry blush on her cheekbones, and the matching gloss on her lips complemented her chestnut-brown complexion. *Not bad*, she thought. She hadn't lost her touch.

Taking up a small round brush, Iris smoothed back the sides of her short, chemically straightened hair before spiking the crown with her fingertips à la Halle Berry. She smiled, flashing straight white teeth. If the style worked for such a beautiful actress, Iris hoped it would do the same for her. The sophisticated makeup and hair, along with a body-hugging red dress and black suede stilettos, were a complete departure from her normal jeans, T-shirt, and apron she wore as the pastry chef at the Muffin Corner.

She left the bathroom, humming under her breath, then

scooped up her phone, clutch bag, and keys. A cool November breeze swept over her exposed skin as she stepped out into the parking lot behind the row of stores where she rented a second-story, two-bedroom apartment above a gift shop on Cavanaugh Island; it was cool but not cold enough for her to go back upstairs for a shawl.

As soon as she slipped in behind the wheel of the late-model Lincoln MKX and tapped the start engine button, her cell phone rang. The name Tracy Daniels appeared on the dashboard screen. Activating the Bluetooth feature, she asked, "Are you ready?"

"Not really," Tracy replied. "My professor wants to go over the entire thesis tonight instead of putting it off for another time. Once I revise according to his suggested changes, he'll review it again so I can submit it before the end of the semester. I'm saying all of this to let you know you'll have to go to the club without me."

Iris groaned inwardly. It'd been Tracy's suggestion to hang out together. She claimed they needed to dance and kick up their heels, to let off some steam.

"Iris, are you there?" Tracy asked while Iris stared out the windshield.

"Yes."

"Are you still going?"

Iris's first instinct was to say no. What self-respecting woman went to a club by herself? Then again, she'd been really looking forward to an evening with a little flirtation...and more. When would she have this opportunity again?

She closed her eyes and sighed. "Yes, I'm going," she answered. After all, she'd taken the time to put on makeup and a hot outfit. The red color and narrow bands criss-crossing her bared back were a welcome departure from the requisite modest black dresses she'd worn to her ex's fund-raisers and dinner parties.

"Good for you," Tracy said. "Remember, you don't have to look for Mr. Right—just Mr. Right Now."

"I know. I'd even settle for Mr. Tonight."

Picking up a man only for sex had never been Iris's style, yet she wasn't going to rule out a little harmless flirting. She also wasn't looking for a relationship. Been there, done that. A whirlwind courtship and subsequent marriage to a man who'd revealed the ugly side of his jaded personality within an hour of exchanging vows made her wary of forming any lasting relationships.

Tracy laughed. "Have fun."

The smile tilting the corners of Iris's mouth reached her eyes. "I plan to. I'll see you tomorrow." She ended the call, taking one last glance at her reflection in the rearview mirror.

Twenty minutes later, Iris entered the town limits of Haven Creek, maneuvering into a parking space adjacent to the Happy Hour. It was minutes before seven, still early enough for her to find a parking spot close to the club's entrance. A group of women, walking arm in arm in an attempt to maintain their balance in four- and five-inch stilettos, made their way across the parking lot, giggling uncontrollably. Her eyebrows lifted a fraction. It looked as if she wasn't the only one exposing a lot of skin tonight.

Iris had come to the club for Thursday karaoke and Sunday brunch, but this would be her first Tuesday Ladies' Night. The club's greeter secured a fluorescent pink plastic band around her left wrist after he'd checked her ID.

"Welcome to Happy Hour's Ladies' Night."

Iris flashed her best smile. "Thank you."

He winked at her. "Enjoy, beautiful."

Cradling her small evening bag, she managed to wend her way through the crowd to the bar. Even though it was Ladies' Night, there were just as many men in attendance. The twenty- and thirty-something males coming directly from their offices in Charleston had shed their ties and suit jackets, while their female counterparts preened in power suits and designer dresses with shoes to match.

Prerecorded music blared from numerous speakers, making it virtually impossible to carry on a conversation without shouting to the person close by. The U-shaped bar, which was the club's centerpiece, and mirrored walls made the space appear larger than its actual square footage. Tables seating two, four, and six were positioned closely together, maximizing capacity as waitstaff moved from table to table, taking orders from those who'd elected not to take advantage of the prix fixe buffet and salad bar. Iris planned to order a cocktail and then become a spectator, and if no one caught her eye, then she planned to head home. Raising her hand, she caught the attention of one of the three bartenders pouring, shaking, and mixing drinks.

Deeply tanned with a long, sun-streaked blond ponytail, the bartender gave her a practiced professional smile, exhibiting shockingly white teeth. "What are you drinking, miss?"

"I'll have a cosmo." Opening her bag, she took out a bill and placed it on the bar. Iris went completely still when she felt body heat and the woodsy scent of a man's cologne sweep over her. He was standing so close she couldn't turn around even if she wanted to. His hand grazed her waist as he placed a fifty-dollar bill on the bar next to her twenty.

"That'll be on me," said a deep voice in her ear.

Iris shivered despite the warmth of the man's chest molded to her back. She closed her eyes. Apparently the heels and dress were working even better than she'd anticipated.

Channeling her inner Halle Berry, she smiled and opened her eyes. "Would you mind stepping back a little bit, so I can see who's offering," she said.

He complied, and Iris glanced over her shoulder to meet the most stunningly virile man she'd ever seen. He was beyond gorgeous. The black pullover sweater he wore emphasized broad shoulders tapering to narrow hips. And it was as if the gold flecks in the brown depths of his eyes had hypnotized her. Iris studied his face like an artist, taking in each distinct feature one by one. He reminded her of wrestler-turned-actor Dwayne "The Rock" Johnson. Her gaze moved up to his cropped straight black hair. He exuded masculinity, making her dizzy and unable to draw a normal breath.

When Collier Ward walked into the club, his intent was to have a couple of drinks and catch up with old friends before driving back to his hotel. Then the woman in red caught his eye. As she turned to face him, he saw she was just as scrumptious from the front as she was from the back. His eyes lingered on her full, parted lips, which practically begged to be kissed. Now he stood a hairbreadth away, inhaling her vanilla-infused perfume, fighting to keep himself from reaching out to stroke the skin he knew would feel like pure silk. Everything about this woman was a definite turn-on.

He extended his hand. "Collier Ward," he said. He counted off at least three seconds before she placed her hand on his outstretched palm.

"Iris Nelson."

His fingers closed over hers. "Well, Iris, will you allow me to pay for your drink?"

There came another moment of silence before Iris said, "Yes, but only if you let me pay for yours."

"My drinks are on the house, compliments of the owners." The fact that he was a silent partner in the club was a closely held secret on Cavanaugh Island, where keeping secrets was as scarce as hen's teeth.

He picked up the twenty, handing it back to her. "Please put that away."

The bartender placed a coaster on the bar, set a cosmo on it, and then leaned over and bumped fists with Collier. "Long time no see, Scrappy. What's up?"

"Not much, Billy."

"Are you having your usual Jack and Coke?" the bartender asked Collier.

"I'm going to try a boilermaker tonight."

With wide eyes, Iris gave him a sidelong glance. "Scrappy?"

A woman stepped away from the bar, creating a space for Collier as he shifted and stood close to Iris. "I'll tell you about it later."

"After you get your drink, let's find a table so we can talk," she suggested.

What Iris didn't know was that Collier wanted to do more than talk. He wanted this woman in his bed tonight.

Collier led Iris along the perimeter of the dance floor to a small round table tucked in an out-of-the-way corner and lit by a single votive. He set his shot glass of whiskey and the beer mug on the table, then pulled out a chair for Iris. Once she was seated, he shifted his chair closer so they could talk without having to shout over the ear-shattering music.

Pouring the shot of whiskey into the mug, he touched his glass to hers, staring at Iris as she took a sip of the pink concoction. "How's the cosmo?" Collier held his breath when she looked at him through lowered lashes, wondering if she was aware of the seductive expression.

"It's perfect."

He took a long swallow of his drink, enjoying the smooth taste of whiskey and beer on his palate. His gaze shifted from the woman, who'd managed to enthrall him even before he was given an opportunity to see her face, to the couples dancing to a popular dance club hit. "How often do you come here?" he asked.

"This is my first Ladies' Night."

His head came around and he met her eyes in the diffused light. "Are you here to meet someone?" The last thing Collier wanted was a confrontation with another man. Something about Iris stirred up emotions he hadn't felt for a while. And he didn't want to let that go anytime soon, because with Iris he wanted a little more than a one-night stand.

Iris took another sip of the icy cocktail. Alcohol always lowered her inhibitions, and she had to decide whether to be coy or brazen, figuring the latter was preferable if Collier was to become her Mr. Tonight. "My friend was supposed to meet me, but she couldn't make it. And before you ask, I don't have a boyfriend, lover, or a husband."

"What about an ex?"

"That's ancient history."

"What happened?" Collier asked.

Iris paused as she contemplated her response. "We didn't see eye-to-eye on a lot of things, so we ended it."

"So, you're just here to check out Ladies' Night."

She flashed a sexy moue. "You can say that, but my actual reason for coming is to meet someone new."

"Have you met this new person?"

She ran the tip of her tongue over her lower lip, bringing his gaze to linger there. "I'd like to think I have," she said, successfully biting back a smile when Collier's eyebrows rose. Iris knew she'd shocked him with her candor.

He leaned closer, his muscular shoulder pressing intimately against her bare one.

"Where is he?"

There came a beat. Now she was ready to lower the boom. Either Collier would take the bait or he would run in the opposite direction. "I'd like to believe he's sitting next to me. That is, if he isn't married." There. She'd said it. There was no way Collier could misinterpret her intent.

"Then this must be my lucky night," he whispered in her ear, "because I'm a free agent." He held up his left hand. "No ring, no wife, no girlfriend."

Bracing an elbow on the table, Iris rested her chin on the heel of her hand. She'd waded into the waters of seduction instead of flirtation, and now there was no turning back. She glanced down at the same time, a mysterious smile parting her lips. "You have no idea just how lucky you are."

Collier smiled, an elusive dimple appearing in his left cheek. "Now I know I must be living right."

The teasing smile that played at the corners of Iris's mouth didn't waver as she applauded herself for her spontaneous, witty repartee. "I take it that's a good thing."

"It is," he confirmed. "I wasn't expecting to meet someone so incredibly beautiful, intelligent, *and* sexy."

His compliment buoyed her confidence. "By the way, how often do you come here?" she asked, steering the conversation away from seduction. She didn't want him to misinterpret her flirting with the desire to get him into bed, despite having been celibate for the past three years. Iris thought of her self-enforced celibacy as penance for marrying someone who was so wrong for her.

Collier's left hand covered Iris's right, his calloused thumb caressing her fingers. "I haven't been here in a couple of years. I'm just visiting for the holidays."

Iris suddenly realized Collier wasn't the only one living right. Unwittingly he had become the perfect candidate for her Mr. Tonight. Thanksgiving was two days away, and then he would be gone. "Where's home?"

"North Carolina," he replied. "Where do you live?"

"Sanctuary Cove."

Collier's thumb stilled. "Where in the Cove?"

"Downtown."

"Downtown where?" he asked.

"I rent an apartment above the sweetgrass basket shop." She gave him a direct stare, flickering light from the candle throwing long and short shadows across his lean face. "Where are you staying?"

"I've checked into a hotel in Charleston."

Collier pointed to her half-empty glass. "Do you want another drink?"

"No thank you. One's my limit when I'm the designated driver."

His fingers tightened on her hand, then eased. "What if I become your designated driver tonight?"

Iris's confidence soared. Collier had a quiet assurance, a sense of strength. She was thrilled that he had made this night so easy for her.

"Did you drive here?" she asked. Collier nodded. "What are you going to do with your car if you drive me home?" she asked Collier.

"I'll arrange for someone to bring me back to pick it up later."

Iris was certain Collier detected her wildly beating pulse under his fingertips as his gaze met and fused with hers. "If that's the case, then I'll have another one. But first I want to know why folks call you Scrappy."

Collier released her hand and leaned back in his chair. "I

used to fight a lot as a kid. Hardly a day went by when I didn't scrap ass."

"You were a bully." She meant it as a question, but it came out as a statement.

He shook his head. "I never bullied anyone. I just didn't back down when it came to a fight. If someone stepped up to me, then they got popped and dropped. It ended once my father sent me to military school. The structured environment taught me discipline and to control my quick temper. At thirteen I left home a tall, skinny kid and came back at eighteen, twenty pounds heavier and confident enough to know that I didn't need to use my fists to settle a conflict. Even though I've changed, folks still call me Scrappy."

Iris digested this information, wondering whether the anger and aggression from Collier's childhood lay dormant where it could surface without warning, praying she hadn't targeted a crazy man. "Does it bother you that you're still called Scrappy?"

He ran his forefinger down the length of her nose. "No, only because it reminds me of what I used to be like." Pushing back his chair, Collier stood. "I'll go get your drink now."

*   *   *

Collier hadn't known what to expect when Iris invited him to come upstairs to her apartment, but it wasn't the furnishings in the living and dining rooms resembling luxurious lodgings for those on African safari. The colors of white, tan, and black predominated. Rattan chairs, a sofa, and a love seat covered in Haitian cotton cradled accent pillows in animal prints. Zebra-, leopard-, and giraffe-printed area rugs were scattered about the wood floor, and intricately carved mahogany masks and framed watercolors of African women in native and ceremonial dress were exhibited on stark white walls above the wood-burning fireplace.

"I like what you've done with your place."

Iris slipped off her shoes, leaving them on the straw mat near the door. "Thanks." She smiled at him. "Would you like some coffee?"

A slight frown creased Collier's forehead. Maybe he'd misread her signals. Did she want sex, or was she just looking for someone to talk to? After all, she'd admitted she'd gone to Happy Hour to meet someone new.

"Sure," he said.

"How do you take it?"

"Black. The stronger the better."

Iris smiled. "Come talk to me while I make it."

Collier stared at the gentle sway of her hips as he followed Iris into the galley kitchen. The all-white space was spotless. Lounging casually against the entrance and crossing his arms over his chest, he watched as she switched on a single-cup coffee brewer.

"Why did you invite me home with you?" He knew his question had taken her by surprise when she nearly dropped one of the mugs she'd taken off a rack.

"You want the truth?" she asked.

He didn't move. "Of course."

She pulled back her shoulders. "I went to the club tonight with the intent of meeting someone."

He blinked slowly. "How often do you pick up men?"

A nervous smile trembled over her lips. "Tonight was my first time."

"Why tonight?"

Iris assumed a similar pose, crossing her arms under her breasts. "You're the first man in more than three years I could carry on an intelligent conversation with and not worry about him trying to get me into bed with him and—"

Collier held up a hand, stopping her words. "Don't say anything else."

"Don't you want to know why?" she asked.

"No, because I also have a confession to make. When I saw you standing at the bar, the first thing that went through my mind was what did I have to do or say to convince you to sleep with me."

Iris frowned. "I suppose I was wrong about you."

Collier took a step toward her and cradled her face between his hands. He lowered his head, brushing a light kiss over her mouth. "No, you're not. But there's nothing wrong with two consenting adults sleeping together."

Iris's eyelids fluttered. "You're right, but I'm not ready to sleep with a stranger."

He kissed her again. "I don't have a problem with that." After a military career spanning eighteen years and seeing many of his buddies die in combat, he believed in living in the moment. And because of his career, the thought of a relationship with a woman was something he'd avoided for most of his adult life.

Releasing her face, he walked over to the coffeemaker and turned it off. "I think I'm going to pass on the coffee." Turning on his heel, he walked out of the kitchen and the apartment. He took out his cell phone and punched in a number. Fifteen minutes later one of the owners of Happy Hour maneuvered into the parking lot to drive him back to the club.

Collier managed to forget about Iris as he caught up with people at the club he hadn't seen in years. But the image of her beautiful face and her sexy body kept coming back to him once he was alone again in the hotel bed. He was able to recall with vivid clarity the sound of her smoky voice, the scent of her perfume, and the softness of her lips when he touched his mouth to hers. He fell asleep with a smile on his face just thinking about it.

During the night Collier opened his eyes, his heart pounding painfully in his chest, his body drenched in sweat as he struggled to surface from the invisible demon holding him in its vicious grip. The nightmare had returned. It'd been several weeks since the last one, and it was always the same. The blast, a ball of fire scorching the earth, the shrapnel from the exploding Humvee, and the horrendous screams from the men burned beyond recognition by a roadside bomb. Gritting his teeth to keep from screaming for the horror to stop, he sat up, swung his legs over the bed, and stumbled in the direction of the bathroom.

He lost track of time as he sat in the tub with a spray of icy-cold water beating on his naked body. It was only when Collier began to shake uncontrollably that he turned off the water and rested his head on the side of the tub. His mind cleared and he realized he was no longer in Afghanistan, but stateside where he was safe from sniper fire and improvised explosive devices. He didn't remember climbing out of the tub or returning to the bedroom to fall facedown across the bed. This time when he fell asleep, it was without the dreams that kept him from a restful night's sleep.

Chapter Two

BUTTER PECAN SHORTBREAD COOKIES

- 1 cup butter, softened
- ½ cup firmly packed brown sugar
- 2¼ cups all-purpose flour
- ½ cup finely chopped pecans

Cream the butter; add the brown sugar, beating until light and fluffy. Add the flour, mixing well. Stir in the pecans. Divide dough in shalf. Cover; chill one hour. Roll one portion of dough to ¼-inch thickness between two sheets of waxed paper; keep remaining dough chilled until ready to use. Remove the top sheet of waxed paper. Cut the dough into desired shapes with two-inch cookie cutters;

remove excess dough. Place a greased cookie sheet on top of the cookies, greased side down. Invert cookie sheet, allowing cookies to transfer to sheet; remove the remaining waxed paper. Bake at 300°F for 18 to 20 minutes or until lightly browned. Put on wire racks to cool. Repeat rolling, cutting, and baking procedure with remaining dough. Yields about three dozen.

Iris woke at four thirty, opting for a warm bath instead of her usual shower. As she played the sponge over her body, she couldn't help wondering what it would feel like to have Collier's hands following the same path. It was hard to imagine letting an utter stranger into her house, but he'd made certain she made it home safely and left without making a scene. Too bad he was only going to be in Charleston for the upcoming Thanksgiving holiday weekend.

The transformation from seductress to working woman was complete when she pulled on a pair of jeans and a long-sleeved tee; she'd exchanged the stilettos for running shoes, and a rich moisturizer for her skin type and clear lip gloss replaced the dramatic nighttime makeup. Today, her hairstyle was more Peter Pan than Halle Berry. Nothing about her outward appearance bore any resemblance to the woman from the night before.

Locking the door to her apartment, she walked down the staircase, opened the outer door, and stepped out into darkness. Sunrise was still more than an hour away. Streetlights revealed the Christmas decorations that had been put up along Main Street by the local chamber of commerce.

Meanwhile, merchants had gotten a jump on the holiday season by decorating their doors and plate glass windows with colorful lights and decorative wreaths a week following Halloween. A few had placed pots of poinsettias on tables and countertops. The residents of the island were also into the upcoming Thanksgiving holiday spirit, with a steady stream of customers coming into and calling the Muffin Corner, placing orders for cakes, pies, and cookies.

It'd taken a year, but Iris's lifestyle had become the personification of simplicity since relocating from Baltimore, Maryland, to Cavanaugh Island, South Carolina. Instead of getting into her car and driving ten miles to work, she now walked three blocks from her apartment to the Muffin Corner. Here on the island there were no traffic lights, stop signs, or traffic jams. Her sound sleep wasn't shattered by honking horns or an emergency vehicle's wailing sirens. The streets and roads were safe enough to navigate regardless of the hour. After spending her childhood as an Army brat, moving from one base to another, she had finally put down roots in a place that actually felt like home to her.

Forty-five minutes before she was scheduled to begin working, Iris opened the rear door to the bakeshop tucked into a row of stores off Moss Alley. An early start meant she could finish early and then return home to make her own desserts and prepare side dishes for Thanksgiving dinner. Light from the kitchen illuminated the floor in the storeroom, while cool jazz blared throughout the shop. She knew who'd come in early by the music choice. Mabel Kelly preferred jazz while her husband, Lester, favored new age.

She took off her running shoes, pushing her sock-covered feet into a pair of white clogs, and then slipped on a white chef's jacket with an embroidered muffin over the breast pocket. Covering her hair with a matching cotton cap and with several pairs of latex-free gloves filling the patch pockets of her jacket, Iris entered the industrial stainless steel kitchen.

A smile parted her lips as she watched Mabel sway to the melodious sound of a soulful sax. Mabel stood barely five foot and claimed a pair of wide hips and slightly bowed legs. She flaunted her Gullah roots as a direct descendant of slaves brought to the island to cultivate rice when South Carolina was still a British colony. Mabel's fifth-generation grandfather had been credited with developing a method for draining swamps and diverting the water to irrigate rice paddies.

Although Mabel and Lester had been married for nearly twenty years, the couple didn't have any children. Iris never asked, yet Mabel did feel comfortable to disclose she never wanted children because from the age of fourteen she had to help her father raise six younger siblings after her mother got hooked on drugs. Iris thought perhaps Mabel had opened up to her because she wanted Iris to reveal her own past, but she hadn't. Once she'd closed the door on her marriage, she vowed never to open it again. Only Tracy knew what she'd gone through after a year of abuse from her ex-husband, and with no help from her mother-in-law, she finally found the strength to start life anew.

"Good morning!" Iris shouted over the music.

Mabel turned around, flashing a gap-toothed grin. "Mornin'! Let me turn down the radio so we don't have to shout at each other." Like Iris, she'd covered her braided hair with a white bouffant cap. She lowered the volume on the radio that rested on a table near the walk-in refrigerator/freezer.

"It's nice to see the Christmas decorations up on Main Street."

Mabel made a sucking sound with her tongue and teeth. "Folks belonging to the chamber cut the fool at the last meeting when they told the board they wanted Main Street decorated before, not *after* Thanksgiving. Personally, I feel that it puts everyone in a more festive mood when seeing the decorations."

Iris nodded in agreement. In some of the larger, more populous cities she'd noticed Christmas decorations going up in early November. "Where's Lester?"

"He'll be along directly," Mabel reported as she resumed cutting out piecrusts. "I told him he'll have to handle the customers today while you and me fill pie orders. What do you plan as the cookie of the day?"

"Butter pecan shortbread."

Closing her eyes, the older woman shook her head. "I love me some shortbread cookies."

"They're also my favorite," Iris confirmed. At least once a week she made up a large batch of basic shortbread and sugar cookie dough.

When first hired, Iris was given the responsibility of assisting Lester in making pies and decorating theme cakes, while Mabel's repertoire included muffins, doughnuts, scones, and quick breads. Now, Mabel's muffin of the day and Iris's cookie of the day were customer favorites. She glanced over at the bulletin board littered with order slips.

"How many pie orders do we have?" she asked Mabel.

"Eighteen."

Iris estimated it wouldn't take more than four hours to make eighteen pies. The Kellys had devised a method of putting the ingredients for the crusts in an industrial mixer with a dough hook, then running the dough through a large machine resembling a pasta maker, turning the kneaded dough into thin, flaky, buttery sheets, which were placed on a flour-dusted butcher-block table and cut in circles to line nine-inch, deep-dish pie plates. Each sheet yielded six crusts. All of the fillings, made on the premises with fresh ingredients, were stored in the refrigerator in airtight, half-gallon glass jars.

Iris removed the pushpins from nine of the orders and sorted through them. "I have two apple, two cherry, one peach cobbler, and four sweet potato."

"Don't forget to make a few for yourself," Mabel reminded Iris as she crimped the edges of a pie shell.

Opening the refrigerator, Iris removed a plastic container labeled shortbread dough and another with finely chopped pecans. "I think I'm going to make a potato pie with a sweet pecan crust."

Mabel's flour-covered fingers stilled. "Oh! That sounds decadent. Can you make one for me?"

"Sure. If I have time, I'll make some tartlets to put in the showcase. If they go over well, then we can add them to the pie choices." Daily Muffin Corner favorites were muffins, doughnuts, and cookies. Pies and cakes were always special orders.

"Remember, we're closing at noon today," Mabel reminded Iris. The bakeshop would open again Thanksgiving morning from seven to noon for customers to pick up their orders.

"I want to leave before noon because I need to make desserts for my dinner, but if you don't mind, I can make them here after we close." Iris knew she had to leave by two, which would give her enough time to return home to shower and change her clothes before driving to Tracy's house to meet the school bus before three thirty.

Mabel sucked her teeth again. "Child, please. You know you don't have to ask. Besides, I know one of these days you're going to leave us to go into business for yourself, and mark my words, you're going to do very well."

Iris went still. How did Mabel know? She'd heard about the Gullah superstition that people born with a caul, or a membrane covering their faces, had the gift of discerning the future. She wondered if Mabel was clairvoyant—because Iris hadn't uttered a word to anyone; not even her parents or brother knew she wanted to start up her own business.

"Why would you say that?"

"You remind me of Lester and me after we graduated from pastry school. For years we worked our butts off at a hotel chain baking for catered parties. I got tired of the frantic pace before Lester did. It took awhile, but I finally convinced him to move back here and open our own bakery. You're much too talented to hide your gift under the proverbial bushel."

Slipping on a pair of gloves, Iris turned the cookie dough out onto a sheet of waxed paper, covered it with another sheet, and rolled it until it was approximately a quarter inch thick. She knew she would have to tell the owners of the Muffin Corner she planned to quit once she bought a house where she'd convert space to use as an industrial kitchen. Mabel had just given her the opening she needed to reveal her future plan.

"You're right. I have thought about it. Eventually I would like to design wedding cakes exclusively."

Mabel cut out another crust. "You can do that here in the Cove."

Iris met her eyes as she picked up a star-shaped cookie cutter. "But wouldn't that compete with you and Lester?"

"Not if we go into business together."

She gave her boss a skeptical look. "Are you talking about a partnership?"

There came a pregnant pause, and then Mabel said, "Yes. Lester and I bought the vacant store next door, believing we were going to expand. We changed our minds when the recession hit everyone hard here on the island. Although we've tried renting it out, no one has come forward."

It was hard for Iris not to cut a dance step at that news. However, seconds later her newfound joy dissipated like a drop of cold water on hot coals. Something just didn't add up. Why would the Kellys hire her, then a year later approve of her becoming a competitor?

"I'm confused," she told Mabel.

"What about?"

"Lester is known as the ultimate cake man. Do you think folks will patronize me if I open a shop next to yours selling cakes?"

Mabel removed her gloves, tossing them into a nearby plastic-lined wastebasket. "I have a confession to make."

Iris listened, stunned, as her employer revealed why she'd hired her. Lester had been diagnosed with the onset of debilitating rheumatoid arthritis, and as it progressed, he wouldn't be able to stand or sit for prolonged periods.

"RA runs in his family," Mabel continued. "His mama, daddy, and several of his cousins also have it; most of them started walking with canes before they were fifty. Dr. Monroe has prescribed anti-inflammatories for Lester, but he doesn't like to take them because they upset his stomach. I can manage making cookies, doughnuts, and muffins, but there's no way I can fulfill all of the pie and cake orders. Even now Lester's not able to keep up. That's why I hired you to help him. Eventually all of our special-order customers will be referred to you, and I'm willing to let you have the space rent-free for the first two years in return for thirty percent of your sales."

Iris paused, replaying what Mabel had just outlined in what sounded to her like a *Shark Tank* pitch. She knew she couldn't give Mabel an answer until she weighed all of her options: operating out of a shop meant she could continue to rent her apartment; the money she would've spent to install an industrial kitchen in a house would be used in the shop; and if Mabel agreed, she could buy the store, using the property as a business tax deduction. Her mind worked overtime, contemplating a business arrangement that could prove conducive and advantageous to both her and the owners of the Muffin Corner.

"Let me think about it over the weekend, and I'll let you know sometime next week."

Iris took a break at nine thirty and left the shop through the rear door. Sitting on a wooden box, she pulled out her cell phone and called her brother, hoping to catch him before he and her niece got on the road to drive up from Florida to spend the holiday weekend with her. As a business owner himself—he taught veterinary surgery at the University of Florida College of Veterinary Medicine, while also running a successful veterinary practice in Gainesville—she wanted his take on Mabel's proposal.

Much to her surprise, Evan actually answered. She listened intently as he outlined the pros and cons of entrepreneurship. "Thanks for the advice," she told him. "You've given me a lot to think about."

"If you're going to incorporate, then you're going to have to come up with a name for your business. I have to go now because I'm scheduled to perform emergency surgery on a champion show dog."

"I thought you were driving up today."

"I was before I got the call to operate."

"What time should I expect you tomorrow?"

"I plan to be on the road before sunrise. Allie likes eating breakfast at the Cracker Barrel, so we'll make at least one stop before we get to Charleston." Evan told Iris he and his daughter were excited about coming to Cavanaugh Island and spending the holiday weekend with her before he rang off.

This year marked the first time Iris would host Thanksgiving on the island. Not only had she invited her family to come to celebrate the holiday with her, but also Tracy and Layla. She'd reserved connecting bedroom suites at the Cove Inn for her parents, brother, and niece during their stay.

Last year she'd joined her family on a cruise to the Caribbean to celebrate her parents' thirty-eighth wedding anniversary. US Army Col. James Nelson, a graduate of the US Military Academy at West Point, who'd served with distinction in the Gulf War and was promoted from the rank of lieutenant colonel to a full colonel, had announced his retirement effective the end of the year, shocking everyone with this disclosure. When seeing the expression on her mother's face, Iris suspected that not even she knew what her husband had planned. Her father, who'd served his country for thirty years, had finally decided at the age of sixty-five he wanted to experience what it felt like to be a civilian again.

Iris noted the time on the phone. She had only a few minutes to talk to Tracy before the teacher began her first class. "Did you meet someone?" Tracy asked before Iris had a chance to say anything.

Pinpoints of heat stung Iris's cheeks. "Yes," she whispered into the mouthpiece.

Tracy screamed. "You didn't!"

Stretching out her legs and crossing her feet at the ankles, Iris watched an elderly woman attempt to park a behemoth sedan with fins dating back to the 1970s between two pickup trucks. The parking lot appeared to be filled to capacity, which meant Christmas holiday shopping had begun in earnest.

"Earth to Iris. Are you there?"

"Yes, I did," she confirmed for the second time.

"You're going to have to tell me all about it."

A knowing smile parted her lips. "There isn't that much to tell."

"Are you going to see him again?"

A slight frown furrowed Iris's forehead "I doubt it. He's only going to be here for the holiday. Enough about Mr. Last Night. I'm calling to ask your opinion about something." She quickly told her about Mabel's business offer.

"If I were you, Iris, I'd go for it," Tracy said, her voice filled with excitement. "We can talk more about it later. By the way, I put some oxtail stew in the slow cooker this morning, so all I'll have to do is make the sides when I get home."

"Don't bother about the sides. I'll fix them once I get to your place." Since becoming best friends, Iris had volunteered to meet Tracy's daughter's school bus and look after the seven-year-old until Tracy came home.

"You don't have to, Iris. You'll have enough to do tomorrow putting together a Thanksgiving dinner."

"Stop stressing. I've got everything under control." Her menu included roast and Cajun deep-fried turkey, corn bread–sausage stuffing, giblet gravy, collard greens, a sweet potato casserole with a praline topping, Parker House rolls, and the quintessential Southern Sunday dinner dessert: coconut layer cake.

"Okay," Tracy conceded. "Remember, I'm going to haunt you until you tell me about your Mr. Last Night."

"Bye, Tracy."

Tracy laughed. "Later."

Iris went back inside. She wanted to tell Tracy that she didn't want to talk about Collier, who, despite her denial, she wanted to see again.

*   *   *

Collier woke for a second time in less than four hours, flailing wildly and drenched in sweat. The nightmare was back, and he was drowning in an ocean stained with the blood of men staring up at the sky with sightless eyes. He'd managed to make it to the sand, where the stench of burning flesh threatened to make him lose the contents of his stomach. Rising to his feet, he started running, but arms like steel bands held him back until he broke free, stopping suddenly when flames erupted before him. He stood helplessly, watching and yelling at the top of his lungs while the firebomb consumed the Humvee.

Collier opened his eyes, staring up at the ceiling in the hotel suite, chest rising and falling heavily, the back of his throat raw from screaming as the images depicting the horrors of his last deployment slowly faded. As Special Forces, he and his team were always called into the most dangerous operations. The nightmares were so vivid Collier could recount every day of the thirteen months he'd been in Afghanistan, the sights, sounds, and smells lingering with him like he was still there.

By midafternoon, he'd finally shaken off the nightmares. Pulling into Sanctuary Cove Elementary and Middle School, he saw several parents waiting in their vehicles for the end of the school day. He'd come to the school to see his niece before she boarded the school bus. The highlight of his deployment in the Middle East had been their sporadic exchanged e-mails.

As soon as his deployment had ended, Collier put in for an official leave. Once it had been approved, he decided to use five weeks of his accrued leave time to surprise his sister and seven-year-old niece by coming home for the holidays. He knew it wouldn't have been much of a surprise if he'd checked into the Cove Inn instead of a hotel on the mainland. If someone on Sanctuary Cove spotted him, word that he'd returned home would've spread like a wildfire. Collier knew he'd also run the risk of someone calling his sister when he showed up at the club, but meeting Iris had been more than worth that risk.

He walked to the entrance of the school and rang the bell. The school safety officer opened the door, and when asked for identification, Collier showed him his driver's license. The man typed his name into a computer, printing out a visitor's badge with his name and his niece's name. He pointed to his left. "Go to the end of the hallway. Her classroom is on the right."

He peered through the glass on the door to the second-grade classroom. His niece, dressed in the requisite school uniform, had raised her hand to answer a question. Collier opened the door and walked in, seeing shock in the eyes of the teacher who'd grown up on the same block as him and his sister. All eyes were fixed on him, and seconds later his niece, realizing who he was, raced from her desk, launching herself against him when he knelt down to hug her.

"Uncle Collier! You didn't tell me you were coming home."

He kissed her neatly braided hair, struggling not to lose his composure. Homecomings were as emotionally heart-wrenching for returning soldiers as for their family members. "I wanted to surprise you," he said in her ear.

"You did surprise me," she whispered back.

Collier felt his heart turn over when he saw the tears in her eyes. He knew he had to leave before both of them started crying. "I'm going to wait for you outside, so don't get on the bus."

Collier stood up, nodding to his niece's teacher. "How are you, Miss Patience?"

Patience Parker smiled. "I'm well, Scrap—Collier."

He gave her a pointed look. She'd corrected herself before referring to him by his childhood nickname. "Thank you for letting me say hello. I'll let you get back to your lesson." Closing the door, Collier retraced his steps. He handed in the visitor badge and walked out into the warm November afternoon.

Sitting on a bench in the playground, he breathed in the distinct smell of Cavanaugh Island. He'd missed seeing the palmetto trees and the Spanish moss hanging from the branches of ancient oaks. He missed the hot, sultry summers, hanging out on the beach, swimming in the ocean, the mild winters, and listening to the older residents speaking the distinctive Gullah dialect that was slowly dying out because the younger generation refused to speak it. Collier also missed the dishes unique to the region, and for the first time since he'd enlisted in the US Army, he was able to admit that he missed his home.

His last deployment had changed him. He'd lost buddies in combat, men who'd become his brothers in every sense of the word, and he'd had to watch helplessly as one died in his arms. Two deployments to Iraq and a subsequent one to Afghanistan had given him his fill of war, of death, and of dying.

Fortunately, he had a little more than a month to distance himself from anything resembling the military. Coming home to celebrate Thanksgiving and Christmas on Cavanaugh Island with his family was an added bonus. And if he were to run into Iris again, then it would make his homecoming even sweeter.

Chapter Three

COUNTRY-FRIED CABBAGE WITH HAM

- 1 medium head of cabbage
- 2 tablespoons oil
- 1 pound cooked ham, sliced about ¼ inch thick or thinner
- 1 onion, cut into wedges
- Salt and pepper to taste

Peel off the outer layer of the cabbage and discard. Cut the cabbage into quarters, then halve each quarter again, and then again. Wash and drain thoroughly. Heat the oil in a medium pot, fry the ham slices on both sides for a minute or two until browned and remove from the oil. Lower the heat, allowing the oil to cool some before adding the drained cabbage and onion. Stir-fry the cabbage and onion over medium heat until they're as tender as you like (some folks prefer their cabbage and onions fairly crisp) and add the ham, then the salt and pepper. Serve the cabbage on its own or over rice.

Iris mounted the steps of the porch to the one-story Lowcountry plantation house. She always made it a practice to arrive at Tracy's house twenty minutes before the school bus was scheduled to drop off Layla. She opened the screen door, then unlocked the inner door, leaving it slightly ajar.

Her friendship with Tracy had begun last year when Tracy came to the Muffin Corner and placed an order for an assortment of scary desserts for her daughter's birthday party, which coincided with Halloween. The desserts were a big hit with Layla's classmates and their parents, and a week later Tracy left a gift basket for Iris at the bakeshop filled with scented candles, body creams, lotions, gourmet chocolates, and bath salts.

Iris reciprocated by inviting Tracy out to dinner in Charleston, and the two discovered they had much in common. Both had teaching backgrounds—Iris had taught art and Tracy was an English teacher—they were only a year apart in age, and both were divorced. While Tracy became a mother during her marriage, Iris made certain not to bring a child into the hell she'd had to endure until she found the strength to leave her abusive husband.

Several months ago, Iris had volunteered to watch Layla

after Tracy's elderly babysitter fell, fractured her hip, and was eventually confined to a Charleston nursing facility. The schedule fit perfectly since Iris worked at the bakeshop from six in the morning until two in the afternoon, and Tracy, assigned to her school's extended session, taught from ten to four. Now they regarded each other as an extended family, sharing meals, going to the movies, and attending church services together.

After washing her hands in the half bath, Iris walked into the kitchen. Lifting the top off the slow cooker, she checked the oxtail stew. It smelled delicious and the meat was fork-tender. She lowered the temperature to simmer, then searched the refrigerator, discovering a head of cabbage in the vegetable drawer. Iris thought about making steamed cabbage until she saw a ham steak. Stir-fried cabbage with ham, rice, and corn bread would go nicely with the stew. She'd learned within days of moving to South Carolina that rice and grits were staples in Lowcountry pantries.

Iris removed the outer leaves of the cabbage and cut them into quarters, then halved each quarter again, and then again. She glanced at the clock on the microwave as she reached for a large bowl, filled it with water, and placed the cabbage in it. The bus driver always dropped Layla off at exactly three thirty. Wiping her hands on the dish towel, she walked out of the kitchen to the front porch.

I don't believe it!

She thought she had to be hallucinating when she saw Layla skipping alongside her Mr. Last Night. Stunned, she took in everything about him: baseball cap, black sweatshirt, relaxed-fit jeans, and running shoes. He hadn't shaved, and the stubble only intensified his masculinity.

"Miss Iris, come meet my uncle! He just came home," Layla shouted excitedly, racing up the porch.

It was then that Iris noticed the Army duffel Collier carried. He was in the military?

A mix of emotions ranging from embarrassment to mortification roiled inside her. *Get it together, girl*, she told herself as she saw Collier's stunned expression. It was apparent he was as shocked to see her as she to see him.

She extended her hand. "Welcome home, soldier. I'm Iris Nelson, Layla's babysitter." It'd be better for everyone if they played this like they'd never met. Too many awkward explanations otherwise.

Collier took off the cap, his shocked expression turning into amusement when he took her proffered hand, dropping a kiss on her knuckles. "Thank you. I must say this homecoming has been quite remarkable. Collier Ward. I'm Tracy's brother and Layla's uncle."

Iris wanted to ask if he meant "Fraud" and not Ward. He'd had plenty of opportunity to tell her he had family in Sanctuary Cove.

Easing her hand from his firm grip, she pointed to the duffel bag he'd set down on the porch. "Are you staying for dinner?" she teased.

His eyebrows lifted questioningly. "Are you cooking?"

"Miss Iris cooks everything good, Uncle Collier," Layla chimed in. "She's teaching me to cook. And you have to taste her cookies. Mama says they are the best in the world."

Collier's gaze was fixed on Iris. "Miss Iris sounds like she's very special."

"Layla, why don't you go in the house and change out of your school clothes? After you wash your hands, you can help me with dinner."

"I know. You don't want me to listen to grown folks' business. Mama tells me that all the time when she's talking on the phone."

Collier winked at his niece. "Go on, pumpkin, and do what Miss Iris tells you." His eyes followed Layla as she stomped across the porch and went inside the house. Tracy claimed Layla should've been his daughter because both were strong-willed and fearless.

Once the door closed behind her, he studied Iris with a curious intensity. She looked nothing like the temptress who'd seduced him with her killer body and stunningly beautiful face. And now, with her standing before him, he wasn't certain which he liked better—the dramatic makeup, quirky hairdo, and sexy revealing dress, or the fresh-faced woman in a pair of skinny jeans, tee, and flats. His gaze lingered briefly on the outline of her breasts under the cotton top. There was so much he wanted to know about her. "You're a cook?"

Iris smiled. "A pastry chef," she corrected. "My specialty is cake design."

"No wonder you smell so delicious." His eyes sparkled with desire.

Her jaw dropped slightly with his comeback, but she recovered quickly. "I wish I'd known you were related to Tracy."

"Why?" Collier asked.

"Because I never would've flirted with you."

He smiled. "I was the one who came on to you, not the other way around. You don't have to worry about me telling Tracy that we met last night because I've never been one to kiss and tell."

The tense lines around her mouth disappeared. "Thank you for being a gentleman." Iris pointed to the duffel. "Did you really stay in Charleston last night?"

He knew he'd lessened some of Iris's tension when the smile parting her lips reached her eyes. Bending, he picked up the bag. "Yep. I checked into a hotel because I wanted my homecoming to be a surprise for Tracy and Layla."

"Where's your car?"

"I parked at the end of the cul-de-sac so Tracy wouldn't see the North Carolina plates. I don't know how well you know my sister, but she's the ultimate worrywart. If I'd called and told her I was coming in yesterday, she wouldn't have gone to work. Either she'd be calling or texting me every hour, and then, if she couldn't reach me or if my flight was delayed, she'd blame me for making her crazy."

Iris glanced over her shoulder at Collier when he reached above her head and held the screen door open for her to precede him inside. "I've never seen that side of Tracy."

"Good for you," he drawled, "because she can be a hot mess."

Collier knew his sister's anxiety was the result of having lost their parents within a year of each other; all the while she'd been going through a contentious divorce with a vindictive soon-to-be ex-husband. He'd requested a personal emergency family leave to be there for his sister and niece, but when it came time for him to return to duty for his second deployment to Iraq, Tracy had to be sedated because she feared losing him too.

After this last deployment, Collier promised Tracy it would be his last combat mission, and barring any unforeseen national threat, he planned to spend the last two years of what would become a twenty-year military career stateside. Physically he could easily put in another ten years as a member of the Army Special Operations Forces, but he doubted whether he would be able to perform at peak capacity emotionally. The recurring nightmares were obvious indicators of post-traumatic stress disorder. He feared that if it continued, he'd become a danger not only to himself, but also to others.

"How long is your leave?" Iris questioned.

"I'll be here through Christmas."

She stopped abruptly in the middle of the living room, her brow furrowing. "That's almost five weeks."

He smiled. "Five weeks to find out more about you other than your name and that you live in the apartment above Rose Walker's A Tisket A Basket."

Iris folded her hands at her waist. "How long will it take for me to find out everything I need to know about you, Mr. Special Forces?"

Collier's body stiffened in shock; he was momentarily speechless. How had she known? Had Tracy told Iris about his military background? "I don't know what you're talking about."

Iris took a step, bringing them within inches of each other. "Yes, you do, Collier. I grew up an Army brat. My father retired last year as a full bird, so the fact that you're in the military and Tracy has been as closemouthed as a clam about you speaks volumes." She rested a hand on his chest. "There are no photographs of you anywhere in this house, and she's never mentioned you by name. That means you're Delta Force, Green Beret, Ranger, or Navy SEAL. Please don't insult my intelligence by denying it."

He covered her hand with his free one. "If you know so much, you also know it's not something we can talk about. What do you want me to say?"

She rose on tiptoe. "Just tell me I'm right."

Collier stared at her mouth under lowered lids. He wanted to kiss her. Really kiss Iris with the passion he found hard to control whenever they were together. "You're right," he whispered.

"Thank you," she drawled, barely able to keep the laughter from her voice. She executed a snappy salute, then turned on her heel and walked in the direction of the kitchen, Collier's eyes fixed on her hips in the fitted jeans.

Oh, this was going to be interesting. Time to step up his game.

*   *   *

"Something smells delicious."

Iris's head popped up. She hadn't heard Collier come into the kitchen. He'd exchanged the sweatshirt for a white tee, the power in his upper body blatantly on display. "I'm sautéing ham for stir-fried cabbage." He peered over her shoulder as she stirred finely diced ham in a large pot, removing the shreds to a plate to drain on a paper towel once they were browned.

"Is Layla still changing her clothes?"

Iris pointed to the closed door off the kitchen. "She's in the bathroom scrubbing her nails. I told her cooks have to make certain their hands are very clean if they're not wearing gloves."

Collier chuckled softly. "I used to tease her when she was a toddler, daring her not to touch me with her little grimy hands because she loved playing in dirt. Her response was to chase me, and whenever I stopped, she would wipe the dirt off on my clothes. I lost track of the number of times I had to change because of her dirty handprints."

"If you hadn't challenged her, she probably wouldn't have done it."

He opened the refrigerator and took out a container of milk. "I learned that the hard way."

"There are cookies in the jar on the other side of the coffeemaker."

Collier met Iris's eyes. "Did you make them?"

Nodding, she turned off the burner. "I make a different cookie every day for the Muffin Corner and bring a few home for Layla and Tracy."

"Which ones are good, Cookie Lady?"

Iris cut her eyes at him. "*All* of my cookies taste good."

"No shit," he mumbled under his breath.

"Ooh, Uncle Collier. You said a curse."

Iris turned to find Layla with her hand over her mouth and knew she had to clean up Collier's expletive. "No, he didn't. He said, 'no slip,'" she lied smoothly. Iris realized she would have to lie again later that evening. There was no way she could tell Tracy she'd flirted with her brother. "Layla, you may have one cookie with a glass of milk as a snack before dinner."

Collier blew Iris an air-kiss, pantomiming "Thank you."

"You know you owe me," she said sotto voce.

He moved closer. "I always pay my debts. What time do you guys usually sit down to eat?"

Iris took a quick glance at the microwave clock. "Anytime between five thirty and six. Barring traffic delays, Tracy usually gets home before five."

Layla set the cookie jar on the table in the breakfast nook. "Are you having cookies and milk with us, Miss Iris?"

Iris studied the upturned face of the young girl with a flawless café au lait complexion, black pigtails, and large, round sherry-colored eyes, wondering how different her life might have been if her husband hadn't been abusive and she'd had his child. She probably would've continued to teach rather than go to culinary school and definitely wouldn't have moved to Sanctuary Cove.

Her expression softened. "Of course, sweetie."

Picking up a gingerbread man, Collier bit off the head. "Please don't eat me," he pleaded in a plaintive cry through closed lips as if he were a ventriloquist. "But I have to eat you because you're so good," he said in his normal baritone. He was about to take another bite when his voice changed again, this time mimicking the iconic horror movie doll Chucky. "You'll be sorry if you take another bite."

"Bite him, Uncle Collier!" Layla screamed hysterically.

"Eat, eat, eat," Iris chanted in between peals of laughter.

Collier took two bites and then collapsed to the floor, holding his stomach and writhing as if in pain. Layla joined him on the floor, tickling him as he begged her to stop.

"Come help me, Miss Iris," Layla shouted. "We need to make Uncle Collier tap out."

Iris joined Layla and Collier on the kitchen floor, holding on to Collier's arm and bending it in an attempt to make him give up. They'd become combatants in a free-for-all tag team, Layla screaming for Collier to give up as Iris labored to keep him from moving. She knew he could've easily freed himself but he pretended to struggle. Layla's shrieking escalated to ear-piercing screams. Collier lay partially atop her, not permitting her space to wiggle.

Iris jumped on his back, clamping his head in a sleeper hold, a move used by professional wrestlers. She felt an instant flare of desire with her body pressed so intimately against Collier's. "Pretend you're going to sleep," she said in his ear. He went limp, rolling off Layla as Iris continued the pretense of applying pressure to his temples. Seconds later, he lay, eyes closed, on his back.

Layla, scrambling off the floor, twirled around and around. "We did it, Miss Iris! We are the tag-team champions of the world!"

"What's going on here?"

Recognizing Tracy's voice, Collier jumped to his feet. Her expression changed, going from confusion to shock as he closed the distance between them, sweeping her up in his arms. The last time he'd seen Tracy, she wore her hair in tiny twists. Now the twists were long enough to graze her jaw. Burying her face against his throat, she cried without making a sound.

"Why didn't you let me know you were coming home?" she sobbed, shaking uncontrollably.

Collier turned around, staring directly at Iris. She'd gathered Layla close to her side. They exchanged a subtle look of understanding.

"Why don't you guys hang out on the porch while Layla and I finish cooking? We'll call you when everything's ready."

He nodded and walked Tracy out to the porch, settling her on the love seat and sitting down beside her. Reaching into the back pocket of his jeans, he took out a handkerchief and dabbed her moist face.

Stretching an arm over the back of the wicker sofa, Collier stared out at the encroaching darkness. Porch lights had come on and light shone through the windows of the six homes lining Coosaw Court. He'd learned to ride a bike and played baseball, basketball, and football in the cul-de-sac where homeowners parked their vehicles in driveways or on lawns in order to provide a safe space for their children to play.

Extending his legs, he pulled Tracy closer. "I wanted to surprise you," he said after a comfortable silence. "I knew if I'd called you—"

"I know," Tracy said, interrupting him. "I would've acted a fool like I did when you told me you were coming back from Iraq, but when I didn't hear back from you for almost a week, I had a meltdown."

Collier tugged on her twists. "Let the choir say amen," he teased.

Tracy slapped at his hand. "Very funny," she drawled. "How long are you staying this time?"

"I'll be here through Christmas."

Two deep lines of concern appeared between Tracy's eyes. "Are you on medical leave? Because you've never come home that long. What are you hiding from me, Collier?"

Chuckles beginning in Collier's throat bubbled up as he threw back his head and laughed loudly. "I'm not hiding anything. Do you want to conduct a strip search to check for wounds?"

Tracy punched him softly in the shoulder. "Don't be gross." She looped her arm through his. "I'm glad you're home. I've just about worn my knees out praying for you."

Light from the lanterns flanking the front door cast a flattering glow over Tracy's face. Collier stared at his sister's profile, smiling. A boy who'd lived in the house across from the Wards used to torment Tracy, saying she was adopted because she looked nothing like their Vietnamese French mother or African American father. The harassment ended when Collier caught him alone and threatened to knock his teeth out if he ever bad-mouthed his sister again. The boy didn't know that Tracy looked exactly like her paternal Gullah grandmother who'd been one of the island's official griots.

He smiled. "You can continue to pray for me but not on your knees. I've been told I'll be stationed stateside unless—"

"Please don't say it," Tracy said, interrupting him again. She rested her head on his shoulder. "I love you, Collier, and I worry about you. I know you've made the Army your career, but what about your personal life? Do you ever think about having children?"

Collier closed his eyes for several seconds. "Not really."

"What happened to our promise that if I made you an uncle, you'd make me an auntie? Layla will be eight next year, and I'm still not an auntie. How long do you expect me to wait?"

"Not too much longer."

Tracy hugged his arm. "I'm going to hold you to that." A flash of humor crossed her face. "What's with you, Layla, and my friend rolling around on the kitchen floor?"

"We were having an impromptu wrestling match."

She made a sucking sound with her tongue. "What would folks say if they found out that Scrappy challenged a little girl to a wrestling match?" Tracy teased.

Collier smiled. "Layla loves wrestling."

"Layla loves having you home."

Collier sobered up. "I like being home."

Tracy sat straight, giving him an incredulous look. "Who is this stranger masquerading as my brother? The last time you came back, you complained you couldn't wait to leave. What changed?"

He pondered his sister's question for several seconds. Two days before celebrating his thirteenth birthday, he'd sat in the lecture hall for an orientation at the elite military school, certain he was going to hate being away from home and all that was familiar. Collier resented his father's decision to send him to what he thought of as a quasi juvenile detention center, but a month into his stay he realized he'd found his niche. He'd fallen in love with all things military. He knew he disappointed his mother when instead of enrolling in college he enlisted in the Army. His father had secretly wanted him to apply to West Point, but Collier redeemed himself when he followed in his father's footsteps and became a Green Beret.

Life in the military wasn't colored in shades of gray, but

in black and white. He loved the success he had achieved and knowing he'd protected his country. But what would happen when Master Sergeant Ward returned to civilian life? What, if anything, would give him as much satisfaction? It was something he thought about constantly. And so far he hadn't come up with an answer.

"I've changed, Tracy."

She frowned again. "How?"

"I only have two years left in the service. I have to decide what I want to do with the rest of my life." He didn't tell her he also had to focus on taking care of her and Layla, although Tracy constantly reminded him she wasn't his responsibility. That she was able to take care of herself *and* her daughter.

"Is getting married and having children in your future plans?"

Collier successfully concealed his annoyance behind a closed expression when he met Tracy's accusing eyes. "I'm in no rush to get married."

"You just said not too much longer. How old do you want to be before you become a father?"

His jaw tightened as he clamped his teeth together. Tracy was like a dog with a bone whenever she wanted to prove a point. "I didn't know there was an expiration date on fatherhood."

"There isn't, and I shouldn't have to remind you that you're the last male Ward on Cavanaugh Island."

The tense lines on Collier's face relaxed. "I can't concern myself with situations I can't control at this time in my life. Did you finish your thesis?" he asked, changing the topic.

"Why do you always change topics when you don't want to talk about yourself, Collier?"

"Changing the topic is the alternative to telling you to mind your business."

"Oooo-kaaaaay," she said, drawing out the word into two long syllables. "We'll talk about me, then."

Tracy launched into a lengthy discussion of the impact of nineteenth- and twentieth-century women's literature on their respective epochs. She'd chosen Mary Wollstonecraft, Toni Morrison, Agatha Christie, Edith Wharton, and Anaïs Nin as the main subjects of her thesis. As a child, Tracy had spent all her free time reading, and Collier knew she would eventually choose a career involving books. They sat on the porch talking until Layla announced it was time to come in and eat.

A short time later, Collier refilled his plate with a second helping of rice, cabbage, and oxtail stew, smiling at Iris across the dining room table. "This food is amazing."

Layla wiped her mouth with a napkin. "I told you she cooks good."

He wanted to tell his niece that Iris was better than good. "If I eat like this every day, I'll have to run at least five miles to burn off the extra calories."

Iris glanced up at him through her lashes. "Well, you better prepare yourself, since I've invited your family to join mine for Thanksgiving dinner tomorrow."

Collier swallowed a bite of corn bread. "It looks as if I came home just in time to get my gobble on."

"Brother, that's so lame," Tracy said while shaking her head.

"Gobble. Turkey," Collier intoned.

"We get it, Collier." Tracy laughed.

"Killjoy," he mumbled under his breath. "Iris, do you need me to help you with anything?"

Smiling, Iris shook her head. "I don't think so."

"Are you sure?"

She nodded. "I'm *very* sure."

An expression of supreme triumph flitted across Collier's face. When he'd left Iris's apartment, he wasn't certain if he would run into her again. Now he was assured of at least three consecutive days with her.

"I need you to get the card table out of the storeroom and put it in Iris's truck," Tracy told him.

"My dining room table seats six; I'll need the card table for Layla and my niece," Iris explained when he gave her a questioning look.

"Where do you live?" Collier asked.

Iris had to give the address to Collier. He was giving an award-winning performance. "I have an apartment above the sweetgrass shop."

His gaze moved from her eyes to her mouth, lingered on her chest, and then back to her eyes. "Will you be able to carry the table up the stairs by yourself?"

Iris met the bold stare with one of her own. "It can't be that heavy."

Collier's eyebrows rose a fraction. "You're going to carry a table *and* chairs?"

She gave him a smile usually reserved for placating young children. "I don't need the chairs." When she'd moved to the island, she'd used a tray table, two folding chairs, and a sleeping bag for two weeks until a moving company delivered the furniture she'd stored with a Baltimore storage company.

Tracy looked at her brother, then Iris. "Collier can follow you in his car and carry it up for you."

"He can bring it tomorrow," Iris said in a quiet voice she didn't recognize as her own after a noticeable silence. The notion of being alone with Collier would prove much too tempting, given her prolonged period of celibacy, much too easy for her to get caught up in sex and not the man.

Growing up on the base had left Iris behind her civilian counterparts socially when it came to dating. The boys of the noncommissioned officers adopted a hands-off approach when it came to dating an officer's daughter, while the sons of the officers were as appealing to Iris as a case of poison ivy. It wasn't until she enrolled in college that she had her first serious boyfriend. Sleeping with the second-year medical student wasn't as exciting as it was satisfying. Then there had been Derrick—her loving, moralistic ex-husband who'd refused to sleep with her until their wedding night. He called it rough sex. She called it rape.

Collier angled his head, a grin parting his lips. "What time do you want me to come by tomorrow?"

"I've planned for everyone to sit down around three, so you can drop by anytime between two and two thirty." Pushing back her chair, she picked up her plate and stood.

"Nah, nah, nah," intoned Tracy, waving a hand. "Put that plate down. You've done enough. I'll clear the table."

Iris hesitated. "I don't mind."

Tracy stood. "But I do. You're on your feet all day baking at the Muffin Corner; then you come here and cook some more. I'm sorry, girlfriend, but beginning now you're banned from the premises until Monday."

Tears welled up in Layla's eyes. "Why can't Miss Iris come here, Mama?"

"Wrong choice of words, sis," Collier said under his breath.

Iris tugged gently on one of Layla's braids. "Your mother's joking, sweetie. I'll see you tomorrow when you come to my place. I have a niece who's eight, so you'll have someone to play with."

"What's her name? Is she going to sleep over?"

Iris hadn't thought about her niece spending the weekend. After all, she didn't have to go back to the Muffin Corner until Tuesday. She didn't work the weekends, and the bakeshop closed on Sundays and Mondays. "Her name is Allison, but we call her Allie."

Layla gave her mother a pitiful look. "Can I sleep over at Miss Iris's, Mama? Pul-lease."

Tracy and Layla had spent a week at Iris's apartment over the summer in the spare bedroom when Tracy had the floors in the house replaced. Iris had taken a week's vacation, and the three of them spent the time touring the Sea Islands, visiting historic plantations, botanical gardens, and soaking up a little Gullah culture when a weaver taught them to weave sweetgrass baskets. It ended with everyone several pounds heavier and blissfully relaxed.

Iris caught Tracy's gaze, surreptitiously tapping her forefinger against her lips, indicating she would handle the situation. "I'm going to call my brother to find out if he's made plans for Allie to hang out with her grandparents. If not, then you girls can have a sleepover."

Layla slid off her chair, looping her arms around Iris's waist. "Thank you, Miss Iris."

Iris rubbed the girl's back in a soothing, circular motion. "You're welcome, baby." Rounding the table, Iris hugged Tracy. "I'll see you tomorrow."

Tracy pulled Iris away from the table. "You know my brother likes you," she whispered in her ear.

"What are you talking about?" Iris said through clenched teeth, praying Collier hadn't overheard. Other than exchanging an occasional glance, there was nothing in their body language to indicate they'd known each other before today.

"I can just tell," Tracy whispered. "Are you certain you don't want me to come over tomorrow and help you?" she asked in an audible voice.

"I'm very certain," Iris reassured her. She planned to get up early, do a little light housekeeping, prepare side dishes, and set the table. Extending her hand, she smiled at Collier, her eyes photographing his lean, dark-skinned, incredibly handsome face. "It's been a pleasure." He took her hand in a gentle grip, thumb caressing her knuckles as he'd done when they shared the table at Happy Hour.

"The pleasure has been all mine." Releasing her hand, Collier splayed his fingers at the small of her back. "I'll walk you out."

Iris went still, her spine ramrod straight. "It's okay. I'm just parked out front."

Reluctantly, Collier dropped his hand. Having her freeze under his touch made him wish he could turn back the clock to where they could've met under a different set of circumstances. He knew without a shadow of a doubt they had a physical connection, and the more he saw her, the more he wanted to see her. Collier knew if he'd been seated next to Iris during dinner, he would've been tempted to concoct any excuse to touch her.

"I have to go out anyway to bring my car around."

Collier waited for Iris to gather her tote before walking her out of the house, watching until her truck disappeared from view. A nearly full moon silvered the landscape as he strolled along the dead-end street to retrieve the rental; minutes later he maneuvered into the driveway, parking under the carport behind Tracy's Chevy hybrid.

He went back inside, closing and locking the doors. The sound of rattling pots and plates greeted him when he entered the kitchen. Tracy had changed out of her pantsuit and into a pair of pajama pants and an oversize tee. She'd also taken out her contact lenses and put on a pair of glasses, which reminded him of their mother. "Sit down, sis, and I'll finish cleaning the kitchen."

Tracy dried her hands on a towel, then sat on a stool at the cooking island. "Thanks. You just have to put the pots in the dishwasher."

Collier stood at the sink rinsing pots and serving pieces. "I like what you've done with the house." Tracy had added the half bath off the kitchen, modernized the kitchen with state-of-the-art appliances, updated the plumbing and electricity, installed ceiling fans in all of the rooms, and removed the worn carpeting and replaced it with gleaming oak floors. Even the exterior hadn't escaped the makeover with new siding and shutters, and she'd replaced the sagging porch floor.

"Once I made the decision to move back home after leaving Larry, I didn't want to be reminded of what Mom went through when Daddy got real sick." Tracy slipped off the stool. "I'm going to make coffee. Do you want some?"

"Sure," Collier said, plunging his hands into the sink filled with warm, soapy water.

He knew Tracy didn't like talking about their parents. Their deaths had impacted her much more than him because he hadn't been there to see the gradual changes in his father's physical appearance before he was finally admitted to the VA hospital. However, he did remember coming home on leave to find the kitchen sink filled with dirty dishes, unmade beds, and trash cans overflowing with garbage. When he broached the subject with his fastidious mother, she admitted cleaning her house was secondary to caring for her husband.

Garrett had become a mere shadow of himself before succumbing to the disease he'd contracted when exposed to

Agent Orange in Vietnam. Grief-stricken because she'd lost the man who'd been responsible for saving her life after the fall of Saigon, Nicole Ward refused to eat, and within three months she had lost half her body weight. Collier, approved for a second emergency personal leave, returned to Sanctuary Cove to bury his mother alongside her husband.

Tragedy had struck his family not once or twice, but three times when Tracy found herself in a legal entanglement with her estranged husband, who'd wanted full custody of Layla. Collier found a barracuda of a divorce attorney who exposed Layla's father's past arrest record and drug history, resulting in the judge's denying him custody. Larry waived his right for visitation and moved out of the state, but he continued to pay child support. Tracy sold her Charleston condo, moved back to Sanctuary Cove, and contacted a contractor to renovate the house where she'd grown up.

The distinctive aroma of brewing coffee wafted through the kitchen when Tracy asked, "What do you think of Iris?"

Collier's mouth curved into a smile. He didn't think his sister would want to hear what he actually thought of her sexy friend. "I think she's delightful."

Tracy gave him a sidelong glance. "Delightful? That's a word I've never heard you use before when describing a woman."

"That's because she's the only woman I've met who is as delightful as she is refreshingly beautiful."

"She's single."

Bending slightly, Collier rearranged several plates on the lower rack of the dishwasher to accommodate the pots. "What are you trying to say, sis?"

"I'm saying maybe you should ask her out while you're here."

He stood straight, his gaze boring into Tracy's. "Why

are you matchmaking?" There was a thread of hardness in his voice. He'd never had a problem meeting women and certainly didn't need his sister acting as a go-between.

Tracy pulled herself up to her full five-three height. "Don't get your nose out of joint, Collier. I'm only suggesting you ask her out because she's had a rough time with men."

"Rough how?"

"Her ex-husband was abusive. It started with emotional abuse, then progressed to physical. Iris said she tried to make a go of her marriage, but once he hit her she knew she had to get out before things got worse. And because she's not looking for anything long-term or a commitment, I thought you taking her out would help restore her trust in men. Come on, Collier," Tracy pleaded softly. "You're not going to be here long enough for the two of you to get *that* involved, and I know you'd never hurt her."

Collier didn't mind dating Iris if she was willing to go out with him, but the revelation that she'd been in an abusive relationship made him uneasy. Her glib response that she and her husband didn't see eye-to-eye on a lot of things so they'd ended it hadn't been an indicator that she was abused. Tragically, seeing him in the throes of one of his nightmares could elicit a flashback of what she'd experienced with her ex.

"I'll have to give it some thought," he said. He wanted to date Iris for the duration of his leave, yet his repeated violent flashbacks were certain to make even a short-term relationship problematic. And hurting her was not an option.

Chapter Four

CORN-BREAD STUFFING WITH SAUSAGE

- 1 pound ground sausage
- 2 cups chopped celery
- 2 large onions, chopped
- 5 cups crumbled corn bread
- 5 cups seasoned bread crumbs
- 2¾ cups chicken broth
- 1½ teaspoons poultry seasoning
- 1 teaspoon sage

Preheat the oven to 325°F. Place the sausage, celery, and onion in a large deep skillet. Cook over medium-high heat until evenly browned. Drain, crumble the sausage, and set aside. In a large bowl combine the sausage mixture with the corn bread, bread crumbs, chicken broth, poultry seasoning, and sage. Mix well and transfer to a 9 x 12-inch baking dish. Bake covered for 45 minutes or until well set and cooked through.

Collier detected movement at the top of the staircase and saw Iris standing in the doorway leading into her apartment. He moved off the top stair, angled his head, and brushed a light kiss over her lips. The kiss ended as quickly as it'd begun, her moist breath whispering over his jaw.

"Happy Thanksgiving, beautiful."

Collier hadn't lied when he called her beautiful. Her light makeup, short hair brushed back off her face, and the orange-and-black color-block dress that hugged every curve of her slim, toned body threatened to send his libido into overdrive. His gaze shifted lower to her bare legs and feet in a pair of snakeskin leather wedges in variegated colors of black, red, and orange.

"Happy Thanksgiving to you too," she said softly. "Please come in and I'll show you where to set up the table."

Collier bit down on his lower lip as he followed Iris across the living room to the dining area. *Damn*, he thought, *even her walk is sexy*. Iris's experience as a chef was on full display. Along one wall were three serving tables, which held a variety of warming trays. The delicious aromas coming from them made his mouth water. Plates were stacked at the end of one table, while the dining room table, covered with a lacy tablecloth, was set with crystal water goblets, wineglasses, silver place settings, and place cards bearing the names of her guests written in a flowery calligraphy.

A vase of bright autumn flowers and leaves in shades of red, orange, and yellow, in keeping with the holiday theme, doubled as the table's centerpiece.

"How early did you have to get up to do all of this?" he asked, pulling out the legs to the card table.

"Five. I get up at that time every morning because I start work at six. You can put it right over here." Iris pointed to a spot several feet from the dining area table.

He positioned the table in front of the window looking out onto Main Street. Collier and Iris looked at each other, then out the window when they heard a tapping sound against the glass. It was raining. Whereas most people complained about rain, Collier welcomed it because he'd spent too many years living and fighting in arid countries where daytime temperatures exceeded triple digits.

He reached for Iris's wrist, pulling her close. "I know we didn't meet the conventional way, but I'd like to start over."

She blinked. "How?"

His gaze lingered on her soft parted lips. "I'd like to ask you whether you'd consider going out with me."

Her eyebrows rose. "You mean dating?"

He smiled and nodded. "Yes. Dating."

It'd been much too long since she'd dated, and she needed to recapture the normalcy that should've been so much a part of a single, thirty-one-year-old woman's social life.

"Okay," she said after a pause. "But let's do this right. Tell me a bit about Scrappy. I want to know you better."

Collier's arms went around her waist and his eyes darkened with desire, gold flecks sparking. "Scrappy wasn't very nice. Collier is a much more interesting character."

Anchoring her arms under his shoulders, Iris leaned into

his hard body, enjoying his warmth through the crisp pale blue cotton shirt. "I'll let you know which one I like best."

Collier chuckled. "Please don't tell me you're into bad boys."

"Good guys are boring." She patted his back. "We can talk more about that after dinner."

Collier pressed his mouth along the column of her silken neck. "I've been called a lot of things, but never boring."

The sound of someone clearing their throat reached Iris and Collier at the same time, and they sprang apart like teenagers caught doing something wrong. Her mother and father stood in the doorway, their expressions speaking volumes. It was obvious they hadn't expected to see her in the arms of a man when she'd told her parents that she'd sworn off men for the rest of her life.

She approached her parents, kissing her mother and then her father. "Welcome." She didn't see her father glaring at Collier. "Mom, Dad, I want you to meet my friend." It was when she made the introductions that she noticed the twitching muscle in her father's jaw. She groaned inwardly. He'd become somewhat overprotective since her divorce.

Collier was the first to offer his hand. "It's nice meeting you, sir."

James, tall and still slender at the age of sixty-five, eyed the younger man with a narrow squint. He still wore his salt-and-pepper hair in a military cut. James grasped the proffered hand, holding it longer than necessary. "What is it you do, son?"

"Daddy!" Iris gasped.

James smiled at her. "It's all right, baby girl. The man doesn't have to answer if he doesn't want to."

Collier returned Iris's father's direct stare. "Right now I'm in the US Army."

James shook Collier's hand vigorously and then dropped an arm over his shoulder. "We need to talk, son. Baby girl, do have anything stronger than beer and wine in the house?"

Iris shared a knowing glance with her mother. Iris was a younger version of Esther Nelson. Her parents complimented each other when they claimed their son was a clone of his father and their daughter her mother.

"Dad, the liquor is in the cabinet under the buffet server."

Esther took off the jacket to her pantsuit and hung it on the wall coatrack near the door. "You know he's going to talk your young man's ear off."

Iris looped her arm through Esther's, ignoring the reference to Collier being her man. "Better Collier's ear than yours, Mom."

Esther smiled. "You're right about that. Where did you meet him?"

"He's my friend Tracy's brother."

"He's exotically gorgeous," the older woman whispered. Iris nodded in agreement. She'd discovered that the moment she turned to look at him at the Happy Hour. "You left the door open," her mother reminded her when Iris steered her in the direction of the kitchen.

"I'm still expecting Tracy and her daughter. By the way, where are Evan and Allie?"

"They were getting dressed as we were leaving." Esther shook her lightly graying hair. "I still can't get used to folks around here leaving their doors open or unlocked."

Iris gave her mother a reassuring smile. "I'm the only one who lives up here, so there's no reason for anyone to come unless they're invited. Don't forget, we left our doors unlocked when we lived on the base," she reminded Esther.

"That's different because the base is secure. I know you love living here, but I still worry about you, darling."

"Stop worrying, Mom. There's virtually no crime on Cavanaugh Island." Esther's expression indicated she didn't believe Iris.

"Iris is right, Mrs. Nelson. I grew up here, and there's never been a problem with feeling safe. Everyone looks out for one another."

Iris turned to find Collier standing only a few feet away. She had a brief moment of longing for him to be the one looking out for her before she chased the thought away. "See, I told you, Mom."

Esther smiled at Collier. "Well, that does make me feel better."

He returned her smile. "I'm glad."

Iris pressed her palms together. "We'll sit down to eat as soon as the others get here."

* * *

Iris felt as if Collier had become a part of a blended family when he joined her at the table. Dinner conversation was lively at the adult table, while Allie and Layla sat together, giggling nonstop. Evan kept everyone entertained with his wicked sense of humor and some of the more outlandish cases he saw at his veterinary practice. Layla, who'd changed her mind about sleeping over at Iris's house, begged Tracy to let Allie stay with them. Tracy, whom Iris suspected had taken a marked interest in Evan, said she didn't mind watching the two girls.

Everyone went back for more than one helping of her turkey and all the side dishes. They ate so much they decided to wait before eating dessert: sweet potato pie and a towering coconut layer cake.

It was after eight when Iris closed and locked the door

behind her dinner guests, all except Collier, who'd offered to stay to bring back the card table. Tracy and Esther had helped with the cleanup before she'd shooed them out of the kitchen to the spare bedroom that doubled as her family room. Collier lingered in the living room with James and Evan watching football games on the wall-mounted flat screen, while she joined the women in the family room where they'd watched *Frozen* and *Tangled* with Allie and Layla.

Collier dropped a kiss on her hair and undid the ties to her bibbed apron. "Go and get off your feet. I'll finish up here."

Tilting her head, Iris smiled up at him. "There's not much left to do."

Lowering his face to hers, he brushed a kiss over her mouth. "Whatever is left I can do it."

She affected a sexy moue. "You must like KP."

"I'm used to picking up after myself. But it seems as if we have something in common."

"What's that?"

"We're both a tad bit compulsive when it comes to everything being in its rightful place."

Supporting her hip against the countertop, Iris reached down and slipped out of her shoes. "I can't function or think when things are out of place. It's a habit I picked up while in college."

Rolling back the cuffs to his shirt, Collier ladled stuffing into a glass container, snapping the cover with a loud click. "I suppose old habits die hard."

Standing behind him, she wrapped her arms around his waist. "I can think of a lot worse habits. Speaking of clothes, I'm going to take a shower and change into something more comfortable."

He went still in her embrace, then relaxed. "Okay."

"Don't run away," she whispered.

Collier smiled at her over his shoulder. "I won't."

*   *   *

Iris lay beside Collier on the living room rug in front of the fireplace, holding hands and listening to slow jams while a driving rain slashed the windows. She felt more comfortable with him than she ever had with her ex-husband.

The buffet dinner was a rousing success, the Wards and Nelsons interacting as if they'd known one another for years. Iris had given the seating arrangement careful consideration when she put Tracy next to Evan, her mother and father at opposite ends of the table, and Collier on her left and her father's right.

"You and my father looked rather intense over predinner drinks," Iris said after a long, comfortable silence.

"We had a lot to talk about," Collier admitted.

"Really? Like what?"

"It's classified."

Iris lifted her head, looking down at him as he stared up at her. "You're kidding?"

Collier's impassive expression didn't change. "No, I'm not."

"It can't be classified if you discussed it with my father because he no longer has military security clearance."

"It doesn't matter, beautiful. It's still classified."

She gave him her best stink eye before sinking back to the rug. "Are you ready for coffee and more dessert?"

Collier snorted under his breath. "You must be mad, woman. How can you talk about food after all we ate for dinner?"

Iris stared up at the flickering shadows on the ceiling. "I guess you can say I am a little crazy to have picked up a stranger."

Turning to face Iris, Collier asked, "Do you regret it?"

"No! Never," Iris countered quickly. "It's just that I ask myself why now when I'd never done anything like that before."

"Sometimes we need to exorcise our demons, and the only way we can accomplish that is to do something that's totally out of character."

Collier was spot-on when he mentioned demons because her ex was an evil spirit masquerading as a moral, upright good guy. "Tracy was supposed to go to the club with me but had to bow out."

"I can't explain it, but I feel we were destined to meet."

"Are you saying we have a psychic connection?" Iris teased.

"I don't know about psychic. What are the odds I would walk into a club and pick up a woman who just happens to be my sister's best friend?"

"I don't have an answer to that," she admitted truthfully. Iris didn't question why certain people had come into her life when she needed them most and yet there were others she should've kept at a distance. When talking to her mother about this, Esther's comeback was for her to not be impulsive and to weigh her options before deciding whether someone or a situation would benefit her in the long run. She wished she'd listened to her mother before marrying a man so unworthy of her love and fidelity.

"What do you want, Iris?"

Letting go of his hand, she shifted to look directly at him. There was enough light coming from the hanging fixture in the dining area to make out his features. "Want for what?"

"Your future."

Propping her elbow on the floor, she rested her cheek against her fist. She smiled. "That's easy. I want to buy a house and turn a portion of it into an industrial kitchen for a cake-decorating business."

"You want to stay on Cavanaugh Island?" he asked.

She nodded. "Yes, but if that's not possible, then I'll probably consider moving to Charleston."

"You get the house, but what about a husband and maybe a couple of kids?"

A wry smile twisted her mouth. "I can't think that far ahead."

Collier shifted on his side. His calloused fingertips grazed her forehead as he leaned closer and pressed a kiss over each eye. "What did he do to you?"

Iris felt as if she'd just turned on a faucet that hadn't been used in years, letting the water flow until it turned from black to rust and finally clear when she told Collier about meeting high-profile DC litigator Derrick Harris and marrying him six months later. "Even though I wasn't a virgin, we made love for the first time on our wedding night."

Collier froze. "Is that something you both agreed to?"

She nodded. "He insisted on it because of his very strict Christian upbringing, and I had to respect that. But what should've been one of the most enjoyable nights of my life was essentially rape. No matter how much I screamed that he was hurting me, he refused to stop. The next day he pleaded with me to forgive him because he'd waited so long to make love to me that he'd gone temporarily insane.

"It was another month before we tried it again, and the result was the same. It was like he felt he needed to dominate me in and out of bed. That's when I moved into the spare bedroom and put a lock on the door. It was all about appearances when we were out in public together. No one would've ever suspected we weren't sleeping together. Soon Derrick began scrutinizing everything I wore. It couldn't be too tight or reveal too much skin, and most of the clothes in my closet were either navy blue or black. No reds because he didn't want people to think he'd married a harlot."

She told Collier that the only time she felt totally free was at the Baltimore high school where she taught art to a small group of very talented students. She hated coming home where her overcritical husband complained that he'd married the wrong woman because she refused to measure up to his standards, and whenever she talked about divorcing him, he threatened to ruin her life so she'd never teach again.

"There were times when I'd asked myself what I could have done to make my marriage work, but in the end I realized I could never become his ideal. I wanted so much to confide in a few of my colleagues, but I knew they wouldn't understand. They kept telling me they were jealous because I'd managed to snag one of the Beltway's most eligible bachelors. If they'd known the hell I was going through, their jealousy would've turned to pity.

"We'd just celebrated our first anniversary when his mother asked when I was going to make her a grandmother. I told her never, and then she went into a rant that my role as a wife was to submit to my husband and give him children. I was past being polite and respectful when I told her if she wanted grandchildren, then she should've taught her boy that rape isn't the same as lovemaking.

"Later that night, I found myself completely blindsided when he came home earlier than usual and sucker punched me, breaking my nose and fracturing my left cheek. He started to strangle me, but I managed to escape and make it to my bedroom where I locked the door and called the police. By the time they got there, he was gone. They took me to the hospital where I contacted my father and told him what had happened. I don't know how Daddy got from Fort Benning, Georgia, to Baltimore so quickly, but when he saw my face, he swore he was going to kill Derrick. Once he calmed down he asked if I was going to file charges for spousal battery."

Sitting up and cradling her face in his hands, Collier asked, "Did you?"

"No. All I wanted was my freedom and my name. I hired a prominent divorce attorney, telling her everything about my wedding night, the subsequent rape, and the assault. Even though I didn't report the assault to the police, hospital records documented what had taken place. I was granted an annulment and a significant settlement if I swore never to disclose the details of our marriage because Derrick had decided to go into politics.

"The money allowed me to start over when I applied to the Art Institute of Raleigh-Durham for culinary arts. After graduating, I got a position with a popular Charlotte restaurant chain, but I left four months later because the executive chef verbally abused his staff. Once again I loaded up my car and hit the road. After a while I knew I had to stop running, realizing my inability to stay in one place for any extended period of time stemmed from moving from base to base as a child.

"That's when I stopped in Charleston. I spent a week there touring the Sea Islands. Then one day I took the ferry to Cavanaugh Island. It had to be karma when I saw the HELP WANTED sign advertising for a pastry chef at the Muffin Corner. Lester said he would hire me on the spot if I could make three fondant leaves, flowers, and hearts, unaware I'd excelled in cake decorating. He kept his word and hired me. I lived at the Cove Inn for two months before this apartment became available." She exhaled an audible sigh. "So now you know all of the sordid details of my short-lived marriage and why I hadn't slept with a man in years."

Collier brushed his mouth over hers. "Didn't you realize he was the sick one, not you?"

"Sick or not, I blamed myself for not leaving him the first time he raped me; I'd stayed too long and if he hadn't hit me, I probably would still be married to the sicko. I know inviting you to my place was risky, but somehow I felt safe with you. And if you'd turned out to be crazy, all I had to do was tell Sheriff Hamilton that Scrappy did it."

Collier laughed loudly. "Damn. Poor Scrappy can't seem to catch a break."

Her laughter joined his. "But didn't you tell me Scrappy has been redeemed?"

"Yes." His smile vanished, his expression becoming a mask of stone. "But unlike your ex-husband, Scrappy would never hit a woman. My father taught me real men don't hit or abuse women, and that's something I've never forgotten."

Iris felt Collier withdraw from her, although he hadn't moved. She'd just bared her soul and now she needed him to do likewise. "What do you want for your future, Collier?"

The popping sound and the shower of burning embers flared behind the fireplace screen, temporarily garnering Collier's attention. He still couldn't believe Iris's ex-husband had raped her; that despite everything she still hadn't fallen apart. He stood up, reaching down and bringing her up to stand.

"Come dance with me."

Iris wrapped her arms around his waist. She recognized the song. Brenda Russell's "Piano in the Dark."

The smile parting Collier's lips slipped into a wide grin

as he spun Iris around and around in an intricate dance step. "You smell good enough to eat."

Iris leaned back, her grin matching his. "Didn't you just say you'd eaten too much?"

They continued to dance without moving their feet. He pressed his mouth to her ear. "I left a little room so that I can taste you." It took a full minute before Iris caught his meaning. "Did I embarrass you?"

"Of course not," she said quickly. "You didn't answer my question."

Collier groaned inwardly. Now he knew why Tracy and Iris were such good friends. Both were unyielding when they wanted something. He couldn't have been more explicit; he wanted to make love to her and she wanted to know about his future. "I want to give the military two more years before hanging up my uniform."

"What do you plan to do after that?"

Collier stared down at her. "I have a few options. I have a one-third share in Happy Hour, but I'd rather remain a silent partner. I'm thinking about buying the auto body shop in the Cove. The owner's looking to retire in a couple of years."

"You want to become a mechanic?" Iris questioned.

Collier thought he detected a note of incredulity in her question. Did she believe dating a mechanic was beneath her social station? After all, her father had graduated from West Point, her mother was an aspiring artist, and her brother a veterinarian.

After enlisting, he'd taken advantage of many of the incentives and benefits the Army offered, and one was earning a college degree, something his mother had always wanted for her children. "Yes. I can take apart and put a car's engine back together, but I prefer restoring classic cars."

"Like *Classic Car Restoration*?"

He nodded. She'd mentioned the reality TV show that had become one of his favorites. "Yes. My father had '64 and '68 Mustangs, and I filled in as his apprentice when he restored them to mint condition."

"Did he sell them?"

"He sold the '68 but wouldn't part with the '64. It was one of the first to come off the assembly line during its inaugural year. It's parked in the garage behind the house. As soon as I check it out, I'll take you for a drive."

Cradling her face in his hands, Collier's tongue traced the fullness of her lower lip. "It's getting late and you need your sleep, so I'm going to head on home."

He'd mentioned going home when it was the last thing he wanted. Sharing Thanksgiving dinner with his sister, niece, and Iris's family had made this homecoming even more momentous. If he stayed over tonight, he'd never hear the end of it from Tracy. The last thing he wanted was for his sister to believe he was taking advantage of her friend's vulnerability.

"Do you have an extra set of keys?" he asked Iris.

Her forehead furrowed in confusion. "Yes. Why?"

"I want to come over tomorrow morning to make breakfast. Afterward you're going back to bed where I'm going to give you the extra-special Ward full-body massage to help relax you."

Her eyes grew wide. "But my folks are coming over?"

"James told me they're not coming until six, so don't try to wiggle out of my wanting to take care of you." Collier kissed her forehead. "Remember, we're not going to have a lot of time to be together, so what do you say? Yes or no?"

When Collier walked into the apartment earlier that afternoon asking to date her, Iris had felt as if she'd been enveloped in a cocoon with a happiness expiration date stamped on the outside. Collier would be around for another couple of weeks and then he'd be gone. And yet, here he was, offering her a chance at...She didn't want to say love, because falling in love with him wasn't an option. But trust perhaps. If nothing else, maybe Collier could finally teach her to trust a man without looking for an ulterior motive in his interest.

"Wait here," she told him.

Iris went into her bedroom and retrieved a second set of keys to the apartment, knowing her life was about to change. She planned to give a man the keys to her sanctuary.

Returning to the living room, Iris reached for Collier's hand, placed the keys in his palm, and closed his fingers over them. "Yes." Going up on tiptoe, she kissed his cheek. "Good night, and thanks for making this Thanksgiving one I'll remember for a very long time."

Collier ran a finger down her nose. "Good night, babe. Sleep well."

Chapter Five

GULLAH-STYLE GRITS

- 4 cups water
- 1 tablespoon salt
- ¼ cup butter or margarine
- 1 cup old-fashioned grits (not instant)

Bring the water to a boil in a heavy pot. Add the salt
and butter. Once the water is hot, add 1 cup cleaned and
rinsed grits. Cook and stir for about 10 minutes until
creamy. Cover and let the grits bubble for 20 minutes on
medium heat.

SAUSAGE GRAVY

- 6–7 sausage patties
- ¼ teaspoon salt
- ¼ teaspoon ground black pepper
- ¼ teaspoon sage
- 1 cup self-rising flour
- 1 cup milk

Place the sausage patties in a cast-iron skillet and use a wooden spoon to crumble them as they cook. Turn heat to medium-low. Stir until the sausage cooks through and drippings appear. Add the seasonings. Add the self-rising flour. Mix well until there is no dry flour or lumps left. Pour the milk into the skillet and continue to stir until the mixture reaches the desired texture.

Collier walked into the kitchen, stopping short when he saw Tracy sitting at the breakfast nook, sipping coffee while flipping the pages of a magazine. He thought she would've slept in because schools were closed.

Her head came around when he moved closer. "What are you doing up so early?" she asked, smiling.

Reaching into an overhead cabinet, Collier took down a coffee mug. "I could ask you the same thing." He filled the mug with coffee from the carafe on the countertop.

Tracy pushed several twists off her forehead, her eyes narrowing behind the lenses of her glasses. "You know I'm a creature of habit. I tried to force myself to stay in bed, but once the sun came up, I decided to get up."

Slipping onto the bench seat opposite his sister, Collier peered at her over the rim of the mug. "The girls were still up giggling when I got in last night," he said, then took a sip of the steaming brew. "What's up with girls that they have to giggle so much?"

"You'll know the answer once you have a daughter. And don't look at me like that, *Scrappy*, because I ain't scared of you."

Collier struggled not to laugh. "You just can't let Scrappy rest in peace, can you?"

Tracy stuck out the tip of her tongue at him. "Nope, because underneath the spit shine and polish, Master Sergeant Ward, you'll always be Scrappy." She paused. "What time did you get in last night?"

He lifted broad shoulders under his faded sweatshirt. "It wasn't late, maybe around ten."

"Did you ask Iris if she would go out with you?"

"What's this, sis? An inquisition?"

She pushed up the glasses that had slipped down the bridge of her nose. "No."

Collier drained the mug, rinsed it, and placed it in the dishwasher. Then he walked to Tracy, leaned down, and kissed her hair. "Yes, I did ask her," he whispered. "And she said she would." He stood up straight. "I'm going out."

"Where are you going?" Tracy asked, grinning.

Turning on the heels of his running shoes, Collier waved to her as he walked out of the kitchen. "See you later, Tracy," he drawled. He didn't need her monitoring his whereabouts. But then he had to remember that Tracy was always in mother mode and a tad overprotective when it came to him and Layla. If he'd managed to survive serving in two war zones, then he had nothing to worry about while on his home turf.

Opening the front door, he stepped out onto the porch. The rain had stopped and the warmth had returned. Minutes later he backed the rental out of the driveway, heading for the business district. Collier slowed when he spied the banner hanging from lampposts as he maneuvered onto Main Street: WELCOME HOME, M.SGT. COLLIER WARD.

"Damn," he swore under his breath. His name and rank were strung across the street among the colorful Christmas decorations. He knew it would be only a matter of time before everyone in the Cove knew he was back. Cavanaugh Islanders had always loved traditions and honoring those who'd served in the military, beginning with the Revolutionary War and up through the war in Afghanistan.

There was another sign advertising caroling and sleigh rides for children under ten. New York City had its Macy's Thanksgiving Day Parade, Philadelphia their Mummers Parade, and for Sanctuary Cove it was a Winter Wonderland Festival held the weekend before Christmas. It began at five in the evening and ended at midnight, weather permitting. The festival brought out locals and tourists alike.

The merchants belonging to the chamber of commerce went all out when they hired a company to spray fake snow on the streets and sidewalks. Vehicular traffic was replaced with horse-drawn sleighs, and vendors lined the sidewalks selling carnival-type foods; the carnival rides were the only thing missing.

The single event to eclipse the post-Thanksgiving celebration was the summer island-wide celebration, which began July 1 and ended with a spectacular fireworks show at midnight on the Fourth of July. The carnival-like events included amusement park rides, picnics, and fun and games for all ages. Even when he'd attended military school,

Collier always returned home for Thanksgiving and the Cove's Winter Wonderland Festival weekends.

He'd missed the past three celebrations, but this year he looked forward to sharing it with Tracy, Layla, and Iris. The clock over the bank read seven o'clock, and with the exception of the supermarket and the Muffin Corner, none of the other stores were open for business.

Collier had traveled the world, and still he felt more at home on an island where everyone knew everyone and their business. He maneuvered into the parking lot between Jack's Fish House and the variety store and walked the short distance to the rear of A Tisket A Basket.

Unlocking the door to Iris's apartment, he recalled the conversation he'd had with her father. James had asked if he was aware of what his daughter had gone through with her ex-husband. Collier was forthcoming when he repeated what Tracy had told him, but at that time he hadn't known the full extent of the abuse. That's when the retired colonel told him in no uncertain terms that he would willingly spend the rest of his life in jail for killing the next man who hurt his daughter.

Collier hadn't blinked an eye when he told James he'd walk away from Iris before hurting her. She'd suffered enough. However, Collier suspected Iris didn't know her own emotional strength. She'd survived and started over with a new career, new friends, and a place she could call home.

He opened the door, encountering silence, and left his running shoes on the mat. Helping to put away leftovers had afforded Collier a glimpse of the contents of Iris's well-stocked refrigerator. He planned to prepare a traditional Gullah breakfast with grits, scrambled eggs, and sausage gravy.

Collier had grown up eating Asian-fusion and Lowcountry

cuisine. However, it was the Gullah dishes he favored most. His paternal grandmother had taught all her sons to cook the dishes indigenous to the region, and Garrett in turn taught his wife. His parents would occasionally compete to see who made a particular dish the best. His father usually won, because his wife invariably included an Asian spice, which subtly changed the flavor.

Making his way to the kitchen, he heard singing coming from the bathroom. Slowing, he peered inside to find Iris in the shower, singing loudly. Collier could make out the outline of her body through the frosted glass, and it took all his willpower not to strip naked and join her.

Without warning, the singing stopped and the door to the shower opened, Iris stepping out onto a mat, dripping wet. She didn't notice him standing there like a deer caught in the headlights until she reached for the towel from a stack on a low bench. With wide eyes, she watched his approach. Collier took in everything about her in one sweeping glance: firm breasts perched high above a narrow waist; a flat belly; firm, slender thighs and legs. Moisture shimmered on her hair and face, turning her into a bronze statue.

The quiet storm beginning in his groin roared to life so quickly Collier had to grit his teeth to keep from moaning. If only he'd come ten minutes later, he wouldn't have caught Iris naked.

He heard a sound, then realized he was gasping in order to catch his breath. "Oh, sweet heaven," he moaned aloud. Collier stood inches away from Iris, their gazes meeting and fusing. "Iris?"

She closed her eyes against his intense stare. "What is it, Collier?"

"Can we do this?"

She opened her eyes, nodding and smiling. "Yes, we can."

With a body like that, with the look of shocked desire in her eyes, he had no choice but to sweep her into his arms and carry her to the bedroom. It took mere seconds to muss her neatly made bed and shuck off his jeans and T-shirt. Reaching into his pocket, he took out a condom and placed it on the nightstand.

Collier got into bed and turned Iris on her belly. Resting his hands on her shoulders, he lowered his head and trailed a series of kisses beginning with the nape of her neck and down her spine to her buttocks. He heard her breathing quicken at the same time a tremor swept over her body.

Collier wanted to be inside her, but he also wanted foreplay. His mouth and tongue tasted every inch of her damp skin, and then he repeated his exploration when he turned her over to face him. Resting his hands on her shoulders, he massaged the muscles there before giving her neck and scalp the same attention, smiling when she let out a soft moan. His hands charted a course down her body to her hips, thighs, legs, and feet, then reversed direction.

"I did promise to give you a massage," he whispered in her ear.

"That feels so good," Iris gasped when his fingers gently kneaded her shoulders.

Collier brushed a light kiss over her parted lips. "Let me know if I'm hurting you."

A dreamy expression crossed her features. "It's perfect."

He kissed her neck, then moved lower across her breasts and down her ribs to her stomach and lower.

Soon he was inside her, and together they found a rhythm that quickened, slowed, and increased again as shivers of giddy desire and ecstasy turned into explosive currents shaking them from head to toe as they climaxed at the same time.

Collier's weight was a welcome comfort when he collapsed on top of her. She felt a distinct sense of loss when he withdrew to take care of the condom. She languished in a cocoon of completeness she hadn't known possible. And for the first time in her life, she had experienced the full range of her femininity. Waiting for a man like Collier to make love to her had been more than worth it. He had taken her to a place of exquisite sexual ecstasy that she'd never experienced.

She smiled up at Collier when he returned to the bed. Her Mr. Last Night had become her Mr. Right Now, and she looked forward to enjoying every moment they would spend together until it was time for him to return to North Carolina.

He slid between the covers, smiling, and stared deeply into her eyes.

"Good morning." His voice still rumbled with a promise of even more pleasure.

"Good morning. It seems we can't keep our hands off each other," she said with a smile.

"What's wrong with that?" he asked.

"What happened to dating?" she countered. "I know you only have a few weeks here, but last night you said you wanted to 'do things right.'"

"Is it so wrong that I find you completely irresistible?"

Iris dug her fingernails into his back. "Collier, I'm serious."

"Okay, babe. I'm sorry." He pressed his forehead to hers. "Do you like going to the movies?" She nodded. "How about a dinner date?" Iris nodded again. "Then there's the Winter Wonderland Festival. Will you go with me?"

"Yes."

"Are you willing to go back to Happy Hour for date night or Sunday brunch?"

Her smile was dazzling. "Yes and yes."

Collier winked at her. "I guess that takes care of the few things we can do in your spare time."

Iris traced his eyebrows with the tip of her finger. "Starting Tuesday, I'm not going to have a lot of spare time until the end of the year. Christmas is the busiest time of the year for the Muffin Corner. If we're not filling orders for the locals, then it's corporate gifts. Last year I lost count of the number of trays of cookies and gingerbread houses we shipped overnight to customers as far away as Connecticut. I'd come home every afternoon and collapse, sometimes not waking up until the next morning."

"I think I can help you out."

"How?"

"Now that I'm home, you don't have to come over and wait for Layla's school bus. I can also start dinner for Tracy and make certain Layla does her homework. So if you want to come home and go to sleep, you can without having to get up for Layla. If you don't mind, I'll come by every night and check on you."

Iris snuggled closer to Collier. "I don't mind, and thank you, sweetie."

"Am I really your sweetie?" he teased.

"Only if you want to be."

Collier knew Iris had put him on the spot as to their budding relationship. They were lovers poised to become friends. "I do." He wanted to be her sweetie, lover, friend, and more. But he didn't want to acknowledge what the *more* was. "Are you ready for breakfast?"

Iris covered a yawn with her hand. "I will be after I take another shower."

Collier cupped the back of her head, his fingers massaging her scalp. "That makes two of us. We'll shower together."

She looked up at him through her lashes. "What's on the menu?"

"Grits, scrambled eggs, and sausage gravy."

"Yum! Where did you learn to cook?"

"My parents taught me. Mom made Vietnamese dishes, and Dad cooked good old Southern food."

"How did your parents meet?" Iris asked.

Collier was about to reveal things to Iris about his parents he'd never told a woman. "My father met my mother when serving as a Green Beret during the Vietnam War. Born Nga Minh Nguyen, Mom changed her name to Nicole after becoming an American citizen. She was the illegitimate daughter of a Vietnamese mother and a French businessman. As a teenager, she was recruited to spy on the Americans for the Vietcong, and when captured by a team of Green Berets, she became a double agent after the Americans promised to take her to the United States once the war ended.

"A few days before the fall of Saigon, the North Vietnamese discovered she'd collaborated with the enemy and she was scheduled to be executed along with a number of other defectors. Dad disobeyed orders, risked being court-martialed, and went to look for her. He found her in a Vietcong prison camp. She was one of the last South Vietnamese refugees to be airlifted to safety ahead of the advancing army. It took almost a year before they reunited and eventually married. Mom taught Tracy and me to speak French and her native dialect. After that, learning a new language came very easily for me."

"What other languages do you speak?"

"Arabic, Pashto, and Farsi. Pashto is spoken in Afghanistan and Farsi in Iran."

Iris rested her head on his shoulder. "Have you ever thought about becoming a foreign language teacher or an interpreter for a government agency?"

"No, babe. I've had enough of bureaucrats. If I'm going to work for the next twenty years, then it's going to be for myself."

Sitting up, he swung his legs over the side of the bed. In telling Iris about his parents, Collier had stripped off a layer of his protective shield he'd hidden from those with whom he didn't share blood ties. He and Tracy never told any of their friends their mother had been a spy in fear of reprisals from both Americans and Vietnamese. Nga Minh had languished in a federal prison for a year before her activities were verified, proving that her spying for the Americans had saved thousands of lives.

He extended his hand to Iris. "Are you coming, babe?"

She crawled off the bed and together they made their way into the bathroom. Under the spray of the shower, they indulged in one more round of lovemaking, then cleaned up and got dressed. Forty-five minutes later, they sat in the dining room to eat a traditional Lowcountry breakfast.

It was early afternoon when Collier parked his car on the street in front of the house on Coosaw Court. Tracy's car was missing, and in its place was a Mercedes-Benz with Florida plates. Evan had probably come by, and he and Tracy had taken their daughters with them.

Spending the morning with Iris was akin to entering an alternative universe where everything was perfection. Having sex with her, preparing breakfast and sharing it with her, and their lounging in the family room watching movies had become the antidote to the horrors of war he'd witnessed that continued to lurk along the fringes of his mind whenever he relaxed enough to fall asleep. Collier had come to look for her spontaneity and openness to talk about anything. She was real, and in turn he kept it real.

Standing in front of the house, crossing his arms over his

chest, Collier stared up at the house with so many good and a few not-so-good memories. His gaze shifted to the other houses in the cul-de-sac, many decorated with wreaths and lights. He exhaled a breath. It was time to get the box of decorations out of the storeroom and put them up.

After finding the supplies he needed, Collier stood on the ladder, stringing solar lights along the top edge of the porch. The sound of tires on the graveled driveway caught his attention above the shrieks and screaming of a group of young boys playing football in the street.

Descending the ladder, he waited for the driver of the Jeep to alight and mount the porch steps before walking over to greet him. He extended his hand, smiling. "I thought I'd snuck back undetected, but it's apparent I couldn't avoid the sharp eye of the law."

Cavanaugh Island sheriff Jeffrey Hamilton took the proffered hand and then pulled Collier close in a rough embrace. "I didn't know you had until I saw the sign the guys at the American Legion put up across Main Street," he admitted. "Welcome home, Scrappy."

Collier nodded. "Thanks, Jeff. What's going on with you?"

"I just got off duty, and I promised your sister I would stop by every once in a while to check on Layla and Iris."

He stared at the retired US Marine captain who'd returned to Sanctuary Cove to take care of his grandmother and had subsequently taken over as sheriff of the entire island. Collier had always looked up to Jeff, four years his senior, whose high school record of sacking opposing teams' quarterbacks still stood after more than twenty years. Tall and muscular, with deep-set dark eyes in an equally dark face, the lawman had been a much sought-after bachelor until he married Kara Newell, heir to the Angels Landing Plantation. The largest parcel of privately owned property on the island had given the town its name, and the historic landmark house and land were currently undergoing a complete restoration.

"Thanks, man. My sister is blessed to have so many folks looking out for her."

Jeff crossed his arms over a black waffle-weave sweater. "Even though Iris is a relative newcomer, she's fit in quite well here."

"Layla really likes her."

Jeff grunted softly. "Layla isn't her only admirer. Since she started working at the Muffin Corner, their business has doubled. And most of the customers are men who would do anything to get her attention."

Collier didn't physically react to this disclosure. "Is she biting?" he asked.

A grin spread over the sheriff's face. "Much to their disappointment, she acts as if they don't exist."

Collier had to work to conceal his satisfaction. "Hmm, I wonder why?" he lied smoothly.

"Are you on leave or back for good?"

Collier's head popped up, meeting the sheriff's intense gaze. "I'm on leave until after Christmas."

"How many more years do you have before you put in your papers?"

He exhaled an audible breath. "Two."

"No more combat?"

"I'm done fighting," Collier said wistfully. He couldn't handle any more roadside bombs, sniper fire, or suicide bombers, though he was still fighting his own personal war with the recurring nightmares.

"Good for you," Jeff countered before pushing his baseball cap off his forehead. "How old are you now? Thirty-five or thirty-six?"

"Thirty-six. Why?"

Leaning against a column of the porch, the sheriff stared at the late-blooming yellow roses climbing the trellis on the opposite end of the porch. "You'll be thirty-eight when you get out and still young enough to start a family of your own and have a second career."

Collier nodded. "Are you and your family planning anything special for Christmas?"

"Kara's folks are coming in from Little Rock on Christmas Eve, and they plan to stay until just after New Year's. What about you?"

"I overheard Tracy and Iris talking about doing something together here or at Iris's place."

"Either way, you guys are welcome to come by and hang out awhile."

"I'll definitely think about it. It's been too long since I've seen Miss Corrine." Jeff's grandmother had been his second-, third-, and fifth-grade teacher before she became principal of the Cove's elementary and middle school.

Jeff adjusted his cap, pulling it lower. "Enough talk. I'm going on home now." Reaching over, he patted Collier's shoulder. "See you around, Sergeant."

"Copy that, Captain."

Collier waited until Jeff drove away and then sank down to the top step, hands sandwiched between denim-covered knees. First Tracy and now Jeff. It was as if everyone wanted to see him married with children. What was so wrong with being single? Resting his head against the post holding up the porch, he closed his eyes. Spending time with his sister and niece, not to mention Iris, had him wanting to stick around and perhaps start a family of his own once his tour of duty ended. He planned to make Sanctuary Cove home and he was serious about buying out the owner of the auto body shop, but there was still his uncertainty about Iris.

He liked her, but they weren't ready for marriage. And even if he were to fall in love with her, there was the possibility she would never agree to marriage after everything she'd been through.

Collier ran a hand over his face. Life had just thrown him a vicious curve. He'd met a woman with whom he could bare his soul and possibly share a future, and she wanted no part of it. And each passing day brought him closer to the time when he would have to leave her and return to his base.

Collier opened his eyes and stood up. Brooding about his budding relationship wasn't going to help anything. Instead, he focused on finishing the Christmas decorations before Tracy and Layla returned home.

*   *   *

Iris answered her cell phone when she recognized Tracy's ringtone. "Hey, stranger." It'd been a couple of weeks since Thanksgiving when she'd last seen her friend, and now Christmas was only two weeks away.

"Yeah, right. I know you've been busy, but you could've sent your BFF a text telling me you're okay instead of me having to hear it from my brother."

"I'm okay, Mama."

Tracy's laugh came through the earpiece. "I miss seeing you when I come home after classes. I love my brother to death, but I can't talk to him about certain things."

"Like what?"

"Like Evan inviting me and Layla to come to Florida over the Christmas break. I've promised Layla I would take her to Disney World if she kept her grades up, but Gainesville isn't Orlando."

"Do you like Evan enough to spend a week with him?" Iris asked her friend.

"Of course I do."

"Then trust him not to put you in a compromising position. I can assure you he has enough space in his house where you and Layla can sleep in one wing and he and Allie in the other. And then there's Evan's eagle-eyed, overprotective live-in housekeeper who'll make certain your virtue will remain intact."

"Now you sound like a character from a Regency novel. What you don't understand is that I'm tired of being virtuous, Iris. I'm ready for my Mr. Right Now, but I don't want to use your brother like that."

Iris closed her eyes and counted to five. "Are you calling me to get my approval to sleep with my brother? Because if you are, then you have it, Tracy. Evan's a grown man and you're a grown-ass woman who doesn't need anyone's permission or approval to sleep with whomever she wants. Now, I'm going to end this call because I don't want to be late for my date with *your* brother, who I just might sleep with tonight. Good night, my friend."

She took a quick glance at her watch, remembering she'd told Collier she would meet him downstairs in front of the sweetgrass shop at six thirty. It was to become their first official date because of her hectic work schedule.

They were going to see *The Best Man Holiday*, a comedy-drama plot spanning the Christmas holidays, which coincided with the current holiday season. It didn't matter to Iris that the Cove's single-screen theater showed movies three to six months behind the first-run feature films on the mainland. She preferred viewing movies in the small theater. Putting on a jacket, she left the apartment.

With Thanksgiving behind her and Christmas quickly

approaching, time was a luxury she could ill afford to squander. The shop was so busy Mabel asked if she would work weekends and come in on Mondays when the shop was closed to keep up with the mail orders. Iris couldn't refuse her now that Lester had reduced his work hours to half days. This left Iris with just one day, Sunday, during which she would go to church, clean her apartment, do laundry, and unwind. Usually she attended the eleven o'clock church service with Tracy and Layla, but this time she opted for the eight o'clock service to get a jump on all she had to accomplish in one day. After a lot of thought, she'd also decided to accept Mabel's offer to go into a partnership with her and Lester. She could hardly believe she was going to have her own specialty cake business in the adjoining shop.

As promised, Collier came over every night to check on her. He made no attempt to initiate having sex, preferring instead to cuddle with her either in bed or on the daybed in the family room. They talked at length about the countries and cities in which they'd lived or visited, while discovering both were partial to music from the sixties, seventies, and eighties. Collier had insisted they share one dance before leaving, and while Iris knew her feelings for Collier were intensifying, it took herculean strength for her not to beg him to spend the night.

"Are you looking for someone, gorgeous?"

Iris jumped as if she'd stuck her finger into an electrical outlet. Collier had come up behind her without making a sound. "You can't sneak up on me like that."

Collier took her hand, tucking it into the bend of his elbow. "I'm sorry, *sweetie*," he apologized in falsetto.

Iris couldn't help but laugh, although the situation wasn't funny. If she'd had a weak heart, there was no doubt she would've had an episode. However, Collier's ability to mimic her and others was uncanny. "Very funny, Mr. Mynah Bird."

"Can mynah birds really mimic the human voice?"

"Yes, they can. I knew someone in Hawaii who had one, and I didn't believe it until I heard it for myself."

She moved closer to Collier when she saw a group of rowdy boys coming in their direction, trading punches and cursing one another.

Collier eased her closer to the storefronts lining Main Street as the boys sauntered down the sidewalk as if they owned it, three abreast. "They look like trouble," Iris said in a quiet tone.

"They're probably kids from the mainland," Collier replied. "If they're looking for trouble, then they've come to the wrong place tonight. I saw Jeff and one of his deputies with two kids who looked like they were high on something. They couldn't have come from here because everyone knows there's zero tolerance for any type of substance abuse on Cavanaugh Island."

Iris shook her head. "If they get locked up, then somebody's mama or daddy is going to be real pissed tonight."

"Word," Collier drawled.

It was a Friday night, and all or most of the stores were open later than normal for holiday shopping; the business district was teeming with people intent on making purchases and those who were more than content to browse.

Two vehicles with the capability of making snow were parked on either side of the wide cobblestone street despite the NO PARKING signs. In less than twelve hours, Sanctuary Cove would resemble a winter wonderland landscape with sparkling Christmas lights and Hollywood-created fake snow. It'd been awhile since Collier saw or felt snow, even of the fake variety, because it rarely snowed in the desert.

"Do you think they'll run out of tickets?" Iris asked when seeing the line outside the theater.

"It doesn't matter. I stopped and bought two tickets earlier."

She smiled up at him. "I think I'm going to keep you."

Collier's eyes widened. "Were you thinking of leaving me?"

Iris fell silent. She didn't want to remind Collier that he would be the one leaving her, not the other way around. "No."

He patted her hand. "Good." Collier held open the door to the theater, handing their tickets to the usher. The aroma of freshly popped popcorn filled the lobby. "Do you want anything?"

"I'll have a small bag of popcorn."

Collier rested a hand at the small of Iris's back as they neared the concession counter. "Why don't I get a small bucket, and then we can share it."

"Sure."

"Butter?"

Iris smiled. "Of course." She stood off to the side to make room for others ordering candy, buffalo wings, hot dogs, crab cakes, popcorn, pizza, and soda. Ticket prices were discounted, while the food at the concessions was slightly higher than comparable items sold in mainland movie theaters.

She watched as two women, wearing knitted hats and ski jackets over black leggings, practically jumped Collier, holding him captive as he struggled to extricate himself. Iris shook her head. Even when she seduced him at Happy Hour, it'd been with words, not action.

"Oooh, Collier," the shorter one squealed. "I heard you were back. How long are you staying?"

Collier drew back when she rested her hands on his cheeks. "Not long."

"I heard you were in Iraq. It must have been awful for you."

Iris contemplated whether she would have to rescue Collier, but he preempted her notion when he managed to free one of his arms and pointed in her direction. Smiling, she blew him an air-kiss; the crestfallen expressions on the faces of the women were priceless.

She recognized both women as Muffin Corner customers. "Hello, ladies." One was a librarian and the other a teller at the local bank. Her facetiousness was lost on them when they returned her saccharine-sweet smile with friendly ones. Approaching Collier, Iris put her arm around his waist. "I'll help you carry something, *darling*." The endearment prompted the women to move to the opposite end of the counter.

Collier kissed her ear. "You know gossip about us will be all over the island before the sun comes up tomorrow."

"You think?" she joked.

Lowering his head, Collier brushed a kiss over her parted lips. "And frankly, my dear, I don't give a damn."

Iris took delight in their brief shared moment, his pronouncement echoing what lay in her heart. She didn't give a damn either, because she was falling in love with Collier Ward.

After the movie ended, Collier and Iris left the theater, and instead of heading home, they sat in the town square along with a number of other couples. It was as if no one wanted to go home despite the hour and the mercury hovering around freezing. The lights, decorations, and traditional Christmas music flowing from speakers attached to poles proved infectious when several older couples in the square sang along, their voices blending harmoniously.

Iris and Collier applauded with the small crowd that had gathered to listen. They sang several more songs, including her favorite, "O Holy Night," took their bows amid thunderous applause, and left.

"Aren't you cold?" Iris asked Collier.

Everyone wore winter jackets while he'd forgone a jacket for a long-sleeved tee and a ski sweater. "Nah. I'm used to desert temperatures going from over a hundred during the day to freezing at night."

Iris huddled closer to his side. "I don't know about you, but I'm freezing."

He stood up, extending his hand and bringing her up with him. "Come on, darling. I'll take you home and warm you up real nice."

Chapter Six

RUM PUNCH

- 3 cups water
- 1 pint passion fruit sorbet, melted
- 1 (12-ounce) can frozen orange juice concentrate, thawed
- 1 (12-ounce) can frozen pineapple juice concentrate, thawed
- 1¼ cups white rum
- ¾ cup golden rum
- ¼ cup plus 2 tablespoons grenadine
- 3 tablespoons fresh lime juice
- ½ teaspoon freshly grated nutmeg

In a large punch bowl or pitcher, combine the water with the sorbet, orange and pineapple juice concentrates, white and golden rums, grenadine, lime juice, and nutmeg. Fill tall glasses with ice, pour in the punch, and serve.

Collier unlocked the door, standing aside as Iris walked into the welcoming heat. "This is what I'm talking about," she crooned. She'd turned on the heat before she left because she loathed walking into a cold house. Living in the Lowcountry had spoiled her; she'd gotten used to not having to drive in snow or navigate ice and slush.

Turning, she smiled at Collier. "I'm going to brew some tea. Would you like a cup?"

"If it's not too much trouble, I prefer coffee."

She took off her jacket and left it on a chair in the living room. "You can make the coffee, while I put on water for tea. I didn't see your car in the parking lot," Iris said over her shoulder as she entered the bathroom.

"That's because I walked."

She stuck her head out of the bathroom, watching as he moved around the kitchen. "Why did you walk?"

"I need the exercise," Collier replied.

"I'll drive you back whenever you're ready to leave."

He gave her a long stare. "What if I don't leave until tomorrow?"

Iris blinked. "That's not a problem. Don't forget I have to go in to work tomorrow. You can use my truck if you don't want to walk back." Tracy lived about a half mile from the downtown business district.

"What time do you get off?"

"I'm only working until two."

Collier nodded. "If that's the case, I'll come back around four thirty and we can go together."

"Sure. Can you please take out the container of cream for me while I wash this makeup off my face?"

Collier opened the refrigerator. "What's in the glass carafe, Iris?"

She stuck her head out the door again, her face covered with a layer of makeup remover. "That's rum punch. I made up a sample to see if I'm going to serve it for Christmas. My folks want to come back here for a Christmas Eve dinner, so I thought I'd serve the punch instead of wine. Pour yourself a glass and let me know what you think."

"I hope you're not going to work yourself ragged at the Muffin Corner while planning a Christmas dinner."

"This week coming up is the last week, and then I'm going back to my regular schedule." Using cotton squares, Iris gently removed her makeup, then scrutinized her reflection in the mirror. How would owning part of her own business change her?

She'd spoken further with Evan about how she should draw up her business proposal with the owners of the Muffin Corner. Once completed, she gave a copy of it to Mabel to discuss with Lester. That had been more than three weeks ago, and they still hadn't gotten back to her. Iris knew she had to broach the subject but had decided to wait until after the holiday. Although she was paid well for working the extra hours, she couldn't help thinking how much better things would be if she worked for herself. She could set her own hours, and aside from the initial investment of installing an industrial kitchen and buying the supplies needed to run a bakery and the cost of utilities, her overhead would be negligible.

"Hey, babe! Did you taste this?" Collier called out.

She joined him in the kitchen. He held a glass of punch, grinning like a Cheshire cat. "No. Why?"

He handed her the glass. "Take a sip."

Iris took a sip from his glass. "That's real good. It's also a little strong."

Collier took down another glass from the cabinet, filled it with ice from the refrigerator's in-door feature, then added a liberal amount of punch. He touched his glass to hers. "Here's to wonderful days and glorious nights together."

Iris's smile was as brittle as thin ice. What was he talking about? They had less than two weeks before whatever they had would end. "Copy that," she whispered, using military jargon, then took a long swallow of the fruity concoction. The mixture of the rums and fruit juices went immediately to her brain, and she swayed slightly before righting herself.

Collier eased her fingers from around the glass, setting it on the countertop. "Easy there, baby."

Resting her forehead on his chest, Iris felt like crying. It was hard to imagine going back to the loneliness she'd experienced before he'd gotten there. How could she have been so foolish to continue to see him when she knew if they did have a future together she would become a copy of her mother—following her husband from base to base. And what about their children? Did she want to uproot them to live a vagabond lifestyle of moving to a new home every two or three years? Her entire body trembled when his hand searched under her sweater and covered her breast. They were so sensitive she couldn't help shivering.

"What's the matter, babe?" he asked.

"Just sensitive, I guess."

He grunted deep in his throat. "Is that good or bad?"

Iris smiled. "Good."

Then, coffee and tea forgotten, he swept her up in his arms and walked into the bedroom.

Iris had wanted this every night for the last two weeks. Collier had come to see her every night, and she had wanted him to make love to her, but he knew her increased work schedule was taking its toll. If he hadn't pressured her to go to the movies with him, she probably would've come home and gone to sleep. She needed a break from the routine or she would eventually burn out, and Collier admitted he cared too much for her to stand by and let that happen.

He took his time removing her clothes, then his own. And after showing Iris just how much he treasured her, Collier pulled her against his body and they fell asleep like nestled spoons.

Iris woke at five and managed to slip out of bed without waking Collier. He lay on his back, chest rising and falling in an even rhythm. She gathered a set of underwear, a T-shirt, socks, and jeans and left the bedroom, closing the door quietly behind her.

She brushed her teeth, showered, and dressed in the bathroom, and when she walked out, she found Collier in the kitchen making breakfast. Droplets of moisture clung to his broad back, and she knew he'd showered in the minuscule shower stall in the family room.

Collier smiled at her. "Come sit down and eat."

"You made breakfast."

"You need breakfast," he said, beckoning to her. "Come on, sweetie," he urged when she didn't move. "It's only five twenty-five, so you have time to eat something."

The scene was one she would remember for years: Collier standing barefoot in her kitchen wearing only a pair of jeans riding low on his slim hips. "Are you going to join me?"

He pulled out a chair at the dining area table. "Of course."

Iris moaned under her breath when she took a bite of bananas Foster French toast. Slices of crisp slab bacon, orange juice, and coffee completed the surprise breakfast. "You're spoiling me, Collier."

He smiled across the table at her. "You deserve to be spoiled. You're so busy pleasing other folks that you neglect yourself."

"I take care of myself," she said defensively.

"Really? You're working like a beast for Lester and Mabel."

She stared at his stubble, thinking it should be illegal for a man to look that sexy so early in the morning. "That may change soon."

Collier drained his glass of juice. "How?"

Iris told him about the proposition and the possible business agreement between her and her current employers. She didn't know what to expect, but it wasn't his stern-faced expression. "Why didn't you talk to me about this? I told you I'm a silent partner in Happy Hour."

She ignored his accusatory tone. "Evan was giving me advice."

"Your brother is a college professor."

"My brother teaches *and* has a veterinarian practice."

Leaning back in his chair, Collier stared down at his plate. "Forgive me for being presumptuous."

"There's nothing to forgive, Collier. I really appreciate you looking out for me."

He glanced up, and the tenderness in his eyes made her heart turn over. "As long as we're together, I'll always look out for you."

Iris knew if she didn't get up from the table, she would embarrass herself and start bawling like a baby. She cleaned her plate, gulped down the juice, and reached for the coffee cup, when Collier caught her wrist, holding it in a loose grip.

"Slow down, baby."

She tried shaking off his hand, but he tightened his hold. "I have to leave now or I'm going to be late." They engaged in a staredown, neither wanting to give in first. "Please let me go, Collier." Seconds ticked by before he released her wrist.

Rounding the table, Iris stood behind him and wrapped her arms around his neck. His hair was growing out of the military-style cut. "Thank you for breakfast."

He covered her hands with one of his. "You're welcome. I don't want you to think I'm trying to run your life."

Iris kissed his hair. "It's okay, babe. I know you're trying to look out for me."

Collier nodded. "That's because I care about what happens to you."

She kissed him again. "I know that. I'll see you later."

Collier felt as if he were losing Iris even before it was time for him to return to North Carolina. Their lovemaking wasn't the same as it had been before she changed her work schedule. And he'd made a grievous mistake when chastising her for not informing him of Lester and Mabel's proposal, because for a nanosecond he thought he glimpsed a glint of fear in her eyes before it vanished. Had he reminded her of her ex, who sought to control every aspect of her life? He prayed he hadn't.

His concern for Iris went beyond wanting the best for her. It was because he loved her, loved her enough to want their relationship to continue beyond the end of his leave. He needed her well physically and mentally because he was broken, and he'd need her love to help him to heal. He hadn't had more than three flashbacks since his return:

the two he'd had the night he'd stayed over in Charleston and another a week following Thanksgiving. Fortunately he hadn't woken up screaming or he would've frightened Tracy and Layla. He'd fallen in love with Iris; she'd taught him it was okay to laugh, and, like her, it was possible to overcome his demons to start life anew.

He left the table and crossed the room to where she stood at the door. Pulling her close, he kissed her hair. "I'll clean up here, go home and change, and then I'll be back around four thirty."

Tilting her chin, Iris offered him a hint of a smile. "Thank you."

Collier watched Iris until she descended the staircase, then closed the door. The apartment was as quiet as a tomb, reminding him that it was the first time he'd been there alone. All of the furnishings reflected Iris's carefree, artistic personality, but without her presence they were as unappetizing to him as used newspaper in the bottom of a birdcage. She'd become his Christmas, Thanksgiving, and all of the festive holidays in a year. Somehow he had to conjure up the nerve to let her know that.

He was scheduled to return to Fort Bragg in less than ten days where he'd await his new assignment. And because the base was fairly close to Charleston, he could make the drive in about three hours. Coming home on weekends would allow him to spend time with his family and Iris. Collier knew if he continued to be with her, there was the hope that they could possibly plan a future together.

*   *   *

Iris felt like a young child experiencing snow for the first time as she and Collier strolled hand in hand along the snow-covered sidewalk. Portable spotlights powered by generators lit up the entire business district as if it were the middle of the day. Even the weather seemed to cooperate with the faux wintry landscape with below-forty temperatures. Children riding in horse-drawn sleighs squealed at the top of their lungs when they saw their parents and friends standing on the sidewalks waving at them. The smell of roasting chestnuts lingered in the air along with the aromas of freshly popped popcorn and grilling meats on charcoal-fired hibachi grills. Carolers dressed in nineteenth-century costumes stood in the town square, joined in song by the crowds. Gasps went up from the assembly when the snow-making machine roared to life, spewing more fake snow and creating blizzard-like conditions.

Collier pulled Iris into the doorway of the ice cream shop and kissed her passionately. She anchored her arms under his shoulders over a waist-length black leather jacket, leaned into him, and devoured his mouth, her tongue dueling with his for dominance.

"Yo, Scrappy, get a room before I tell the sheriff and have you arrested for lewd behavior."

Iris went completely still, then managed to relax when Collier chuckled softly. "Get the hell outta here, Leon, before Scrappy decides to whoop yo' ass."

"Yo, Scrappy, ain't you going to introduce me to your woman?"

"Beat it, Leon." This time there was no teasing in his voice.

"Okay, man. Be like that."

Iris kept her face averted until the man Collier called Leon walked away. "What was that all about?" she whispered.

Palming her face between his hands, Collier smiled. "It was just a little harmless fun."

Her eyebrows shot up. "It didn't sound like fun to me."

"Leon's harmless. He had a brilliant career as a commercial airline pilot but messed up when he couldn't stay sober. Now he's teaching aeronautical aviation at one of North Charleston's trade schools. I would've introduced you to him, but I could smell the alcohol on his breath."

"Did he relapse?"

"He's what you would call a functioning alcoholic. I've heard that they won't sell him liquor at the store here in the Cove, and they won't serve him any at Happy Hour, so he probably got someone to buy him a bottle."

"How does he get to his job?"

"He takes the ferry, then a bus. Every town, no matter how small, has its share of drunks, deadbeat dads, and cheating husbands and wives."

Turning around, Iris leaned back against Collier's chest. "I must be an ostrich with my head in the sand because I never met anyone like those folks."

Collier wrapped his arms around her. "That's because you're a newcomer. Live here for the next ten or twenty years, and you'll see everything that happens in a larger city."

She shivered slightly when his breath feathered over the top of her ear. "I can't think that far ahead."

"Didn't you tell me you wanted to buy property here?"

"Yeah."

"Well, that means you intend to put down roots."

Iris smiled. "That sounds about right." She wanted to put down roots, marry again, and have a couple of children. She wanted all of the things she'd fantasized about as a girl, but only with Collier. She'd fallen in love with him, knowing their relationship would end in less than two weeks. She wanted to become Mrs. Collier Ward, have his babies, go to bed with him every night, bring their children to the Winter

Wonderland Festival, celebrate holidays with friends and family, and grow old together. But she knew that wasn't possible because just when she'd found a man to love, he wasn't available for anything long-term.

Resting his hands on her shoulders, Collier turned her around to face him. "Why do you sound so doubtful? Either you are or you aren't."

"I can't answer that until I buy the house. Let's go, sweetie. I want to stop at Jack's and get a bowl of okra gumbo; then I want to see if we can find Tracy and Layla in this crowd before we go home."

The year before, Iris had watched the festival from her living room window, wanting to join in the festivities, but she had held back when she saw couples and families together. It had been the first time in her life that she experienced what it felt like to be totally alone. Like a child with her nose pressed against the window of a department store, she'd watched carolers moving along Main Street, singing the traditional and a few modern Christmas songs, horse-drawn sleighs filled with children laughing and squealing in delight, and while not one to engage in self-pity, Iris drew the drapes and went into the family room to watch several of her favorite comedic movies.

"This reminds me of New York City during Christmas," Collier said quietly. "The last time I was there it was snowing heavily, but that didn't seem to bother the skaters at Rockefeller Center."

Iris huddled closer to Collier. "It's been awhile since I've been to the Big Apple."

"Maybe we'll get to go together whenever I get my next leave."

She glanced up at him. "That will depend on my work schedule."

"Of course."

They hadn't gone very far in search of Tracy when Iris's cell vibrated in her jacket pocket. "Hey," she said when she saw Tracy's name come up on the screen. "Where are you?"

"We're in the square hanging out by the carolers."

"Collier and I are going to Jack's. Why don't you meet us there?"

They managed to get a table at the celebrated seafood restaurant, Iris sitting next to Layla, who couldn't stop talking about how she missed seeing her after school. "Uncle Collier is all right, but you're the best, Miss Iris. I don't have cookies and milk with him," she said sotto voce.

Iris pressed her mouth to the girl's ear. "I'll talk to him about that."

Tracy glanced around the crowded restaurant. "This place is a mob scene. It's worse than New Year's Eve when everyone comes here for hoppin' John and chitlins."

Layla scrunched up her nose. "I don't like chitlins, Mama."

"It's an acquired taste, sweetheart," Tracy explained.

Collier stared directly at Iris. "Do you eat chitlins?"

"No."

His expressive eyebrows lifted a fraction. "Have you ever tried them?"

"Yes."

A shadow fell over the table. Luvina Jackson stood with her arms crossed over the front of her bibbed apron glaring at Collier. "I should take a switch to yo' fine behind fo' not coming by to see me, Scrappy. How long you been back?" she admonished him.

Collier stood and picked up Luvina as if she weighed twenty pounds instead of two hundred. He kissed her cheek. "How are you, Miss Vina?"

Luvina screamed, and the restaurant fell silent. "Put me down fo' you drop me."

Collier lifted her higher. "I'm not going to drop you. I can bench-press four hundred pounds, and a fine woman like you don't weigh no four hundred," he said, lapsing into dialect.

Luvina pounded his back. "Put me down, boy. I'm 'fraid of heights."

Collier kissed her cheek, then set her on her feet. "You still the best-smelling woman in the Cove." Miss Vina was famous for wearing lily of the valley perfume.

Luvina's broad dark face, with features that bore her Gullah ancestry, softened as she smiled. "The devil sho nuf gave you a silver tongue when he was handing them out. Now, what can I git you and yo' family?" She waved a hand. "Famemba, we don't take no money from those in the active military, so keep yo' money in yo' pocket."

Iris had watched the interchange between Collier and the woman who'd run Jack's Fish House with her husband for more than two decades, struggling not to laugh. He was as charming as he was handsome—a heady combination, indeed. She and Collier ordered okra gumbo, and Tracy and Layla selected fried catfish with a side order of hush puppies. When it came time to settle the bill, Collier gave Tracy the money.

They returned to the festivities along Main Street. Layla finally convinced Tracy to take a sleigh ride with her while Iris and Collier lingered to watch a juggler toss four pins into the air, catching them before they fell. There was a face-painting station for children and several clowns perched high on unicycles.

Collier noticed when she tried to smother a yawn behind her hand. "Let's go, babe. Off to bed with you. I'm going to make sure you sleep past five tomorrow."

"Okay." Iris needed no further urging. She hadn't realized how sleepy she was until she sat still for more than a few minutes.

It took longer than usual to walk back to the apartment. Crowds had even gathered in the parking lots behind stores. Groups of teenagers sat around talking, texting, or listening to music on their electronic devices. As they neared the sweetgrass shop, Iris saw Collier's Mustang for the first time. He'd promised to take her for a ride, but that was before she changed her work hours.

"The Mustang is beautiful."

Collier smiled as if she'd complimented one of his children. "We'll go for a drive after church and brunch."

"Will you let me drive it?"

"We'll see."

She slowly shook her head. "Please don't tell me you're one of those guys who love their cars more than their families?"

Collier preceded her up the staircase, unlocking the door. "I'll have to wait and see when I have a wife and children to find out if that's the case."

Iris took off her boots, leaving them on the mat. "I'm going to brush my teeth, and then I'm going to bed."

She lowered the thermostat, brushed her teeth, undressed, and slipped into a nightgown and got into bed while Collier lingered in the family room watching the news. Her eyes felt heavy, and when she couldn't keep them open any longer, she fell into a deep, dreamless sleep, not stirring even when Collier slipped into bed next to her.

Suddenly, Iris woke in a panic, struggling to breathe. She tried to move, but something held her down. She opened her eyes to find Collier with his hands around her throat, yelling at her in a language she couldn't understand or identify.

She struggled mightily, trying to push him away, but he was two hundred pounds of solid muscle. Suddenly, she was trapped in her memories, desperate to get away from the husband who'd tried to kill her once before. She tried to scream but couldn't draw a breath. Black spots swam in front of her eyes from a lack of oxygen. Finally, she managed to loosen his hands enough to suck in a lungful of air.

She scrambled out from under him and out of bed, screaming in horror. Even after she turned on the light, Collier didn't wake up, just continued to twitch and shout in a foreign language.

She took several deep, calming breaths before working up the nerve to touch him. "Wake up!" she shouted. "Collier, come back to me."

Without warning, his eyes opened, staring at her as if she were a complete stranger. "What's the matter, baby?"

"What's the matter?" she whispered as tears flowed down her face, landing on the sheet. "You almost strangled me. Why didn't you tell me you have PTSD? You were yelling at me in some language I've never heard before, and your hands were around my throat. I—I couldn't breathe. It was like Derrick all over again."

Collier felt as if he'd been knifed in the gut as he watched Iris cry. He wanted to touch her but knew he couldn't because she feared him hurting her. The nightmare had returned, and this time he couldn't remember any of the details. He gently cupped her face in his hands and lifted her chin. That's when he saw the imprint of his fingers on her neck, already turning into an ugly purple bruise.

"Baby, I'm sorry. I—"

"Please go, Collier," she pleaded softly. "I can't go through this again." A sob escaped her. "I need to be with someone who makes me feel safe. And right now you're not the one."

Collier reacted like an automaton, moving in slow motion as he put on his clothes. It took all of his strength and self-control not to break down. His limbs felt like lead, and he was so cold that he could've been in Alaska in the dead of winter as he slipped behind the wheel of the classic car. The parking lot was empty, the throng that had lined Main Street gone. Only the winking Christmas lights and a few wisps of dirty fake snow remained.

Staring through the windshield with sightless eyes, Collier made it home without wrecking the car. He didn't remember putting the key in the door or walking into his bedroom and falling across the bed fully dressed.

A soft knocking on the bedroom door roused him, and when he turned over he saw daylight coming through the blinds on the window. "What is it?"

The door opened slightly and Tracy stuck her head in. She frowned. "What happened to you?"

"Nothing. What do you want?"

"It's ten thirty. Are you going to church with us?"

"No. Now get out and close the damn door."

The door swung open, bouncing off the doorstop. "I don't know what happened between you and Iris, but don't you dare take that tone with me, Collier."

He waved at her. "Please close the door. Is that better?"

His facetious tone wasn't lost on his sister when she walked into the room and sat on the chair in a corner. "No, it's not better. I don't know how many times I've told you that I love you and worry about you, Collier. And because there's only the two of us, we need to trust each other. There isn't anything I keep from you and I expect the same from you."

"Like you spending the Christmas week in Florida with Dr. Evan Nelson?"

"Yes," she spat out, "like me spending a week with a man and his daughter. I told you because as long as you're here I owe it to you to let you know my whereabouts."

Collier felt as if he'd gone ten rounds with a heavyweight boxer. His body hurt, his head hurt, and his heart ached. "It's over between me and Iris."

Tracy stared at him as if he were a stranger instead of her brother. "What happened?"

He told her everything. "I almost killed her, Tracy. First her husband punches her out, then tries to strangle her, and in a flashback I did the same thing."

"Don't you dare compare yourself to her ex-husband! The man deliberately made her life a living hell. You're different, Collier."

"Different, Tracy? I hurt her." He'd punctuated the three words. "She's had enough pain in her life, and she doesn't need any more with me."

"Do you love her?"

"What does love have to do with this?" He ran both hands over his head. "The bottom line is I should've told her about the flashbacks."

"How long have you had them?"

Collier sank down onto the pillow cradling his shoulders. "They started about six months ago. I had to watch three of my men burn to death after their Humvee hit an IED." He closed his eyes. "I can recall everything about that day and..."

He told his sister what he'd witnessed firsthand during his repeated deployments, seeing disbelief in her eyes as she stared at him. It was as if the floodgates had opened and the demons he'd held in check had escaped along with the tears he was helpless to stop. It was as if their roles were reversed when Tracy moved off the chair to hold him while he cried.

When he'd come home to make funeral arrangements for their parents, he'd been the stoic one while Tracy had been an emotional wreck.

Tracy hugged him tightly. "It's going to be okay, Collier," she said soothingly. "You're going to have to get some help or the nightmares are going to get worse."

"I'm tired, Tracy. I'm really, really tired."

She pressed a kiss on his damp hair. "Try to get some sleep. I'll come and check on you after Layla and I get back from church."

Chapter Seven

CLASSIC DEVILED EGGS

- 8 hard-cooked eggs
- ¼ cup mayonnaise
- 2 teaspoons sugar
- 1 teaspoon sweet pickle juice
- 1 teaspoon prepared yellow mustard
- 1 teaspoon cider vinegar
- ⅛ teaspoon dry mustard
- Salt and Tabasco to taste
- Paprika, parsley, and chives, for garnish

Shell eggs and halve lengthwise. Carefully scoop the egg yolks into a mixing bowl. Mash yolks, then mix in the mayonnaise, sugar, pickle juice, yellow mustard, vinegar, and dry mustard with a fork until smooth; season with salt and Tabasco. (If the mixture is too thick, add extra mayonnaise.) Spoon or pipe the yolk mixture into 12 of the 16 egg halves. (The two extra eggs were cooked for the yolks; discard remaining whites.) Garnish with paprika, parsley, or chives; serve immediately or chill, loosely covered.

The next morning, Iris untied the scarf holding the ice packs in place around her neck, examining the angry bruises in her bathroom mirror. Three years ago, it had been a broken nose and a fractured cheekbone. But what hurt most of all was her heart, and unfortunately, there was no remedy in the world to heal that.

Just as she finished getting dressed in a set of sweats, the shrill of the doorbell echoed throughout the apartment. She couldn't remember the last time someone had rung the bell. Peering through the peephole, she saw the distorted face of Tracy staring at her.

"Go away, Tracy."

The doorbell shrilled again. "I can't do that, Iris. Open the door."

Pressing her back against the door, Iris closed her eyes. "No."

"I'm not going away until you do."

The bell chimed over and over until Iris unlocked the door and flung it open. She would never forget the look on her friend's face when she saw her neck. Tracy looked as if she was going to faint before she recovered quickly. Seconds later, Iris found herself in Tracy's arms.

"I'm sorry, Iris. I'm so very sorry he did this to you."

Iris eased out of her friend's embrace. "Please stop or I'll start crying again. And my throat hurts too much for that."

Tracy held Iris's hands. "Come sit down. You don't have to talk, but I need you to listen to what I have to say. Okay?"

Iris nodded. Sitting, Iris pressed her head back against the sofa and closed her eyes.

"I didn't know Collier was suffering from PTSD," Tracy began. She told her about what Collier had gone through during his deployments, her voice breaking with emotion. "My brother loves you. And it's breaking him up inside to know he hurt you."

Iris shook her head. "I can't."

"You can't what?"

She inhaled, holding her breath, then let it out slowly. "I can't deal with him as long as he's like this. I thought he was going to choke me to death."

"What if he gets help?"

Iris's hands were shaking when she brought them up to cover her face. "I don't know."

"Do you love him, Iris?"

Lowering her hands, she gave Tracy a long, penetrating stare. She was asking her the same question that had nagged at her as she sat in the bathtub this morning. Did she truly love Collier or was she infatuated with him?

"Right now I don't know," she answered honestly.

Tracy reached for her hand, threading their fingers together. "You've become more than a friend, Iris. You're like a sister to me, and knowing what you've been through, you deserve someone who will love and protect you."

Iris recalled telling Collier he was supposed to love her, not hurt her. "Are you saying Collier is that someone?"

"He can be."

"He can be, but right now he's not because he needs help."

Tracy stood. "What you and Collier have is worth fighting for. It tore my heart out to see my brother cry. He never cried when we buried our mother and our father. But he cried because he knows he's lost you."

Iris sat in the same spot long after Tracy left, her mind in tumult. She was familiar with the term "PTSD" and knew several veterans who'd served under her father who had undergone treatment for the disorder. Collier *had* to get help before he hurt someone or himself.

*   *   *

Collier waited on the porch for Tracy to come out of her house. He'd seen Layla off to school that morning, but his niece had no way of knowing it would be the last time she would see him for a while. It was four days before Christmas, and he'd decided to return to the base earlier than planned. If he remained on the island, he knew he wouldn't be able to stay away from Iris.

The screen door opened and closed with a soft click. Pushing to his feet, he forced a smile. "It's time for me to leave."

Tracy's face fell. "What are you talking about? You have another week here."

"I'm going to get help, sis. I can't continue to live like this." Collier extended his arms, and he wasn't disappointed when Tracy walked into his embrace. "When you see Iris, tell her that I'm sorry and that I love her."

Tracy patted his broad back. "I will. You take care of yourself."

"I will," he whispered. "And you take care of my niece."

"I will," she promised.

Collier kissed Tracy's forehead, picked up his duffel, and walked down the porch to the rental car. He could feel his sister's eyes boring into his back as he got into the car and headed toward the causeway. Barring traffic delays, he expected to arrive at the base within three and a half hours. He knew he had to begin the process of exorcising his demons if he hoped to have a healthy relationship and possibly a future with Iris.

Tracy's meeting with Iris had left him with a glimmer of hope. She'd recognized he needed help and he was going to get that help. Collier didn't know if he could be completely healed, but he was going to do everything possible to begin the healing process.

Iris surveyed the dining room table, pleased with her handiwork. It was the second time in a month that she would host a holiday dinner. It was Christmas Eve, and her family and friends would be coming to the apartment for a cocktail hour followed by a sit-down dinner at the stroke of midnight. She'd put up a lifelike artificial tree and decorated it with tiny white velvet bows and lights. A number of gaily wrapped gifts were positioned on the red tree skirt.

She'd forced herself to keep busy in order not to think about Collier. Tracy had called to ask her if she would meet Layla's school bus because her brother had cut his leave short to return to his base. Tracy had reopened an emotional wound that was just beginning to heal when she gave Iris Collier's parting message: "*Tell her that I'm sorry and that I love her.*" He loved her and she loved him, yet their lives were going in different directions.

He'd returned to active duty, and she had settled back into the routine she'd kept before his arrival. But it wasn't the same.

Her parents had come down from Virginia and Evan and Allie from Florida earlier that morning, checking into a Charleston hotel because the Cove Inn was filled to capacity with snowbirds.

Tracy walked into the kitchen, holding a plastic cup half-filled with rum punch. "Girl, you outdid yourself with the punch. This stuff is potent." She executed a mambo step. "We need to go to the Caribbean and let our hair down."

Iris thought her friend looked lovely with her hair pulled back from her face and pinned atop her head. A red-and-green plaid silk blouse and a black pencil skirt, sheer black stockings, and matching strappy suede stilettos transformed the schoolteacher into a seductive siren. She knew Tracy had paid special attention to her appearance for one special person: Evan.

Iris took the cup from Tracy and took a sip She held it in her mouth before swallowing the icy concoction that exploded in a fireball of heat when it settled in her chest. "Whoa!" she gasped. "That's lethal. Maybe I should add a little more juice."

"Don't you dare," Tracy threatened. "It's fine the way it is. Folks will just have to put on their big girl panties and big boy boxers if they're going to drink. Speaking of folk, I think I hear them coming up the stairs."

Iris removed her bibbed apron, placing it on the stool in the kitchen, and went into the living room to greet her guests. Her father and brother were carrying shopping bags filled with colorful gifts. She pressed her cheek to her father's, then Evan's. "Please come in. You can put your coats in the family room."

She hugged her mother. Esther's hair was beautifully coiffed, the salt-and-pepper curls framing her smooth round face. "You look beautiful, as usual."

Esther held Iris at arm's length, eyeing her critically. "You've lost weight."

"It's the dress." Iris didn't want to get into a debate with her mother about her weight. Esther always believed she was too thin. Her outfit was a black sleeveless sheath dress, with the addition of a wide tartan plaid silk belt to break up the somber color and a pair of black suede kitten heels. A pair of diamond studs had replaced her usual small gold hoops.

She helped Esther out of her coat. "I've put out appetizers and punch to tide you over before we sit down to eat at midnight."

Iris had given careful consideration to making up the menu for her Christmas dinner. She'd decided on an orange-glazed ham, roasted asparagus with a jalapeño hollandaise sauce, corn bread, and candied sweet potatoes. She'd baked two pies: apple with a walnut topping and a Southern pecan pie.

"What's wrong, Mom?" she asked when Esther glanced around the living room.

"Where's your boyfriend? He told James he'd be here through Christmas."

She didn't react to her mother's reference to Collier as her boyfriend. "He had to return to his base early." Iris wasn't about to tell anyone what Collier had done to her, because in hindsight she realized he wasn't responsible for his actions. She'd worn a scarf every day to conceal the bruises on her neck until they finally faded. Mabel teased her relentlessly that her attempt to hide Collier's love bites didn't fool her. Word had gotten around that the pastry chef at the Muffin Corner was Scrappy's girlfriend, and the men who'd previously flirted with her when she worked the front of the shop ignored her as if she'd come down with the plague. She missed Collier, while at night her longing for him intensified. The longing had nothing to do with sex; rather, she missed his companionship.

James tuned the radio to a station playing classic Motown hits, then took his wife's hand and dipped her as they swayed to Smokey Robinson and the Miracles' "Ooo Baby Baby."

Allie laughed hysterically when she saw her grandparents dancing. "Daddy, why don't you dance with Miss Tracy?"

Evan made a big show of bowing before Tracy, who giggled like a little girl, then moved into his arms. Iris felt hot tears prick the backs of her eyelids as she watched two generations of Nelson men dance. She'd felt Tracy's excitement as she filled her luggage with clothes for her and Layla to take on their weeklong Florida vacation. They would ride down with Evan and Allie, and he'd made arrangements for a chauffeur to drive them back to South Carolina because he wasn't able to book a flight this late in the holiday season.

Iris made her way over to the buffet table, filling a cup with punch. After several sips, she was swaying in time to the Temptations' upbeat hit "Papa Was a Rollin' Stone." Evan came over, easing the cup from her hand, and swung her around and around until the ceiling started spinning. James turned up the volume, singing and clapping to the music from his youth.

Allie patted Iris's arm. "Auntie Iris, somebody's ringing the bell," she shouted to be heard above the driving bassline beat.

"I'll get it," James volunteered.

Iris watched her father gyrating across the living room. She didn't know who could be at the door. She wasn't expecting anyone. Her heart skipped a beat when Collier walked in wearing his fatigues. Her eyes followed his every motion as he and James exchanged rough hugs. Layla jumped up and raced into his arms as he knelt down and pulled her close to his chest. Tracy, who appeared as shocked as Iris, approached her brother, holding on to his neck as if she feared he would disappear before her eyes.

Iris caught Collier's eyes over his sister's head, and the smile he gave her just about leveled her right there. She wasn't even aware of him crossing the room, but suddenly he stood before her, offering his hand. Without conscious thought, she slid her palm against his.

"I'd like to talk to you for a few minutes. In private," he said.

"You can kiss her, son," James called out. "After all, it is Christmas."

Iris stiffened as he pulled her against him. As much as she wanted to sink into his familiar warmth, she knew she was playing with fire.

Lowering his head, Collier touched his mouth to hers in a chaste kiss. "Merry Christmas."

She took his hand, winding their fingers together as she led him across the living room. Her heart was beating so fast she feared fainting. "Merry Christmas, Sergeant Ward."

He squeezed her hand. "There's no need to be so formal, darling."

Her heart skipped a beat. He'd told Tracy to tell her he loved her, and it was apparent his feelings toward her hadn't changed.

Iris smiled. "Merry Christmas to you, too, darling. Is that better?" She closed her eyes for several seconds, hoping to buy time to slow down her pulse. "We can talk in the family room." She led the way to the smaller of the two bedrooms, flipping on the wall switch.

"Please close the door."

She hesitated, then closed the door, shutting out some of the music and raised voices. "Shall we sit?" Iris asked Collier, lowering her eyes. If she'd lost weight, so had he. His face was much leaner and she wondered if he was eating.

He shook his head. "No. What I have to say won't take that long. I know I should've told you I was experiencing flashbacks, but I was too afraid I'd lose you."

"Have you forgotten that I'm an Army brat, Collier? I know some soldiers come back from combat needing medication and psychotherapy in order to function somewhat normally. The problem is you didn't trust me with your secret."

Collier stared at her under lowered lids. "That's something I'll regret for the rest of my life. I was evaluated by a psychiatrist who prescribed prazosin for the nightmares, but the side effects were counterproductive."

"Do you still have nightmares?"

"Not since the one I had with you. There are times when I can go weeks without having them, and then sometimes they recur one after another. I'm in therapy, and I've scheduled weekly sessions with the chaplain, who claims forgiveness is the best medicine for anything and anyone." Holding her hands, Collier went down on one knee. "Please forgive me."

Iris sank to her knees, pressing her forehead to his as she fought back tears. "Yes, sweetie, you're forgiven."

"Do you mind if I come to visit you from time to time? The drive from Fort Bragg is just a few hours."

She sniffled. "No, I don't mind. I think it's time we put aside our pasts and start over. We've been given a second chance, so let's try not to mess it up."

"I'm not going to mess it up," Collier said quickly. He stood, pulling her up with him. His eyes made love to her face as he lowered his head and kissed her with all the passion he could possibly feel for a woman. "Merry Christmas, my love."

Iris clung to him as if he were her lifeline. "Merry Christmas, love of my life. I think we'd better get back before someone comes looking for us."

Collier increased his hold on her hand, stopping her from leaving. "I love you."

Iris felt like crying. And if she did, they would be tears of joy. Her lids fluttered wildly. "I love you too." They returned to the living room, their arms around each other.

"Are you guys all right?" Esther asked.

"We're good," Iris and Collier chorused together.

"How good, Sergeant?" James questioned.

"Hopefully good enough, Colonel, to convince your daughter that spending her life with a retired master sergeant doesn't have to be boring." His pronouncement was met with applause as Esther kissed his cheek and James pumped his hand. Evan slapped his back, while Tracy clasped her hands and mumbled a silent prayer.

Iris said her own silent prayer of gratitude. Collier hadn't proposed marriage, but they had time to right the wrongs, work through their misunderstandings, and share a love that promised forever.

Also by Rochelle Alers

The Cavanaugh Island Series

Sanctuary Cove
Angels Landing
Haven Creek
Magnolia Drive
Cherry Lane

About the Author

With nearly two million copies of her novels in print, best-selling author Rochelle Alers is also the recipient of numerous awards, including the Gold Pen Award, the Emma Award, the Vivian Stephens Award for Excellence in Romance Writing, the Romantic Times Career Achievement Award, and the Zora Neale Hurston Literary Award.

*　　*　　*

Learn more at:
   RochelleAlers.org
   Twitter @RochelleAlers
   Facebook.com

Joy to the World

Hope Ramsay

Chapter One

Rudolph the Red-Nosed Reindeer had been flying across Harbor Drive every Christmas since Brenda McMillan could remember. But this morning he was dangling by his hind foot as a crew of workmen hoisted him into place. Their crane was positioned smack-dab in the middle of the busiest intersection in town, while Deputy Ethan Cuthbert ineffectively directed traffic.

Brenda drummed her fingers on the steering wheel. "Come on," she muttered, inching forward. When she finally made the turn onto Magnolia Boulevard, Ethan shouted "Merry Christmas" at her. Brenda stomped on the urge to tell Ethan he could take Christmas and shove it up the chimney.

She pushed the speed limit to the post office and dashed into the building, ignoring Cathy Fonseca, who waved and said "Good morning." There was nothing good about this morning.

Brenda pulled her mailbox key out of her purse and held

her breath as she slipped it into the lock. *Please let there be a postcard*, she silently prayed.

She opened the door to find a wad of Christmas catalogs jammed into the tiny space. Lillian Vernon, Balsam Hill, L.L.Bean, and a half dozen other retailers were already advertising Cyber Monday, which was still three weeks away. Where the heck did these people get her address, anyway? She'd never bought a thing from Balsam Hill or L.L.Bean.

As she pulled out the catalogs, a postcard fluttered to the floor like a dry leaf and landed in a wet spot where people had tracked in some of last night's rain.

She picked up the card, wiping a smudge of mud away with the sleeve of her black parka. On the front of the card the words *Greetings from Arizona, the Grand Canyon State*, were printed in big block letters across a photo of rusty red buttes.

She turned the card over, recognizing the long, neat lines of Isabella's handwriting. Her heart rate spiked. Was her daughter coming home? Finally?

Brenda read the message through the still-wet stain. There were only six words in the tiny space allowed, but they were sufficient to convey the point: Ella was not coming home for the holidays. Again. She hadn't even signed the card with love.

Brenda's throat closed up, and she struggled to draw breath. This year her daughter had sent a grand total of five postcards, each containing one sentence each. Such was the depth of Ella's anger.

Brenda flipped through the catalogs as she headed toward the door and dumped the whole lot of them in the trash can by the parking lot.

She checked her watch. She was going to be late for

work, but she didn't give a damn. Let Louella Pender, the owner of A Stitch in Time, where Brenda worked, behave in her usual passive-aggressive manner. Nothing mattered now that Brenda knew for certain Ella wouldn't be coming home.

It was just another reason to hate Christmas. But then she'd hated the holiday for a very long time, and not one thing had ever happened to change her mind about the whole jolly season. In fact, it was sort of a sign that she'd gotten a postcard today, on the same day they'd hung that tacky reindeer over Magnolia Harbor's main street.

* * *

Jim Killough laughed right out loud the moment the work crew swung Rudolph into position. Tonight the reindeer's red nose, along with the ethereal light coming from his insides, would cast a glow over the town's central business district.

A few years back, Patsy Bauman had tried to retire the glow-in-the-dark Santa and his reindeer. It was a testament to the good people of Magnolia Harbor that her efforts to "upgrade" the holiday decorations had failed.

Santa's sleigh and reindeer had been flying over the main street since the 1960s, and there were lots of folks, Jim included, who viewed his arrival as a harbinger of the holidays. A memory of Julianne, laughing as she stood in the middle of the road looking up at Rudolph, came to mind. He'd fallen in love with her that night.

He still loved her, even though she'd been gone for a long time.

No, not completely gone. Standing there, with the South Carolina sun warming up the morning, Julianne's memory rode shotgun in his mind. He would never stop loving her, or missing her, even though more than twenty years had passed. Memories of her never failed to buoy his spirit, especially around Christmastime.

He turned away and continued his walk up to Bread, Butter, and Beans. The coffeehouse smelled like cinnamon and fresh baked croissants as he stepped up to the counter and accepted a dark roast coffee in a to-go cup from Brooklyn, Julianne's younger sister. His morning visit to his sister-in-law's business had become a ritual for him. He'd been stopping in for coffee before heading off to his medical office for years.

As usual, Brooklyn had something to say the moment she handed over the paper cup. "Do you really think you can convince Brenda McMillan to fill in for Simon as the director of the Christmas Chorale this year?"

Boy, the Magnolia Harbor rumor mill had been working overtime. He'd only decided to ask Brenda last night after a long conversation with Donna Cuthbert about Simon Paredes' health issues. But then again, Donna was the oil that made the gossip machine work in this town, and she had given him less than a ten percent chance of convincing the town Grinch to lend a hand. So he shouldn't be surprised. Everyone would know his plan by now, even though he hadn't yet put it into action. He wouldn't even be surprised if the guys down at the firehouse had started a pool on whether he'd succeed or not.

He took a sip of his coffee and chose his words carefully. "Brenda McMillan isn't as scroogey as people say. She's lonely is all. And right now she's the one person in town with the skills necessary to get the Christmas Chorale in shape."

"She'll never do it." Brooklyn crossed her arms over her chest.

"We don't know that until we ask."

"And you, dear man, are a dewy-eyed optimist. That's what Julie loved most about you."

He shook his head but didn't argue the point. In truth, Julianne had been the optimist. And for twenty-one years, he'd been keeping her alive by remembering the way she used to say, "Things will work out. You wait and see. I have faith."

There was only one time she hadn't used that saying— when she'd been diagnosed with glioblastoma, a deadly form of brain cancer. That time she'd known better than to make a promise she couldn't keep.

"Well, you can't fail if you don't try," he said.

Brooklyn shook her head. "I'm not sure I even understand that. But good luck. I don't know what the clinic will do if we have to cancel the Christmas Gala."

"We'll do without, I guess. And things will work out. I'm sure. I have faith."

Brooklyn gave him that sad, happy look. She clearly remembered too.

"Have a wonderful day," Jim said and turned away, pushing through the coffee shop door out onto the sidewalk, where the work crew had started to hang red bows on the streetlamps.

He continued down Harbor Drive, in the opposite direction of his medical office, under Rudolph's watchful eye. He reached A Stitch in Time, the local yarn and fabric store, and paused a moment on the sidewalk. It was a bit manipulative to corner Brenda at work. But it was probably the only chance he had of shaming her into helping out.

If he had merely driven out to her house and asked for help, she might have given him a swift kick in the butt and told him never to darken her door again.

This sneak attack might not be very nice, but sometimes the ends justified the means. And the benefit gala, featuring the town chorale's performance of Christmas music, along with a silent auction and a visit from Santa, was the main fund-raising event for the Jonquil Island Free Clinic, which provided medical care for indigent people and those without insurance.

A lot of kids depended on that clinic. And the clinic depended on its Christmas concert. And the Magnolia Harbor Choral Society depended on its musical director, who was currently in the hospital and unlikely to recover in the next few weeks.

So Jim drew in a big breath, squared his shoulders, winged a little prayer to the man upstairs, and headed inside.

A couple of gray-haired ladies occupied the comfy chairs in the shop's front sitting area, their needles clicking away. Joyce Kalnin and Paulette Coleman had their heads together and their mouths running a mile a minute, but they both stopped talking, seemingly in midsentence, as he walked across the floor to the checkout counter.

"What on earth are you doing here, Doc?" Paulette asked to his back.

He turned. "Would it surprise you if I said I was taking up knitting?"

"Yes, it would." She frowned. "Oh my goodness, you're here to talk Brenda into standing in for Simon."

"What?" Joyce asked in an astonished voice. "What's wrong with Simon?"

God bless, there was hope. Some people didn't actually listen to Donna Cuthbert and the town gossips.

"Oh my word, you didn't hear?" Paulette said in a breathless voice. "Well, I guess not, since you're a member of Heavenly Rest Church. But it's all over Grace Methodist.

I'm afraid our choir director had a stroke day before yesterday. He's in the hospital on the mainland. Sally said it was mild, and he'll recover with a lot of therapy and whatnot. But he's in no shape to direct the Christmas Chorale this year."

"Oh, the poor dear. Does Sally need anything?"

"The altar guild has it covered, honey." Paulette turned back toward Jim. "Good luck trying to convince that scrooge to do anything for anyone. She's—" Paulette stopped abruptly as Brenda emerged from the stockroom at the back of the store, carrying a plastic bag filled with a dozen skeins of red yarn.

Paulette turned back to her knitting and pretended that she hadn't just been unkind. But the words had been spoken firmly and a bit on the loud side, since Paulette was slightly deaf and didn't wear her hearing aids. Jim was pretty sure Brenda had heard them.

Good! This was exactly what he needed.

* * *

Brenda clutched the bag of Cascade 220 Superwash Merino wool to her chest as heat flushed across her skin. She wasn't a Scrooge. She wasn't even a Grinch. She just didn't like Christmas. There was a big difference between not feeling celebratory and the fictional characters who were mean and cruel or tried to steal everyone's joy.

She just wanted to be left alone at this time of year. She wanted to hide out before some new bad thing happened to her. What the hell was wrong with that?

And why was Doc Killough here listening to Paulette's loudly spoken opinions? Men didn't drop by A Stitch in Time very often, and certainly not the town's busiest family doctor and goodwill ambassador. How on earth could one man be that happy all the time?

In fact, the doctor was grinning at her right this minute, his blue eyes twinkling. And damn if he didn't have dimples that were kind of merry and unruly salt-and-pepper hair that curled over his collar.

She wanted to step around him and take the bag of yarn to the proper cubby on the other side of the room. There'd been a run on red and white yarn recently, since everyone seemed to be knitting Faire Isle mittens for their grandkids this Christmas.

But the man blocked her path.

"Hello, Doc," she said in her best customer service voice. "Is there something I can help you find?"

"As a matter of fact, yes. I'm in desperate need of a musical director for the Christmas Chorale."

The tiny hairs stiffened on the back of Brenda's neck, and she fumbled the bag of yarn as her fingers spasmed. "Oh," she said as the yarn hit the floor. She and Jim simultaneously bent over to retrieve the wool, and she bonked her head against his. Well, one thing was clear, the good doctor had a very hard head.

"I'm sorry," Jim said, handing her the bag of yarn.

She took the yarn with the numb fingers of her left hand while she rubbed her forehead with her right. She took a little step backward because the man was invading her personal space. It wasn't far enough. If Paulette hadn't been watching, she might have turned and run like a scared rabbit.

"I can't," she said, averting her gaze. She wanted nothing to do with the twinkle in his eyes or his Christmas Chorale.

"Please," he said.

Her gaze bounced around the store. She wasn't going to

let him talk her into this. Or goad her into it. Or shame her either. She hated Christmas. She hated wintertime. She even hated the damned winter solstice that the public school systems celebrated in lieu of Christmas. No, she didn't want to direct any kind of musical event tied to this time of year.

"I'm sorry. I can't," she said, stepping around him and heading toward the cubby where the yarn belonged.

"You can't, or you won't?" he asked, following her like a pesky shadow.

"Both," she said, not bothering to turn around.

"But we need you. Simon Paredes had a stroke and—"

"I know. But surely there's someone else. I know Heavenly Rest doesn't have a formal choir but doesn't the AME church?"

"They do, but Jesse Cardwell, the choir director at Living Water AME Church, had a heart attack a month ago. He doesn't want the stress. And as his doctor, I agree with him about that."

"I'm sorry to hear that, but the answer is still no." She shoved the yarn into the cubby with a little more force than was necessary.

"Come on, Brenda. You're the only person in town with a degree in musical education. Your mother recommended you highly."

Momma. Of course Momma had recommended her. Momma also wanted her to ditch the dead-end job at A Stitch in Time and apply for a teaching position at Rutledge High. And when Brenda had refused to do that, Momma had gone behind her back to suggest to Rev. Micah St. Pierre that Brenda would make a perfect choir director for Heavenly Rest.

Brenda turned and faced the doctor. "Leave my mother out of it. The fact is, I was a high school orchestra instructor, not a choral director," she said. It was a weak argument, because in the Muncie school district, where she'd taught for years, she'd done double duty when budgets got tight. She'd even taught elementary school music for a while.

"Your mother told Donna Cuthbert that you've directed choirs before. She even said that the folks at Heavenly Rest have been after you to organize a more formal choir there."

Damn, damn, damn. She gripped the edge of the cubby as the room swam. The gossips of Magnolia Harbor were ganging up on her.

"I'm not going to direct the Christmas Chorale," she said.

"But what about the people who depend on the—"

She turned on him and his twinkly blue eyes. "What part of 'no' do you not understand?"

"I was just saying that it's for a good cause, and—"

"Look, I hate Christmas music. If you must know, I hate the whole season."

"Why?"

"Just because. Trust me. I'm no good at Christmas."

Across the room Paulette said the word "Scrooge" under her breath, but with Paulette that meant she practically shouted it out loud. The woman was deaf as a stone.

Brenda finally met Jim's impossibly blue eyes. "I'm not Scrooge. I'll gladly give you a donation for the clinic. I'm not the Grinch either. If you want to celebrate Christmas and sing like the Whos in Whoville, be my guest. I don't want to steal your merrymaking. Just don't ask me to participate."

She turned and ran for her life.

Chapter Two

"I old you so," Paulette said as Brenda hightailed it into the back room. "That woman is a lost cause. Just the other day I heard her complaining about people buying Christmas fabric."

"That was back in August, Paulette, before the shipment of holiday fabrics came in," Joyce said. "You remember, don't you? Millie came in here complaining about the dearth of Christmas fabric and blamed Brenda for it. You know how Millie can be when she's irked."

"Still, it shows a woman who is incapable of understanding the joy of the season."

Jim tried to tune the women out as they continued to gossip about Brenda. He'd certainly started a snowball down the hill, hadn't he? Now he wished he hadn't taken this tack. Bullying Brenda would probably not work. He'd been wrong.

Something else was bugging that woman. His sixth sense

niggled at him. That uncanny feeling had led him to medical solutions many times in the past, especially when a patient would come to him complaining about not feeling well but was unable to name specific symptoms.

Something was going on inside Brenda's head. Some painful memory or deep loss stood between her and the joy of the season. He understood this well. There had been times in his life when all he'd wanted was to hide from the holidays. What had turned Brenda so sour on Christmas? He wanted to know. Not merely because he needed her help, but because he suddenly wanted to help her.

He turned and gave Paulette a little wink and said, "I haven't given up on her yet," before he headed through the shop's door. As he walked up Harbor Drive, his son, Dylan, called. Jim fished his cell phone out of his pocket and connected the call.

"Hey," he said as he continued up the street at a brisk pace.

"So? Did she say yes?" Dylan's tone was faintly smug.

"Not exactly."

"Ha. Told you so. We need to rethink. Patsy Bauman suggested that we do a talent show instead. We wouldn't have to organize much for that."

"Oh, heaven forbid. If we have a talent show, Harry Bauman will insist on playing the harmonica. I'm sure that's why Patsy suggested it."

"We could have tryouts."

"What? And hurt Harry's feelings when we say no to him? Now that I think about it, could we even say no to him? I mean, he's on the town council and he's a platinum-level donor to the clinic."

"You have a point there. And Patsy would get huffy if we didn't let him play the harmonica."

"Exactly my point."

Dylan blew a breath that vibrated in Jim's ear. "You aren't going to change Brenda McMillan's mind. Everyone says she's utterly immovable."

"Interesting. I wonder why."

"Come on, Dad, the answer to that is simple. She's just a grumpy old lady."

"No. I don't think so. For starters, I'm sure she's younger than I am, so she isn't old. And I'm not sure she's grumpy. There's something else going on. A musician doesn't give up music, even when he decides it's not going to be his vocation."

"She isn't a patient."

"I know. She's a neighbor."

"Stay out of it. And don't go putting on rose-colored glasses either. Your optimism about people is often misplaced."

Jim swallowed back his argument. Dylan had not grown up to be an optimistic person. He tended to see the bad side of every situation and often missed the important things that patients *didn't* say. He had much to learn about human nature if he was ever to become a really good family doctor.

"Well," Dylan said a moment later, his tone as exasperated as his words, "if we can't have a chorale performance, and we don't want to do a talent show, what do you suggest?"

"I'm going to give Brenda a day to think about it."

"Dad. I just said—"

Jim arrived at his office door and waved at Lessie, his receptionist. He headed down the hall and popped his head into Dylan's office as he disconnected the line.

"I've heard all your arguments, Dylan," he said. "But my plan is to let Brenda think about it for a day. And I also need to talk to her mother and figure out why she's so angry about Christmas."

"She's a scrooge, and you'll soon discover that," Dylan said.

Dylan was thirty years old now—the same age Julianne had been when she'd passed away. To this day, it took his breath away sometimes when Dylan would look up like he was doing now. He was so much like Julianne, with the same sandy brown hair, the same unruly curl that dipped over his forehead. Oh, what would his mother have to say about him now? Would she be as worried as Jim was about the boy's glass-is-half-empty view of the world?

"We need to make a decision on this," Dylan said. "We can't keep the members of the chorale hanging."

"We can. For just a couple of days more."

Dylan rolled his eyes. "Dad...people are not as nice as you think they are."

Jim turned away and headed down the hall to his own office, worried about the man Dylan was becoming.

* * *

Later that day, Louella sent Brenda to the back room to check inventory, but since Brenda had done a full inventory at the beginning of the week, this banishment was either punishment for being late this morning or, more likely, a ploy to get her off the sales floor, where customers had been coming in all afternoon to give her the stink eye.

Doc Killough, who knew everyone in town, had purposefully uncorked the evil gossip genie. What was he trying to do? Shame her into helping out?

Probably.

She was in a truly awful mood when her phone buzzed around three in the afternoon. She stopped counting skeins of baby yak yarn and glanced at the caller ID.

Momma. That was predictable.

Her mother had been pushing her ever since she could remember. First it had been to earn a scholarship to the Juilliard School, then it had been to ditch Keith and come home, then it had been about Ella. The fact that Momma had been right about everything was irritating as hell.

Momma might be soft-spoken but she was pushy as hell.

Brenda connected the call. "Yes, Momma, I did refuse to help Doc Killough."

"Of course you did," Momma said in her infernally measured tones. Momma never raised her voice.

"So, are you calling to tell me that I'm being stupid, or emotional, or what?"

"I'm not the enemy," Momma said. "I understand why this time of year is hard for you. But honey, if you'd let just a tiny bit of Christmas joy into your heart, maybe…" Her words trailed off into a sigh.

Brenda had heard this speech for decades. Ever since the night of the Christmas Blizzard back in 1989, when she'd been sixteen. She would never forget that morning, two days before Christmas, when Chief Cuthbert had knocked on their door, grim-faced and red-eyed, to tell them that Daddy, a volunteer with the Magnolia Harbor rescue squad, had been killed in a freak car accident as he was trying to help someone out of a snowdrift.

Brenda pushed the skeins of yak yarn back into their shipping box. If only she could push that horrible memory to the back of her mind where she could forget it forever.

"I understand, you know," Momma said into the silence.

No, she didn't. Momma may have overcome the loss of her husband, but that didn't make her an authority on Brenda's grief. And besides, if Brenda hadn't yet gotten over the loss of her father, then it was Brenda's business and no one else's. Not even Momma's.

"Okay, I know you don't want to talk about this, honey. But I think it would be much healthier if you did," Momma said.

"I got a postcard from Ella," Brenda blurted. "She's not coming home for the holidays."

"Oh."

Silence drifted between them like wind-driven snow.

"Honey, you know how people feel about the clinic," Momma finally said, ignoring Brenda's attempt to change the subject.

Brenda opened a box of merino and silk sock yarns and started counting.

"People care about the clinic," Momma continued. "And the Christmas Chorale performance gets people to the fundraiser. It's become an important part of our town's holiday celebration."

Brenda made scratch marks on her legal pad as she counted skeins and colorways but made no argument.

Momma went on in her quiet way. "The word on the street is that you're just being mean."

"I'm not mean."

"I know that. You know that. But the rest of the town is calling you Ebenezer behind your back."

"Paulette Coleman practically called me Scrooge to my face," Brenda said. "I wonder how that happened? I mean, Doc Killough said you were the one who recommended me to stand in as the chorale's director."

"I didn't exactly recommend you. It's common knowledge that Reverend St. Pierre has been trying to get you to organize a choir at Heavenly Rest. I'm sure Doc Killough heard about that."

"Okay. And who's been nagging me about organizing a choir at the church?"

Another long silence welled up between mother and daughter before Momma said, "Okay. Maybe you don't care about what people say about you. But for once in your life, could you think about me? My phone has been ringing off the hook all morning. And Christmas isn't always easy for me either."

"Oh. So this is about you then?"

"No. It's about the sick people, especially the kids, who depend on the clinic."

Momma certainly knew how to play her trump cards.

"You know, Momma," Brenda said, "Doc Killough isn't playing fair. He could have called me on the phone. But no, he comes waltzing in here with his happy twinkly eyes and launches a sneak attack right in front of Paulette Coleman, one of Magnolia Harbor's biggest gossips."

"You have to hand it to the man for being in tune with the way things work around here. The truth is, you've become a scrooge, and everyone in town has known it for quite some time. This is merely confirming their beliefs about you. And I never noticed that Doc Killough has twinkly eyes. I'll need to check that out the next time I see him."

"Momma. He's manipulating me."

"Yes, he is. And maybe that's a good thing. Maybe you should let some of that twinkle into your life. It might be good for what ails you."

"I've got to go. Louella has me doing inventory again."

"Well, that's a sign," Momma said in her gentlest of voices, and then disconnected the line.

Chapter Three

Brenda decided that recounting the stock was a royal waste of time. The rest of the afternoon would be better spent marching down to Doc Killough's office and explaining to him, in excruciating detail, all the reasons she hated this darkest time of the year. It would be like bearing the black secrets of her soul, but she had to believe that once he understood her grief, he'd back off.

So she left the back room and told Louella that she had a headache and needed to go home.

"That's not surprising," Louella said as Brenda gathered up her parka and headed for the door. "I'd have a headache, too, if I were you."

It was truly astonishing how cruel people could be in the name of charity. She stepped out onto the sidewalk, where the skies had opened up in a depressing drizzle. Brenda had left her umbrella at home today so she pulled up her hood and headed off down Harbor Drive toward the medical building on Palmetto Street, which housed the Jonquil Island Free Clinic as well as Doc Killough's family practice on the second floor.

By the time she arrived, her parka was nearly soaked through. She found herself standing in an expanding puddle of water as she faced down the doctor's receptionist, Lessie Blackburn, one of A Stitch in Time's regular customers. Lessie didn't look particularly happy to see her.

"Is Doc Killough in?" Brenda asked.

"Which one?"

Brenda blinked. "There's more than one? Heaven help us."

"Doctor Jim's son joined the practice two months ago," Lessie said with a hostile lift of her chin.

"I guess I want to speak to Doctor Jim then."

"He's downstairs seeing patients at the clinic." Lessie paused a moment before adding, "Which depends on the funds raised at the Christmas Gala."

Brenda backed away from the reception desk. Did everyone in town think she hated sick children?

Nothing could be further from the truth. She'd been a teacher for two decades. She cared about children. But she didn't have to direct the Christmas Chorale. And besides, wouldn't it be better for Doc Killough to choose a Christmas-loving choir director?

She headed down the stairs and into the clinic, which was surprisingly crowded with preschool kids and their mothers. By the number of runny noses, it looked as if an upper respiratory infection was running rampant through the community.

She stepped up to the reception area where a harried Nita Morrison was juggling files. "Take a number," Nita said without looking up. She nodded toward the bright red ticket dispenser near the door.

Clearly, Doc Killough was too busy to talk right now, and Brenda wasn't about to cut in line when so many kids needed medical attention. So she helped herself to a number and took a seat beside a woman with a little boy of about six on her lap and another one a couple of years younger playing on the floor with a Matchbox car.

The older child was obviously ill. He rested his head on his mother's shoulder, and even at a distance, Brenda could hear the rattle in the kid's chest. His little brother looked like the only healthy kid in the waiting room. He was making little-boy motor sounds as he drove his car around the end table. When Brenda took her seat he turned and gave her a big smile.

"Are you sick too?" he asked.

"Hush, Donovan. Don't be asking strangers about their health. It's not polite," his mother said, turning toward Brenda, her expression a study in anxiety. "I'm sorry. He has no boundaries."

"It's okay." Brenda gave the kid a smile. "I'm not sick. I just need to talk to the doctor. But he's pretty busy right now."

The boy nodded. "Yeah, 'cuz there are lots of kids like Harper who have asthma 'n stuff. I don't have asthma. I'm not the sick one." He said this last bit in a little whisper, as if he'd heard grown-ups talking about his older brother.

"What did I just say, Doni?" The boy's mother glared.

The kid turned his back and flopped down to the floor, sitting tailor-style, with his elbow on one knee and his chin in his hand. "How much longer, Momma? I'm bored," he said.

"I don't know."

An ancient memory stirred in Brenda's mind, of that long winter when Ella had been five and had suffered one ear infection after another. At the time, Brenda had been working two menial jobs and going to school. She hadn't had health insurance in those days. She was a lot like the mothers in this room. She and Ella used to sing kid songs to make the time pass on those days when they'd ended up at the emergency room. Ella had loved music from the first moment she'd drawn breath.

Brenda squeezed her eyes shut and swallowed back a knot of longing, just as little Doni got up and started jumping around the room like a puppy who hadn't been allowed to run free in a long time.

"Doni, please," his mother said.

"Hey Doni," Brenda said. "Do you know the song about the wheels on the bus?"

The kid shook his head.

"Come here. I'll teach it to you."

The kid was ready for any kind of distraction, and Brenda reached back into her memory from the years she'd taught elementary music.

By the time Nita called Doni's mother's number, they had sung the song at least half a dozen times. "Bye," the little boy said with a wave as he followed his mother into the examination room. To her surprise, after Doni and his mother and brother left, Brenda got smiles from several of the other mothers in the room. It was the first time anyone had smiled at her all day.

Brenda remained in the waiting room until almost six o'clock because, every time someone new showed up, she traded her ticket for the newest one. So when Nita finally called her number, the waiting room was empty.

The receptionist gave her a frown. "Brenda, you know you shouldn't be here. This is for people who—"

"I'm here to see the Doc. And I've waited my turn several times over." She held up her number. "I'm next in line."

"Are you sick?"

"Well, I guess that depends on how you define sick. Based on the things people have been accusing me of all afternoon, I would venture to say there are many people in this town who think I'm crazy as a loon for not getting on board with the whole Christmas spirit thing."

This earned her a bona fide glare. "Follow me," Nita said, ushering her around the reception desk and down a long wall painted a sunny yellow.

Nita stopped at the first exam room. "Wait in here."

Brenda sat down in another hard-plastic chair. Bernice Cobb, the nurse practitioner, poked her head in the room a few minutes later. "Sorry," she said, "we had another kid just show up. It will be a few more minutes."

So she settled in. A few more minutes turned into almost half an hour before Doc Killough opened the door. "Hello, Brenda. What seems to be ailing you?" he asked in a disgustingly upbeat tone.

"I'm not sick. I want to—"

He turned his twinkly eyes in her direction, and it was like getting hit by a Merry Christmas cruise missile. She lost her train of murderous thought and stopped speaking midsentence.

"Well, that's a matter of debate," he said, jumping into the silence. "I think you have a case of Christmasitis."

She was not going to rise to his bait. "You have to stop," she said.

"Stop what?" He gave her an I'm-up-to-no-good look that might have passed for innocence, except that Brenda had taught school for decades and wasn't buying it.

"You know good and well. It's only taken eight hours, but I've become Magnolia Harbor's public enemy number one. Lessie, your receptionist upstairs, as much as accused me of supporting cruelty to little children."

"She did? Really?"

"Yes. Because, evidently, not wanting to have anything to do with the Christmas Gala is the same as wishing harm on all of Magnolia Harbor's little ones." She folded her arms across her chest. "And don't tell me that wasn't your intent."

"That was never my intent. I just want you to help out with the choir portion of the program this year."

"Okay. So the thing is, I have a good reason for not wanting to direct the Christmas Chorale, and if you'd—"

"Would you like to have dinner with me?" he interrupted.

"What?"

He checked his watch. "It's almost seven o'clock, and I haven't had anything to eat since around eleven. I'm famished. How 'bout I take you down to Aunt Annie's Kitchen for some chops, and you can tell me all about it."

"I don't want to have dinner with you. I just want you to understand why I can't direct the Christmas Chorale."

"Okay. I'm willing to listen. Over dinner. Come on, let's go."

He turned and strode out of the room, leaving her with no other choice but to follow. He was annoying. And dictatorial. And manipulative.

And for a fifty-something man, he was outrageously handsome. But then she'd only just now noticed that fact.

Chapter Four

Jim glanced once to see if Brenda had followed him. To his delight, she had, albeit with a frown turning down the corners of her mouth. How could this grumpy puss be the same woman who, according Donovan Jephson, had managed to get a group of sick kids singing in his waiting room?

A minor mystery he intended to solve. And besides, if she would quit frowning, everyone in town would notice she was beautiful, with curly auburn hair that she wore in a carefree style and a pair of eyes the color of Moonlight Bay on a stormy day.

He snagged his raincoat and umbrella on the way to the door. The afternoon's drizzle had turned into a steady rain, and Brenda didn't have an umbrella so he found himself huddling close to her as they made their way around the corner to Aunt Annie's Kitchen.

Brenda wasn't a tall person, so he had to hunch to make sure the umbrella protected her from the rain. That brought his face a little closer to the top of her head, where he got a whiff of her scent. And damn if she didn't smell like tangerines—an aroma that always made him think of Christmas back in western New York. Mom had always put a tangerine in the toe of his stocking. Back in those days, tangerines were rare and wonderful. How interesting that the town's Scrooge should smell like Christmas morning.

Aunt Annie's Kitchen was crowded, even on a rainy midweek night. And since it was November, the crowd was mostly locals, many of whom stared at Brenda as they crossed the dining room.

Once they were seated, Jim took a moment to study his adversary. Brenda had a fragile quality about her that had nothing to do with bone structure. The impression came from the way her gaze flitted around the room like a hummingbird in flight, never landing on anything for very long and never really making eye contact.

So he wasn't surprised when she picked up her menu and hid behind it until Annie came over to take their orders.

"Hey Doc," Annie said. "I heard Bonelle Jephson had to take Harper to the clinic. Is that baby all right?"

"He's got a bad cold, but I gave Bonelle some medicine to help him breathe. I see she's not working tonight."

Annie shook her head. "No, sir. I told her to stay home. Trevor has to be over to the mainland every night until nine o'clock. He's got a holiday job at the Value Mart, and her babysitter has come down with whatever's going around. Harper and Doni need their momma tonight."

"Annie, you have a heart of gold."

Annie laughed and then turned toward Brenda. "Hey Miz Brenda, what can I get you tonight?"

"I'll have pork chops and some okra and tomatoes on the side."

Jim handed his menu off and said, "I'll have the same thing."

"I'll have sweet tea and hush puppies on the table in a minute," Annie said, turning away.

"So Doni's mother works for Annie?" Brenda asked. "I don't think I've seen her here before."

"She just started a few weeks ago. She had to take the job in order to make ends meet this year because Harlan Cantrell called it quits on shrimping and Trevor, Bonelle's husband, worked on Harlan's boat. There are several families who are suddenly in need because of that. Annie has a soft spot for shrimpers' wives. She used to be one awhile back before she opened her chophouse."

"You see a lot of shrimpers' kids at the clinic?"

"Yes, I do. And I see a lot of people who only have seasonal jobs. The clinic is an important part of the island's safety net."

Brenda interlaced her fingers and stared down at her hands. "You really know these people, don't you?"

"I've been taking care of them for decades."

"I'm sure you think I'm an awful person. But I told you this morning. I'm not against the clinic. I'll happily give you a contribution."

"It might surprise you, but I know you're not a bad person. To me, you're the person who could take over the Christmas Chorale and help the clinic raise money for kids like Harper and Doni."

"I can't."

Annie came back with their iced teas and a bowl of hush puppies. Jim snagged one of the little fried corn-bread balls and popped it into his mouth. It was one of his guilty pleasures.

"Have a hush puppy, Brenda," he said as he chewed.

She shook her head. "They're so bad for you. I can't believe you're eating one. How many times a day do you tell your patients to cut down on saturated fat?"

He laughed. "Too many to count. And you know what they say in response?"

"They probably hang their heads and tell you they'll do better next time."

"Well...that's true. But if they truly spoke their minds, they'd tell me that it's the holiday season, and we should all live a little because life is short."

She cocked her head and met his gaze, her glance landing long enough for him to realize that her eyes had little shards of amber in them. Like a pair of twin kaleidoscopes.

She dropped her gaze to the hush puppies but she didn't take one. "Look," she said in a tight voice, "I realize you're in a bind. But don't ask me to do this. I hate Christmas."

"Why?"

She looked away, turning her head and focusing on one of the many pieces of African artwork lining the restaurant's walls. "There are so many reasons. Bad things happen to me this time of year. And I'm sorry, but I can't get over the negative memories. When the holly and the ivy goes up, I just want to disappear and not come out until after New Year's."

* * *

Brenda hunched her shoulders and tried to hide behind her shaggy hair. It suddenly seemed as if everyone in the dining room was staring at her, condemning her for not wanting to be happy at this time of year. She almost pushed away from the table but Jim covered her clenched fists with his warm hands. The touch sent a shock through her system, and she looked up at him.

The twinkle had gone out of his eyes. "My wife died on Christmas Day," he said, holding her gaze for a long instant.

"I'm sorry," Brenda muttered, pulling her hands away from his warm touch and reaching for her purse. "I think I should go."

"Running away again?" One of his salt-and-pepper eyebrows arched, and she had the feeling the man possessed ESP or something.

"I'm sorry for your loss. I lost someone around Christmastime too. And I can't forget it or get over it."

"And you've let this loss color your life?"

She shrugged. "Among many other losses. Look, I don't want to—"

Just then, Annie returned with their food, placing it on the table and then retreating.

"Seems kind of silly to run away when one of Annie's chops is right there for the eating, and I'm picking up the tab."

"I can't do what you want me to do."

"What, eat the chop?" He laughed.

And damned if the corner of her mouth didn't twitch involuntarily. "I don't understand you," she said in a near whisper.

He leaned forward. "I guess we're even."

She picked up her steak knife and sliced a piece off the chop. "I don't understand how you can be so merry," she said, before popping a bite into her mouth. As always, Annie's food had a way of comforting, right down to Brenda's wounded soul.

"Why, because Julianne died on Christmas Day?" Doc Killough asked.

She nodded.

"Well, it's like this," he said, his gaze drifting a little.

"We thought she wouldn't make it to Christmas Day, so Dylan and I were happy that she woke up on Christmas Eve and was able to see Dylan open one of his presents before she lapsed into a coma."

"Dylan is your son?"

He nodded. "He was only ten when Julianne died."

"Oh." A twinge of pain lanced through her. The poor kid. She knew how he felt. But she didn't want to talk about that. Instead, she asked, "You never remarried?"

He shrugged. "The right woman never came along. And you? I understand you're divorced."

"I divorced my husband twenty-seven years ago. He wasn't much of a husband. Ella, my daughter, was only three at the time."

"And you never remarried?"

She shrugged and then realized that she'd mirrored his body language. What was up with that? And why had a man as handsome as Doc Killough never found another wife? Julianne must have been something.

She concentrated on eating her chop, and the conversation stalled. She suddenly had a zillion questions she wanted to ask about his dead wife, about raising a kid on his own, about how he'd managed to remain so merry and bright even with that tragedy in his past. But mostly she wanted to know how Dylan felt about Christmas.

Her own sad relationship with the holiday had only started when Daddy died.

The saga continued another Christmas when Keith had gotten wasted and then belligerent. He hadn't done anything to hurt her or baby Ella, but Brenda had become truly frightened of him. On Christmas Day, she'd moved out of the house and fled all the way from Chicago to Indianapolis, where she hired an attorney and initiated the divorce.

Nine months later, she'd enrolled in the music education department at Indiana University as a part-time student. It had taken her years to earn her degree, but she'd done it. Money had been tight in those years so their holiday celebrations had been low-key. Momma would send enough money for Brenda and Ella to come home for Thanksgiving. But besides that, Christmas hadn't been a big thing. Which probably explained why Ella never felt the need to come home for the holidays.

She looked up from her food to find Jim studying her, a sly look in his eye. "What?" she asked.

"I can see the wheels turning in your head."

"So you're a mind reader now?"

He shook his head. "No. I'm just an old country doctor. And I've seen cases like yours before."

"Oh, really? This Christmasitis you were talking about earlier."

He nodded. "Yup. In my opinion, you need a dose of joyful music."

"Why? Because you think I should be joyful this time of year?"

"No. Because I think whoever you lost would be so unhappy to see you miserable during the holidays."

"You sound like my mother."

"She's a wise woman."

Brenda cut another slice of pork chop and popped it into her mouth. "My father died the night of the big snowstorm. You know, the Christmas Blizzard in 1989. I was sixteen, and he was the light in my world."

"I'm sorry."

"He could have saved himself. A lot of other members of the volunteer rescue squad stayed home that night. No one here has the first clue about driving in the snow. But Daddy had a four-by-four pickup. So he went and some other idiot lost control and plowed right into him." Her lip trembled. "It wasn't fair."

* * *

Brenda looked up at Jim, pain shimmering in her kaleidoscope eyes. He wanted to pull her into a hug, but the table stood between them.

"So," he said, "you've been running from Christmas ever since?"

"Sort of. When Daddy died, I lost my way for a while. I got involved with a boy, Keith. And I got pregnant out of sheer stupidity, lost my opportunity to try out for a place at Juilliard, and ended up living in Chicago, married. I left Keith a few years later. He was no good for me or Ella." She looked down at her food, the picture of unhappiness.

"Did you really have an audition date at Juilliard?" he asked.

"Yes. But I canceled it."

"So did I."

"What?" Brenda's head snapped up.

"I had an audition date at Juilliard, but I canceled at the last minute because I was offered a full scholarship to UNC's premed program."

"You willingly walked away from Juilliard?"

He nodded.

"Why don't *you* direct the choir?"

"I'm a reasonably good pianist, but I have no clue how to direct a choir. And besides, I get called away on emergencies all the time."

"You walked away from Juilliard? I can't believe it."

"It wasn't what I wanted."

"Well, that certainly makes us different. Because I wanted that audition more than life itself, but I screwed up so badly." She looked away.

"If things had been different, we might have met in New York years ago."

Her gaze zipped back and held. "How did you end up in Magnolia Harbor? You didn't grow up here," she asked, changing the subject.

"I met my wife at college. When I was finished with med school, she wanted to move back home."

"And you stayed after she died?"

He shrugged. "It was one of many ways to stay close to her."

Brenda let go of a mirthless laugh. "Funny. When I left Keith in Chicago, I went to the place he was least likely to find me. I didn't want him following me home. That's how I ended up in Indiana."

Jim leaned forward. "So I get that you made a mistake as a young girl, but you did eventually go to college and become a music teacher, right? Why are you throwing your music away now?"

"You're going to make me spill my guts, aren't you? While simultaneously manipulating me. You're a piece of work."

She was right about that. "You said you wanted to explain. I'm listening," he said.

"The last time I directed a winter concert," she said, "was two years ago in Muncie, where I was the orchestra and choral director for a magnet school. On the night of the concert, half of my violin section was injured in a car accident. It was snowing that night—not much for Indiana where they don't close schools at the drop of a hat. Just some light flurries and a little sleet. Enough to make roads slippery.

"I will never understand why one of the parents let their child drive in that weather. Her inexperience contributed to the accident, and my first-chair violinist, a girl name Katie Liao, was killed."

Brenda's voice got thin and thready, and the sheen in her eyes turned into tears that spilled over her lower lids. "I couldn't direct anything after that. Katie was so talented. She had such a bright future. And what? She lost her life a week before Christmas because of sleet and snow. I should have canceled the concert, even though school hadn't been canceled that day. But if I had called off the performance, it would have meant no concert. And we'd worked so hard. And I ." Her voice trailed off.

Jim reached across the table and took her hand. "I can't imagine what it must be like to lose a student. But I have lost patients over the years. I always feel as if I didn't do enough. But I've learned to accept that there are some things beyond my control. The weather is one of those things. Katie's death was never your fault."

Brenda dashed a tear from her check. "I know that. But it doesn't change how I feel."

"Not even if you were to get back in front of a choir and let the music in?"

She looked up at him and gave a small head shake.

"Okay, but one last question. How did you feel today when you were teaching the song to the kids in the waiting room?"

Her lips parted. "You know about that? I thought—"

"Nita told me the moment you arrived."

"But she acted like she didn't see me. She made me wait."

He shrugged. "There's a cold virus going around. And it was sweet the way you kept giving up your place in line. You are a great big fraud, you know that?"

"And you are incredible."

"Thanks." He smiled. "But if you really think you have nothing to give despite the obvious, then I'll stand down. We'll come up with some other plan for the clinic and the kids who depend on it."

She dropped her head into her hands. "You are impossible," she muttered.

"Does that mean you've changed your mind?" he asked, a little spark of joy swelling in his chest.

She looked up with rounded shoulders. "I'm going to hate myself in the morning. But okay. I give up. I'll do it."

"You will?" He gave her a big smile that bounced right off her frowny face.

"Yeah. If I don't, I'm never going to be able to walk through town without someone whispering behind my back. So let's get one thing clear. I'm not doing this because I love Christmas or Christmas music. You cornered me. And I'm giving up."

"Clear as glass," he said, stifling a smile.

"I'll need to talk to Simon or figure out what music he had planned."

"No problem. I've got his notes for this year's performance as well as the music the chorale has collected and paid for over the years. I can bring them out to your house on Saturday."

Chapter Five

On Saturday afternoon, directly after clinic hours, Jim headed out on Magnolia Boulevard to deliver Simon's box of music to the new choral director.

The pieces had already been chosen and the music distributed to the chorale's members weeks ago. Rehearsals had also started before Simon had gotten sick, and Jim hoped his new director wouldn't want to make a lot of changes. The rehearsal schedule was already in turmoil. Even worse was the fact that at least half of the chorale had called him up to complain that they didn't want the Grinch as their director.

Proving that sometimes a person just couldn't win when it came to the court of public opinion. And also, Jim should never have let the gossip get so badly out of hand. It would be up to him to make sure this didn't end up in a full-out disaster for Brenda. He owed her that much, now that he understood the reason she was so reticent to get involved.

He pulled into the Paradise Beach community, a group of cottages that had been built on the ocean side of the island back in the 1960s. The houses out here weren't nearly as large as the new ones springing up along the coast north of town. These were small two-bedroom homes, built up on stilts and shoved cheek by jowl behind the primary dunes. Over the years, palmettos and pines had grown up between them, giving them a well-established feel that the bigger vacation homes lacked.

Brenda's cottage was typical. Painted a medium blue with white trim, it had a screen porch on one end and a deck on the other. Above the door to the porch hung a piece of gray driftwood with the words "Cloud Nine" hand-lettered in blue paint.

He stifled a smile as he carried the box of music up the stairway and rang the bell. Brenda came to the door looking as comfortable in her skin as Jim had ever seen her. Her beautiful auburn hair curled around her face, and she wore a pair of worn jeans that hugged her hips, although the frayed-at-the neck Indiana University sweatshirt hid some of her curves. But the worn-out jeans and old sweatshirt told him a lot. Evidently, she was the sort of person who hung on to things.

He liked that about her, even though he had a feeling her biggest problem was the grief she was clinging to.

Her house was like her, somehow. It had never been renovated and still retained the original 1960s tongue-and-groove wood ceiling and paneling. The walls were covered with beach art, and a comfy couch and a big armchair rounded out the furniture.

"I come bearing music," he said with a smile.

She stepped back from the door and ushered him all the way into her front room. It was only then that he noticed the

Steinway upright piano along the back wall. A violin case sat open atop the piano, and a stand to one side held the music for Amy Beach's Violin and Piano Sonata.

"Amy Beach, huh?" he said, nodding to the music stand as Brenda took the cardboard box and placed it on the coffee table.

"What? Oh." She glanced at the music. "Yeah. A particular favorite."

"Very romantic music."

"And obscure. Because, you know, female composers." She frowned a little. "You know Amy Beach?"

"Yeah. I do. I've even played that piece."

"Recently?"

He shook his head. "No. Years ago, when I had a neighbor who was pretty good on the violin."

He didn't wait for her to respond. Instead, he crossed the room and inspected the music open on the piano. "Shall we practice?" he said, sitting down on the bench.

He flipped the pages to the opening chords, stretched his fingers, and rested them on the piano keys for a moment before playing. The beginning of the piece, written in A minor, was dark and brooding.

He expected her to pick up her violin and join in, but she remained behind him. No doubt she was judging his less-than-stellar playing. It had been years since he'd played anything quite as difficult as this piece.

When he finally stopped and turned, she was wearing that little frown of hers.

"Aren't you going to play with me?" he asked, giving her his best smile.

"You weren't kidding, were you? You could have been a Juilliard-trained concert pianist."

"No. I would have hated every minute of it. I like playing

music because it gives me joy. Not because I make my living at it. And besides, I made a bunch of mistakes."

"You sight-read the music, and you didn't make that many mistakes."

"Okay, so it was good enough for an amateur. Why don't we play the sonata together?"

She continued to frown at him, grumpy as ever.

"What? Don't you think you can keep up with me?" he asked.

Oh, that got her. "I can keep up."

"Then show me."

* * *

Brenda took her violin out of its case and rosined her bow, all the while avoiding eye contact with the incredibly annoying, but supremely talented, Dr. James Killough. She shouldn't have let him challenge her like that. She shouldn't have let him goad her into agreeing to anything.

But here she was, tucking the fiddle under her chin and finally looking over at him. Good gracious, he was one handsome man, with a slightly wild mane of salt-and-pepper hair and those merry eyes that were twinkling at her right now, sparking anticipation for the music to begin.

Or maybe for something else she hadn't felt in way too long a time. Dammit, she was attracted to him. To his long fingers resting on the piano keys and his blue eyes that seemed to see right into her soul.

She nodded, and he turned and played the first few chords of the sonata. The opening theme was dark and rich and almost dirgelike, until the violin joined in, taking the musical variation high above the piano in a swirling, romantic style reminiscent of Brahms.

They played the movement through to its end, which took ten minutes. During that time, Brenda became utterly lost inside the music. Jim was a stellar accompanist.

What was it about music? Sometimes, when she least expected it, music could make the world and all its troubles fade away until only the notes and the rhythm remained. Once upon a time, before she had lost so much, Brenda had told Momma that playing the violin was like praying. God lived inside the music.

This time, though, it wasn't God she felt. It was Jim.

When the last note of the movement faded away, they turned toward each other. His eyes were shiny, and her heart pounded like timpani in her chest.

For an instant, the connection held, and then he burst into a bright laugh. "That was fun," he said.

She tucked the violin under her arm as heat crawled up her cheeks. She was an idiot. She'd promised herself, long ago, never to let anyone into her life who could push her around. And suddenly it seemed as if she had.

She put her violin in the case, avoiding eye contact. "So...," she said on a long breath, "I guess I should get busy looking at the music for the concert."

"I guess maybe you should, unless you want to help me and Dylan decorate a boat for the Festival of Lights."

She cocked her head. "You have a boat?"

"No, but Jude St. Pierre just bought a new one. It's a 150-foot gaff-rigged schooner. Built back in the 1930s. They just christened it *Synchronicity Too*. He must have spent a fortune fitting that boat out, but I reckon he'll earn it back with more people on his sunset cruises. Anyway, the boat has two masts and a bunch of yardarms. It's going to take a lot of twinkle lights to make it shine during the Christmas boat parade. I'm sure he wouldn't mind extra help."

"No thanks. I'm not climbing up any boat masts. I'm afraid of heights."

"Really? Or is it just Christmas lights you have a problem with?" He winked.

"I really need to get ready for the rehearsal on Monday."

"All work and no play...," he said.

"Jim, do you want me to direct your chorale, or do you want me to suddenly have a magical transformation and throw myself into Christmas like the rest of the people in this town?"

"Well, actually, I'd love to see both."

"Why?"

"Because you need a little Christmas."

"And now, thanks to your Christmas Gala, I have exactly that. A *little* Christmas. A little Christmas goes a long, long way."

"So, I guess you wouldn't want to actually ride on *Synchronicity Too*."

Brenda blinked. What the hell? "Are you asking me out on one of the sunset cruises?" she blurted.

He laughed. "No. I'm asking you to participate in this year's Festival of Lights. Jude's invited some of the kids from the clinic, and he wants to go full-out pirate for this."

"Pirate?"

"Jude is advertising his pirate cruises, and you know how the kids love pirates in this town. So anyway, everyone on the boat is going to dress up like a pirate...or a wench. And there will be lots of fun for the clinic kids."

"Pirates and Christmas? Together? Really?"

"Yup. Which is why taking a ride on *Synchronicity Too* would be perfect for you."

"Perfect how?"

"It will get you out of the house, and I promise there will be no elves or Santas involved."

"But it's a Christmas parade."

"Okay, if you want to get technical..." He rolled his beautiful blue eyes, and damn if she didn't suddenly want to dress up like a pirate wench.

"Are you dressing up?" she asked.

"In a tricorn hat and a big frock coat."

The idea of seeing him dressed up like that appealed to her in a completely forbidden way. He'd look really good in a frock coat and knee britches.

"Okay. I'll think about it," she said.

He grinned, and she melted a little.

"Good," he said, and then headed toward the door. But he stopped before he opened it. "I loved playing music with you. Maybe we could get together again sometime?"

A fire ignited in her middle. "I'd like that," she said.

Chapter Six

Brenda stood in the middle of the Rutledge High School cafeteria checking her watch. It was five minutes to seven, and half the chairs set up at the end of the room were empty. Where was everyone? Had they boycotted the first rehearsal because she'd agreed to be the choir director?

Even her accompanist, the talented and infuriating Doc Killough, was MIA. She wasn't entirely sure what she'd do if Jim didn't show up. She could play the piano, but she was no accompanist, and playing the piano while simultaneously trying to direct would be difficult.

She dug into the box of music Jim had given her on Saturday and pulled out thirty sets of an arrangement of "Joy to the World" and "He's Got the Whole World in His Hands." It was easy to learn and upbeat—a perfect song for the opening of their program. She was scratching the song Simon had selected because it was one of the pieces her choir had planned to sing the night Katie Liao was killed.

There were too many bad memories associated with "In the Bleak Midwinter."

She passed out the music to the choir members who were sitting in their chairs. But at 7:03 p.m., a quarter of the chairs were still empty.

"Where is everyone?" she asked Jim, who had finally arrived at the stroke of seven and seated himself at the electronic piano they were borrowing from the high school's music department. He took the sheet music and began studying the piece. His presence sent an electric hum through her body that she tried, without any success, to suppress.

"They'll be along, eventually," he said.

She pulled her gaze away from the doctor and checked her watch again, irritation mounting. She had only one hour each Monday night to get the group ready for their concert. How the heck was she supposed to whip these people into a choir if folks didn't show up on time?

Just then, Donna Cuthbert and Leanne Milford strolled into the room, talking and laughing.

"I'm so glad you could join us," Brenda said, glaring at them.

They stopped and stared at her with surprised faces.

"You're late. Rehearsal starts at seven o'clock."

The two women glanced at each other and then shucked their coats as a few more choir members wandered in.

Brenda waited, grinding her teeth as they found their seats. There were still a few empty chairs. She glanced over at Jim, who was giving her a little frown. What? Did he expect her to be nice to everyone and not rock any boats? She stomped on the urge to ask his permission to take charge. She didn't need permission. Choirs were not democracies. Either the singers followed the director or the result was cacophony.

Brenda took her place in front of the music stand facing the choir. "Let me make my expectations clear. I don't know how Simon managed this group in the past. But I'm not Simon. I'm…" She paused a moment because she almost referred to herself as Ms. McMillan, as if they were a class of high school students and not adults.

"I'm Brenda," she said. "And I expect you to be here at 7:00 p.m. Not five minutes later. And I expect you not to talk while I'm talking." She turned and glared at the soprano section where Donna Cuthbert was whispering something into Lori Colbert's ear. The ladies snapped to attention, and Donna's face flushed red.

"How many of you can read music?"

The majority of the group raised their hands.

"Good. Because we're making a few changes in the program. We're dropping 'In the Bleak Midwinter' and adding 'Joy to the Whole World.' I also want to add an arrangement of 'Silent Night' toward the end of the program, but I will need to find and purchase some music before next week. So stand by."

There was an audible hum of distress among the group.

"None of the new songs will be difficult to learn. I'm sure you're all capable."

But after an hour of working with them, she wondered just how capable any of them were. They had been working with Simon for three weeks before he'd been stricken, and yet they didn't know their parts, even for the easy pieces. She was able to get through only two of the songs, and there were a few more audible grumbles as the choir members filed out of the cafeteria when rehearsal was finished.

Well, too bad. It was a classic case of be careful what you wish for.

She was collecting her music from the stand when Jim walked up behind her. She felt his approach long before he arrived. The man seemed to generate heat wherever he went.

"So," he said, "that went well."

She turned. "You think?"

"You took charge. That's important."

A little frisson of relief washed through her. "Glad you understand."

"I never expected anything less. Simon used to annoy me sometimes. He always took his work at Grace Methodist more seriously than what we did here."

"I see," she said, wondering why Simon would do something like that. A choir director needed to make sure his performers didn't make fools of themselves.

So," Jim said cocking his head, "have you thought about my invitation?"

"To dress up like a pirate wench?"

His mouth curled, and the twinkle in his eyes deepened. "Yup."

She'd all but decided to tell him no, but standing there, looking up into those incredible blue eyes, she suddenly wanted to say yes. It had been a long time since she'd wanted to say yes to anything. But she couldn't say yes, could she?

"What's stopping you?" he asked as if he could read her mind.

So many things. "People are going to laugh at me for dressing up like a pirate wench," she said. "And besides, I'm too old for something like that."

"No you're not. You're younger than I am."

"It's not the same. I'm going to be wearing one of those

bodies, you know, and…" Her voice faded away. She was not about to say something stupid like her cleavage was too old to be on display like that.

"Yeah. I know," he said, a flirty smile lighting up his face.

She blinked and blushed, the heat climbing her face.

He rushed into the awkward moment with more words. "And no one is going to laugh. People love pirates in this town. It's part of our history. And even if they do, they'll be laughing along with us, right? I mean, Yo ho ho."

She laughed. Because it was funny. And it struck her right then that Keith McMillan would never have dressed up as a pirate. Not in a million years. Because he wasn't comfortable with his masculinity.

"I guess it is kind of funny in a good way," she admitted.

"There you go. Say yes. Please."

"Why? Because I need a little Christmas?"

He shook his head. "No. Because I'd like you to come." He paused for a moment. "And I'd like to see you wearing that costume."

For an instant, she might have been riding on the Tower of Terror. Her stomach dropped, and she was free-falling. She certainly didn't want to fall in love, and she was probably too old for lust. And besides, if she had to fall into anything, it would be best not to do it during the holidays. That would be just plain dumb and risky. "I don't know," she said in a strangled tone.

"Please," he murmured.

She drew in a sharp breath filled with his scent, which was one-part vanilla and another part clean and astringent. She closed her eyes. Would it be so bad to say yes? She opened her eyes and found herself trapped in his twinkly gaze. "Okay." She breathed the word.

"Great. I'll drop by with your costume in the next day or

two. Maybe we can play the Amy Beach again. I'd really like that."

"I would too."

And then he turned and headed out the doors, leaving her alone and weak in the knees.

Chapter Seven

Dylan was furious about something, but Jim couldn't figure out what. They were sitting in the middle of Rafferty's dining room grabbing a bite after work, and his son hadn't said one word in the last fifteen minutes. That wasn't like Dylan. He would talk about sports or his passion for fly-fishing, but he rarely sat rigid like that, with a pinched look to his mouth.

"You want to tell me what's bugging you?" Jim asked.

Dylan leaned forward, shoulders hunched. "Have you lost your mind?" he asked in a harsh whisper as if he didn't want anyone at the next table over to hear him.

Jim glanced in that direction. It looked as if Kerri Eaton was having a nice evening out with her girlfriends. He didn't think Kerri, the proprietor of the Daffy Down Dilly boutique on Harbor Drive, cared one whit about the discussion happening at Jim's table. The girls seemed to be having a lovely time.

"I don't think I've lost my mind. What's the problem?"

"I heard from Debbie Shane that you've been visiting Brenda McMillan out at her place. In the evenings. Are you sleeping with that woman?"

Jim almost choked on his beer.

"Dad, are you okay?"

Jim waved Dylan away as he coughed. What the hell? Did Dylan think he was romantically involved with Brenda?

He leaned back in his chair, wiping his mouth with his napkin, and the idea opened in his mind like a beautiful rose. A romance with Brenda might be fun. It had been a very long time since he'd had a romance with anyone. And he had thoroughly enjoyed the couple of times he'd gone out to her place to work on the Amy Beach sonata.

"Dad? Are you with me?" Dylan asked in an urgent tone.

"I'm fine."

"So? What's the deal with you and that woman?"

That woman? Wow. "I'm not sleeping with her," Jim said. "We've been working on a piano and violin sonata. It's been a long time since I had anyone to play classical music with."

"So it's true. You have been going out to her house at night."

"Is this an interrogation?"

"No. But there's a lot of gossip, Dad."

"There always is."

"And I just heard from Jude that you've invited Brenda to join you on *Synchronicity Too* during the Festival of Lights. You can see how people are putting one and one together. Are you serious about this woman?"

"I guess so. We're playing *serious* music together."

"Really?" Dylan rolled his eyes, clearly not enjoying Jim's lame dad joke.

"Look, I'm serious about trying to help Brenda find a way to enjoy the holiday. I thought it might be fun for her to join me on Jude's boat and wear a costume. There are psychological benefits to—"

"A costume?" Dylan sounded deeply distressed. "What costume?"

"Jude didn't tell you? He wants everyone dressed up as a pirate or a wench. It's a shameless piece of marketing on his part. But for a variety of reasons, getting Brenda to dress up like a pirate wench is going to be good for her."

"Oh my God. People are going to laugh. At both of you."

"So?"

Dylan cocked his head. "You don't even care, do you?"

"About what?"

"Your reputation."

"My reputation is fine, thank you."

Dylan huffed out an exasperated sigh. "I don't think she's good for you."

"That's not the point. I'm trying to be good for her."

His son blinked and stared. "What does that even mean?"

"Give it up, Dylan. She's coming with me on the Festival of Lights cruise." He paused a moment to pop a shrimp into his mouth and chew. "And we'll both be wearing costumes."

Dylan's mouth dropped open. "You're too old for this."

Oh boy. Dylan rarely annoyed him, but being told that he was too old to enjoy dressing up and having some fun was irritating as hell. He leaned forward, catching Dylan's stare. "How old is too old?" he asked.

Dylan shrugged. "I don't know. But..."

"I'm over the hill at fifty-one? Is that it?" Jim's voice sounded tight.

"No. But..."

"Then why did you say I was too old to dress up as a pirate or enjoy being with a woman dressed up as a wench?"

"Damn. I'm digging a big hole, aren't I?" Dylan said.

"All the way to China, boy."

"Just be careful, okay? The last time you had a lady friend, she turned out to be a witch."

"Yeah, well, Brenda isn't a witch."

"No? From what I've heard she's downright scary at choir rehearsals."

Jim stifled a smile. He could see how people might be intimidated by her because Brenda was the epitome of a tough and demanding high school teacher. Simon had never imposed any discipline on the choir, but Brenda was cut from different cloth. So there were some grumbles. But there were also a lot of others who were relieved to have someone who knew what they were doing. The whole town would soon discover Brenda's talents. This year's performance was going to give people goose bumps.

"Well, call me foolish," Jim said, dipping another shrimp into cocktail sauce, "but I like a good challenge."

"Oh my God. You aren't even denying it, are you?"

Jim said nothing because his son was behaving like a petulant child who didn't like the idea of his widowed father dating someone. But damn, if he was going to date anyone, Brenda would be right there at the top of his list.

* * *

Momma had stopped roasting a turkey for Thanksgiving the year after Daddy died. And for the last thirty years, Thanksgiving dinner had featured a roast chicken instead.

Brenda hadn't missed many Thanksgivings after she'd

left Keith in Chicago. Momma always sent gas money, and Brenda made the long drive from Indiana year after year.

So Thanksgiving at Momma's house was a habit, or a tradition, or something. But for years now, ever since Ella had followed in Brenda's footsteps and run off with a man, Ella's chair at the end of the table had been empty. Cody Callaghan, a handsome country-and-western singer, had convinced Brenda's daughter that she could make a living playing fiddle in Nashville rather than studying classical music in New York.

"Lord, make us truly thankful for what we are about to receive." Momma said grace, and Brenda bowed her head, trying to count her blessings. But the emptiness of the chairs on each side of the table overwhelmed her.

"Amen," Momma said.

Brenda raised her head and picked up her knife and fork. But before she could cut a slice out of her chicken breast, Momma said, "They're gossiping about you all up and down Harbor Drive."

Brenda squeezed her silverware and met her mother's gaze. "When have they ever stopped?" she asked.

"Honestly, honey, I don't understand why you have to be so negative all the time."

Brenda swallowed back a retort. Momma was a sweet woman who never raised her voice or said a harmful word to anyone. She was a peacemaker and a member of the Piece Makers, the local quilting club. Which meant she heard all the gossip in town.

So Brenda counted to three and reached for the same calm voice Momma used. "They asked me to do a job, and I'm doing it the best way I know how. I have no idea how Simon managed the chorale in the past without losing his temper. The sopranos think they're in charge, and the tenors aren't much better. The poor altos get lost when the basses start to bellow. And you know how it is with altos, they always lack confidence."

Momma smiled, the corners of her eyes wrinkling up. She had a lot of wrinkles these days, but then, she was pushing seventy. The thought was mildly discomforting. Momma had had a few health issues recently. A detached retina and some serious trouble with arthritis that made it painful for her to quilt. She was getting old, and one day she'd be gone too.

And then Brenda would be utterly alone. Except for Ella. But her relationship with her daughter was strained at best.

"I'm not talking about the Christmas Chorale," Momma said, pulling Brenda from her negative thoughts. "In fact, Donna was saying, just this past Tuesday at the Piece Makers, that you might not be as likable as Simon but she feels as if the chorale is in good hands."

"Really? I don't think she likes me much."

"Well, she doesn't have to like you, honey. But she definitely respects you, and that's more important."

"Then what are they gossiping about?" she asked, finally slicing into her chicken breast.

"Doc Killough."

"What about him?"

"Is it true that he's been coming out to your house on Thursdays?" Momma leaned in, a strange, almost avid light in her eyes.

"Oh, good grief. Momma. No. I mean, yes, he has been coming out on Thursday nights the last few weeks, and he was out on Tuesday of this week as well. We're working on Amy Beach's Violin Sonata."

"Working on?"

"He's a gifted pianist. Did you know that?"

"Well, I know he plays piano. I mean, everyone knows that."

"He was accepted to Juilliard. He chose not to go."

"What?"

Brenda nodded, something warm and odd spreading through her chest. Momma might be a saint, but she'd never truly forgiven Brenda for messing up her one chance to study at the nation's foremost musical college. What would Momma think about a man who walked away from that chance?

"He wanted to be a doctor more than a musician."

"Oh my word. I didn't know."

"So we've been playing this piano and violin sonata."

"What? Like rehearsing it?"

Momma's question was obvious but Brenda had no answer. They hadn't been rehearsing it. They had no plans to perform it for anyone. They'd just been playing it because...

And the warm feeling in her chest expanded to include her whole body. Yeah. Okay. She was an idiot.

"I guess," Brenda said, not quite telling the truth.

"Oh. Are you going to play it at the Christmas Gala?"

She shrugged one shoulder. "No. I don't think we're going to be ready. And it's a very long piece so..." Her voice faded out.

Momma nodded, her mouth twitching a little. Was she amused? Did she see through Brenda's dissembling? Probably.

"I also heard from Jenna St. Pierre on Tuesday that you're going to be on Jude's boat for the Festival of Lights tomorrow night."

Oh boy. Momma had been working herself up to this,

hadn't she? It wasn't just the gossip about how Jim was stopping by the house to play music. It was the whole pirate wench thing. Momma had probably heard it all.

"Yeah, I guess," Brenda said.

"You guess? You don't know?"

"Yes, Momma. I'm going to dress up in a ridiculous pirate costume and ride on *Synchronicity Too* in the Festival of Lights. And when that happens, I think the head of every gossip in Magnolia Harbor is going to explode."

Momma chuckled. "I never thought I'd see you ride on one of the boats in the Festival of Lights."

"Yeah, well, that makes two of us."

"Doc Killough must be a very persuasive man."

Brenda met her mother's gaze. "He is."

Momma nodded. "Just be careful, okay? I don't want to see you hurt again."

Brenda said nothing.

"The folks in this town love Doc Killough."

Brenda could see why. He was eminently lovable and handsome with a killer bedside manner and serious musical chops.

"Yeah, I get it, Momma. People don't like me the same way."

Chapter Eight

Jim stood at the bottom of Brenda's front stairs trying to catch his breath. She was utterly magnificent dressed in an eighteenth-century costume with a tight, lace-up-the-front bodice. He'd known for some time that she was hiding a nice figure under her big sweatshirts, but... wow.

His mouth went dry, and his whole body responded to the way the costume accentuated the curves of her body. He couldn't help but smile. No, he was definitely not too old to feel the pull of sexual attraction.

He took the cheesy tricorn hat off his head. "Milady," he said, giving her a sweeping bow.

And she laughed.

Oh, good lord, Brenda had a wonderful laugh. Where had she been hiding it? She should let it out more often, because the sound made him happy and light on his feet.

"You don't think I look ridiculous?" She tugged at the

low neckline and then noticed where his gaze had gone. An impressive blush crept up her neck to her cheeks.

"No," he said.

She laughed again. "Well, you also look pretty spectacular." Her gaze took in his frock coat, ruffled shirt, and knee britches. "But you need boots," she said, looking down at his Sperry boat shoes.

"Yeah, well, not aboard Jude's boat." He gave her his arm and escorted her to his Jeep.

Twenty minutes later, they boarded *Synchronicity Too*, a gorgeous schooner with mahogany decks and gleaming wooden masts and yardarms. Jude St. Pierre was doing a pretty good impression of Johnny Depp in a killer pirate costume except that he'd traded his tricorn for a fuzzy red Santa hat. "Avast, me hearties," he said from his spot behind the captain's wheel. "And Merry Christmas to all."

"You said there wouldn't be any Christmas on this boat," Brenda muttered.

"And you were foolish enough to believe me," Jim said, hoping she wouldn't back down now. He relaxed when the corners of her mouth twitched in an almost-smile.

"Doctor Jim, Doctor Jim, lookit." Jim turned to find Donovan Jephson standing at the bow of the boat with a group of other kids from the clinic and their parents. All the kids and parents wore life vests and tricorn hats. The kids had each been given a gift bag with a toy spyglass, some clip-on-the-shoulder wooden parrots, and eye patches.

At the moment, Topher Martin was up there dressed like Captain Hook and looking like a total badass, real-life pirate with his real-life eye patch.

"Hey, singer lady," Doni called, waving. "You look pretty."

Brenda waved back and curtsied. A smile broke out on her face again, and something hitched in Jim's chest.

Maybe he should give the gossips something real to talk about. The dress made her look so beautiful and enticing. He had an itch to touch her that was almost adolescent.

Unfortunately, for safety's sake, like all the other guests on tonight's cruise, Brenda had to cover up all that pretty cleavage with a personal flotation device.

"I think you should rescue the little kids. Topher is scaring some of them," she said, buckling the big orange vest around her bodice.

He glanced at the kids. "I don't think they're that scared. Or, if they are, it's fun scared, like going to a scary movie."

"Well, the boys are definitely lapping it up, but I think some of the little girls might be kind of intimidated. And speaking as a girl, I've never been a fan of scary movies."

He snorted a laugh. "You know, people have the wrong idea about you. You aren't anything like Ebenezer Scrooge. Why do you let people get away with thinking those things about you?"

"I don't let people get away with anything. They think what they want."

"And you do nothing to change their minds."

"I don't know if that's true. After all, I agreed to direct the choir, but it didn't change anything. I guess I'm not naturally lovable like you," she said, turning and pretending to explore the beautiful sailboat.

"Okay," he said to her back. "I understand that you don't want to talk about it. Holidays are hard for you. But—"

She faced him. "But you think I'll eventually come around, huh?"

He shrugged. "I'm known for my perseverance."

She huffed out a sigh. "I used to make an effort, when Ella was little. I didn't have much money so there wasn't a mountain of gifts or anything. But we had a little tree and some lights."

"And what happened?"

She looked up at him, her eyes a little shiny, her mouth quivering with emotion. "Ella ran away when she was seventeen. Just walked right out of my life following after this man who told her lies and promised her things he wasn't ever going to deliver. And I should have been like Momma. I should have held my tongue, but I didn't. I tried to tell her she was making a big mistake, but Ella didn't take that well."

Brenda strolled down the deck toward the bow of the boat. "That's not the whole story, though, is it?" Jim said, following her.

She stopped again and turned. "No. It's not. Because I was wrong. She's been with Cody for thirteen years. They've made a life for themselves."

"You have grandkids?"

She shook her head. "No. And Ella and Cody have never married, but that doesn't matter; they've committed to each other. So who am I to judge? And she's never forgiven me for what I said the day she left home."

She looked out at the shoreline as *Synchronicity Too*'s engines started. Slowly, they headed out into the channel.

"All I wanted was to stop her from making the same mistake I'd made. If you think I'm a good violinist, you should hear her play sometime. She was my one crowning achievement. The child who would have the life I threw away because of a stupid boy."

"I can see why you didn't want her to run off when she was seventeen."

"Did you have a big fight with your parents when you opted not to go to Juilliard?"

"There were doors slammed. My mother cried. But they let it go."

"Good for them." She exhaled deeply. "I suppose if Ella had wanted to go to college or join the service or something, I might have come around. But she ran off with a guy I didn't like. And to this day, I feel as if I should have made more of an effort to get along with Cody. Maybe if I hadn't disliked him so much, she might have come home to visit from time to time. But I didn't, and she's gone, and without her, Christmas doesn't feel like Christmas."

The pieces of the puzzle suddenly fell into place. Brenda had every reason to be sour on the season. The light of her life—the daughter she'd sacrificed for—had abandoned her.

Jim couldn't imagine spending the holiday without Dylan. His son had been his reason for living each day after Julianne died. If someone took Dylan away from him, he might end up the same way. Sad and lonely and not terribly interested in celebrating a holiday that was supposed to be about joy.

There was nothing joyful about feeling abandoned and alone.

* * *

Heat crawled up Brenda's face. What was she thinking to spill out her unhappiness that way? Now Jim would know how badly broken she was. Not sick or in need of medical attention, but damaged beyond repair.

She closed her eyes and breathed in the salty scent of the bay and then turned toward the doctor. He was really something, standing there wearing that red frock coat with the brass buttons up the front and over the cuffs. What did he want to do? Heal her hurts? Make her happy?

Good luck with that.

She turned away from him, making her way to the front of the boat while he followed behind saying nothing. And she thanked heaven when Jenna St. Pierre pulled him away to tell stories to the kids. Brenda found a little corner on deck protected from the chilly breeze, and she watched as Jim gathered the clinic kids around him and started telling the story of the dread pirate William Teal, whose ship had gone down in the inlet back in 1713.

It took about half an hour for the boat parade to form and begin its sail south along the coastline. There was a pretty big crowd on the public dock by Rafferty's as they sailed by. But then they circled around Lookout Island for a northward tack along the mainland where the crowds were much larger.

At that point, the kids had grown tired of pirate stories. Jenna St. Pierre herded them belowdecks for hot chocolate in the boat's state-of-the-art galley. Freed from storytelling duty, Jim found Brenda's hiding place and tugged her to the railing.

"I'm not sure I want to get too close to the edge," she said, resisting him.

"Don't worry, I've got you," he said, linking his arm with hers. "Now wave."

"What?"

"The people onshore are waving at us. They think we are very cool in our pirate costumes. It would be rude not to wave back."

She waved. And waved. And after about fifteen minutes of waving, her arm was tired.

"You're almost smiling," Jim said after a while.

"I am not. I'm grimacing."

His hand touched her back, below the annoying life vest. "You're cold."

"Only a little."

"Come on, the parade is breaking up. Let's go see what Jude's new boat is like belowdecks."

They headed down the companionway into a salon that had a Christmas tree in the corner where the clinic kids were opening presents.

"No Christmas, huh?" Brenda muttered.

"I'm incorrigible," Jim said. "But we don't have to stay here. Jude and Jenna are playing host. And you can lose this," he said, turning her toward him and unbuckling the flotation device. "We only wanted to make sure people wore them abovedecks in case someone fell overboard."

He drew the life vest over her head and then his gaze dropped to the neckline of her ridiculous dress. She stifled the urge to tug at her bodice. Meanwhile, Jim licked his lips like a hungry wolf.

Her insides took a wild free fall. For a crazy moment, she thought he might actually kiss the top of her breast or maybe bury his nose in the prominent cleavage created by the costume's ridiculous bodice. But he didn't.

"Come on." He captured her cold hand in his warm one and pulled her down a passageway that led to a series of staterooms.

The rooms were small, except for the captain's quarters at the back of the boat. That room was nothing short of gorgeous, fitted out with burled wood on the bulkheads and luxury linens on the queen-sized bed.

One glance at the beautiful bed and Brenda's heart took off at a full gallop. For a moment, she wondered if Jim might ravish her like a pirate.

Good God, she didn't really want to be ravished. Did she? No. But somehow the idea of being seduced by a man in a frock coat was terrifying in an absolutely sexy way.

Like the little girls who had been pretend-scared of the pretend pirate earlier this evening.

She leaned against the doorway to the stateroom, not trusting herself to step inside the bedroom with him. When she stopped he turned, his blue eyes darkening and his laugh lines deepening. He cocked his head for a moment, and then his gaze shifted upward. A ridiculously jolly smile touched his lips right before he said, "I'm afraid you have made a tactical mistake."

"What?"

"You're standing under some mistletoe."

She looked up. Damn. But before she could escape, Jim took her by the shoulders, slanted his head, and moved in.

The kiss was surprisingly rich and dark for a man who appeared to be yo ho ho–ing his way through life. He tasted like cinnamon and vanilla in their unsugared form. A little hot on the tongue. A little untamed.

He pulled the mob cap from her head and ran his fingers through her hair, and she became unmoored in time and space. The touch of his hand against her overexposed breast set off fireworks that were more suited for the Fourth of July than Christmas.

She leaned into the touch and emitted a deep hum from the back of her throat. But that little noise pulled her back down to earth. Wait a second. This was idiotic. And dangerous. If she didn't run now, Jim might unleash a tsunami of yearning and insanity that would leave nothing but wreckage in its wake.

She braced her hands on his shoulders and gave him a gentle but firm push. He stepped back, his eyes dark, the look on his face more solemn than she'd ever seen before.

"I—" he began.

"Don't," she interrupted, turning her body sideways in

the small passageway and hurrying back to the main salon. He didn't follow right away, which was just as well. The kids were out of control, and Jenna and Jude St. Pierre had no idea how to corral them.

She cleared her throat and dropped right into teacher mode. "Come, children," she said in that authoritative classroom voice that cut right through the roar. "Let's sing some songs. Who knows 'Frosty the Snowman'?"

Chapter Nine

Jim sat down at the piano and blew into his hands to warm them up. The weather had taken a surprising turn toward cold since the Festival of Lights on Saturday. And he'd managed to lose his gloves somewhere.

Today the Christmas Chorale was rehearsing in the Rutledge High auditorium, where the performance would be held in just two weeks.

There was a lot to accomplish before then, but he had faith in his new choir director. He checked his watch. It was five to seven, and almost every member of the chorale was present with music folders in hand.

Brenda had the choir exactly where she wanted them. He studied her for a moment. She stood at her music stand in front of the group, studying her notes with a deep frown on her face.

Jim knew well enough now that the rumple in her forehead had nothing to do with her frame of mind. She always frowned when she concentrated. He'd played enough music with her to know that she frowned even when she was in the groove—the magical place every musician reaches for, where the sound gets inside your head and you stop thinking.

She looked up from her notes and met his gaze. Electricity hummed along his synapses. He wanted to kiss her again. Hell, he wanted to get her naked.

She blushed and turned away, telling him everything he already knew. She'd enjoyed the kiss. She could probably be convinced to kiss him again. If only he could prove that he would never abandon her. If only he could restore her faith in love and family.

It was a pretty tall order. And she'd been hurt so many times. He'd heard the pain in her voice when she talked about her daughter. She was still hurting. And winning her trust would be difficult. Maybe impossible.

"All right, it's seven o'clock," she said in her high school teacher tone that caught everyone's attention. "We need to run through all the pieces tonight. And just remember that next week, we have a rehearsal on Monday and then a soundcheck on Friday, the night before the concert. Attendance at the soundcheck is mandatory. If you know ahead of time that you won't be able to come, you need to let me know.

"Now, let's begin with the Vaughan Williams, shall we?"

Jim arranged the music on the stand and then looked in her direction. For a short moment, before she began counting out the beats, their gazes met, and another jolt ran through him. But she never missed a beat. He, on the other hand, almost missed his cue to start playing. He fumbled, which earned him another little glance that almost melted his bones.

He could fall in love with her. The notion was kind of life-altering. He'd never met anyone since Julianne who had so captivated him. She wasn't sweet. She wasn't always happy. She wasn't anything like his late wife. But she was interesting, and funny, and talented. And playing music with her was an unspoken but intense joy they shared.

He watched her, taking his cues from her. That was his job. She set the beat, and he followed.

She was on a tear tonight. When the bass section tried to run away with the meter on "What Child Is This?" she had to stop the performance and help them practice their part several times. The basses had a part like a deep-sounding bell that set the rhythm for all the other sections. If they didn't keep the beat, the rest of the choir would be left high and dry.

When she finally got the performance she was looking for, she said, "Okay, let's turn to 'Joy to the Whole World.' This one is easy." She raised her baton, gave Jim the cue, and the chorale started singing.

But right in the middle of the performance, which had been pretty good in Jim's opinion, Brenda stepped off her podium, folded her arms across her chest, and gave the choir a chilling look. And since at least a quarter of the choir was *still not paying attention to her*, it took a moment before the singing stopped. Which proved her point.

"People, please, get your heads out of the music," she said in a surprisingly soft voice.

The choir shuffled and murmured.

"I know y'all think I just want you to look at my pretty face," Brenda continued. "But you need to watch me. And even more important, you need to look as if you actually believe what you're singing."

This caused the murmur to increase into a little hum.

She pulled her half-moon reading glasses from their resting place on the top of her head, tilted her head back, and read the lyrics out loud. Then she looked up, her blue gaze like ice. "It says joy to the world."

The hum turned to silence.

"So why are all of you frowning?" she asked.

Jim almost laughed out loud but managed to button his lip.

Donna Cuthbert didn't have nearly as much discipline. "Because you are?" she said in a tentative voice.

"I'm frowning?"

Everyone nodded.

"Oh," she said, and then looked over at him. "Am I frowning?"

"You always frown when you concentrate," he said in a low voice, his mouth twitching beyond his control.

"Oh, well, that's a good point, Doc. I think we're all concentrating too hard. We know this piece, and we know the words, don't we? I mean, we don't have to look at the music to sing 'joy to the world,' do we? So, everyone, put your folders on the chairs behind you. We're going to sing this without looking at the music or the words. And let me feel the joy, okay?"

The choir did as she directed, although several members in the always-opinionated soprano section glanced sideways at each other. Since Brenda had never said one word about emoting any joy, Jim reckoned the choir had a right to be skeptical.

"All right, from the beginning," Brenda said, waving her baton, counting out the beats. Jim began to play and the choir began to sing.

And behold. They made a joyful noise.

* * *

When the choir sang the last few notes of "Joy to the Whole World," goose bumps rippled over Brenda's skin. Man. These people could really sing. They were, despite the rocky beginning, capable of a great deal more discipline than her high school students ever had been. And to her amazement, once they'd put their music down and just sang, a contagion of smiles broke out.

She wasn't immune. Somehow, for a short moment, the joy of the music seeped into her grinchy heart, which, unlike Dr. Seuss's character, didn't need to grow any bigger. Brenda's heart wasn't small; it was just fragile. It had been shattered so many times in the past, and sometimes the glue that she used to patch it back together seemed brittle.

But as the chorale ended on the phrase "He's got the whole world in his hands," she felt something knit back together. Somehow the music had made its way into her chest like some healing medicine.

"That's more like it. Well done," she said when the last vibration ebbed away. "Let's end on that high note. I'll see y'all next week."

The choir headed for the doors, but most of them had smiles on their faces, and it reminded her of those good days in Muncie when the kids had performed well. Funny how she'd forgotten that half the battle was making the choir believe in itself. She'd been so drawn down by the tragedy of Katie's death that she'd blocked out the happy moments.

In any case, she felt confident that the chorale was ready for their performance. Even more important, *they* knew they were ready, and that confidence showed. When the lead soprano waved good-bye and wished her a good week, that was a major turnaround.

Her insides warmed a little more, as if she'd just taken a

sip of warm mulled wine. And maybe that was why she was so unprepared when Jim strolled up to stand right in front of her podium.

"You got a minute?" he asked.

She looked up, her body sending her conflicting messages. Fight, flight, or wait until the auditorium cleared and kiss him one more time?

The flight instinct took over. "I'm sorry, I need to get—"

"I was wondering if you had time to work on the sonata this week," he interrupted in his typical Jim manner. The man didn't take no for an answer. It was a proven fact. Besides, she loved playing music with him. Maybe she loved it too much.

She didn't want someone who was determined to charm her into doing his bidding. Maybe that was the big hurdle. She'd been charmed before. She'd been used. She'd been filibustered, and bullied, and had lost her way.

So she gathered up her music. "No, Jim, I—"

"Brenda, are you going to let a little mistletoe get in the way of a new friendship?"

She looked up at him. Big mistake. That twinkle in his eye was so adorable, and sexy. It reminded her of . . .

No, wait. No.

It didn't remind her of Daddy. It was just hard to resist. But she was going to resist. She had to. She couldn't afford to have another man in her life, unbalancing things, making her care and then hurting her or, worse yet, leaving her. "Is friendship what you want?" she asked, her voice hard.

"If that's all I can have."

She shook her head. "You're a terrible liar."

"Okay, so I admit it. I liked kissing you, Brenda. It's been a long time since I've kissed anyone and enjoyed it. And if you tell me you didn't enjoy it, then you're a liar."

She looked away from those twinkly eyes. "I did enjoy it," she said in a soft voice. "But I can't trust it."

"Because you were hurt before?"

She shrugged. "Of course. Why else? And besides..." She pulled her music from the stand and walked away from him down the aisle to the seat where she'd left her coat and purse.

"Besides what?"

She plucked her coat from the seat and turned. He was still standing up by the stage. "I can't afford that kind of thing. I've learned how to live without it. And I just want to be left alone. I thought I made that clear from the start." She pulled on her puffy down coat and headed for the exit.

But he wasn't about to let her get away so easily. "You should follow your own advice, you know."

She stopped and turned. "What advice?"

"The advice you gave the choir tonight."

"What?"

"Put the music down. Get your head up. And smile, Brenda. Fake it until you can make the feeling real. Look at me; I'm a walking example of that."

She shook her head. "What are you talking about?"

He crossed the now-empty auditorium until he stood just in front of her, so close that she had to look up to meet his gaze. "I'm talking about how, when Julianne died, I was so lost inside my head and my grief that I didn't think I could make it through another day," he said in a low, emotion-laced tone. A telltale sheen glimmered in his eye, and it struck her that Jim Killough was not always Mr. Happy. He could ho-ho-ho like any respectable Santa, but beyond the bedside manner was someone with a great deal more emotional depth.

"I had a little boy to raise," he continued. "I couldn't

abandon him. I needed to help him get over this monumental loss. So I just pretended. I used to think about Julianne sitting on my shoulder with her always-optimistic view on life. I would mouth her words all the time, and then one day, out of the blue, Dylan said something funny, something Julianne would have loved. And I laughed. And then I laughed again. And pretty soon I was laughing all the time."

"Yeah, well, it's different." She turned her back on him.

"It's not."

"Yes, it is," she said, her feet stubbornly rooted to the auditorium floor. She should run, but the urge to turn back was starting to overcome her justifiable fear. "I don't have a happy button I can just switch on, okay? I'm not like you. I don't charm people. I'm not naturally gregarious and lovable. I'm notorious for dragging everyone down, and you're—"

"You don't."

She turned then. "What?"

"You don't drag people down. Brenda, after you pointed out the choir's lack of emotion tonight, the performance they turned in was quite a bit more energetic. It gave me shivers."

"Me too," she whispered. "But that's just performance energy."

"No, it's not. It was joy. And you made them feel it."

"The music made them—"

"No. You did. And when they walked out of here, most of them were smiling. You were smiling. You don't drag people down. I don't know why you think that."

She stared down at her toes for a long moment, letting his words percolate through her. Why did she believe this thing about herself?

Short answer: Because Ella had said it so many times. Because Ella's father had accused her of the same thing. Because even Momma sometimes said she was a grumpy puss.

"You're blind," she said, not looking up as emotions tumbled through her like a rockslide, bruising her from the inside out.

With a single warm finger, he lifted her chin, his touch shocking her down deep. "Look at me, Brenda. Listen. I am not blind. I saw what I saw today. And I saw you on the schooner the other night singing songs with the children. You are not a grump or a grinch or a scrooge. But you have been hurt, and it's only natural for people with wounds to curl up and protect themselves."

"I'm afraid."

"I know. But I promise. I will never hurt you."

"That's not a promise you can keep," she said with certainty.

"So you won't give me a chance?"

She closed her eyes. "I can't."

"No, you *won't*."

"I'm afraid," she repeated.

"Of course you are."

And then he stepped closer and lowered his head and kissed her for the second time in as many days.

* * *

As Jim's mouth captured hers, Brenda wondered if this fluttery hot feeling in her core was fear, or confusion, or something else altogether stupid and adolescent. He knew how to kiss, and pleasure sparked through her like electricity.

She reveled in it for a long moment: the pressure of his body next to hers, his broad shoulders, his rough palm where he caressed her cheek. She ran her fingers up into his mane, the texture wiry and deeply masculine. Her core started to overheat, and the blood rushed so fast that she could hear it as it moved through her body.

For a moment, she almost understood those crazy people who willingly dove off high cliffs into tiny pools just for the thrill of it. If she jumped, the ride would probably be exhilarating but the landing might kill her. When she'd jumped in the past, she'd always fallen badly.

And that old saying about difficulties making a person strong was BS. Bad experiences made people brittle. If she fell hard this time, she might never put herself back together again.

And even knowing this, her stupid heart wanted to take Jim home.

She pushed him back a little, and he broke the kiss but didn't retreat very far.

"I wish I knew where this was going," she murmured.

"Well," he said on a long breath, "not back to my house, because Dylan is there."

Oh yeah, Dylan. Who didn't like her much. The few times Brenda had crossed Dylan's path over the last few weeks, the young doctor had been barely civil. Another good reason to turn around and run for the hills.

But she couldn't move. She was scared of being hurt, but not nearly as frightened as she was at the prospect of spending the rest of her life alone. It came as a sudden realization: Life is short and this was one last turning point.

"I guess we could go to my place," she said, her words coming out in a whisper.

"Are you sure?"

She looked up into his bright blue eyes and shook her head. "No."

The corner of his mouth twitched. "It's okay. We can—"

"No," she said pressing her palms against his chest. The soft cotton of his shirt felt like a barrier. She suddenly wanted to touch him. Skin to skin.

The thought was terrifying and electrifying.

"No?" he asked, one eyebrow rising.

She closed her eyes and drew in a deep breath to steady her runaway heart. "I guess I'm confused, you know. My head tells me to run away and my heart…" Her voice got thin and she opened her eyes and gazed up at him. The twinkle in his blue eyes had gone dark and serious. That wide-eyed look gave Brenda the impression that Jim was actively listening to her.

"Can I tell you a secret?"

He nodded. "I was hoping we could get used to sharing secrets."

"I want to…" She hesitated, feeling like a teenager in a forty-something body.

"What?"

"To be honest, I really want to undress you," she said, playing with one of his shirt buttons. "But I don't want you to…"

"What?"

"Oh, crap, I'm just an old lady," she said, "I never had very many good body parts, and now most of them are somewhat worse for the wear."

He leaned in, the twinkle returning to his eye. "For the record, I've seen some of your body parts in a low-cut dress, and I would like to get better acquainted with them."

Every square inch of her skin heated in that moment and her knees almost gave out. She had to lean against him, forehead to sturdy chest. And damn if it didn't feel as if she fit there. As if that spot had been made for her.

They stood that way for a long time, until the sound of someone out in the hallway pulled them apart. "Come on, let's go," he said.

"Where?"

"Wherever you want to take this."

"My place." It wasn't a question.

"Your place," he repeated as he took her by the hand and led her out to school parking lot, where they kissed again for a long time before he followed her home.

Chapter Ten

Jim slept at Brenda's house five out of the next seven days, and now he felt as if he was walking on air. All these years, he'd mourned his wife and thought that love would never happen again. And here he was, discovering that even a guy his age wasn't too old for love.

It was a little past five thirty in the morning a week later when Jim left Brenda's house, dashing to his Jeep in the predawn cold.

Cold was not really a good enough word to describe the freezing temperatures that had settled in over the weekend. The tips of Jim's fingers were almost numb by the time he fired up the Jeep and started the heat. He still hadn't found his gloves.

The heated seats kicked in, warming his butt as he drove back to town and the house on Redbud Street that he shared with Dylan. He'd made this drive five times since last Monday, but today he'd overslept. Brenda's bed had been warm, and the weather outside was frightful for coastal South Carolina, which rarely saw temperatures in the teens.

So it had been particularly hard to wake up this morning. And Brenda hadn't been in any hurry to kick him out. She'd even offered to cook him breakfast. But he'd declined because he was worried about Dylan.

In a role reversal, he found himself sneaking around like a teenager, trying to keep his suddenly intimate relationship a secret from his thirty-year-old son. But the inevitable confrontation was waiting for him this morning.

"Where have you been?" Dylan demanded as Jim came through the door to the mudroom.

Dylan was standing in the middle of the kitchen, his hair wet from the shower and a look of disapproval on his face.

Busted.

"Uh... well..." The words dried up in Jim's mouth. This was damned awkward, wasn't it?

"Never mind. I know where you've been." Dylan paced to the coffeemaker and began to savagely scoop grounds into the brew basket.

"Um, look—" Jim began.

"Have you lost your mind?" Dylan turned and threw the coffee scoop across the room. "People are going to gossip about you. You know that, don't you? I mean... really?"

Of course they were going to gossip. But Jim didn't care. Why did Dylan?

The question nagged. Jim had a hard time accepting that his son was that concerned about public opinion. No, something else was bugging him. What the hell?

Jim straightened his shoulders. "I'm sorry. I should have told you I wouldn't be home until early in the morning. I didn't mean for you to worry."

"I wasn't worried." Dylan stalked across the room to pick up the scoop he'd just thrown.

"Okay, I get it. Brenda isn't the woman you'd choose for me. But here's the thing: It's not your choice. I care about her. A lot. I'm . . ." He let the words fade out because he wasn't quite ready to tell Dylan that he'd fallen in love. Especially since he hadn't told Brenda that yet.

It was on his to-do list. But he was in no rush. Saying the l-word would probably scare the crap out of her.

"I can't believe you," Dylan said, stalking off through the door to the garage without turning on the coffee maker. A moment later, the garage door opened, and Dylan headed out on his motorcycle.

Well, that hadn't gone well, had it?

Jim sucked back a few choice cusswords before starting the coffeemaker and then heading into his bedroom, where he turned on the television and tuned into the local news. He took three steps toward the bathroom when the weather report froze him.

"The National Weather Service has issued a winter storm warning for Georgetown County," the local weatherman said.

Jim turned back toward the TV as the local weather expanded right into the news hour. The weatherman was standing beside a map of the East Coast, which showed an ominous weather front with a big L located just off the coastline. The animation showed the classic track of a nor'easter— the kind of storm that could flood the island, but which might do something much more unexpected this time.

"We've got lots of cold air in place," the weatherman said. *"Last night the citrus growers in Florida experienced the lowest temperatures since 1989—the year of the Christmas Blizzard."*

The news anchor asked, *"Are we expecting a storm of that magnitude?"*

And the weatherman replied in a somewhat gleeful tone of voice that confirmed him as a Yankee, *"All the models suggest that this could be a repeat of that storm. People should take precautions now, because in 1989, coastal portions of Georgetown County got fourteen inches of snow. We could see totals that big with this storm. The Weather Service is predicting that snow will start sometime around three this afternoon and continue through the night. Here's a map showing the expected snowfall totals."*

They flashed a map, and Jonquil Island looked as if it sat in the middle of a multicolored bull's-eye.

An urgency coursed through Jim. Fourteen inches of snow was serious business anywhere, but in Syracuse, New York, where Jim had grown up, they got more than a hundred inches of snow every winter. Folks up there knew how to deal with fourteen inches of snow because snow-storms like that happened multiple times a year. But down here, a dusting was enough to scare people half to death.

Even worse, the community had no resources or budget for snow removal, and snow wouldn't stop people from getting sick. Worse yet, idiots would go out in it and hurt themselves trying to shovel it or drive in it or walk down a slippery street.

And then he remembered Brenda's father.

Damn. They might even get themselves killed.

* * *

At seven thirty on Monday morning, Brenda stood in her front room, drinking a cup of coffee and staring out at the angry winter ocean pounding along the sand. She didn't need a weatherman to know that a storm was coming. The northeast winds were driving the surf up the beach and whipping the waves into foam. She should probably close the hurricane shutters before she headed off to work. She shivered. It was freezing out there.

She was just pulling on her parka when her phone rang. It was Momma.

"Have you seen the weather report?" Momma said when Brenda connected the call.

"You know I don't have a TV out here."

"Well, you should turn on the radio then. They're saying we could have another blizzard, you know, like the last one."

"The last one" was understood as the Blizzard of 1989. Over the decades, South Carolina had seen occasional snowstorms that left trace amounts of the white stuff. But the big storm would forever be the one that took Daddy away from them.

"Oh," Brenda said before the words dried up in her mouth.

"Honey, you need to put up the storm shutters and pack a bag. You're staying in town with me tonight. They say the snow will start this afternoon, and we could get inches of it. I'll bet Louella closes A Stitch in Time early today."

"Oh," Brenda said again.

"Honey, are you okay?" Momma knew her fears.

"Yeah. I was just going out to put up the shutters. The ocean looks angry today. I'll be over after work."

"If it starts snowing early, you leave your car in town and walk home, you hear?"

"Yes, ma'am. But what about you? Do you have supplies? Do I need to stop at the market?"

"Honey, the store is sold out of anything worth having. We'll have to make do with what's in the freezer." Living alone all these years, Momma had become a champion at freezing leftovers. They wouldn't starve, assuming they didn't lose power and the ability to run the oven and microwave.

"I'm going to have to cancel tonight's rehearsal," Brenda said, disappointment nipping at her. Funny how she'd been looking forward to it all week, and to the performance this coming Saturday.

"If we get a foot of snow and it stays cold like it's been, the whole show might have to be canceled or postponed."

Brenda stared out at the pounding surf. It would take days to clear a foot of snow. They'd have to wait for the sun to come out and melt it all, and if it got below freezing, then they'd have to deal with black ice. A deep sense of regret or guilt or sorrow—she couldn't quite name the emotion—settled into her head, making her feel heavy and useless.

Momma was right. They might have to cancel. And she would err on the side of safety every time. She didn't want anyone else getting hurt trying to make it to a performance she was directing.

"You might be right," Brenda said, the heaviness weighing down her shoulders.

"And then you'll be free of this obligation."

Brenda swallowed back a retort. She probably deserved that soft-spoken comment after the way she'd refused Jim at the beginning. But it wasn't her wish to have a foot of snow fall on the woefully unprepared town. And after agreeing to direct the chorale, she didn't want the performance canceled either. Jim had somehow infected her with his Christmas spirit—or something. But she wasn't ready to tell Momma that.

"I'm going to get the storm shutters up. I need to go," she said instead. "I'll see you after work."

Brenda pushed the guilt and regret to the back of her mind and got busy boarding up the windows and packing a bag with enough clothes to last a week. When she had the bag stored in the back of her car, she stopped and gave Jim a call, which went straight to voice mail.

She left a message telling him she would send out an email canceling tonight's rehearsal and asking him his opinion about canceling or postponing Saturday's event.

The snow hadn't started by the time she reached work, but the sky had gone the color of gray flannel, and the temperatures continued to hover in the low twenties. It was too cold for rain.

"Looks like we're going to have a white Christmas," Louella said as Brenda settled into work.

"White Christmases are highly overrated," Brenda grumped, remembering the snow that lay on the ground the day of Daddy's funeral. It had been just a few days after Christmas and five days after the blizzard.

Louella shook her head. "As grinchy as ever, I see," she said.

Brenda didn't argue. She had a good reason to see the negative side of the storm bearing down on them, but she was certainly in the minority. A stream of customers came through the front doors that morning, all of them kind of excited about the snow. There was a lot of talk about watching their kids and grandkids building snowmen for the first time ever.

Brenda eventually escaped into the back room and called Jim again. And for the second time, she was shuffled off to his voice mail. She wanted to talk to him, not just about the Christmas Gala but about the snow. About her fears. About...

Hell, she just needed to hear his voice. The arrival of this storm was like some cosmic sign in her life. She pushed the unreasonable fear to the back of her head and taught her midmorning knitting class.

The first flakes of snow started falling around two in the afternoon, and they immediately stuck to the ground and the road. Louella shut the store at 2:30 p.m. and told Brenda to go home and be safe.

But instead of going up to Momma's house, Brenda decided to walk down Harbor Drive to the clinic. It was crazy of course. Jim was probably busier than a one-armed paper-hanger. But she needed to see him, just to reassure herself.

Or something.

She hadn't quite reached the clinic's doors when the snow began to fall in earnest, blown sideways by a persistent wind. The icy motes stung her nose and cheeks and made her eyes water.

She was cold by the time she reached the clinic, but before she could step inside out of the wind, Jim came barreling through the front doors, his hands jammed in the pockets of his coat because he'd lost his gloves.

"Brenda," he said, gingerly coming to a stop. The sidewalks were already starting to get slippery. "What are you doing here? I thought you were going to your mother's."

"You got my message?"

"I'm sorry I didn't call you back. It's been crazy. But I've got an emergency. Harper Jephson has a bad respiratory infection, and with his asthma, I think he needs to be hospitalized. But the ambulance service refuses to come out here from the mainland. So I—"

"You're going to drive to the mainland in this?"

He cocked his head, a kind smile curling the corner of his lips. "I grew up in Syracuse, New York. A foot of snow is like a flurry up there."

"Really? Because even in Indiana it's a lot of snow."

"Syracuse is in the New York snowbelt. So don't worry. I've got lots of experience and a four-wheel drive. And I don't have any other choices. I have to take care of that little boy."

She did understand. She'd made a career out of teaching kids of one age or another. But it didn't change the way she felt about Doc going out into a raging snowstorm.

"I do understand, but..." Her voice broke.

He stepped up to her, the snow falling all around them. "I'll be okay. I promise you." Then he leaned in and kissed her, his lips so warm in the freezing cold. "I love you, Brenda McMillan. I don't intend to lose you now that I've found you."

The words stunned her and opened her heart and flayed her all at the same time. She loved him too, but she couldn't say the words out loud. They froze in her throat, along with a paralyzing fear that he should never have spoken his feelings out loud because it was probably bad luck.

"I'll see you later," he said, then turned and sprinted down the snow-covered sidewalk, slipping once and almost falling.

Her heart lurched in her chest, and she wanted to follow after him, but she stood there stiff and unmoving as he fired up his Jeep and drove off into the storm.

Chapter Eleven

Many hours later, the old shade tree in Momma's front yard collapsed under the weight of the snow. It fell with a kind of death rattle, more sigh than crack, and it awakened Brenda from a fitful sleep a fraction of a second before one of the tree's large branches came down through the roof with a deafening crash that shook the house to its foundation.

In one terrifying moment, Brenda found herself caged by branches that had pierced the ceiling, missing her by mere inches. And now, like some surreal dream, snow came drifting down through the hole above her, lit up by the streetlamp outside.

It took a moment for Brenda to process what had happened. This was not a snowy nightmare. A frigid wind swept through the room she'd occupied as a child. The snow landing on her cheeks as she looked up was cold and wet and real. She shivered.

And then, like an aftershock, the fear struck. A black,

nameless panic welled out of her. "Momma!" she hollered at the top of her lungs.

Silence and the whine of the wind answered her.

"Momma!" she hollered again, this time like a frightened three-year-old, as a sob erupted from her chest. "Momma!"

She struggled against the quilt and sheets. The limbs had trapped her, so she had to bend herself like a pretzel to wriggle her way through the cold, wet branches. Piles of snow had cascaded into the room, and by the time she'd gotten away from the branch, her pajamas were soaked, and her feet were almost numb from walking through the icy piles on the floor.

"Momma!" she shouted again, pulling open the door just in time to see her mother, coming down the dark hall using her cell phone's flashlight to negotiate the darkness. Brenda reached for the hall light switch but it didn't work. Obviously they'd lost power.

"Momma?" She raced down the hall and hugged her mother like she didn't ever want to let her go.

"Good lord, you're soaked. What happened?"

"You didn't hear?"

Momma cocked her head. No, of course she hadn't heard. Momma was going deaf. And evidently only the shade tree in the front yard had fallen. Momma slept way in the back of the house.

"The tree fell," Brenda said.

Momma took a couple of steps into Brenda's old bedroom and let out an audible gasp. "Praise the Lord. Are you okay? Are you hurt?"

"No. Yes," she answered the questions in reverse order as she started to shiver. Momma sprang into action then, proving that, despite the hearing loss, seventy was the new forty. Momma might have arthritis but she wasn't feeble. Not by a long shot.

In short order the Magnolia Harbor Fire Department was summoned, dry pajamas were found, and half an hour later, Brenda sat wrapped up in two handmade quilts in front of a fire burning brightly in the living room fireplace at the Heavenly Rest rectory. She clutched a cup of hot Earl Grey tea in her hands and leaned back in the old couch while Ashley Scott got Momma settled down in Rev. St. Pierre's guest bedroom.

Ashley would have put them up at Howland House if there had been even one room available. But there was no room at the inn because a number of year-round residents with homes along the coast had chosen to ride out the snowstorm in town.

Now if Brenda could only reach Jim, she might get some sleep. But the man had yet to respond to her text about the tree falling on Momma's house. He had sent a text earlier in the day saying he'd made it over the bridge, but the roads were bad and it might take some time before he got back home again.

She hoped to heck that he'd booked himself into a hotel room or something and was just sound asleep. But she couldn't help spinning one disaster after another in her mind. Visions of him being stuck all night by the side of the road, running out of gas, his cell phone battery dying, and his hands going numb because he'd lost his gloves. Or worse yet, being buried and then having some jackass plow into his car and...

"You're going to be okay."

She looked up as Rev. St. Pierre sat down on the ottoman in front of the couch. "You need another cup of tea?" he asked.

"No, thank you. I'm really sorry we've descending on you like this."

He cocked his head. "I have an extra bedroom and a couch. There's nothing to be sorry about."

She shivered.

"Are you still cold?"

She could lie. But this was her minister. So she opted to tell the truth. "I don't know. I can't stop shaking."

"I can imagine. You came very close to being seriously hurt."

She pulled the edges of the quilt closer around her shoulders. "Can I tell you a secret?" she whispered.

"That's why I'm here."

"I wouldn't have minded."

He frowned and leaned forward. "What do mean?" His words had a dark urgency.

She waved his concern away. "I'm not suicidal. That's not what I mean. What I mean is…" She stopped as an emotion swelled in her throat. It took a minute to swallow it back, and the minister gave her the time she needed.

"Right after the tree fell, I had this feeling that I was utterly alone. I thought Momma might have been hurt or killed. And then I kind of flashed back to the night Daddy didn't come home. And I'm just so worried about…" Her voice faded out.

"What are you worried about?" the minister asked gently.

"Not what. Who." She looked up at the preacher. "Jim Killough." Her words were a confession.

"What about him?"

"He went off to the mainland this afternoon. Harper Jephson needed to be taken to the hospital, and there wasn't anyone else to do it. I haven't heard from him since the tree fell. I mean, I called him a little while ago, when Grant Ackerman was bringing us up here in his four-wheel drive. The call went right to his voice mail. And he hasn't answered my texts either. And I..." She had to stop because her eyes welled up. If she kept talking, she would probably start bawling like a baby.

"So." The minister leaned forward and took her hand in his. He had big hands, but not nearly as big as Jim's. He squeezed. "What you're saying is that a life without connection isn't worth much at all. If you lost your mother, or Doc Killough, you'd be lost altogether?"

She nodded and bit her lip, the tears running down her cheeks.

"You know, to get love you have to give it," he said, his big brown eyes soft and earnest in the firelight.

She took a deep breath. "Yeah, that's what everyone says. But every time I give love, someone finds a way to take it from me. And the worst things always seem to happen in the middle of a snowstorm a few days before Christmas. Why is that?"

"I don't have an answer except to say that nothing bad happened tonight. In fact, from my perspective, either you got lucky or God intervened. Why do you think He might have done that?"

"What? God? I'm not qualified to answer that."

"Well, I have a theory. I think He still has a purpose for you on this earth."

She blinked.

"Life is all about perspective, Brenda. From my perspective, I'm mighty glad you weren't hurt tonight. Because you have things to do. Gifts to give. Christmases yet to celebrate." He had the temerity to say this with a big smile.

"You're almost as persistent as Jim is," she muttered, shaking her head.

"Flattery will get you everywhere. But I'm serious. You had a big scare tonight, and I hope you can see that you were spared because you're needed and wanted and loved. I heard that you gave the choir a pep talk about joy the other night. And I've heard people say that you're tough but the Christmas Gala is going to be better than it ever was. And my own brother told me all about how you stepped in on Saturday and had a group of unruly children singing holiday songs. So don't tell me that you weren't spared for a purpose. 'Tis the season for gift giving, and it seems to me you've been working overtime in that department."

"You heard about all that?"

He chuckled. "There isn't much that happens in this town that I don't know about, even if Donna Cuthbert is a Methodist."

She stared down at the worn carpet in his living room. "None of that would have happened without Jim," she said in a small voice as her fear closed in.

"You want me to sit up with you while you wait to hear from Jim? I'm certain that he's all right. He's a Yankee who's used to the snow. I'll bet he's either sound asleep in some hotel room waiting out the storm or he got pressed into service by the hospital. I heard they put out a call for four-wheel-drive vehicles."

The last thought didn't make her feel any better. Daddy had answered the call and paid for it with his life. But she also knew that Jim would always be the first to volunteer. And that was one of the reasons she loved him.

She nodded and tried hard not to cry. "I know I'm being silly."

"No. You're not being silly at all. You are deeply worried about someone you love. That's all. And he'll get in touch in the morning. I'm sure of it. But if you want me to sit up with you, I'll go make a pot of coffee."

She shook her head. "No. It's okay. I'll be fine. No

reason you should lose sleep. I'll just hang out here on your couch."

"All right. If you need me, just holler. I'm right down the hall."

He headed in that direction but stopped before he left the room. He turned and looked over his shoulder. "When he does finally check in, don't hold back, Brenda. Tell him how you feel about him."

Micah pinned her with a somewhat stern look, and she found herself nodding.

* * *

The sun was peeking over the horizon when Brenda and her mother made the somewhat treacherous walk across Lilac Lane from the rectory to Howland House. The snow had stopped hours ago, leaving about eight inches on the ground and a bit more in places where the wind had drifted it. Lilac Lane hadn't seen a plow, and by the looks of it, neither had any streets in Magnolia Harbor.

Rev. St. Pierre had gotten up before dawn to shovel a path between the rectory and the bed-and-breakfast. Thank goodness Heavenly Rest's minister was a young man. Otherwise, Brenda and Momma might have starved. The bachelor minister obviously didn't do much cooking. His cupboards were bare. Although he did seem to have a large coffee stash.

The walk was freezing-cold, but Momma got halfway across the street and stopped in her tracks. "Oh, isn't that lovely," she said, looking up at the old mansion. "Howland House looks just like a Currier and Ives Christmas card."

Brenda followed her mother's gaze, and even her grinchy self had to agree. The snow clinging to the inn's roofline and portico provided a sharp contrast to the red bows on the wreaths that adorned every single window. Inside, Howland House looked as if it had been staged for *Southern Living*'s Christmas issue, and Momma spent the next five minutes waxing poetic about all that pine roping.

Brenda had just shucked off her boots in the entry vestibule when a high piping voice asked, "Do you want to build a snowman?"

Brenda turned to find Jackie Scott, Ashley's nine-year-old son, sliding down the hallway on a pair of what appeared to be hand-knitted wool socks. The kid was already bundled up in a bulky sweater and wool hat, clearly anxious to go play even though the sun was barely up.

"No playing in the snow until I get some breakfast," the minister said, yanking Jackie's hat off his head and holding it beyond his reach. "Have you had breakfast?" he asked.

The boy rolled his eyes.

"Exactly what I thought. We need oatmeal before we go out into the cold. Playing in the snow is hard work."

"Is it?"

The minister chuckled. "Yes, it is."

"Okay. Let's get some breakfast," Jackie said in a loud voice as he rushed ahead, leading the way into the dining room, which wasn't crowded at this early hour. Ashley was there, welcoming them with coffee and biscuits and a home-cooked meal. Momma and Brenda lingered over the food while the minister finally gave in and let Jackie pull him outside for what turned into a snowball fight.

"He'll sleep well tonight," Momma said as Ashley joined them.

The innkeeper patted Momma's hand. "I'm so glad you weren't hurt last night," she said. "I just wanted to let you know that the folks renting the cottage are supposed to be checking out today. We'll see if that happens, but I'm sure they'll be gone soon. And I don't have Rose Cottage rented again until spring break. You can stay there for as long as it takes to fix your roof."

Momma dashed a tear from her eye. "Thank you so much. I've been worried."

"You know you can stay in my guest room out at the cottage if you want," Brenda said.

Momma reached out and squeezed her hand. "I'd like that very much."

"Even though it's not close to town?"

Momma nodded.

So it was settled. As soon as the roads cleared, Momma would go stay at Brenda's, which might put a crimp in plans for Jim's visits.

And just like that, she fell back into an ocean of worry. Where was he? Why hadn't he called? She obsessively checked her cell phone again. Nothing.

Momma and Ashley continued to chat while Brenda pushed up from the table, taking her coffee and phone into the library where she had a bird's-eye view of the minister behaving exactly like a nine-year-old boy. You had to love Micah St. Pierre; he was thoughtful and sensitive. It was kind of surprising that no woman had yet snagged the man.

Sort of like Jim.

She resisted the urge to pull out her phone again. It would beep if anyone sent a text.

Little pieces of her heart began to shatter, and a lump formed in her throat. There had to be an explanation she told herself as she squeezed her eyes shut and leaned her head against the cold windowpane.

"Oh my word. Brenda. Brenda, come quick."

She opened her eyes at Momma's summons. How long had she been standing there feeling sorry for herself?

"Brenda! Where are— Oh, there you are." Momma came flying into the library. "Come back to the kitchen, girl."

"What?"

"Don't be asking questions now; just come quick." Momma reached out her hand palm up, and Brenda took it like a little girl, letting her mother pull her down the hall to the back of the house, sure that a member of Magnolia Harbor's police force had arrived with very bad news.

But before that fear could completely overwhelm her, Momma said, "Look who's come home for Christmas."

Brenda raced the last few steps into Ashley Scott's large, modern kitchen and found Ella, wearing a pair of faded blue jeans and an Indiana University sweatshirt that had once been Brenda's. Seeing Ella was a huge shock, but finding Jim standing behind her, with one of his big hands resting on Ella's shoulder, took a moment to fully process.

"Hey, Mom," Ella said. "Jim picked me up from the airport. But the roads were bad, and we had to stop, and then Jim's cell phone charger died, and we didn't want to ruin the surprise by having me call. But honestly, we almost freaked out when we got to Granny's and saw the tree through the roof. I thought…" Her voice trailed off and her lips trembled.

"I'm fine," she said, and then glanced at Jim. "Your cell phone charger died?"

He shrugged. "Yeah. Bad timing, but I guess it made the surprise more surprising, huh?"

"You brought her home to me." And then Brenda couldn't say anything else because Ella ran the last few steps and threw her arms around Brenda and gave her a bone-crushing hug. "I missed you," she whispered into Brenda's ear. "I just didn't know how to say it. And when I saw that tree... I thought I might have waited too long."

When Ella pulled back, tears were running down her cheeks, and for the first time Brenda noticed the hollow places in her daughter's face. She'd aged in the last few years, and not in a good way.

Brenda pushed a lock of Ella's chestnut-colored hair aside. "Are you okay?"

Ella shrugged. "I'm here. For a while. Is that okay?"

And Brenda hugged her again, fiercely. "Oh, baby, it's okay. You can stay as long as you like."

Epilogue

Jim took his seat on the piano bench. The auditorium at Rutledge High was completely sold out, even though the Christmas Gala had to be postponed for a week because of the snowstorm, which had knocked out power to half the town, including the high school.

But it was okay. The word on the street, carried by the gossips of Magnolia Harbor, was that Brenda McMillan had whipped the Christmas Chorale into shape. Even more astonishing was the news that the town Grinch had experienced a holiday change of heart and had finally agreed to form a choir for the Episcopalian congregation at Heavenly Rest Church.

Of course, Rev. Micah St. Pierre might have helped that news along. The man was practically crowing about his persuasive abilities.

Jim said nothing to disabuse the man. But Jim knew good and well that Brenda's change of heart came about because of his treatment of her Christmasitis.

And then again, the man upstairs may have had a hand in the whole thing, because Jim hadn't had a lot of trouble finding Isabella McMillan's cell phone number. A quick Google search had led him to her page on LinkedIn, of all places, where she was trying to build relationships with music industry executives. And maybe that's why she'd answered his out-of-state phone call.

It had been a gamble of the highest order, to just cut through the crap and reach out to the girl who was slowly breaking her mother's heart. He'd halfway expected his gambit to fail, either because he couldn't find her, she wouldn't answer his calls, or she'd flat out refuse. But none of those things happened.

He'd called and chatted with her. And a day later, she'd called him back. Giving him the feeling that the young woman might have been looking for an excuse to break away from her boyfriend. Maybe his call had come at the right moment.

Who could say?

The only wrinkle in Jim and Ella's plans had been the snowstorm. He could hardly have told Brenda where he was going that snowy afternoon without ruining the surprise. So he'd made up the emergency. Harper Jephson was doing just fine. His asthma was under control, thanks to the clinic. And even if there had been an emergency, the guys down at the firehouse would have moved heaven and earth to transport a patient to the mainland. Even in a snowstorm.

But the snow had almost ruined everything, and he'd done a whole lot of second-guessing when he'd arrived at Brenda's mom's house and saw the tree lying across the roof. Nothing had scared him more than the thought that he could have lost Brenda that night. Luckily, one of the neighbors was able to tell him that Brenda and her mother were okay and spending the night at Rev. St. Pierre's rectory. And the minister himself told Jim where to find Brenda when they finally made it up the snowy road to the inn.

It brought a tear to his eye when mother and daughter finally embraced. It was maybe the best Christmas gift he'd ever arranged for anyone. But really, the best part was afterward, when Brenda pulled him aside, wrapped her arms around him, and told him that she loved him.

Yeah. He'd gotten a pretty good Christmas present too.

And now there Brenda stood on the podium, wearing a lovely black dress with a sequined top and a shiny new Christmas tree brooch that her mother had given her right before the performance. She raised her baton and turned toward him.

There was a twinkle in those twin kaleidoscope eyes as she counted out the beats, her baton rising and falling. He began to play, and then the choir joined in, singing without looking at their music.

And man, did they ever make a joyful noise.

Also by Hope Ramsay

The Last Chance Series

Welcome to Last Chance
Home at Last Chance
Small Town Christmas (anthology)
Last Chance Beauty Queen
Last Chance Bride (short story)
Last Chance Christmas
Last Chance Book Club
Last Chance Summer (short story)
Last Chance Knit & Stitch
Inn at Last Chance
A Christmas to Remember (anthology)
Last Chance Family
Last Chance Hero
A Midnight Clear (short story)

The Chapel of Love Series

A Fairytale Bride (short story)
A Christmas Bride
A Small-Town Bride
Here Comes the Bride
The Bride Next Door

The Moonlight Bay Series

The Cottage on Rose Lane
Summer on Moonlight Bay
Return to Magnolia Harbor

About the Author

Hope Ramsay is a *USA Today* bestselling author of heartwarming contemporary romances set below the Mason-Dixon Line. Her children are grown, but she has a couple of fur babies who keep her entertained. Pete the cat, named after the cat in the children's book, thinks he's a dog. Daisy the dog thinks Pete is her best friend except when he decides her wagging tail is a cat toy. Hope lives in the medium-sized town of Fredericksburg, Virginia, and when she's not writing or walking the dog, she spends her time knitting and noodling around on her collection of guitars.

* * *

Learn more at:
　HopeRamsay.com
　Twitter @HopeRamsay
　Facebook.com/Hope.Ramsay

Fall in love with these charming contemporary romances!

A VERY MERRY MATCH
by Melinda Curtis

Mary Margaret Sneed usually spends her holiday baking and caroling with her students. But this year, she's swapped shortbread and sleigh bells to take a second job—one she can never admit to when the town mayor starts courting her. Only the town's meddling matchmakers have determined there's nothing a little mistletoe can't fix...and if the Widows Club has its way, Mary Margaret and the mayor may just get the best Christmas gift of all this year. Includes a bonus story by Hope Ramsay!

THE TWELVE DOGS OF CHRISTMAS
by Lizzie Shane

Ally Gilmore has only four weeks to find homes for a dozen dogs in her family's rescue shelter. But when she confronts the Scroogey councilman who pulled their funding, Ally finds he's far more reasonable—and handsome—than she ever expected...especially after he promises to help her. As they spend more time together, the Pine Hollow gossip mill is convinced that the Grinch might show Ally that Pine Hollow is her home for more than just the holidays.

*Find more great reads on Instagram with
@ReadForeverPub*

CHRISTMAS ON REINDEER ROAD
by Debbie Mason

After his wife died, Gabriel Buchanan left his job as a New York City homicide detective to focus on raising his three sons. But back in Highland Falls, he doesn't have to go looking for trouble. It finds him—in the form of Mallory Maitland, a beautiful neighbor struggling to raise her misbehaving stepsons. When they must work together to give their boys the Christmas their hearts desire, they may find that the best gift they can give them is a family together.

SEASON OF JOY
by Annie Rains

For single father Granger Fields, Christmas is his busiest—and most profitable—time of the year. But when a fire devastates his tree farm, Granger convinces free spirit Joy Benson to care for his daughters while he focuses on saving his business. Soon Joy's festive ideas and merrymaking convince Granger he needs a business partner. As crowds return to the farm, life with Joy begins to feel like home. Can Granger convince Joy that this is where she belongs? Includes a bonus story by Melinda Curtis!

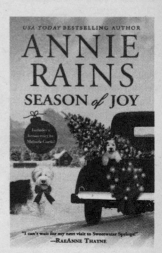

Connect with us at
Facebook.com/ReadForeverPub

HER AMISH WEDDING QUILT
by Winnie Griggs

When the man she thought she would wed chooses another woman, Greta Eicher pours her energy into crafting beautiful quilts at her shop and helping widower Noah Stoll care for his adorable young children. But when her feelings for Noah grow into something even deeper, will she be able to convince him to have enough faith to give love another chance?

THE AMISH MIDWIFE'S HOPE
by Barbara Cameron

Widow Rebecca Zook adores her work, but the young midwife secretly wonders if she'll ever find love again or have a family of her own. When she meets handsome newcomer Samuel Miller, her connection with the single father is immediate—Rebecca even bonds with his sweet little girl. It feels like a perfect match, and Rebecca is ready to embrace the future...if only Samuel can open his heart once more.

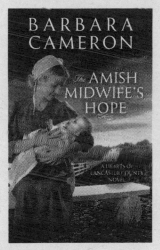

Discover bonus content and more on read-forever.com

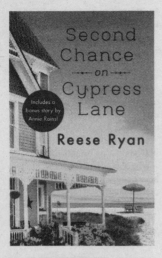

SECOND CHANCE ON CYPRESS LANE
by **Reese Ryan**

Rising-star reporter Dakota Jones is used to breaking the news, not making it. When a scandal costs her her job, there's only one place she can go to regroup. But her small South Carolina hometown comes with a major catch: Dexter Roberts. The first man to break Dakota's heart is suddenly back in her life. She won't give him another chance to hurt her, but she can't help wondering what might have been. Includes a bonus story by Annie Rains!

FOREVER WITH YOU
by **Barb Curtis**

Leyna Milan knows family legacies come with strings attached, but she's determined to prove that she can run her family's restaurant. Of course, Leyna never expected that honoring her grandfather's wishes meant opening a second location on her ex's winery—or having to ignore Jay's sexy grin and guard the heart he shattered years before. But as they work closely together, she begins to discover that maybe first love deserves a second chance...